Solar Express

SOLAR EXPRESS

L. E. MODESITT, JR.

A TOM DOHERTY ASSOCIATES BOOK
NEW YORK

This is a work of fiction. All of the characters, organizations, and events portrayed in this novel are either products of the author's imagination or are used fictitiously.

SOLAR EXPRESS

Copyright © 2015 by L. E. Modesitt, Jr.

All rights reserved.

Designed by Mary A. Wirth

A Tor Book
Published by Tom Doherty Associates, LLC
175 Fifth Avenue
New York, NY 10010

www.tor-forge.com

Tor® is a registered trademark of Tom Doherty Associates, LLC.

Library of Congress Cataloging-in-Publication Data

Modesitt, L. E., Jr.
    Solar express / L. E. Modesitt, Jr.—First edition.
        p. cm.
    "A Tor book."
    ISBN 978-0-7653-8195-8 (hardcover)
    ISBN 978-1-4668-8551-6 (e-book)
    1. Unidentified flying objects—Fiction.   2. International relations—Fiction.
I. Title.
    PS3563.O264S65 2015
    813'.54—dc23

                                                            2015023318

Our books may be purchased in bulk for promotional, educational, or business use. Please contact your local bookseller or the Macmillan Corporate and Premium Sales Department at (800) 221-7945, extension 5442, or by e-mail at MacmillanSpecialMarkets@macmillan.com.

First Edition: November 2015

Printed in the United States of America

0   9   8   7   6   5   4   3   2   1

FOR LINNEA CHRISTINA DUKES,

UNFETTERED BY MERE GRAVITY

INBOUND FROM APHELIA

DAEDALUS BASE
23 MARCH 2114

Alayna Wong-Grant turned her head from the screen wall that could hold more than a dozen displays at once and glanced down at the antique console before her that contained the controls for COFAR—the Combined Farside Array, both the sprawling radio telescope whose rows of polyimide film and its embedded dipole antennas stretched over most of the comparatively flat surfaces of Daedalus Crater and the fifteen-meter optical mirror, if a dish created from powdered lunar regolith, nanitic epoxy, and sprayed aluminum with a limited range of movement could accurately be called a mirror, unlike the ten-meter liquid mercury mirror that it had replaced some twenty years earlier and that had never worked as designed. While those were the main components, COFAR also had a separate dedicated full-spectrum solar optical array as well as the requisite spectrographic and interferometry capabilities.

"Dr. Wong-Grant, image processing is completed for sectors four through seven, with complete comparison to February nineteenth." The AI's voice was a pleasant baritone, one of the first changes Alayna had made after arriving at Daedalus. Luis had programmed the AI with what he must have thought was a sexy and husky alto that had grated on Alayna's nerves with every word uttered. He'd also called the AI "Marcelina." She'd shortened it to Marcel.

"Thank you, Marcel." Her words were not quite perfunctory as she scanned the messages that had piled up while she'd slept, not that she slept all that much during the two-week-long Farside night, since that was the most valuable observational time, and there were seemingly always schedule changes, particularly for the optical telescope. With the heavier usage then, there were also always minor maintenance problems, and given the charges users incurred for every minute of observational time, and the precarious financial position of the Farside Foundation, sleep came second to accommodating schedule changes and getting the comparatively few repairs made. Her eyes continued to travel down the message queue, although she knew that Marcel would have awakened her earlier had there been anything truly urgent.

The heading on the next message stopped her—"BSF"—Basic Science Foundation. *Should you open it?* With a wry smile she touched the console screen, another antique, dating from before neural headsets or implants for those who could afford them.

> Dr. Wong-Grant—
> BSF has not received your latest semimonthly report. Missent?
> Or are you behind on maintenance?

The authentication was that of someone she'd never heard of, doubtless another underpaid postdoc working for anything that had a vaguely scientific aura to its name or operations.

She checked the calendar. "Shit!"

Marcel, clearly deciding that comment was not required, remained silent.

The last thing Alayna needed was to antagonize BSF, since they were the ones paying half her stipend. The Farside Foundation paid for the other half, as well as her transport and support costs at Daedalus Base, and granted her full access on a limited basis to observational array—when the array was free or when the array's user permitted use of the observations.

Alayna immediately created an open file with the proper headings, and copied her previous report into the file so that she could edit and add whatever was necessary once she ran through the rest of the messages. She still wasn't used to the fact that standard off-Earth messages contained no graphics or images, just text and standard symbols—a result of both economics and security. Sending graphics and images cost more, a lot more, and the various global media consortiums had little interest in "overserving" on a money-losing basis the comparative handfuls of off-Earth space-types, that is, those not on Earth or in Earth orbit.

The next five messages were routine confirmations of future time slots from various Earth-based organizations. The one after that was not addressed to her, but to COFAR. She thought about discarding it unread, since most messages addressed to the array were either pleas for "free" observational time, requests for access to data or archives, again requesting the information without payment, or high-level crackpots.

> Dear underpaid postdoctoral professional—or the equivalent:
> Would you like to work on the cutting edge of solar astro-

physics, doing something beyond trying to explain the alpha effect? Even proving that laminar electric current flows do in fact exist along the borders of solar granules? If so . . .

Alayna shook her head and checked the sender—Solar Electric Research. With that, she deleted the message. She couldn't blame the electric sun crowd for trying, but denying that thermonuclear reactions occurred in the solar core wasn't something that she wanted any part of . . . even if the pay was reputed to be outstanding.

From what Alayna had seen in her first three months, COFAR wasn't quite the white elephant the resurgent Noram Conservative Party politicians claimed. Nor was it still the vanguard of astronomical observation proclaimed in the last gasp of American Democrats before the Continental Consolidation of 2089, a date that the vanquished American Republican Party had declared would live in infamy. The problem was that almost thirty percent of COFAR's funding came from the Noram government, and only half from its operations, which left twenty percent coming from the dwindling coffers of the Farside Foundation.

"Dr. Wong-Grant," Marcel said, "there is an anomaly in sector five optical data to be addressed."

"Is the data from client observations or from Foundation reserve observations?"

"It's from shared observations with the Williams Observatory consortium."

"I'll get to it in a moment."

"Anomalous observational data cannot be transmitted until it is reviewed, Dr. Wong-Grant." The AI's voice was apologetic, as if he hated to remind Alayna. She couldn't help but think of the AI as "he," although Luis had always considered it female.

Alayna did not reply, instead quickly scanned the rest of the messages, stopping at the one from Alfen Braun, the Director-Generale of the Farside Foundation.

Dr. Wong-Grant:
This is to inform you that on March twenty-eighth or twenty-ninth, possibly the thirtieth depending on shuttle transport from the WestHem Earth elevator, an inspection team from the Office of the Noram Inspector-General will be visiting lunar facilities supported in whole or in part by Noram government funds. Due to funding constraints, the Foundation is unable to dispatch an escort . . .

Alayna stopped reading. *You've only been here a little over a month, and you're going to have to host a government inspection team?* She forced herself to keep reading.

> . . . trust that you will assure that everything is operating at full efficiency and that the installation is in compliance with the Memorandum of Understanding (MOU) between the Foundation and the Noram Department of Off-Earth Activities [DOEA]. Please find attached briefing information for your use . . .

Meaning that you'd better memorize and know it cold before the inspectors arrive.

There was more, much more, including a summary of the MOU, which included the requirement that, as necessary and physically possible, the Foundation was to make available quarters and food for DOEA and other governmental personnel engaged in official duties, such availability not to exceed ten individuals for more than one month total in any calendar Earth year. There were also several lengthy enclosures with background facts and figures on COFAR, and an imperative to acknowledge receipt of the message. It was almost a quarter of a standard hour before Alayna straightened and stretched, realizing that, despite the low lunar gravity, her shoulders were tight and cramped. After several moments, she hurried through the rest of the messages.

Nothing else urgent and nothing from Chris. Then she straightened and took a swallow from the bottle that held lukewarm tea before saying, "Display the anomaly and explain."

Alayna was not supposed to make judgments on *what* was observed, but on how the data/images were observed, and to review anything that appeared strange to make as certain as possible that such an anomaly had in fact been observed and that it was not an artifact of the system or the result of some form of outside interference with the observation—such as an unauthorized crossing of the Farside observation zone.

An image appeared on the larger screen to Alayna's left. After a moment, a red arrow appeared, its tip almost touching a point of light.

"That is the anomaly," said Marcel.

The screen split, displaying two almost identical images, if each half the size of the first. The image with the arrow was on the left. The one without was on the right.

"The right-hand image shows the same part of sector five on February nineteenth."

"What's the apparent magnitude?"

"Apparent magnitude is sixteen."

"Sixteen? Did you do a spectrographic analysis?" Alayna had to wonder if the anomaly was a distant nova. In-system bodies were usually detected earlier and at fainter magnitudes.

"The available analysis shows no extrasolar stellar origin. Reflected solar radiation with an indication of silver . . ." There was a pause. "And silicates."

Silver and silicates? "Are there any previous records . . . anything that possibly matches?"

"No, there are not, Dr. Wong-Grant."

"How far away is it?" That was Alayna's immediate question, and she regretted the careless wording as soon as her words were out. She immediately added, "Assuming a cometary albedo and a solid diameter of fifteen kilometers."

"Assuming your parameters, the object would be five point five three AU from Sol. From the spectrographic results, the albedo is likely closer to point five with the body having a small diameter, at close to six AU."

"Could it be on such a high inclination orbit that . . ." She broke off the question. "Cancel that." Even at a ninety-degree inclination, something that faint at that distance would still have been in the same observational frame two weeks earlier. Alayna had more questions, but none of them could be answered, not with any degree of accuracy, from the two observations.

That was the thing about observational astronomy. The distances were so vast that even objects moving at comparatively high speeds didn't show much positional change in short time periods, not when viewed from six AU away.

"Do you have any other requirements, Dr. Grant-Wong?"

Alayna would have loved to track the object, whatever it was, but she didn't determine the COFAR viewing priorities. Still . . .

"Send a complete report on the anomaly to Foundation headquarters and note the spectrographic analysis, especially the silver and silicates."

"The report has been transmitted."

"Also, take an observation in twelve hours and another in twenty-four hours." If, on the off chance the object showed discernible motion, Marcel might be able to determine if it might be an outer system body or a comet.

"If it meets the parameters for a discovery, do you want me to submit a report to the International Astronomical Union?"

"When you have another solid observation, prepare the report. Then let me know."

"I will do that."

"Thank you." Even though Marcel was an AI, he deserved professional courtesy . . . or rather, she needed to observe professional courtesy.

"You're welcome."

Alayna returned to the message screen, and her reply to Director-Generale Braun. That was an immediate personal and professional priority. After that, she could complete the report and reply to Basic Science, a definite personal priority. She tried not to think about all the reasons why the Noram Inspector-General might be interested in COFAR.

And, at some time, she needed to send a message to her father, especially before he got worried. If she didn't message at least once every week, preferably more often, he'd message her, wanting to know if she happened to be all right. After all that had happened, she couldn't exactly blame him, but she'd rather do the messaging on her timetable.

2

ONEILL STATION
25 MARCH 2114

Chris Tavoian rose from the briefing console in the cramped ready room with the languid grace of experience, a grace learned through more than a few painful reminders that, in the station's approximation of lunar gravity, apparent "weight" did not equate to mass. He wasn't sure whether to smile or shake his head—a frigging investigating team from the Inspector-General's Office of the Noram Assembly. While he doubted that they were terribly interested in pilots, at least not ones currently assigned to Earth-Moon runs, from what he'd heard they asked both hard questions and stupid ones.

As Tavoian moved toward the open hatch leading to the rim walkway to the mess, Liam Keiser, one of the more senior pilots on the station, and a major in the Space Service, gestured. "That's quite an expression, Chris. When's your next run?"

"Late tomorrow. Lunar Low Orbit Station. Three-person team from the Noram Inspector-General's office."

"You're lucky they're not the Sudam inspectors."

Tavoian nodded politely. He'd heard some of those stories, although he suspected they were exaggerated. But then, he'd never had to deal with the Policia Espacial, because all the FusEx burners fell under the authority of DOEA, with all pilots holding officers' commissions, and the pilots and other DOEA personnel used the high-speed magline to and from ONeill Station, both under DOEA, as opposed to the elevator's standard climbers and main station, which were under the authority of the Sudam AES, and the Policia Espacial, who tended to be somewhat excessively enthusiastic in dealing with those of an Anglo background.

"Do you know what the inspectors are looking for?"

"The briefing just said periodic and routine inspections of lunar facilities receiving DOEA funding."

"That's just about everything." Keiser shook his head, then grinned. "You ever hear from that astronomer you ferried out a couple months back? The one you didn't want me to see?"

"We've exchanged a few messages." More than a few, but Tavoian wasn't about to admit that. "I'm not getting to Farside anytime soon, and she won't be leaving there until her tour is up."

"Anyone sent to Farside doesn't do tours. They're one and done, to avoid the rad limits. Cheap highly educated labor."

"They're almost completely shielded at Farside and at most of the lunar bases."

"Still cheaper that way. She wasn't bad-looking."

"She also wasn't interested in anything short-term. She made that very clear." Tavoian grinned. "If you think otherwise, you could always look her up."

"I'm not headed that way. If I were, I'd have better things to do than spend my pay on elevator fare down to Nearside and a maglev halfway around Luna."

"Two maglevs, I hear. The second one's more of a coffin express. Makes the control space of a burner look like a lux-suite."

"No thanks. Watch out for the slowboats."

"They have their uses," replied Tavoian. "Would you want to lug all that stuff?"

"It'd get there faster," countered Keiser.

"At ten times the cost." Except that Tavoian knew that transporting something by fusionjet cost more like a hundred or two hundred times that of the vasimr slowboats that shuttled various cargoes between the Earth elevators and the nearside lunar elevator, a structure that actually predated even the first partial Earth elevator. "Where are you headed?"

"Phobos."

"Slow or fast transit?"

"Middling. Something like a week each way. DOEA's worried about Hel3 stocks, and the Service has to listen."

Tavoian wondered how Keiser knew that, or if the older pilot were merely speculating. "Inside squib?"

"Don't you read?"

"Read what? I haven't seen anything that mentions that."

"The financial sheets. Commodity exchanges. The futures price of Hel3 has been up every month, more than twenty percent higher now than at the end of last year. It could be that the Sinese are buying up whatever they can get besides what they're getting from the northern craters."

"I thought . . ." Tavoian was about to say that selling Helium three to unauthorized sources was forbidden by the Space Accord, but he knew better, particularly since there was always some multi-type, more often than not, but not exclusively, one from Sudam, who could find a way to make the illegal legal. "Why, do you think?"

"Do you think the lunar Hel3 stocks are unlimited?"

"That might be the beginning of something less desirable. If things don't get better, we might end up being military pilots for real."

"Things won't get that bad. Not after what resulted from the Middle East Meltdown."

"That was more than thirty years ago."

"People forget, and the ones who remember get old and die." Keiser stretched slowly, then rose. "I'm off to meet with Associate Director Xun Sun."

"A Sinobloc team? Why are they using a Noram burner? The Sinese burners are almost as fast as ours." *If not faster.*

"It's a joint Noram/Sinese investigation team. Xun Sun is the head of the Noram side."

"About the nanotech meltdown?"

"Your guess is as good as mine. I was told not to ask anything about their mission, and no one's saying."

"Good luck. When do you break orbit?"

"Early tomorrow. After the last Sinese arrives." Keiser moved toward the briefing console that Tavoian had left.

As he left the briefing area, Tavoian wondered if he'd ever be as cynical as the older pilot, or if Keiser had just been born that way.

Back in the cubicle that was technically his "cabin," a space on the innermost section of the habitat wheel, and the one that had the lightest "gravity," although after all the years in space the spacers and the physicists still argued over whether the spin-created force that approximated gravity was centrifugal or centripetal, Tavoian composed a message, then read it over a last time before he linked to the pilots' network to send it. On Earth or on Luna, they could have linked and talked directly, but personal transspace links weren't allowed, at least not on DOEA installations, ostensibly for reasons of both bandwidth and security, not to mention the costs of real-time, full-image communications . . . or even burst-sent full-image comm.

Alayna—
Nothing new here. Headed your way—LLOS—with some bureaucrats late tomorrow. Strange how space changes perspective, that I'd think half a moon away is "your way." I'm still on the local shuttle runs. Hel3 worries have DOEA cutting back on everything. The thing is—I don't see any slowdown in vasimr slowboats bringing it back from the lunar elevator, and all the burners are topped off before each run.

The good thing about shuttle runs is I get hours and experience with lower rads, and that means I can keep piloting
longer—and higher pay! Maybe I'll even make major one of
these days. Exploration or equipment refit runs in-sys from
Earth pile on the rads. Hazpay doesn't really compensate for
that. But then, after a while, shuttle runs, well, they're all the
same . . . or close to it. From what you've said, you've actually got a wider range of duties than most pilots. You've got
to be astronomer, maintenance tech, ground transporter for
that maintenance, cook, and chief bottle washer. All I have to
do is to deliver passengers and high priority cargo and not
damage anything in the process. Still don't understand why
there aren't two of you there.

He paused. She'd said something about that, that there was a mining
base south of the crater, and that was deemed close enough for backup.
He smiled ironically. It wasn't as though he had any real backup once he
lit off a burner. He glanced back at the text.

I never asked you. Do you get any breaks? If you do . . . where
can you go?

Oh . . . I'm attaching that political book I told you about.
I'd like your thoughts on what he has to say, especially the
second paragraph on page 37 . . . if and when you have a
moment to read and think.

Tavoian double-checked to make sure the book file was attached
before linking, checking the encryption, and sending off the message and
the attachment.

Then he accessed the station database and looked up the powers of
the Noram Inspector-General.

3

Alayna woke to flashing lights in her sleeping cubicle. There was no alarm. That meant a problem, but not an emergency.

"Marcel? What's wrong?" Her voice sounded rough and hoarse, but then it always did when she first woke up, more so at Daedalus Base, with an atmospheric pressure closer to that of Denver than that of New Hampshire.

"A thirty-five-kilometer section of the radio telescope is inoperative. It appears that a hundred-meter section will have to be replaced."

"Where?" She sat up slowly. It hadn't taken her long at Daedalus Base to realize that quick and abrupt movements when still sleep-fogged could be painful in low grav.

"Four kilometers north and fifteen point three kilometers east of the control center."

"Why the alarm?"

"In five hours, Arecibo takes control of the telescope for a deep search. The inoperative section has reduced effectiveness by five percent."

"Frig!" Alayna understood. Unless she could complete the repairs by then the Space Research Institute (Noram) would complain that COFAR's reduced sensitivity had compromised whatever the combined search was investigating. At the least, it wouldn't look good for Alayna. At the worst, SRI headquarters might reduce the payments to the Farside Foundation. She stood and took two steps to the narrow wardrobe, which she opened to locate and extract the one-piece undersuit required for compatibility with the exosuit used for outside lunar surface maintenance.

No matter how sophisticated the system, things happened that needed to be fixed, and decades of experience had shown that a reasonably intelligent and well-trained human being on the spot was far more cost-effective than either excessive redundancy or repeated repair missions, or even AI-controlled robotics. Add to that the fact that sophisticated equipment was more expensive than a nearly endless supply of overeducated young postdoctoral professionals eager to obtain both jobs and experience.

During her first week at COFAR, when Luis had walked her through everything, she'd half wondered if she'd ever remember it all, even with Marcel as backup.

The most frustrating part was being so close to such an array of equipment, and being able to use it so little, at least so far. That thought didn't help Alayna's frame of mind as she prepared for the repair mission. Almost half an hour later, she finished suiting up while breathing a high oxygen mixture in order to accommodate the lower pressure and higher oxygen levels she'd be breathing for the next several hours—if not longer.

When she finished the suit pressurization level tests, she opened the suit comm link. "Marcel, comm check."

"All your frequencies are clear. Ten percent loss on lowband."

"I'm not going far enough for that to matter."

Next came the inspection of the roller. Alayna made certain that the batteries were fully charged, then put a spare in the equipment bin. She couldn't have done that if the break in the antenna had been another ten kilometers farther out. After that came the two prepackaged sections of polyimide film—and its embedded dipole antennas—that barely fit in the open cargo bin at the back of the roller. She couldn't help but notice that there were only ten sections left. Still . . . according to the logs, sometimes years had gone by without the need for replacing antenna sections. As almost an afterthought, she added another package of antistatic wipes to the package already in the equipment bin.

Another fifteen minutes passed by the time she had the roller moving out of the lock. Then she had to guide it through the maze of paths and tunnels, designed so that the rollers could reach every part of the radio-telescope antenna without rolling across any of the meter-wide polyimide swathes. Physically replacing the polyimide film would always require some travel since the rows stretched fifty kilometers in each direction, but going just fifteen wasn't as bad as it could have been. Then, if the damage had been at forty-nine kilometers, the reduction in antenna effectiveness would have been minuscule, unlike the five percent reduction that Marcel had reported. The big problem was that replacing a hundred meters of damaged film was going to be a chore, especially since Alayna had only done one replacement of fifty meters, and that had been of aging polyimide close to the COFAR control center, and had been almost a practice repair, close as it had been to the base center.

Almost forty minutes later, she slowed the roller to a stop. From where she sat on the open vehicle, she couldn't see any damage. "There's no obvious impact, Marcel. Where does the damaged section start?"

"Section fifteen-point-three. There should be a yellow stripe indicating where the sections join."

Alayna forced herself to scan the edge of the film slowly, finally catching sight of a yellow tab, rather than a stripe. Then she checked to make certain she had the antistatic wipes in the suit's belt patch. As soon as she stepped off the roller, her boots sank into the regolith—not that much, perhaps a few centimeters, but a haze of dust rose, almost climbing up her boots and legs.

Walking slowly and carefully, she made her way to the edge of the antenna film, where she inspected the yellow tab, which had the numbers 15.2, indicating that she'd stopped a good hundred meters short. *Which might be why you don't see any damage.* "Marcel . . . the tab indicates fifteen-two."

"The roller's calibration must be off."

Alayna didn't voice, not even subvocally, what she felt about that as she turned back toward the roller. When she got back into the driver's seat to move forward another hundred meters, she had to keep wiping her faceplate with an antistatic wipe in order to see where she was directing the roller. By the time she stopped at the connection/disconnection point another hundred meters farther east, she'd had to discard the first wipe, stuffing it into the waste bag beside the driver's seat, and was using a second.

This time she could see the damage to the antenna, not all that obvious—just a series of punctures in the film. After she took the separator—a short rod that looked like an oversized flat screwdriver—from the tool box, she got off the roller carefully. Her boots went into the dust almost ankle deep. She glanced around. The damaged section of the antenna film had been laid over the dust as well.

"Marcel, there's a lot of dust here."

"Where you are doesn't have any observations on that."

She didn't feel like commenting. Instead, she moved toward the yellow tab, leaning down and verifying the section number before easing the separator into the groove at the end, and moving it slightly. Nothing happened.

She applied more force, cautiously, slowly wedging the two sections apart. By the time she'd separated the connections between the two sections, she was sweating, not heavily, but more than she would have liked, despite the fact that the only humidity in the suit came from her.

Then she had to roll up the damaged section. The film was light enough, especially in lunar gravity, but she was very careful, and moved slowly, until the first damaged section, except for the last few meters, was in a rough cylinder. By then, she was wiping her suit faceplate every few steps. After separating the first damaged section from the next one, she began rolling up the second section.

"Your internal suit temperature is getting too high," observed Marcel.

"That's all I need," snapped Alayna. Nonetheless, she straightened up and just stood quietly, trying to breathe easily. She looked eastward, but could see nothing, given the dust on her faceplate. She slowly and gently wiped the faceplate clear, knowing that even fine class II dust was highly abrasive.

From what she could finally see, she had only another five or six meters left to roll before she could separate the second section. Then would come the even harder work.

After what seemed forever, she cleared her throat. "Marcel?"

"Your temperature's down. Not as much as would be optimal."

"I'll move more carefully." In fact, out of necessity, Alayna made certain her movements were more deliberate as she finished rolling up the last few meters of the second section. Separating it from the remainder of the antenna row was easier than the first and second separations had been. After finishing rolling it up she had to walk back to the roller. There she unloaded the first section of new antenna film, unsealed it, and was about to begin fitting the old and new sections together when she realized that the area around each receiving clip socket was covered with dust . . . and if she pressed the two sections together without cleaning each and every socket first . . . then the dust would work into the socket and before long, perhaps immediately, given the electrostatic properties of the dust, the connections wouldn't be tight, and likely the antenna still wouldn't work.

Cleaning and sealing was tedious . . . and every other receptacle required a new antistatic wipe. Just cleaning and sealing the 120-centimeter-wide section took more than twenty minutes. When she finished, she almost didn't want to link to the AI again.

She did. "Marcel, linkage test, please."

"The links are secure. A reception test is not possible until you unroll the rest of the antenna."

Alayna moved and did that, but because she was moving backward in order to avoid stepping on the film, it took longer to unroll than it had to roll up the damaged section, especially since the dust was clinging to everything.

"Marcel, reception test?"

"Signals being received from the new section."

At least that works. Then she had to walk back to the roller and move it forward to unload the second section, open it, and unroll it enough to be able to connect the two new sections. While she had to wipe down the contact points and the area around the receiving sockets, the connection was easier because there wasn't nearly the dust gathered on the replacement antenna sections.

Her back didn't ache; it twinged painfully by the time she had unrolled the second section. Worrying about that would have to wait.

She was about halfway through connecting the second section to the rest of the antenna row when Marcel pulsed. "You have thirty minutes before Arecibo takes control."

Had she been out almost three hours? *Frig!* "I'll be done with the repairs before that." But there was no way she and the roller would make it back to COFAR center by then.

Twenty-one minutes later, Alayna and the roller, as well as two rolls of inoperative antenna polyimide film, an enormous number of used antistatic wipes, and a coating of dust, headed back toward the COFAR maintenance lock.

Although Marcel had verified the repair had been successful, just before the roller reached the open lock door, she linked to the AI. "Is the antenna still fully operative?"

"It is fully operative, Dr. Wong-Grant. The roller caused a slight interference field on your return, but that was minimal."

And frigging unavoidable.

When the lock closed, Alayna just looked at the dust-coated roller. Her back ached, as did her head, and her eyes were burning . . . and sooner or later she'd have to clean the roller. Otherwise the dust would migrate into places where it could do real damage.

You don't have to clean it this moment.

She did have to get through shutting down the roller, as well as connecting it to the charging system. She unloaded the rolls of damaged antenna film and stacked them in the waste room. She couldn't put them through the reprocessor for another week, not until "day" arrived, and she had full solar power. Next she had to clean the exosuit. By the time she was back inside the installation, she was shivering because her undersuit was soaked.

She did take a warm, if short shower, before pulling on a dry stationsuit, and then heading to the control center. The console alert light was flashing.

When she saw the first message, the priority one that had triggered the alert, she relaxed.

> Your system reports EFA exceeding three hours. Please report reentry.

That was an inquiry request from the Lunara Mining installation south of Daedalus Crater, most likely automatic, although it bore Harris's name as sender. Her response was swift and short.

> Reentry at 1143 UTC. Extended exterior repairs, successfully accomplished. Appreciate your watchfulness. Thank you.

Her next step was to monitor the performance of all systems, but as Marcel had already informed her, all optical and radio systems were operating at close to optimal levels. She nodded, more in relief than approval.

Before she started in on checking the rest of the message queue, she went to the galley and fixed some tea. She also ate several biscuits. Then she carried the sealed mug back to the control center where she settled before the console.

Despite all the early space-age hype about living longer in low-grav, what experience had shown, both on the space elevator and on Luna, was that prolonged low-grav wasn't any form of anagathic, but just created the early onset of muscular degeneration and osteoporosis, not to mention various other conditions that were anything but life-extending. That was why Alayna's first postdoc employment was at COFAR, a job that was anything but glamorous, and a combination of basic maintenance technician, janitor, and second-level astronomer. Being in good physical condition, having an outstanding academic record, and enough publications that had gotten some attention meant that, unlike many other young and largely inexperienced postdocs, she had real and gainful employment . . . if under less than optimal conditions and pay . . . and if only for two years.

Alayna had been sipping the tea for less than a minute when the console flashed again.

The second alert message was from Dorthae Wrae, the Foundation's chief of operations.

> Dr. Wong-Grant:
> The Space Research Institute (SRI(N)) has informed us that for the first ten minutes of the joint Deep Listen operation there was low-level interference at COFAR, the frequency of which was consistent with operation of a roller. How did this occur? Was it absolutely necessary? Please report immediately.

"Shit!" *Ten lousy minutes because there was so much dust that everything needed anti-triboelectric wipedown?*

At least Wrae wasn't demanding a full-comm real-time link, but that was understandable. Given both the cost of full-band face-to-face communications and the annoying two- to three-second delay, the Foundation seldom initiated or authorized direct real-time links. Costs drove everything, and that was another reason why Alayna had a station designed and built to hold ten people all to herself—except on rare occasions.

Alayna reread Wrae's message, then concentrated on framing a reply, forcing herself to respond methodically. Even so, it was almost a half hour later before she was ready to send her reply.

> Director Wrae:
> A micrometeor spray impacted the antenna at 0313 UTC. I was sleeping at that time, and the damage did not trigger a full alarm. When I woke at 0600 UTC, I determined that more than half of antenna row 6NE was inoperative as a result of the damage. I immediately began preparations for an EFA with the roller, since I knew the importance of the SRI(N) Deep Listen event scheduled for 1100 UTC. Those preparations, done as quickly as possible but according to the approved procedures, took ninety-three standard minutes. The roller left the maintenance bay at 0746. Travel time to the point of the damage was forty-one minutes. Higher speed was not possible because of lunar night power limits. Repairs began at 0834.
>
> The damage necessitated . . .

Alayna went on to detail the repairs step by step, checking the roller log to enter the exact times.

> . . . because the impact occurred at a point along the antenna where the local regolith is predominantly Class II dust, both the contacts and connections on both the existing antenna film and the replacement antenna film required careful and time-consuming cleaning.
>
> Repairs were completed before the beginning of the Deep Listen event, but for slightly more than the first ten minutes of the event, the roller was still returning to COFAR maintenance. While I regret the time it took to complete the repairs, it would seem that some slight interference for ten minutes was preferable to degraded antenna performance for the entire event.

While the last sentence wouldn't make the director happy, Alayna wanted to convey the idea, if less than absolutely directly, that she hadn't been responsible for the impact and that she'd done the most that she could.

She sent the reply, then went back to the message queue. There was a message from Chris, but it wasn't flagged, and she kept it as new until she could make sure that there wasn't something else urgent. She'd no sooner finished running through the queue than there was a reply from Foundation ops—again from Dorthae Wrae. The gist of the reply was simple enough.

> Was this repair necessary at this time? Would the client have
> even noticed the difference in signal strength?

Alayna did the math, then checked it. The disabled section of the antenna should only have resulted in a deterioration of less than half of one percent. For some observations, that would make a difference. She frowned. *Except Marcel reported it as five percent.*

"Marcel? The amount of usable antenna lost to impact damage was less than one percent. Why did you report it as five percent?"

"The lost segment was eight tenths of one percent, but the signal loss was five point seven percent."

"Why the difference?"

"Without an analysis of the damaged section, that is impossible to say."

"Would the infiltration of Class II lunar dust have affected the signal transmission?"

"That is impossible to determine at this time."

"I don't believe that. Isn't there any research on that?" Alayna recalled reading something, but not where.

"The electrostatic properties of regolith dust have been studied—"

"Cancel that. What I want to know is whether the triboelectric charging effect could create a field that would affect more than one antenna row."

"There's no research on that, Dr. Wong-Grant."

"Great. A wonderful topic for a scholarly paper . . . as if it would do me any good." Alayna took a deep breath and began to compose a reply.

> Dr. Wrae:
> In regard to your inquiry about the impact on the client's data,
> according to system measurements taken by the AI, approxi-
> mately one percent of the antenna array was nonfunctional,
> but the system status was only ninety-three percent after the
> impact. Once the repairs were accomplished, system status

returned to ninety-nine percent. This suggests that electrostatic loading by the Class II regolith dust in the vicinity of the impact damage had an effect, although I could find no research either supporting or refuting that possibility. Because the measured loss was more than five percent, and because it appeared likely that I could complete the repairs before the beginning of Deep Listen, I went ahead with the repair procedures. Because of the unforeseen high concentration of Class II dust in the vicinity of the damaged section of the antenna, more extensive anti-static cleaning measures were necessary, which extended the repair time. For the record, the system records did not note that that section contained excessive fine dust levels. Under these circumstances, I made the judgment that immediate repairs were in the client's best interests.

What else could she say? After adding a few polite phrases expressing concern and appreciation for the inquiry, Alayna sent off her reply, again glad that she didn't have to explain verbally.

Then she went back to dealing with all the routine messages.

More than two hours after she'd reentered the COFAR control center, she finally opened the message from Chris, half guiltily. *But you deserve a few minutes for yourself.* She began to read, smiling as she did about his description of the bureaucrats.

He's actually thinking about where you are . . . or wanting you to think that he is. She smiled ironically since, either way, it was thinking about her. Given how few bureaucrats traveled willingly to Luna, it was also likely that he was transporting the Noram Inspector-General team. Her eyes went back to the last lines.

> . . . I'd like your thoughts on what he has to say, especially the second paragraph on page 37 . . .

She smiled at the words that followed. *It's as if he knew what kind of day I was going to have.*

When Alayna finished, she glanced at the attached book file, quickly opened it, and read the title—*Observations on Politics.* She frowned. *Why would he send me this? Except for internal Foundation politics, I could care less.* Still, she was intrigued enough to skip to page 37, where she read.

> Good politicians understand one fundamental aspect of human nature—that the concern of most individuals attenuates on a

geometric basis with the distance in time or space. That was the principal reason the successful development of space facilities exclusively by governments was initially limited. The costs were high and the benefits distant in both time and distance. Only the threat of monopolization of the power conveyed by the commencement of the Sinese space elevator, an installation created by a government with greater resistance to popular opinion, spurred the development and completion of the West-Hem space elevator. Without either another threat or immense profits, further and more extensive space development, especially beyond the Martian colonies, is unlikely.

She frowned. She'd have to think about that. Idly she skipped through the pages, when a highlighted phrase—a title, really—caught her eyes.

Those to whom politics is music are most adept with the symbols.

With a smile at the words, one that quickly faded, Alayna read a few of the lines beneath.

In a sense, the "music" of politics reflects current culture, because it embodies the heavy use of symbols, i.e., coded language, and percussion, the continuing, not quite simplistic, heavy and repetitive beat designed to frame apparently new issues in terms of old memes . . .

If he reads this sort of thing, your burner-boy is deeper than you thought. Except . . . he wasn't hers, and at three years older than she was, he was hardly a boy. She closed the message and shifted the letter and the book to her personal directory.

There's something else you need to do. Abruptly she remembered. "Marcel, what about that anomaly in sector five? What can we report?"

"The anomaly has moved, but not enough to calculate either speed or projected path accurately. We're close enough to day that we won't get another observation until April twelfth."

"Then we file a report, and someone else gets part of the credit." *If they haven't already.* "Do the report and let me see it."

"It's already done. It's in your pending file."

Alayna called up the report, in standard format for the International Astronomical Union, and read through it. She had no corrections, not that she likely would have had, since Marcel had years of experience in drafting such reports, and all had been seen and corrected, if necessary, by others, likely with far more experience than Alayna had. Still . . . she wondered what the anomaly might be, although given the odds and how well the solar system had been mapped over the past century it was most likely a long-period comet. *And being a discoverer of a comet wouldn't hurt professionally . . . assuming no one else has reported it.* Even if Marcel was really the discoverer . . . and she was probably the tenth astronomer to report it.

"Go ahead and send it, with copies to Farside Operations."

"Transmission is complete, Dr. Wong-Grant."

She still had to clean the roller, and that needed to be done before the inspection team arrived. *You might as well get that done now.* The way things were going, who knew what might come up if she waited . . . and she still had to go over the briefing materials she'd barely skimmed . . . and get off a message to her father, something she'd put off too long, not that he sometimes wasn't exactly regular in messaging, but he regarded her reporting in as more necessary than his.

And, as had been the case, for most of the time she'd been at COFAR, so far, at least, her duties, her familiarization with the station, and more maintenance than she'd expected had left her far too little time to pursue her own research into the mysteries of the solar photosphere. But then, she'd been told that her research came behind everything else. She just hadn't realized how far behind that would be.

THE NEW YORK TIMES
26 MARCH 2114

[OTTAWA] "Throwing money into space makes no sense when the world's greatest city is drowning." In the debate over the annual appropriations for the Department of Off-Earth Activities, Senator Riccardo Castenada (CP-NY) went on to attack the Yates Administration's request for supplemental finding for DOEA. "Far too many dollars go to the Space Service already. Many of those jobs could be more cost-effectively handled by private industry." Castenada refused to comment on rumors that he had threatened to reveal classified DOEA material to the media if the Administration failed to provide additional disaster relief to New York City in the wake of the destruction caused by Hurricane Teresa.

Senator Tanya Patton (D-SASK) noted acerbically that Castenada had been the one leading the floor fight against funding for restoring New Orleans and who had created the coalition to block appropriations for the San Francisco Bay flood barriers and for disaster relief for Sacramento. Castenada did not reply.

In dismissing Castenada's charges, DOEA Secretary Karl Luvalle stated, "To turn the control over fusion-powered spacecraft to private industry, as the good senator proposes, would invite a return to the aircraft and missile terrorism of a century ago." He went on to suggest that Castenada's views ignored the resurgence of the Sinese effort to mount manned explorations to the moons of Jupiter and well beyond.

There was also no comment from the EC, although Chancellor Rumikov had earlier declared that off-Earth activities would always require careful government oversight, given that excessive reliance on the goodwill of the private sector had been the principal cause of the economic implosion of the 2030s that led to the near-collapse of the United States and Mexico, and that had been so artfully ignored that the full collapse of 2081 had become inevitable. Rumikov has said often that "the Russian Federation avoided economic disasters by careful oversight."

The Sinese Minister for Space declined direct comment, but an official of the Space Ministry is rumored to have previously observed that the Noram DOEA was the handmaiden of the ultra-military Space Service, and that the Space Service was tacitly supporting the Indian Dyaus project and had a hidden agenda. He did not describe that agenda, but sources suggest that he referred to Noram plans for the militarization of space. That charge has been repeatedly denied by both the Noram Secretary of Defense and by DOEA Secretary Luvalle.

An unnamed Indian government spokesperson again denied any coordination or collusion between the Indian Space Administration and the Noram DOEA.

President Yates's office issued a statement praising the Noram Senate for addressing funding issues in a timely and constructive manner.

ONEILL STATION
26 MARCH 2114

At 1513 UTC, Tavoian completed the post-loading check of the supplies for Low Lunar Orbit Station, some of which were for the station, and some of which were for transshipment elsewhere on Luna. The rear/lower passenger cabin was also loaded with supplies, as it often had been over the past four months, with fewer passengers heading to the Moon. He returned to the control deck, going hand over hand along the ladder between decks, easy enough in the null-grav of the station docking ring. Once there, he logged the completion of the inspection, then began the preboarding checklist, taking his time. He finished at 1542 UTC and put the ship's power and nav systems on locked standby.

Because he had a few minutes before his passengers arrived, he called up the last message Alayna had sent—he'd saved them all in his private files, something he wasn't about to tell Keiser or any of the other pilots—and began to reread it.

He hadn't even gotten through the first paragraph when the comm buzzed.

"FusEx three, Ops Control. You're down to three passengers. The two from OutSpace canceled."

"OpsCon, understand cancellation of two passengers. Interrogative cause of cancellation?"

"Three, log it as operational necessity. They departed on FusEx four alpha."

"Interrogative delay in notification."

"Unable to reply. That is all, three."

Tavoian frowned. By all rights OpsCon wasn't required to tell a pilot the reason for a cancellation, especially that a pair of LLO-bound passengers had shifted to a burner bound for Phobos earlier in the day. Keiser's burner, no less. Why would a commercial outfit shift a team from lunar assignment . . . with the penalties involved? *Unless they'd never intended to go to Luna.* But that was an astronomical price, literally, to pay in order to keep their eventual destination hidden. Or had their assignments been changed? OutSpace was a Sinese-controlled multinational, and that meant their scientists and professionals did exactly what the government wanted.

He made the log entries and was still mulling over the oddity when the lock alert chimed, notifying him that his passengers were ready to board. He closed the message he hadn't reread, then ran over the passengers' names in his mind—Antoine Deveau, Geoffrey Hart, and Dominique Perez—names suggesting political compromise more than technical expertise, but then, Noram was more than large enough to accommodate both needs, Tavoian suspected as he made his way aft to the forward/top passenger deck, where he checked the pressures, and then unlocked the outer hatch, opening it to the umbilical. Once the monitors showed that the three and their gear—a small kit bag each—were in the lock, he used the manual stud to close the outer hatch, making sure it was sealed before opening the inner lock.

He waited until the three were all inside the upper passenger deck before closing the inner lock and surveying them. Deveau was the tallest and broadest, perhaps in his early forties, swarthy with receding black hair. For all of her Latino heritage, Perez was almost as tall as Deveau, and trimly muscular, with blue-back hair and a slightly olive complexion. Hart was a good five centimeters shorter than Perez, with the odd combination of thick, coarse, and short-cropped blond hair, a thin face, and fine features. All three wore dark blue shipsuits without insignia.

THEIR AUTHENTICATIONS ARE VALID. THEY MATCH THEIR BIOMETRICS, the ship's AI reported through the pilot's earpiece, since Tavoian had opted out of an implant. All ship AI voices were standard, as a result of experience.

"Welcome." Tavoian offered a smile before asking, "Have all of you traveled on a FusEx before?"

It didn't totally surprise Tavoian that all three nodded.

"Good. You'll have heard the briefing before, but it's required. First, you're required to comply with any order that I give. That's for reasons of safety. Second, you're required to be strapped into your seats at certain times. Those times are during preparation for release from the station, during maneuvering after release, during maneuvering prior to docking, and any other time when the "Restraint" light is illuminated. The actual trip will take about four hours, with anywhere from half an hour to an hour for release here and for docking there. Do you have any questions?"

"How long will it take to get to the surface from the lunar station?" asked Hart.

"That depends on their shuttle availability, your destination, and the station's position relative to that destination." Tavoian offered a rueful smile. "I'm not about to guess. I'm not a shuttle pilot, and I don't know their operations."

"But you're a pilot," said Hart.

"The LLO isn't lunar-centric, unlike the cargo stations at the Lagrange Points. That means it's always at a different distance from any point on Luna. Second, they use chemical rockets for their landers. It's entirely different."

"Isn't that expensive?" asked Deveau.

"Not when they manufacture the fuel on Luna. Also, they don't have to contend with an atmosphere . . . or more than a hint of one, and only one-sixth the escape velocity on the return." Tavoian waited for another question. There wasn't one. "Now, if you'd make sure all your gear is stowed in the rear bulkhead lockers, and that they're sealed. Then strap yourselves in."

Once he was satisfied that everything was as it should be, Tavoian float-climbed up the ladder to the control deck, then sealed the hatch before settling into the pilot's couch and releasing the standby lock.

"Interrogative ship status," he asked the AI.

SHIP IS READY FOR RELEASE.

Tavoian checked the displays, activated the restraint warning, then opened the commlink. "OpsCon, FusEx three, ready for release."

"FusEx three, wait one."

"Three, standing by."

Tavoian wondered how long the wait would be, since his screens showed no objects obviously in the path of the ship, but the screens— radiation combined sensor systems—didn't show anything that might be approaching from beneath or around the station, then asked the AI, "Interrogative traffic?"

OPS IS REPOSITIONING SUDAM LONGLINER.

"Inbound or outbound?"

THAT INFORMATION IS NOT AVAILABLE.

Tavoian wondered whether the rumors about Sudam developing a hidden asteroid habitat had any basis in fact, then shook his head. The energy signature of a burner, or even a high-gee lobbed cargo shell, was too difficult to conceal, especially if you didn't want to take forever to get somewhere. And if Sudam had the capability of the mythical reaction-less drive . . . they certainly wouldn't be still partnering with Noram on the WestHem elevator . . . although they remained anything but pleased with the Noram monopoly and control over the Low Lunar Orbit Station and the lunar elevator and the Lagrange Point stations.

"FusEx three, cleared for release. Release will occur in thirty seconds.

Cleared to use thrusters. Do not activate drive until you are cleared for ignition."

"OpsCon, three green for release. Will await clearance for ignition." Tavoian switched the ship from station power to the ship auxiliary power, then put the AI in maneuvering mode, necessary to ease the ship clear of the station and to align it for the optimal course and trajectory for the Lunar Low Orbit Station . . . or where it would be when FusEx three arrived.

"Three, you're disengaged. Clear to maneuver."

While the announcement of disengagement was superfluous and after the fact, since the ship's systems knew as soon as the physical separation occurred, the clearance was not. "Commencing maneuvering this time."

Tavoian watched as the AI used the thrusters to ease the ship away from the upper ring where the various spacecraft using ONeill Station docked. He could have maneuvered the ship manually, but that was reserved for emergencies or unusual circumstances, since the AIs invariably used less thruster propellant. Even so, he was ready to override the AI at the slightest hint of something going awry. It didn't, of course, and the AI reported, SEPARATION ACHIEVED.

"Commencing orientation." Tavoian switched to the AI. "Destination is Lunar Lower Orbit Station. Begin destination orientation."

After several moments, the AI replied, ORIENTATION COMPLETE. READY FOR IGNITION.

"FusEx three, you're cleared for ignition."

"OpsCon, understand cleared for ignition." Tavoian gave the command to the AI, "Ignite drive."

DRIVE IGNITED.

"FusEx three, you are cleared to activate drive and depart."

"Activate drive."

DRIVE ACTIVATED.

Initially, there was the faintest sense of pressure, pushing Tavoian straight down in his couch. That faint pressure continued to build for the next several minutes until it reached one gee, leveling out at that point. During the buildup of acceleration, the AI switched ship functions from auxiliary power to the bleed-off generator, and Tavoian checked to make certain that the generator was fully online.

Even knowing that the AI was doing the same thing, Tavoian continued to monitor the screens displayed before him, showing in real-time every body of any size that might conceivably pose a problem for the ship. Despite all the near-Earth sweeping operations, there was still too much space junk left over anywhere within the orbit of Luna around Earth and even farther out, and that didn't include chunks of rock too small to be called asteroids that appeared occasionally from nowhere. While they might not be asteroids, except to astronomers, they were pretty much disaster to the burner on a fast Earth-Luna run that happened to meet one, small as the odds were. There had only been one collision with a true rock in the past decade . . . but there had been almost a score of dings, dents, and survivable perforations from space junk, and the resulting damages and near deaths had resulted in lawsuits, international disputes, and a tacit agreement to deal with anyone or anything who added to the problem.

While he'd "seen" small asteroids before on lunar runs, neither he nor the AI detected anything that wasn't supposed to be near them . . . although they passed less than ten kays from a small piece of something metallic less than ten minutes after leaving ONeill Station.

Tavoian thought about reading Alayna's message again, then shook his head. With his luck, something would happen. He kept watching the screens and checking the drive indicators.

After eighty minutes of acceleration, he made the required announcement. "Approaching turnover. Please take your couches and strap in." His passengers were in their couches well before the AI cut the drive, and initiated turnover, using the thrusters to rotate the burner end to end, so the drive nozzles were facing their destination.

Some of the Sinese burners used dual drives, but SpacePlus, the manufacturer of FusEx three and all Noram fusionjets, had opted for the simpler single drive configuration—a far more cost-effective design that eliminated the additional drive system, as well as swiveled couches or the need for passenger restraint during decel. The single drive system did necessitate an extremely precise rotation not required of a dual drive system. All in all, the three-hour trip was essentially eighty-five minutes of one-gee acceleration, ten minutes of changeover in weightlessness, and eighty-five minutes of deceleration.

Ninety-one minutes later, FusEx three floated nearly motionless off the upper docking ring of the Lunar Lower Orbit Station. The lower docking ring, beneath the station, was for lunar landing shuttles.

Tavoian link-pulsed the station. "LunaCon, FusEx three, standing by for docking."

"FusEx three, maintain position this time."

"Maintaining position." *Now what?* "Anything incoming?" he asked the AI.

THERE IS A LANDER DOCKING ON THE LOWER RING.

"That shouldn't affect us."

"FusEx three, this is LunaCon. Interrogative deliverables."

"LunaCon, passengers and clearances, cargo manifest to you."

"Thank you, three."

Did they know you're carrying an inspection team? Tavoian frowned. How could they not?

One minute passed, then two. After another five minutes, the comm buzzed. "FusEx three, cleared for approach and docking."

"LunaCon, three, commencing approach this time."

Once the AI confirmed the grapples were secure and that the station umbilical was connected, Tavoian switched to station power.

"FusEx three, lock secure. You're cleared for disembarkation and off-loading."

"Stet, LunaCon."

After a last check of the station power, Tavoian shut down the ship's aux power before continuing shutdown procedures . . . for everything but habitability. Then he turned off the restraint light. Given that docking rings had no rotation, there was no gravity or any semblance of such, and after opening the hatch between the control deck and the forward passenger deck, he went down the ladder hand over hand.

Even before he was near the deck, all three of the passengers were looking at him.

"What was the delay?" asked Hart.

"There was a lander docking. They might have had problems with that. Luna Control didn't say." As he moved through the air toward the lock, carefully, he didn't say that he wasn't about to ask. "You can get your gear. You're cleared to disembark." After a hesitation, he asked, "Where are you headed on Luna?"

"Where the Inspector-General has sent us," replied Deveau pleasantly. "I'm sure you understand."

"I'm afraid I do." To Tavoian, Deveau's response meant that the man was either excessively self-important, or that someone, or lots of some-ones, were in trouble. Neither was a particularly good thing. He checked the lock pressure, then offered the authentication and pressed the lock stud, standing back as the inner hatch slid open.

The only one of the three who said anything as they entered the lock, awkwardly enough to show that they weren't that experienced in weight-lessness, was Perez.

"Have a safe return trip."

"Thank you." Tavoian closed the inner lock, then opened the outer one. Once he saw that all three and their gear were securely in the station's receiving umbilical, he closed the outer lock.

You need to send Alayna a message. It couldn't hurt, one way or another, but he'd have to wait until he'd dealt with the cargo and deter-mined what his layover was going to be.

On Friday, Alayna slept later. Now that the sun line had reached and passed the COFAR installation, and it was lunar "day," the highest priority use of the various telescopes had diminished, and she needed to catch up on her sleep, especially before the inspection team arrived. But then, part of that lost sleep time had been devoted to studying the briefing materials sent to her, clearly designed to highlight the importance and cost-effectiveness of COFAR.

Even so, she was awake by 0600 UTC. In little more than a half hour, she was seated in the control center. After checking the equipment and getting a report from Marcel, she surveyed the messages. At the top of the queue was one from Alfen Braun, wanting to know the status of the Noram IG inspectors. Alayna immediately replied that the inspectors had not arrived, and that she did not have an ETA, but that she would inform the director as soon as she knew more. Especially after the message she'd received from Chris two days earlier, she had to admit that she was more than a little concerned. If the inspectors found anything wrong that was her fault, and possibly even that wasn't, COFAR might escape relatively unscathed, but she most likely would not. If she fouled up, or there was any hint of that, she could likely forget about a future career in astrophysics. And she had to take care of their food and other needs. That was clearly spelled out in the MOU. It did make sense, of a sort, because there weren't any other quarters in Daedalus Crater.

Speaking of which . . . "Who's using the optical arrays, especially the solar telescope and the associated equipment?" She could have looked up the schedule, but asking Marcel was quicker.

"The Solar Research Institute," replied the AI, as pleasantly as always.

"They don't restrict my right to use whatever data and observations they're making, right?"

"You can use their observational data, but you can't publish without their approval. According to the records, they've never withheld approval."

That's assuming you can develop something worth publishing over the next two years . . . and you ever get enough time to carry it out.

During her doctoral research Alayna had come across a reference to "regular" and longer-lasting solar mini-granulations. For the last two centuries, astronomers had described the solar granulations as the manifestation of convection in the visible reaches of the solar photosphere. From over a century's worth of observations, at least those recorded and published, all but a handful of the mini-granules observed had fit the multifractal model first observed in the early twenty-first century by the orbiting Hinode Solar Observatory and by the Big Bear Solar Observatory before its destruction in 2031, as well as by the ill-fated Advanced Solar Telescope. The short-lived Inner System Solar Observatory (ISSO) had recorded and transmitted a series of observations/data apparently observed at the frequency of Helium 1 that purported to show possible regular mini-granules. Before the consortium backing the ISSO could follow up, a particularly violent coronal mass ejection had effectively destroyed the observatory, and the international funding crisis of 2081 had precluded the struggling EC from replacing it.

One very good reason for an observatory like COFAR. Not that the Moon's shield against a large CME was anywhere near as effective as Earth's, but COFAR had deployable shields . . . and a live human to repair damage.

From what Alayna had discovered, the very few so-called regular mini-granulations had been dismissed as artifacts of the space between the "normal" semiregular granulations and the multi-fractal mini-granulations . . . or possibly as some sort of shape created by the interacting flux lines of adjacent granulations.

Because the magnetic Reynolds number of solar plasma was so high, that allowed the possibility of magnetic structures of a few meters, not that even COFAR could detect something that small, but the possibility certainly was consistent with the observations of mini-granulations, and possibly far smaller magnetic structures . . . the only problem being that a high Reynolds number usually signified turbulent flow and instability, and the multi-fractal mini-granulations didn't appear to have a significant difference in stability from regular granulations, possibly, Alayna thought, because the instability was manifested in the fractal shape rather than in a shorter duration? But then, wouldn't a "regular shaped" mini-granulation exist for a longer period, rather than a shorter one?

There had even been one study showing that the small number of "regular" mini-granulations was simply the mathematical result of the huge number of observations. In short, the study postulated that, occasionally, the fractal mini-granulations and larger granulations would interact in a way that left a regular "space" between them. Not only did Alayna have her doubts about that, but she was working on a line of research that might further investigate the mini-granulations—not that they were actually "mini," since most of those observed and recorded had the equivalent of an "effective diameter" of six hundred kilometers, although virtually none were actually even close to circular. Of course, she had chosen to look into the mini-granulations at the time of a solar minimum, but she had no idea how that might affect her work, even if earlier studies had suggested "quiet sun" areas were more suitable for such study. *But the phases of the solar cycle don't always coincide with the opportunity to do research.*

A faint chime announced another incoming message, from Harris at Lunara Mining. It was short.

> The Noram inspectors will be leaving here at about 1200 UTC with the pack train. The train will wait for their return. Enjoy their company.

The "pack train" was an AI-guided series of lunar rollers from the Lunara base that carried supplies for Daedalus Base. Almost half a century ago, Lunara had built a maglev from their base to the south polar terminal of the lunar elevator. Alayna wasn't so sure that the charges from others using the maglev weren't the difference between Lunara's making a profit and barely breaking even.

Alayna immediately replied.

> Thanks for the heads-up. Please let me know if they're delayed.
> Let's hope the train doesn't have to wait here too long.

Surprisingly, there was an immediate response.

> Better you than us.

Alayna smiled.

She was glad she'd inspected the quarters the day before. They were spartan, but clean, and everything was laid out.

She glanced at the displays again, then asked Marcel, "Have we had any response from the IAU on that anomaly?"

"No, Dr. Wong-Grant. We have not."

"Do you have any thoughts on what it might be?" Although Alayna suspected that the anomaly was most likely a comet, she wanted Marcel's assessment, even as she wondered, far from the first time, if AIs actually had "thoughts."

"It's unlikely to be an asteroid or a body in a regular orbit at that distance from the sun. Jupiter's gravity would have swept it away long ago. That suggests a cometary orbit, but the light composition doesn't come close to matching any known comet, and the observations suggest that its temperature is close to that of a solid body."

"A solid body in a long-period cometary orbit—a burned-out remnant of a cometary nucleus? Maybe a sungrazer with a metallic . . ." She broke off. Silver and silicates hadn't ever shown up as the principal elements of any comet or asteroid, but the lack of heat strongly suggested that it was just a lump of something. As one early scientist was reputed to have said, "Not only is the universe stranger than we imagine—it is stranger than we can imagine." *Eddington . . . or was it Haldane?* Alayna shrugged. Either way, it was likely true. "The IAU should have notified us if it's something already discovered, shouldn't they?"

"It could be that someone else, or several others, discovered it at the same time. Or it could be that the IAU is waiting for more reports from us or others."

Alayna nodded. The IAU would do what it would do. Before she started studying what was coming in from the Solar Institute's programmed observations, she took a moment to call up Chris's latest message and read through it again, and not just to see what he had observed about the Noram IG's inspection team.

> Alayna—
> I'm parked here at Lunar Low Orbit for the next two days, maybe longer, waiting for a high priority cargo of some sort. Deposited the passengers on the LL Orbit Station, and while I'm waiting for two returning VIPs and some sort of high priority cargo, thought I'd send off a message.
>
> My passengers were rather closemouthed about what they will be doing and where they might be visiting. That alone would suggest that anyone they do visit should be rather cautious. These days, it looks like caution is the watchword, especially since the Sinese report of a successful orbit change of an iceberg asteroid toward Mars.

That part of the message bothered Alayna, because changing the orbits of large chunks of ice or rock carried implications that went far beyond science, astronomy, or astrophysics. But while she worried, she couldn't do much about it. Her eyes went back to the message.

Since you're not likely to read much of *Observations* soon, or not until you've been sunside for a while, there's another passage you might find interesting. I'll even include it here.

In politics, looking at the big picture is the most convenient way to avoid getting bogged down in annoying little details, like the facts. That's why politicians always talk in generalities, such as "balancing the budget" or "obtaining justice under law" or "maintaining meaningful employment," when they really mean "massive spending cuts in programs advocated by my opponents," or "creating a religious loophole for my largest contributor," or "keeping open a redundant and wasteful government facility in my district."

Alayna couldn't help but smile. At the same time, she didn't want the citation/quotation thing to become one-sided. Then she smiled. She had just the right book from which to send back her own citations . . . but that would have to wait. She needed to see if what the Solar Institute was doing dovetailed with what she had in mind. If not . . . there was a block of time, almost an hour, available tomorrow morning where she could insert her own program and follow up on what she'd begun during the last lunar day on Farside. Once she had an observational baseline, then she could use the many small segments of unleased observational time that often occurred, as well as piggyback on observations of the solar latitudes she was studying.

After several minutes of examining the Institute's program and observations, she shook her head. All the focus there was on the chromosphere, and what she needed were specific spectro-polarimeter studies of the base of the photosphere, where the magnetic flux lines created the solar granulations.

With that, she turned to refining the observational program she had worked out.

At 1223 UTC, she got another message from Lunara, even shorter than the earlier one.

Pack train left with passengers and cargo at 1219.

She sent back a pleasant thank-you and went back to work.

At 1611 UTC, Marcel announced, "The lead roller has entered the supply tunnel. ETA at the supply lock is 1623."

"Thank you." Alayna stretched, then made a last survey of all the monitors before rising. She needed to change into an undersuit because she'd have to use the exosuit to unload the supplies, given that the supply tunnel—really just a big covered and radiation-insulated trench—was unpressurized. She voice-locked the control center before heading down to the lower level and the supply lock.

By 1641, all three of her visitors were inside the suit locker room adjoining the supply lock. Alayna was wearing her undersuit, and her suit was hanging before her locker, ready to don, once she finished with her welcoming duties.

She had concentrated when they introduced themselves in order to remember their full names—Antoine Deveau, Geoffrey Hart, and Dominique Perez—because no one had sent her anything on who the inspectors actually were. When she could get away from them gracefully, or maybe after they retired to sleep, she wanted to see if there was any information in the databases.

Alayna offered what she hoped was a warm and welcoming smile. "I'm Dr. Alayna Wong-Grant, the duty astrophysicist and general technician here at COFAR. Once you finish unsuiting, I'll show you to your quarters, and to the galley, if you're so inclined. While you're settling yourselves, I'll need to unload the pack train. After that we can eat, or I can show you around the station."

The shorter man frowned. "We're supposed to . . . ?"

"If you trust my cooking, I can fix something, but I'll need to unload the train first." One of the reasons Alayna wanted and needed to do that was because Harris or someone at Lunara usually threw in some fresh vegetables or fruits from the hydroponics and minifarm at the mining facility, but the insulation on that section of the cargo bin wasn't especially good at keeping things from freezing if they were left too long, and the melons she often received, in particular, were far less edible after being frozen solid.

"It's a one-person station, Geoffrey," said Dominque Perez mildly.

"Just be careful with the pressure cooker or the pressure kettle if you want tea."

"There's not an autochef?" asked Deveau.

"The center has been maintained, but not updated with anything that draws more power. We still operate off the original solar array. Individual panels and assemblies have been replaced, of course, and the Foundation has upgraded the power storage capabilities."

Alayna felt like an old-fashioned tour guide as she led the three from the suit locker room. "There aren't any steps here, just ramps. The idea behind that was to be able to wheel anything anywhere, but the station is fairly well designed, and there's never been much need to move much of any mass inside. Outside, yes. There are four unoccupied rooms here. Each has two bunks. My room is the end one, closest to the hatch up to the operational levels."

Hart offered a puzzled expression. "Space for ten people?"

"A larger crew was required to build the facility, and it didn't take that much more effort to factor in the extra quarters once all the power supplies were in place . . ." Alayna gestured. "The showers and facilities are across the hall . . ."

Once she had them on the upper level, she quickly pointed out the laboratory, the technical support space—the workroom, really—and the hatch to the control center. With an apologetic smile, she said, "I'll leave you to clean up, rest, or whatever. I need to unload the supplies." She did not quite flee.

She also made certain that she was linked to Marcel before she stepped out of the receiving lock.

More than an hour and a half passed before Alayna finished unloading the supply train and stowing the various items, although she did take the fresh produce off first and lock it into the station. Then came space-polymer-wrapped containers of various sizes and shape. She did note that there were not any large packages, nothing resembling antenna film . . . and with only two lengths of replacement film left, more would certainly be needed. *Although . . . it might not be required for years . . . or it could be tomorrow.*

She had sent a message to Foundation Operations about the possible shortage when she had discovered it after the repairs, not in time for replacements likely even to be found or ordered. Before she had sent it, she'd checked the message logs, and her predecessor had made a similar observation over a year ago. That bothered her. Was the Foundation that strapped for funds? Or wasn't anyone making the antenna film anymore?

When she finally unsuited and returned to the upper level of the station, the three were seated at one of the two tables in the room adjoining the galley.

"Do you need something to eat?" Alayna really didn't feel like fixing food for others, but she felt that was clearly expected.

"Antoine managed to find some pasta and various other items. We've eaten," said Geoffrey Hart.

Alayna could have added what he hadn't spoken, something to the effect of "if one can call that eating."

"What were you doing?" asked Dominque Perez.

"Unloading and storing—roughly—what was on the supply train. It wasn't quite a full load. Usually, the train arrives a few days before the night line. They didn't want to send it twice. So they loaded it with what was ready."

"The timing is designed so that the solar cells can power the train?" Perez's words were not quite a question.

"It can run on stored power, but it's more efficient with solar power, and it's also to make sure that it doesn't interfere with nighttime observations any more than necessary. Those are usually the most important." *The ones that bring the Foundation the most revenue.* Dr. Braun had been most emphatic about that.

Alayna definitely had the feeling that the next few days would be long, and that was all she needed after the sleep she'd lost during the last lunar day, both to the repairs, the subsequent cleanup, and making sure that the station was as clean and in as good a condition as possible for the Noram inspectors.

THE TIMES OF INDIA
30 MARCH 2114

(DELHI) "India will not brook interference with its Dyaus Improvement Project." Those were the key words from Prime Minister Narahaj Ravindra yesterday, after the Sinese Minister for Space made a statement suggesting that two space elevators were more than sufficient for the world. The Sinese minister had also suggested that greater priority should be placed on regional environmental remediation, especially after the recent tropical cyclone that destroyed another five percent of the coastal lands of Bangladesh.

In response, Ravindra went on to say, "If necessary, India will place its Indra scramjet missiles on immediate alert."

The Indra has a range of over fifteen thousand kilometers at a speed of between Mach 10 and Mach 16, approximately twenty thousand kph, depending on altitude, and can be programmed to strike within a ten-meter square, allowing a combination of high speed and surgical precision. The Prime Minister's statement was read by many as a thinly veiled suggestion that India would not hesitate in targeting heads of states if any action was taken against extension of the partial space elevator currently used by India . . .

Noram President Dyana Yates weighed in on the controversy by stating, "Noram believes that peaceful national economic and technical goals should not be constrained by political or military considerations." Regretfully, that was one of her more unambiguous statements, even as tensions between the Sinese bloc and the nations of southern Asia have risen in recent months . . .

On Friday evening, after Alayna had eaten, she finished giving the Noram inspectors the internal tour of the station, including the control center, where they questioned Marcel far more than Alayna. The questions she answered were largely about her background and about the staffing of COFAR.

Saturday morning, she did fix breakfast for everyone, hoping to keep the edge out of Geoffrey Hart's voice and questions. By keeping busy, she also avoided questions. After they finished eating, and she cleaned up, before the "free time" on the solar and optical array, she had the three suit up. Then, once the "free" block began, no longer quite free, because the system was collecting her data and observations, she put the inspectors on the roller with her, Perez beside her, and the other two in the cargo bin, and eased the roller out of the upper service lock and out along one of the rows of antennas.

"There are dipole antennas embedded in the polyimide film. Each fifty meter length of film can be replaced . . ."

"How often is that required?" asked Hart, his voice still sounding harsh through the double link.

"Whenever there's damage. I had to replace two lengths about a week ago, during the last lunar night. A micro-meteorite burst damaged both. There have been something like twenty lengths replaced over the last thirty years. It doesn't happen that often."

"There's no atmosphere to shield you," Deveau said evenly. "That seems like a low number of repairs."

"That's true, but the antenna film isn't that wide, and there's much more open space between the antenna rows than what the film takes up. Plus, the film is used as a separator and base for the small embedded dipole antennas so that some meteorite strikes may hit the film without causing damage to the antennae. We're also in a crater, and that stops some of the low angle meteors."

"How wide is the film? A meter?"

"A hundred and twenty centimeters."

"Do you have steerable dishes?" asked Deveau.

Did he read any briefing materials? "We only have five. They're comparatively small. That was because of the weight constraints at the time COFAR was built." *And there was never more funding to add to that array later.* "They're placed in a cross pattern with three kilometers between each."

"Not linear?"

"There was great discussion about that, I understand. It took place before I was born," Alayna added dryly.

"Isn't this the largest radio interferometry array ever developed?" asked Perez.

"That depends on how you define large. It's the largest permanent and fixed array to date. The Sinese longline space array had a greater linear dimension, but it only lasted eleven years. The COFAR array has been able to discern more about the behavior of active galactic nuclei than was even anticipated . . . and how AGNs' reactive measures hold large galaxies together."

"Of what importance is that research?" asked Hart.

"I couldn't tell you that right now. Usually scientific importance is realized in hindsight. A number of astronomic observations in the early twentieth century validated the basic aspects of relativity. It's possible that the observations of galactic internal actions may well lead to a unified theory of quantum mechanics, relativity, and black/strange matter. There have been some observations of changes in galactic dark matter discs that parallel certain shifts in AGN activity."

"What might that lead to, if anything?" Hart pressed.

"It's been theorized that it could lead to balance-point energy foci that would permit selective creation of ship-sized Hawking wormholes. Real-time faster than light travel, if you will." Alayna tried not to snap. "History has shown that the impact of basic research can precede commercial application by more than a century. If there's no basic research, then eventually commercialization slows or even dries up."

"I don't think that—"

"Geoffrey," interjected Perez smoothly but firmly. "Dr. Wong-Grant is a fairly junior, if accomplished, astrophysicist. You're asking her to justify the entire field in philosophical terms. We're here to determine what COFAR does and whether the funding the government supplies is being used effectively. We should keep our questions to those of fact."

Alayna winced, even as she understood who was in charge among the three.

For several moments, no one spoke.

Then Deveau asked, "What percentage of those dipole antennae in a fifty-meter section can you lose before the loss attenuates the signal? Was that what happened when you had to replace those sections of film?"

"There's parallel circuitry in each section. So long as that is intact, there's a minimal difference in the overall signal even if every antenna in a given section fails. The problem in the repairs I had to make was that two sections of antennae were struck by what you might call a microme-teor spray that cut through the continuing circuitry. That's very rare."

"How rare?" asked Hart.

"That kind of break has only happened that one time in forty-seven years." Alayna knew that because she'd had Marcel look it up in the rec-ords, just in case someone did ask.

After the brief tour along the antennae rows, Alayna guided the roller back toward the central optical mirror building. "That's the center of the optical system. The solar telescope in the smaller dome is viewing the sun right now, collecting data on solar granulation."

From the lack of reaction she received, Alayna might as well have been talking about the granulation of sugar.

After several moments, Perez said, "If the telescope is focused on the sun . . ."

"There are various filters. We can observe in various wavelengths, depending on the filter . . . or in visible light with a white light filter." Alayna didn't want to get into why the large telescope had a wider range of motion than the solar telescope, but no one asked.

After several more questions, she turned the roller back to the service lock.

Once they were back at the installation, and unsuited, almost an hour later, Perez turned to Alayna. "We do have a few more questions for you, Doctor."

"Over tea or coffee upstairs?"

"That would be fine."

Alayna led the way to the galley, where she refilled the pressure kettle, and then turned it on. She and Deveau had tea. Perez had coffee. Hart had water. Then the four settled around the large circular table in the adjoining lounge/dining area.

"If you have any last questions," announced Perez, "this is the time to ask them."

"According to the background provided to the Inspector-General," Hart immediately began, "the principal values of the COFAR facility lie in the ultra-low frequency radio telescope and in the full-range capabil-ities of COFAR. What does that mean in simple terms?"

"It means that COFAR's users can obtain more comprehensive data than from most other facilities. Because of the Earth's ionosphere, ultra-low frequency radio astronomy isn't possible on Earth or even in orbit around Earth. Long-baseline antennas aren't terribly practical in space, even at Lagrange Points, and repair costs here are far less expensive. The failure of the Sinese longline free space array proved that."

"With a fusionjet, you can put a technician anywhere close to Earth in hours," Hart pointed out.

"The cost of sending a fusionjet rocket from ONeill Station to the LLOS one time is more than the total cost of maintaining COFAR for a year. A repair mission costs more than that. The Noram government only pays part of COFAR's operating costs, and none of the Noram support is for equipment or repairs. All equipment and repair costs are paid by the Farside Foundation," replied Alayna, not that she'd known any of that before studying the briefing materials that Director Braun had sent. "The solar telescope here, and the associated equipment, is the largest in the system and provides an unmatched capability." Even as she spoke, Alayna wondered what, if anything, the system might have picked up while she had been guiding the inspectors around the facility.

"For all that you say," said Deveau musingly, "there are many astronomers who feel that off-planet astronomy offers more advantages and can be more cost-effective."

"There's an argument for that," admitted Alayna, "but not from Noram's point of view. To put a space observatory in place that would exceed COFAR's existing capabilities would cost far more than the share of upkeep paid by the government. Most of the astronomers who want the free space observatories want governments to pay the majority of the costs."

"Some of them claim that the Farside Foundation charges too much and wastes money," stated Hart.

"We charge enough to keep the facility operating." Alayna gestured around the small windowless chamber. "This isn't exactly opulent. We're reliable. Most of the so-called free space observation facilities have come and gone over the past century or so."

"What astronomical breakthroughs has COFAR made?" asked Hart.

"We have supplied the facilities and observation time for a number of astronomers and astrophysicists who have made various discoveries. Without our facilities, that would not have been possible."

"Such as?" Hart's voice was dry.

"Maartan Scheel's work on active galactic nuclei that revealed the links between dark matter and dark energy was accomplished through COFAR facilities. That could lead to revolutionary future scientific breakthroughs. I mentioned that earlier."

Almost another hour passed before Perez looked around the table. "I think we've seen enough, and taken enough of your time, Dr. Wong-Grant." She offered a pleasant smile. "If we leave within the hour, we can stay close to our schedule."

"Do you have any last questions . . . anything else I might be able to answer?" Alayna wanted to preserve the impression of helpfulness to the end.

"I think not," declared Perez firmly.

Alayna couldn't tell whether that was good or bad. Polite as Perez had been, Alayna couldn't tell whether she was for or against COFAR funding, or if she even cared. "Where are you headed for from here?"

"To the next installation we've been assigned to inspect."

"I wish you the best," Alayna replied with a pleasant smile.

Once she had seen the three inspectors off, she immediately secured the station, then returned to the control center, where she wrote a report for Director Braun, detailing everything the three had seen, and the nature of their questions, as well as their unwillingness to say where they were going, and the fact that Dominique Perez seemed to be in charge.

Only after that was she finally able to begin to study the results of her own observations. Even under the greatest enhancement, neither she nor Marcel—or rather his management of all manner of optical and spectral analysis—could see any sign of what she had hoped to at least catch a hint of.

"What if we shifted wavelengths?"

"Your program already did that, Dr. Wong-Grant."

"How about overlaying all the hydrogen . . . or calcium wavelengths?"

Marcel began to create the overlays, and Alayna kept looking at the overlaid combinations of wavelengths, and the more she looked, the more she felt that she was missing something. *But what?*

"Are there patterns buried in those combined wavelengths?"

"There are no discernible shapes recognizable as regular."

That didn't mean there weren't any. It did mean that the AI, or its programming, or its own continually learning self-programming, did not discern any.

You must be imagining things.

Alayna was still thinking that over when she turned to the message queue. The newest message was from the International Astronomical Union.

The object you registered with the IAU has been named C/X/2114 FT2 COFAR-SMOA. IAU would appreciate periodic updates.

Alayna should have recognized the acronym for the co-discoverer.
She didn't. "SMOA? What's that?"

"The Sinese Main Optical Array."

"Oh, SINOP." For some reason, she hadn't recognized the official
acronym of the Sinese deep space array.

"They've classified it as a comet, but they're asking for periodic updates on the object? They don't sound certain."

"The object appears to be on a cometary orbit with an eccentricity
close to one, and an inclination of forty-three degrees. Its albedo varies
periodically and is not characteristic of any known comet."

*Then why are they classifying it as a comet? Because it might be an old
burned out one? Or is the designation provisional pending more observations?* Alayna almost asked about Kuiper Belt or Oort Cloud objects,
but that would have been a stupid question. Eris and some other KBOs
had high albedos, but those were based on icy surfaces, not one that suggested silicates and silver. *And their albedos don't vary. You need to inform
Foundation operations.*

She took care with the report to Director Braun, making sure it was
factual, but less than fifteen minutes after she sent it, she had a response.

> Your discovery may help the Foundation, and we appreci-
> ate your diligence. While not strictly necessary, it might have
> been politic to have listed the Williams Observatory as a co-
> discoverer, since Comet COFAR was discovered during shared
> observation time. If this could be quietly remedied, it would
> be useful.

*Translated loosely, you should have thought of that, because anything
will help with fundraising.*

With a sigh, Alayna went to work composing another message to IAU,
not that it would do much good, given that the IAU naming conventions
only recognized the first two discoverers, but at least she could note that
she had tried and inform Director Braun. Sometime after that, perhaps,
she could finally send a message to Chris, the one person who didn't seem
to be demanding something from her. Then, for a little while, she might
listen to music or even see if any of the realies she brought appealed to
her . . . or any of those left by Luis, although she had her doubts about
whether any of those would appeal to her.

9

LUNAR LOW ORBIT STATION
2 APRIL 2114

Tavoian looked at the message that had come through the encrypted link several minutes before reading it a second time.

> Tavoian, Christopher, Captain, NSC
> FusEx Three, ONeill Station
> Noram Space Service
>
> You are hereby ordered to proceed with your vessel to Lunar Lagrange Station 1, for further assignment. Details for release and travel will arrive via LunaCon Operations. Authorizations to follow.

That was all—no explanation. No details on the assignment, or how long it would be, or what it would entail. Or who his replacement might be. His tour at ONeill Station wasn't due to end until October, and he'd been told it might even have to be extended. So what had changed, or had it been something he'd done?

His first thought was whether he'd offended the Noram IG types. He shook his head. He might have done that, but the originating time and date on the orders were before he'd even linked to LLOS, and the IG types would have had no way to commlink while onboard. So whatever had caused him to come to the attention of detailing hadn't been his passengers. He went back over his past shuttle hops, but he couldn't think of a single incident that might have singled him out for something he'd done in either exemplary or terrible fashion. The one thing he did know was that, whatever it was, someone didn't want the details on the commnet, and that was anything but routine.

He puzzled over the orders for several minutes more, then shrugged. Whatever he'd done, or not done, or for whatever reason Space Command had made the decision, there wasn't much he could do about it. All he could do was let a few people know.

His first message was to Alayna.

> I've just received orders that I'm being transferred to L1 Station, for further assignment. What that means, I have no idea. I've never received orders like that before. Nor has anyone else that I've heard of. Then again, how would I know? As for messaging, keep using the same routing. I should get anything you send, except it might take a little longer.
>
> I only hope it doesn't have anything to do with the mess developing between the Sinese and the Indians. If the Indians want to gamble their future on turning their partial space elevator into a surface-to-orbit operation, with the base link in the middle of the Indian Ocean, which doesn't have the calmest of waters, then that's their business. As I understood it, that was why they initially opted for a partial elevator that didn't descend into the lower atmosphere. I'll let you know what I can when I can.
>
> Have you made any progress in your solar project? Who knows? You just might discover something new about the sun. Or are you still dealing with the Noram IG team? I assume they at least paid a visit to COFAR. If they didn't, count yourself quite fortunate.
>
> I'm still thinking over that selection you sent from *The Passion of Science* . . .

Tavoian could even remember the quote without looking at her last message—"Passion is the genesis of science, but then, passion has been the genesis of everything." While he remembered it, he wasn't ready to comment on the content. Not directly, anyway.

> In return, I'll offer another extract from *Observations*. "'Truth' is a judgment placed on the facts, not the facts themselves, a point irrelevant to both politicians and pathological liars." From what you've said and what I've read, true scientists try to avoid using the word "truth." Maybe the rest of the human race might give that a try . . .

When he finished the message to Alayna, Tavoian sent a second, and much shorter one to his parents, just saying that he was being transferred to LL1 station on temporary duty and that he'd let them know more when he knew. He dispatched a copy to his sister Katherine. Kit continually insisted on knowing where he was stationed, and what he was doing. He always let her and his parents know what he could, and he tried to do so in a way that wouldn't worry them. *Even when you're worried . . . like now.*

Then . . . he looked at his orders—again—trying to read something into them that clearly wasn't there, wondering when LunaCon would release him and his ship for the very short hop to LL1.

10

HOTNEWS!
3 APRIL 2114

[Image Deleted for Off-Earth Transmission]

Another rumor that's no longer rumor. Remember that Sinese "robotic science mission" to investigate Jupiter's moons? It didn't fail. Not from what *HotNews!* has discovered. It found something out there, but the Sinese aren't talking. When they don't talk about science, it's not science.

[Image Deleted]

EC Chancellor Rumikov—he's at it again! Hot-ice and then some. Another non-denial denial by the double-dexed man-around. The woman he visited in Paris on the way back to Moscow from the Madrid meeting of regional EC ministers? She's not his mistress. His daughter? Could be. Accepting that her mother is a male double-sexer. Nothing about rumored billion Euro trust fund set aside in an unnamed hidden overnet bank, either.

[Image Deleted]

As for the question of higher quotas for EC Hel3 coming off the lunar el? Not a word from Noram Prexy Dyana Yates. No Artemis there.

[Image Deleted]

Diva Eleana denies the full-body leaked netwide is her. She shouldn't. Better shape than hers. Could it be that the denial's to make the leaked image seem real? Her career's not the only thing sagging.

[Image Deleted]

Senator Khelsey Armstrong, no Venus there! Not for the Moralist candidate for the Noram presidency. *HotNews!* hears that her ex has let that be known. She can say yes, to the right one. Even no, if only to her ex, unlike Dyana, who speaks a lot and says nothing. Too bad no pics.

[Image Deleted]

Mighty India's PM Ravindra shaking the Indra stick again. Much good that'll do him. The last thunderbolt that had any effect was an American aircraft in a losing war. Sorry about that, antiquarians. Facts is facts.

[Image Deleted]

Latest on the Bollywood scene. Transgen Tanya isn't. Transgen, that is. She's a she... and always has been. Make that "has been." All that surgery... just to make her features and figure match the image...

[Image Deleted]

Noram's DOEA Secretary insists the increase in Noram FusEx production was "strictly for commercial reasons." What about that Memo of Understanding with the Department of Defense concerning transfers of propulsive assets? What assets? Could they be missiles? Naughty, naughty... isn't there a treaty about not militarizing outer space?

11

LUNAR LOW ORBIT STATION
3 APRIL 2114

Tavoian was still waiting for word from LunaCon Operations on Monday morning, sitting alone in the pilots' ready room after having spent a not very restful night in a small cubicle euphemistically called a cabin. The cabin had been vaguely redolent of a disinfecting deodorizer, but Tavoian still preferred to sleep in low pseudo-grav than in weightlessness. Besides, it put less strain on the ship's habitability systems, and he always wanted to have any ship he piloted in the best shape possible. He'd checked messages even before he ate, but there was nothing new. He'd even packed all his gear back into his kit, and stowed it in his ship locker, just so he wouldn't have to worry about that when he reached LL1.

He hadn't gotten a return message from Alayna, but sometimes she did take several days to reply. On the other hand, Kit had replied with a message peppered with questions he couldn't answer, and even if he had known the answers, he likely wouldn't have been able to answer them without revealing things he was required not to disclose. But that went both ways, since Space Command restricted retransmission of the more salacious "news" realies, like *HotNews!* and *Unlimited*, even though they were stripped of video and sound for off-Earth transmission.

At 0814 UTC, the ready room speaker announced, "Briefing information for Captain Christopher Tavoian on console two."

Tavoian had no idea whether the announcement was AI-generated or whether a human had entered the information. He doubted whether it mattered in the slightest as he hurried to the indicated console, where he pressed his hand to the sensor and then entered his personal authentication.

The briefing information revealed only two things more than the orders of the previous day. The first was his scheduled departure time from LLOS—1010 UTC. The second was that he would be carrying two passengers—Valentia Frezza, Senior Technician, LL1, and Martyn Franck, Technician3, LL1. The last line was that further orders awaited him at LL1.

The fact that he only had two passengers was an indication that his departure was not entirely conditioned on waiting for cargo or passengers, as well as a confirmation of sorts that someone wanted him soon at the end of the comparatively short hop—amazing in a way that a distance of from fifty-five thousand kays to more than seventy thousand could be considered short.

From the ready room he immediately returned to FusEx three, where he began the pre-release checklist. He finished that in less than fifteen minutes, even taking his time. Then he waited . . . and waited. At least, that was how it felt.

PASSENGERS ARE AT THE LOCK, the ship's AI announced. THEIR AUTHENTICATIONS CHECK.

"Thank you."

Tavoian pulled himself down the ladder from the control deck to the forward passenger deck, where he opened the outer lock, and then after closing it, the inner hatch. The two technicians were definitely different— a tall woman and a much shorter young man, both in gray shipsuits with Noram Technical Service insignia.

"Technician Frezza, Tech Franck . . . Chris Tavoian." He smiled politely. "I'll be your pilot to LL1."

The tallish woman nodded politely. "How long will it take?"

"The actual transit is less than an hour. That's because we're already mostly above Nearside." It would have been almost another hour, largely because of maneuvering requirements, had the station been above Farside at the time of departure. "Release and docking times . . . that's up to Operations. Usually around half an hour at each end."

"Thank you."

Tavoian looked to Franck, markedly shorter than Frezza, compact and not quite chubby, with an expression like a worried puppy. Tavoian wondered if LL1 was his first off-planet assignment. He cleared his throat before beginning, "You'll have heard the briefing before, but it's required. First, you're required to comply with any order that I give . . ." When he finished, he gestured to the lockers and then the couches. "Please stow your gear securely, and then strap yourselves in. We're scheduled for release shortly."

Both techs nodded, but did not speak.

As he made his way up to the control deck, hand over hand in weightlessness, Tavoian found himself mentally comparing Frezza to Alayna. Frezza had striking jet-black hair, cut short, and hazel eyes. She was willowy and tall. Alayna was definitely shorter and more muscular, with nondescript brown hair. But Tavoian recalled Alayna's eyes, intense green with what he could only call an aliveness . . . and he'd liked talking to her. It was clear enough that Frezza wasn't one for talking. Franck he somehow felt sorry for.

Once in the control deck, Tavoian sealed and locked the hatch to the passenger deck, then strapped himself in and completed the post-boarding check. After another scan of the displays, he activated the restraint warning, switched the ship from station power to ship auxiliary power, then opened the commlink. "LunaCon, FusEx three, ready for release."

"FusEx three, this is LunaCon. You are disengaged. Cleared for immediate release this time. Cleared to use thrusters. Do not activate drive until you are cleared for ignition."

"LunaCon, three commencing release this time. Will await clearance for ignition." Tavoian put the AI in maneuvering mode. "Commencing maneuvering this time."

Once the ship was clear, Tavoian announced to the AI, "Destination is Lunar Lagrange Point One. Begin destination orientation." He watched while the AI oriented the ship for the trip to Luna Lagrange One, a course that would gradually converge to parallel the nearside lunar elevator that ran from the Moon's surface to Lagrange Point One.

After several moments, the AI replied, ORIENTATION COMPLETE. READY FOR IGNITION.

At that, Tavoian commlinked, "Three oriented and ready for departure."

"FusEx three, you're cleared for ignition and departure."

"LunaCon, understand cleared for ignition." Tavoian switched to the AI. "Commence ignition."

COMMENCING IGNITION.

Initially, there was the faintest sense of pressure, pushing Tavoian back into his couch. That faint pressure continued to build for the next several minutes until it reached one gee, leveling out at that point. While he turned off the "restraint" display in the passenger deck, he did not bother to unstrap, not for the less than twenty minutes before turnover and decel.

He still couldn't help but wonder what awaited him at LL1. Lunar Lagrange Station 1 was entirely Noram, funded originally as a means to obtain Hel3 and whatever other lunar resources might prove useful . . . and profitable. After almost a century, Helium three remained the most useful and profitable, although enough light metals, water, and hydrogen had showed up that a small supply and fabricating industry had developed to provide some other supplies and equipment for near-Earth space activities.

After nineteen minutes of acceleration, followed by turnover, and eighteen point nine minutes of deceleration, FusEx three moved slowly toward docking ring two of Lunar Lagrange Station One. Tavoian link-pulsed the station. "EllgeeCon, FusEx three, approaching for docking."

"FusEx three, cleared for docking at lock two. Thrusters only."

"Understand lock two." Tavoian cut the drive. "Proceeding on thrusters this time." He turned over approach control to the ship's AI, although he continued to monitor the rate of closure until FusEx three rested in the locking cradle, and the station umbilical was ready to supply power. Then he switched to station power.

"FusEx three, Ellgee Control. You're cleared for disembarkation. Your replacement is standing by. Please leave your fueling port unsealed."

"Will do, Control. Thank you."

"Thank you."

Replacement? Someone wasn't wasting any time.

Still thinking about that, Tavoian shut down the ship's aux power before continuing shutdown procedures. Then he turned off the restraint light, and once he had opened the hatch to the forward passenger deck, he went along the ladder hand over hand.

Even before he was near the lock on the passenger deck, Frezza and Franck were unstrapped and retrieving their gear. At the same time, the AI announced through his earpiece, YOUR REPLACEMENT IS READY TO ENTER.

Tavoian did not reply to that, but opened the lock hatch and turned to the two techs. "Whenever you're ready."

Frezza moved toward the lock, nodded, and said, "Thank you." She did not smile.

"Thank you, Captain," added Franck, grinning boyishly.

"You're welcome." Tavoian closed the inner lock and opened the outer one to the station. Once he saw that the techs were clear, he watched as a uniformed figure with a kit bag entered the lock with the grace of experience in weightlessness. Then he closed the outer lock and opened the inner one.

Not totally surprisingly, Tavoian recognized the major who pulled himself through the open inner hatch and into the ship, a kit bag in one hand—Drake Gray.

"Good to see you again, Chris," offered the major.

"*You're* my replacement?" That didn't make sense to Tavoian. Gray had been a senior captain when he'd trained Tavoian, and he was probably near his rad limit, if not over it, by now.

"Only for one hop, and I'm not the pilot." Gray offered a crooked smile. "I am in command, though. We're using your ship to pick up some special equipment. Your escort will be here shortly. You'll meet her at lock five, or rather you'll meet the tug she's piloting there."

"Will I need an exosuit?"

"No. They're sending a passenger tug."

"Can you tell me what this is all about?"

"No. You'll find out once she takes you to your new assignment."

"Exactly where is that?"

"You'll see when you get there."

"That's it?"

"You never were the most patient officer, but you'll learn." Gray grinned. "We all do, sooner or later. You'd better get your kit. The colonel doesn't like officers who keep others waiting."

Tavoian decided against asking who "the colonel" was. He'd find out soon enough. He nodded and went to the end locker and pulled out his kit bag. Then he pulsed the signal to the AI that he was delinking, which would require Gray, or the pilot who was presumably on his way, to offer the proper authentication to take control of the ship.

"You have the ship, sir."

"I have the ship, Captain."

There was no gravity in the docking ring, but there was a moving rail on the inner side of the ring corridor. Tavoian grabbed it and let it tow him to lock five. He arrived just moments before the lock door opened.

The outer lock hatch of the tug was low enough that he angled himself forward as he pulled himself into the craft's lock, surprisingly large for a tug, although most tug locks were only big enough for two people in exosuits.

The tug pilot stood, or floated upright, by the hatch to the control deck, since the layout of the tug was more like an aircraft than a burner. She was a fresh-faced first lieutenant, who immediately said, "Courtney Collins, Captain. You can have the right seat up with me, if you want. You're the only one, and if you're like the others, you hate being a passenger."

The others? "Where are we headed, if I might ask?"

"Donovan Base."

Tavoian had never heard of it. "Here at Lagrange One?"

Collins nodded. "Close enough. You don't have to strap in, but it will keep you in place. The lockers are at the back."

Tavoian took the hint, stowed his kit, and then returned to the copilot's couch and strapped in. He doubted that there was a copilot very often. "The number two seat is just for training and familiarization?"

"That's right. There aren't any simulators for this tug."

Tavoian had to admit he hadn't seen any pressurized space tugs before. "Because it's more of a transport, and it saves on suits . . . and notice?"

"Mostly notice, I'd judge."

The other difference was that the tug had both a view plate in front of the controls, with a heads-up display, suggesting that the pilot had to do visual maneuvering in areas where the screen displays either could not be used or were not used, possibly for security reasons. Tavoian kept that thought to himself as Collins commlinked.

"EllgeeCon, Shuttle Zebra, departing lock five this time."

"Zebra, you're clear."

Tavoian was initially surprised when the lieutenant did not turn control over to an AI, but then realized that there wasn't one. That didn't make him feel any better.

The tug's destination was a gray cylinder floating in space. As they neared, Tavoian could see that it was huge, possibly a thousand meters in length and five hundred in diameter, with a docking ring that was a solid disk above. Given the short time it took Collins to guide the tug there, Tavoian doubted that it was more than five or ten kays from LL1, if that, because the effective area of the libration point at L1 was comparatively small.

Interestingly enough, Collins did not request clearance as the tug approached the cylinder.

"Active IFF?" asked Tavoian.

She nodded.

He didn't ask any more questions as she used what were clearly beefed-up gasjet thrusters to maneuver the tug to where the station grapples enfolded it and drew it to the lock. Before that, Tavoian had also seen a far larger cargo lock farther around the circumference of the docking ring. While he couldn't be certain, he thought he might have glimpsed a fusion-jet on the far side of the ring as well.

An angular and narrow-faced tech2 in a plain gray shipsuit waited outside the lock, his boots well above the deck. As in all stations, the docking ring was not rotated.

"Welcome to Donovan Base, sir." The tech reached for Tavoian's kit. "I'll take your gear, sir."

"That's not optional, is it?"

"No, sir. It will be waiting in your quarters after you meet with the colonel."

That was another factor that told Tavoian that Donovan Base was a secure installation. Everything in his kit bag would be scanned, and then some, before it was returned to him.

"This way, sir." The tech moved toward a corridor that led to the center of the docking disk. Once there, he touched a stud, and the transit rail began to move. Following the tech's example, Tavoian grasped the rail and was pulled toward the center of the disk, where an open shaft dropped down, presumably into the center of the cylinder that was the base. Four ladders led down, not that there was any "down" in weightlessness. It could have been "up" as well, but Tavoian preferred to think of it as down. He went hand over hand, just using the ladder rungs occasionally, and joined the tech in front of an open hatch.

"After you, sir."

Tavoian stepped into what seemed like a small room or an elevator car, but what had to be a transfer car that would match the rotational speed of the base. The tech followed, and the hatch to the shaft closed. Tavoian shifted position so that his feet were against the bulkhead opposite the hatch, which would become the floor—sort of, because there would be that much centripetal force at the center of the cylinder, likely only the slightest amount, although that depended on the base's rate of rotation. He could feel the slightest tug almost immediately as what had seemed a bulkhead became a deck. Then a section of the new "deck" opened.

Tavoian moved forward and let himself drop into the transition room, which opened onto a shaft heading outward toward the rim of the base.

"There are belt harnesses on the shaft railing. Please use one of them, sir."

Tavoian understood. While he doubted that the base/station was rotating fast enough to cause him any physical damage if he slipped and was thrown outward to the end of the shaft, it was better not to take unnecessary chances—or to break the rules of a base that he hadn't even known existed, especially one as large as Donovan Base.

They did not pass or see anyone on the trip down the moving rail to the outermost deck. Tavoian did notice that the bulkheads, overheads, and decks were all a pale blue, far easier on the eyes than the gray of LLOS or ONeill Station. When he reached the base of the shaft, he realized that he stood in the equivalent of about a half gee. Given that, the harnesses did make much more sense. It also told him that the base was intended for longer-term tours.

He walked beside the tech2 along a corridor for almost fifty meters, passing several closed doors—doors, not hatches, although Tavoian saw an open pressure hatch some twenty meters farther along when the tech stopped and opened a door. "This is the colonel's office. I'll take care of your gear."

"Thank you."

Tavoian stepped into the office, where a rating sat at a console outside a closed pressure hatch—another oddity, or so it seemed to him.

The rating looked up as Tavoian approached. "Captain Tavoian?" Her voice was pleasant, but even.

"Reporting."

The spacer3 pointed to the biometric ID attached to the wall. "If you would, sir."

That wasn't a request, either, and Tavoian had no doubt that if the biometrics didn't match, he'd be immobilized before he could move. He still felt nervous when he stepped up to the eye reader and placed both hands in the gauntlets.

"Thank you, sir. The colonel will see you in a moment."

There were no chairs, suggesting that there was little loitering in the outer office . . . or that the colonel wanted to make it uncomfortable, although that was likely to take longer in what amounted to a half gee. Tavoian didn't have to wait long, less than five minutes before the hatch opened.

"You can go in, Captain."

"Thank you." Tavoian nodded politely and eased around the console and through the pressure hatch that closed immediately behind him. The colonel's inner office held a console and two chairs . . . as well as one entire bulkhead that was jet-black—most likely a blanked-out dimensional display that could focus on a single image or scores of individual displays, probably from all over Donovan Base. *And from who knows where else.*

The officer who stood by the console chair had short-cut but limp sandy hair shot with gray and a round face that might have been cherubic if there had been a gram of fat in it. His eyes were an innocent-appearing blue.

"You can call me Colonel Anson, or Colonel. Don't bother searching for me under that name. You won't find anything." The colonel's voice was a pleasant baritone. He gestured to the empty chair, then seated himself. "Have you ever heard of Donovan Base before, Captain?"

"No, sir."

"Even a suggestion of it?"

"No, sir." And that was true.

"Would you care to speculate on why it exists?"

"It's obviously for a military purpose, and one that DOEA doesn't want known. I can't think of any other reason. Beyond that, I'd rather not speculate."

"Speculate on why it's located where it is, please."

Tavoian paused, thought for several moments. "The lunar elevator, Ellgee Station, and the LLOS are all strictly Noram controlled. A large featureless cylindrical disk near Ellgee Station might well be a storage or transshipment point. Sometimes, concealing something is easier if it's concealed in plain sight. It's also often easier to get to." He paused. "Is there, by chance, another large seemingly identical disk in the other direction?"

The colonel smiled. "Those who evaluated you said you were perceptive. In time, we'll see how perceptive. What do you think of the political situation, particularly with regard to Earth?"

"I don't like what I see, sir. The situation between the Sinese bloc and India seems especially dangerous, and I wouldn't be surprised if the UAAS isn't up to something. Sudam continues to resent the presence of ONeill Station as a check on their control of the WestHem elevator. I also wouldn't be surprised if EC Chancellor Rumikov doesn't have aspirations to re-create the Russian Empire with himself as tzar."

"I'd be surprised if he didn't. I'd also be surprised if he is foolish enough to ever reveal a hint of that. You're right to be concerned about the Sinese-Indian tensions. Here's a relatively current image of the Indian geocentric orbit station." The colonel gestured toward the wallscreen covering the entire bulkhead opposite the pressure hatch as it lit up with a single image, that of a disc with the Earth below, showing the station's position over the equatorial Indian Ocean.

Tavoian couldn't tell from the image how large the station might be.

"You can't see the cabling up to the counterweight. Almost the entire upper surface is covered with solar panels. Each panel is a film square five meters on a side. The station is 250 meters across."

"That's a fair amount of power, isn't it?"

"A little less than a hundred megawatts at ninety percent efficiency." The colonel offered a lazy smile.

"But they're not beaming it anywhere, are they? That's prohibited under the terms of the Earth Satellite Treaty."

"You don't believe that the Indians or Sinese would be stopped by a mere treaty, do you, Captain?"

"No, sir, but they would be stopped by someone detecting that and making it known . . . and it would be hard to hide that kind of power transmission, if it occurred on a continuous basis."

"Except perhaps over the central equatorial waters of the Indian Ocean." The colonel paused. "You're correct, however. They're doing something else, which is why both the Sinese and the EC are worried, not to mention the Australians. They've likely developed a new form of supercapacitor."

Tavoian had to think about that. A geocentric satellite installation with a massive solar array . . . "Can they deploy an even larger film cell array?"

"Most definitely." The colonel waited for Tavoian to say more.

"Lasers, even pumped lasers, wouldn't be that effective against hardened ground targets. Even a particle beam . . . not that anyone has managed to develop one . . ." Tavoian looked to the colonel.

"Not too bad, but you're thinking about ground targets. The Indian elevator orbit station is just a bit over fourteen thousand kays—orbital distance—from the Sinese elevator station."

Tavoian thought he understood. The Indians could hit the Sinese station . . . if they had either a particle beam or a high powered laser . . . and if they could focus and aim it over that distance.

"You're not saying anything, Captain."

"You're suggesting that the Indians can take out the Sinese elevator and stations without any warning."

"We're fairly certain that they can't . . . yet. No laser or particle weapon can be focused with that intensity over that distance. So far."

"But the Sinese think that could happen, and they want to stop the Indians before that can happen?"

"Wouldn't you . . . if you were the Sinese?" The colonel's smile was ironic. "The entire Sinese bloc, as a whole, has a declining population. They've suffered some devastating economic blows because of sea-level rise. There's little left of Guangzhou, and Singapore is essentially dying behind seawalls that will have to be raised again in another few years. We can't even count the coastal communities and lowlands that they've lost. Or the sections of larger cities."

"So have we." Tavoian couldn't help but think of a third or more of New York City under water, the "Venice of the West," or the ruins of Miami, a totality of disaster that had been compounded by the collapse of so many limestone caverns across Florida, half of which was under water, or New Orleans and Sacramento.

"We gained some productive land in Canada, and access to Arctic Ocean resources. When what remained of the Russian Federation joined the EC, that blocked the Sinese from a northern frontier, especially with the desertification of northern China. India actually benefited, at least comparatively, from the combination of the Climate War and the Middle East Meltdown. With Pakistan eliminated, the reformation of Iran, and the ocean's effective reclamation of most of Bangladesh, the only real threat they face is the Sinese, and the longer they can hold on, the more the balance swings in their favor."

"And the Sinese obviously know this," Tavoian said, suspecting that some commentary was necessary.

"The Sinese have continued to build burners, and there are more docked at their Heavenly Jade Station than we've ever seen."

"And we're stockpiling Hel3 just in case?"

The colonel smiled pleasantly. "How did you come up with that idea?"

"That's an estimate based on the price . . . and various rumors about burner power conservation." None of which Tavoian would have known if Keiser hadn't mentioned it.

"The other aspect of the problem is that the UAAS has approached India about the possibility of developing an orbital tethered power system."

"As a way to get their own elevator or partial elevator?"

"That's a possibility. All of this could lead to a situation where military superiority definitely shifts from a reliance on both Earth and space-based weapons to one where space-based weapons will predominate." The colonel cleared his throat. "That leads to why you're here at this particular time. There are reasons why DOEA has insisted that all fusionjet pilots are also commissioned Space Command officers, and why we've resisted commercialization of space travel. It's not merely a matter of parochial control, not that we mind having that control. It's more fundamental than that. Very much more fundamental than that. The aim of business is to make money. Lots of it. However those sainted business leaders can do it. The aim of military leaders is to protect those they serve. All of those they serve. That's the honest senior officers. The dishonest ones want to protect people in order to rule them. That puts even a dishonest general above an honest businessman. Give business total access to fusionjets, and we'll be under Sinese control in a generation. Or maybe Indian control."

Tavoian understood what the general was saying. He had doubts about some of it.

"... every DOEA fusionjet was designed and built for rapid conversion into a warcraft. Currently, four fusionjets, five including the one you piloted here, are being converted as a precautionary measure. You, and a number of other pilots, will be trained to operate those combat craft."

"Might I ask to what end, sir?"

"To the end that we hope you'll never have to fire a weapon in combat. We want to present a new and powerful weapon to keep either the Sinese or the Indians from attacking each other. Or us."

And to make it clear that Noram is still a power to be respected. Tavoian didn't have to say that. He knew that was really what the colonel had in mind.

Alayna had been able to gather over almost eighty hours' worth of observational solar data over the first nine Earth days of the long lunar "day" . . . and still she was finding nothing new among the scores and scores of multi-fractal mini-granulations. *And you're confining your observations to a narrow band of solar latitude. Still . . . that doesn't mean something's not there.* With that thought, she shook her head. Lack of discovery could well mean that there was nothing. *Except that no one has yet been able to probe beneath the upper surface of the photosphere, and there's a lot beneath that.*

While she hadn't found anything yet, she did have Marcel set aside a special file of the single-element overlays he had created for her. *There has to be something.* Except she was well aware that there didn't have to be. All too many scientists throughout history had felt there had to be "something," and more often than not, they didn't find it. Most of science was disproving, not proving or finding something new, a fact overlooked by most people, and especially by the media and politicians.

She'd put off answering Chris's latest message for several reasons, including the fact that she'd been preoccupied with her own research, poring over the data and observations, looking for the smallest hint of something besides the patterns of granulation and mini-granulation that had been studied and restudied for more than a century and a half. But it seemed that nothing was there. *Nothing was there . . .*

For some reason an old rhyme came into her head.

> *Yesterday, upon the stair,*
> *I met a man who wasn't there.*
> *He wasn't there again today.*
> *I wish, I wish he'd go away.*

Like it or not, one way or another, the data, the observational hints she was seeking, the clues, the whatever . . . she and the solar array weren't finding them . . . or not recognizing them, and she was having trouble dealing with that. She reminded herself that Percival Lowell had looked for Pluto for more than ten years, and after Lowell's death Clyde Tombaugh had searched more than a year. And then seventy-six years after Tombaugh found it, and almost ten years after his death, the IAU decided he hadn't found a planet at all but just another KBO.

With a wry smile, she pushed the thoughts about her project away. She needed to do something else for at least a little while, and she did owe Chris a reply. *Owe?* She did owe him, but she'd found that she liked messaging him, and she also liked that she could think about what she said before sending those thoughts off. It also didn't hurt that he'd given her hints about the Noram inspectors, either.

> Chris—
> I hope this reaches you without too much delay, and that your new assignment is something you'll be looking forward to. If it's not, you do have my condolences, and even a trace of sympathy.

She wasn't about to say what else she thought, that he'd likely have a job with the Space Service or DOEA as long as he wanted it, unlike her. Alayna was well aware that finding a job in her field, even after a stint at COFAR, was going to be extraordinarily difficult, even if she had discovered a comet, if it even turned out to be one. More likely it was an ancient burned-out relic. That might explain the silicon. *But what about the silver?*

She shook her head. In an infinite universe there had to be a cometary nucleus with silver traces. And finding something slightly odd wouldn't distinguish her that much from the hundreds of others who made cometary discoveries, many of whom were dedicated amateurs. Professional-level jobs were difficult to find and even harder to hold, and the last thing she wanted was to have to go into some form of personal service, no matter how dignified the title or remunerative the pay, although most personal service didn't pay that much.

> Almost another week [Earth measure] has gone by. I've got lots more observations and data, but nothing yet along the lines I'm looking for. That's often the nature of observational astrophysics. I wouldn't call it a "truth," especially after your last quotation. I do think there's a great deal of accuracy in those words, though. In terms of the havoc that proclamations of truth cause, is there any great difference between politicians, religious fanatics, and pathological liars, especially when they

say things like, "The truth of the matter is . . ." and then go on to spout some nonsense? Scientists aren't immune from believing in nonsense, of course, but most nonsense from scientists occurs when they venture outside their field. In time, any nonsense we spout within our field is usually discovered quickly. Usually, anyway.

In the spirit of trading thought-provoking quotations, I've enclosed something a bit different.

She called up the more lengthy selection she'd attached. *Lengthy compared to what you sent before, but you don't want him thinking he's the only one who can find longer meaningful passages.* Even as she thought that, she wondered why she cared so much about what he thought. It wasn't as though they'd likely even see each other again. Her eyes dropped to the excerpt.

> *Scientists too often accept the criticism that they don't get excited. We do get excited. We just don't get as excited in print or publication. Nor do we get excited about the everyday. Too many people get too passionate about too little, and not as excited about what matters. Who cares who won what event in the Olympics? Millions! Who got really excited and concerned about the carbon levels in the Earth's atmosphere? Thousands, and they were all scientists. But everyone forgot who won what medal in two weeks, and the entire world was left coping with the disasters caused by the greenhouse effect fueled by increased carbon levels. People remember the great comets they have seen their entire life, or a spectacular view of the aurora borealis . . .*

She smiled, then ended the excerpt and went back to finishing the message.

When she finished, she sent if off and called up her father's latest message, with the formal address of R. James Grant—although his full name was Royster James Grant, and he only answered to James. She began to reread his message, if quickly, before sending a reply. She had time, for the moment, and she might not later.

> Dearest Alayna,
> I was beginning to worry about you when I hadn't heard from you, but your latest reassured me, although I cannot say that

I'm exactly sanguine about having an astrophysicist daughter all alone in a station in the middle of an isolated crater on the far side of the Moon, particularly when tensions appear to be rising between the Sinese Federation and everyone else. There's more talk about Noram and the Sinese Federation militarizing space, and it strikes me that you might be rather vulnerable . . .

Militarizing space? She hadn't seen anything about that, even in the news summaries . . . except . . . hadn't there been something on one of the sensationalist vidloids? *HotNews!* maybe. What would be the point of militarizing space? All that would do would be to raise taxes and put the whole world at greater risk. But then, her father was always worrying, always overreacting. She smiled faintly and shook her head.

I did appreciate your description of the repairs you made to the radio telescope antenna, and I cannot tell you how proud you have made me and how much your mother would have given to know of your accomplishments . . .

Alayna swallowed. She couldn't help it. Her mother had died when Alayna had just finished defending her doctoral thesis at Princeton. She'd visited Alayna and then gone to Boston, or what was left of it, to visit Alayna's cousin Willie. Willie and Wilhemina, except they were both Wilhemina, had died when Hurricane Ernesto had merged with a nor'easter. So many had died that neither Alayna nor her father had ever discovered the exact circumstances. That was understandable, intellectually, given that more than twenty thousand had perished in the extreme winds and flooding, but Alayna's father had pressed for answers ever since. Only in the last weeks had his messages ever referred to her mother.

. . . I can only hope in some vain and impossible way that she must know, unpredictable and unfair as I have come to believe this universe is and has always been.

I also hope that you will have success in your research, and that, even if you do not immediately achieve that success, you will take such satisfaction in your work that eventually you will be rewarded, for, because we are seldom granted recognition for our accomplishments, we should take satisfaction in them, regardless of either recognition or lack of recognition . . .

Alayna smiled at yet another phrasing of the words she had heard since childhood.

> We have another important case coming before the Noram Court of Appeals, this one dealing with residual ground-water rights in the Ogallala Aquifer, although there is little enough groundwater there after the water mining wars of a half century ago . . .

She nodded and began her reply.

Sweat oozed across Tavoian's forehead. He blotted it with the forearm of his shipsuit, just to keep it from drifting into his eyes, trying to focus on the combat screens arrayed before him, half wishing that he had a functioning AI or even a commlink.

He could see that he hadn't corrected enough for the spaceward drift caused by a less than perfectly balanced course shift. He gave a five-second blast to the rear port thrusters to point the burner's nose more to port, trying to gauge what an AI could have done instantly.

He checked his target—zero seven one, negative fifteen, with four minutes to torp release.

Tavoian gave a burst to the orientation thrusters, then followed by adding power to the burner. He kept checking the gee-meter, more properly an accelerometer, making certain that the acceleration remained below three gees. He held the acceleration for less than three minutes, checking the closure rates, his eyes scanning the displays of other craft, as well as the outlying Sinese upper orbit station, none of which were anywhere close to visual range.

Abruptly, all but two of the displays blanked with a flare.

Forward sensors disabled. The warning flashed below the remaining displays.

Now what? The flare suggested he'd been hit with a concentrated laser flash, and that meant it was likely it had been managed from a distance. *You hope.* At least lasers couldn't do much more than blind sensors except at extremely close range.

There was little else he could do, not without aborting the mission, except sit tight, because he needed to maintain course and acceleration in order to boost the release velocity of the torp before firing, and then beginning his own return to base. Even if he'd looked through the emergency porthole, he wouldn't have seen the target, not when the release point was more than ten thousand kays from the impact point—a distance covered in less than three minutes from time of release.

He concentrated on the system indicators, especially the hydraulics. Could he even release a torp? The systems remained green or amber.

At the precomputed time, he fired, manually, hoping that he'd be as precise as the AI, or that the tracking computer on the torp could correct enough.

Immediately after that, using the thrusters, he put the burner through partial turnover, in order to shift his course vector, then began to increase the power to the drive, building a separation, knowing that if he merely slowed the burner on his previous course, he'd end up passing practically in front of the target and any weapons systems they had deployed and surviving around the orbit installation. Once he had separation he could begin to kill some of the built-up speed that was still carrying away from his own base.

After another five minutes, with the distance between him and the target increasing, as indicated by the surviving rear sensors, he repositioned the burner and held the drive at two gees until he could finally determine that he had killed his approach to the Sinese installations and was beginning to pull away. Finally, he dropped the power to maintain one gee. Even so, he'd need to cut the drive before long and then wait more than an hour before he would be able to begin decel to return to base.

"That's enough." The colonel's voice came through his earpiece. "Shut it down."

Tavoian slowly ran through the checklist manually, necessary because the AI was disabled, then finished the shutdown procedures. Only then did he unstrap himself from the combat couch of the simulator. Simulation or not, he was soaked with sweat, partly because there was minimal ventilation in the simulator, identical in all respects, including weightlessness, except for gee forces, to the control deck of a combat burner.

He made his way to the hatch, opened it, and pulled himself through, then used the handrail to guide him to the hatch out of the simulator, located in Donovan Base's docking ring, and into the simulator control center where the colonel waited, loosely belted into the seat in front of the array that controlled the simulator.

The senior officer half turned and tossed a folded towel at Tavoian. "You look like you need this."

"Yes, sir." Tavoian caught the towel and blotted his face before making his way toward the debriefing chair, where he also belted himself in.

Colonel Anson looked at Tavoian for a long moment. "Not bad. Not great, but not bad. You should have cut the power a minute earlier on the attack. You can't afford to waste Hel3, and it would have put you that much closer to the target after the torp release. You ended up having to spend more fuel on deceleration in order to return to base."

"Yes, sir."

"Did you think about just altering heading and doing an elliptical around Earth?"

"Only for a moment."

"Why not?"

"It would have required more fuel to change course and the velocity added by the course change would have required more fuel for decel."

"Why did you do a series of change-overs rather than a turn?"

"Because, without forward sensors, I had no idea what I might be turning into or away from. Also, that used far less Hel3 than a turn." Also there was the fact that, without an operational AI, trying to compute every bit of motion in any direction, any acceleration, got more and more complex with each maneuver, and trying to work that out without sensors would have been an even bigger nightmare. Then, too, without either gravity or air resistance, directional control was a beast. Tavoian knew that from experience, but piloting a burner on a transport run, except in emergencies, was like driving railed maglev. You powered up, and then you reversed power to decelerate.

That didn't even take into account the stresses on the drives and magnetic nozzles. Standard fusionjets—the ones he'd been piloting for the past six years—were designed to provide a constant one-gee acceleration for up to two hours straight without overheating, three perhaps under optimal conditions. The reconfigured combat fusionjet could take three to five gees, but the length of time the drives could operate without overheating or actually melting down dropped in proportion to the time at continuous acceleration. More than an hour at two gees, and the drive system was on the verge of meltdown. Half an hour at three gees was pushing the system. Fifteen minutes at four was likely to inflict maximum structural failure on the drives . . . and incidentally on the entire burner and its pilot.

"What if the sensors had just been overloaded?"

"I thought of that, but there wasn't any way to check that from the control deck. I did cycle the power, but there wasn't any response. Those panels are accessed from the forward bulkhead on the passenger deck. It also didn't seem wise to leave the controls at that moment."

The colonel looked skeptical. "Have you ever checked the sensor panel of a fusionjet, Captain?"

"Yes, sir."

"I suppose you know the location of all of the maintenance panels, too?"

"I've checked out the control system and the lock panels. I know the location of the fuel and drive system panels, but I've never checked them.

Those are beyond me." Not to mention that getting to them required special tools.

"You're one of the ones who needs to know how everything fits together."

"I find it helpful, sir."

"I suppose you can repair an AI, too?" The colonel's tone was sardonic.

"I don't think trying that would be a good idea, especially in combat, sir." Tavoian decided against mentioning that he'd built simple AIs as a way to earn money after university and before he'd been accepted for the Space Service. In some ways, it had been only slightly more difficult than sophisticated black-boxing.

"Why do you think we put you through all of this, when it's likely that the ship's AI will handle it all?" The colonel looked straight at Tavoian.

"I can think of three reasons, sir. First, it gives us a far better understanding of what's entailed. Second, that understanding should enable us to know when to override the AI if it's damaged or scrambled . . . or even hacked. Third, there is always the possibility that the AI might become inoperative."

"Next question. You know that a space installation is a sitting duck to a high speed torp attack. Ours as well as theirs. Once anyone starts such attacks, no one will have any installations left. So why are we training any of you for such attacks?"

Tavoian managed not to frown. The colonel had already made that point before. Was that another test? "You'd mentioned that before, sir. If we don't have that capability immediately ready, they can take out our installations, and they'll have the only ones left."

"Which will require us to destroy their installations Earthside, because the time required for a ground-based missile to reach geosynchronous orbit height is sufficient for antimissile missiles to lock on."

Tavoian didn't say what he was thinking—that an armed standoff wasn't the most secure way in which to avoid hostilities, except he didn't have a better answer. From what he could tell, neither did the colonel.

"Don't you think the Sinese and the Indians know that, Captain?"

"Yes, sir."

"Then why are we spending all the time, effort, facilities, on this training?"

"Because history shows that failure to respond emboldens the opposition."

"Those were my words. Do you believe them?"

"I think that there are often leaders in any field who gamble that their opponents won't prepare for the obvious because that preparation is too costly. And sometimes it is . . . the fall of the USSR . . . or the near collapse of the United States. I don't know where you draw the line."

"It's always a question. We'll be discussing this later. Now . . . your vector analysis and reaction leaves more than something to be desired . . ."

Tavoian nodded and listened intently, unpleasant as he sometimes found the way in which the colonel expressed himself in debriefings.

Almost an hour later, the colonel finished and released Tavoian, who made his way back to his quarters in the main section of Donovan Base. After showering and donning a clean shipsuit, he sat down before the small comm terminal in the cubicle that was his "stateroom."

More than a week had gone by since he'd received Alayna's last message, and almost two since Kit's. He hadn't wanted to send anything until he had a better understanding of the base and his duty and training—especially knowing that every comm was reviewed, and if it revealed something, it was rejected and returned with the offending section highlighted. Then the studies and the simulator training had consumed him, especially trying to estimate combined speed and power vectors almost instantaneously. The colonel's continual emphasis on the fact that the cold equations trumped mere effort and sentimentality every time didn't help much, either.

Tavoian pushed away those thoughts and concentrated on the messages he'd neglected for too long.

Kit first. He squared his shoulders and began.

TO: Hensen Correia Deputy Secretary
Department of Off-Earth Affairs
FROM: Khelson LeMay Lieutenant General
Noram Space Command
SUBJ: Jade Spear
DATE: 18 April 2114

Background:

The Sinese spacecraft [code name: Jade Spear] that departed the Sinese installation at L4 on 19 March 2114 has the exhaust profile similar to an MTF drive. The use of an adapted MTF drive suggests mass/payload considerations. The spacecraft is estimated to be 340 meters in length with an approximate estimated mass of 5,400 metric tons. The crew number is likely seventeen. Multiple shuttle trips from the Sinese space elevator to the Sinese installation [see asteroid 2031 SJ4] indicate extensive equipment/cargo, including extensive hydroponics/organic recycling systems.

Current Situation:

Multi-point analysis from Noram Mars Orbit Cubesat array confirms Jade Spear making course corrections at approximately 4.25 AU from solar center. Course line continues toward Jupiter. Probability exceeds .70 that target is Europa.

Mission Possibilities:
- Establish orbit station with lander to study Europa in depth
- Establish mining base to extract deuterium to obtain fuel for possible DF spacecraft, or to supplement existing deuterium supplies
- Establish a mining base for other reasons, based on results of unmanned 2101 Sinese probe [Pearl Fisher]
- Other undetermined

Thursday morning, Alayna slumped/sat in front of the COFAR displays after dealing with the routine of checking the systems and then the messages. She was tired. How she could be that tired when her legs only had to support a sixth of the weight they did on Earth she wasn't certain, especially since she'd never been overweight . . . and still wasn't. And she certainly hadn't been staying up late trying to stay abreast of the latest realies. She couldn't because the media links to Farside were strictly data and text, and even the newsies were limited to text. Bandwidth was precious, and there wasn't enough commercial traffic to justify full-scale video transmissions. She did have the small realie library of favorites she'd brought with her, and those left by previous resident directors, although many of those Luis had left had been in Spanish. Supposedly, all video transmissions were screened after what events surrounding the Middle East Meltdown a generation earlier had shown—and, again, that sort of screening was far too expensive for the few hundred people spread across Luna. Screening text and data was far cheaper and easier. Of course, the optical images COFAR sent Earthside were screened, but that was through the massive Noram center in Bluffdale. No one ever mentioned the fact that another part of the problem was that there was never enough funding for infrastructure, and no politician wanted to pay for something used by only a few, and no business wanted to invest in anything that didn't offer a solid return.

What else is new?

She stifled a yawn and tried to think about what else she ought to be doing. She didn't have any immediate reports for Dr. Braun, and apparently the Noram IG visit hadn't generated any problems for the Farside Foundation or for Alayna. *Not yet, anyway.* She'd already checked the roller, and it was fully charged. Finally, she asked Marcel, "What should I be doing that I feel too tired to do?" She knew the AI would tell her something, since she'd asked a question.

"The word 'should' implies a moral obligation. I cannot make that judgment for you."

"Some help you are. Have you found any new fractals in the solar scans you processed while I was sleeping?"

"There are numerous instances of fractal patterns in the instances of mini-granulations. There have always been such patterns."

"Display the latest ones please. Along the same latitude band. With their heliographic coordinates."

Marcel began to flash the images before Alayna, highlighting the fractal patterns in green. "Would you like me to create more overlays of the type you have requested before?"

"Why not?"

"Is that affirmative?"

"It is."

The overlays didn't tell her anything except that the fractal mini-granulations looked similar to the previous ones. Still, she studied them intently, almost as if doing so might reveal something . . . anything at all. Once again, all she saw were the latest views of granulations in a Gaussian distribution, with the multi-fractal mini-granulations apparently filling the spaces between.

More than an hour later, with all her pressing and routine duties under control, she decided to reread Chris's latest message.

Dear Alayna—

I've been assigned to a Space Service unit that provides additional pilot training . . . and I'm definitely being trained . . . and then some. I won't bore you with the details except to say that I was a late addition, and I've had to catch up. That's one reason why this message is later than it should be . . . much later . . .

She frowned. He didn't give a second reason.

In your last message, the quote you referenced stated that scientists got excited, but more often over what "matters." That brings up the question of what people feel is exciting and why. It also raises the question of what matters and why. I'm not a scientist. I only hold the far less exalted and less meaningful position of a pilot. At times that's little more than a high-tech or glorified transport driver, and sometimes I'm more like a backseat driver to the AI. But it seems to me that what matters to most people is in the here and now. One of the problems our ancestors had in dealing with global warming was that they couldn't see the problem as something that affected them. It didn't "matter" to their lives.

I have the feeling that if you discovered that the sun would go nova or have a massive solar flare in exactly 197 years, three months, two days, and three hours . . . that it would be news for a few days, a few weeks at most, and then most people would get back to their lives. You scientists would immediately begin to work on ways to mitigate the impact, or build habitats. Half the politicians would immediately denounce the science, and the other half would agree, but not on how much funding to pay for dealing with the problem. On the other hand, if an alien spacecraft appeared—not that anything like that is at all probable given the size of just our galaxy— everyone would throw money at the various space services and military to deal with the alien threat, even before knowing what such implausible aliens intended. When I was in university, I saw an old cinema about an alien artifact. I don't remember the title. It was probably dated when it was created, at least from what I recall from somewhere. But the bottom line was that all the warring nations would unite in the face of a greater power. Leaving aside the doubtfulness of a greater power, if anything like that actually happened, I don't see much hope of unity.

Along those pessimistic or at least cynical lines, here's another quote from Observations:

Complete and total honesty will destroy any politician because government, even a totalitarian government, can never deliver all that its clients desire. Self-serving dishonesty, in saying what each constituency wants to hear to that constituency, was an effective strategy before the age of mass and instant media, and is still useful in addressing those constituencies whose support is ideologically based, rather than fact-based, so long as factual inaccuracies are avoided, but the use of contradicting "statements of fact" results in the political equivalent of the "death of a thousand cuts," unless the politician is interested in only a short term in office.

> *At the same time, more than occasional nonresponsiveness is not acceptable in a media-driven society. Therefore, a successful politician must be truthful, of necessity, the majority of the time. This is not as difficult as it might appear. It does require that a politician use more absolutely verifiable facts than many are comfortable with, but those facts only need to be marginally relevant, and the more facts that can be cited that reinforce already formed stereotypical views, the better. An accurate fact in an incorrect context is an effective lie.*

As she finished reading the quote, Alayna pondered over just what kind of training Chris was engaged in. The cynicism had been there before, but now there was definitely a darker shade to his words.

> I do hope you're making progress in your work, if only by eliminating the impossible in order to find out what's there . . . or what isn't. I admire your desire for discovery and the passion behind it . . .

"I hope that's the scientific passion you admire," she murmured.

Thankfully, Marcel did not ask for a clarification.

She thought about sending a reply to Chris, then decided against it, for the moment. "Marcel . . . do you have any better data on the anomaly?" She really didn't like calling it "Provisional Comet COFAR," not when it could turn out to be something else, even a rogue and strange asteroid flung into a cometary orbit by Jupiter or who knew what else. She didn't know of anything like that, but between the Kuiper Belt and the Oort Cloud there was certainly a chance of just about anything, improbable as it might seem. And Chris's comment about an alien artifact had made her think. *With silver . . . could it be . . . ?*

She shook her head. As he'd said, aliens visiting the solar system were implausible. *More like totally impossible.*

"Provisional Comet COFAR is now almost four-tenths of an AU closer to the sun. The most recent observations suggest more strongly that it is a solid body and that its diameter is less than three kilometers. Its albedo varies periodically and significantly. The probability is greater than eighty percent that the variation results from different surface characteristics exposed to solar radiation as the body rotates."

"Can you calculate its period from the data?"

"Based on current observational data, the period is 11,318 years."

Definitely a long-period something. Probably just a two-faced, gassed-out, rogue comet nucleus, the cometary equivalent of Iapetus. "Is there anything more?" *Another stupid question.*

"That is all, Dr. Wong-Grant."

Alayna turned her thoughts back to her project, her real work, and most likely her only hope of building the body of work necessary to find a "real" job in her field. Should she consider tracking granulations at a higher solar latitude? She shook her head. According to years of observations, except for the latitudes near the solar poles, the granulation activity was similar, and she needed to find something that was an indication of solar processes, not an inexplicable outlier.

ORBITAL MECHANICS

16

Alayna woke up with the nonsense poem or rhyme in her thoughts again—except she'd finally looked it up and discovered it actually was a poem called "Antigonish" and that it had been put to music almost two centuries before. By a poet called Means, no less. Then she corrected herself. *His name was Mearns. It has to mean something if your subconscious keeps bringing it up . . . and even changing the writer's name.* She winced at the semi-pun. *But what?* Why did she keep thinking about the man on the stair who wasn't there?

Even after going through her morning routine, checking the messages, and hoping that there was a message from Chris, which there wasn't, and hoping there wasn't one from her fretting father, which there was, and making certain all station systems were operating within parameters, her thoughts kept drifting back to what wasn't there in all the solar scans and data she kept messaging and analyzing.

"What if what's not showing is what's important?"

"How do you want me to apply that question?" asked Marcel.

"I don't know. Not yet."

She had to think things through, again, and more intelligently. The larger granulations weren't necessarily regular, but they weren't fractal, and certainly not multi-fractal, and she had found only two examples of small mini-granulations that were essentially regular, and those appeared to be affects of the flux lines bordering the larger granules. She keyed in another search. While she could have asked Marcel, she didn't want to seem crazy. After less than a minute she smiled at the lines before her:

> . . . a multi-fractality test reveals that the structures smaller than 600 km represent a multi-fractal, whereas on a larger scale the granulation pattern shows no multi-fractality and can be considered as a Gaussian random field . . .

Maybe she shouldn't be looking for regularity, but for why the mini-granulations came up as multi-fractals and why the standard granulations or the super granulations were essentially "regular" shapes in a Gaussian distribution. If she tried that, the question was, then, how to separate out the random field represented by convective granulation from whatever the multi-fractal mini-granulations resulted from or represented. Had anyone followed up on that? She keyed in another search and waited . . . and waited. It seemed like forever, but it was less than a minute before the display stated, "No results for query."

She tried a number of variations, but the system response was the same.

Theoretically, natural fractals did not exist in three-dimensional form, at least not that she was aware, although she recalled the resurgence of the Mandelbulb—mathematical attempts to re-create Mandelbrot set fractals in three dimensions—but could Marcel do that by isolating a sample of mini-granulations and seeing if there was any way to extrapolate into three dimensions?

It wouldn't be a good idea to have him do that until it was day on Farside, when the demands on the system were less and when the solar cells were all online. She put a reminder to herself into her calendar, then asked, "What do the latest observations of our provisional comet show?"

"It is highly unlikely that provisional Comet COFAR is a comet. Its brightness increased as it neared the orbit of Jupiter, but that increase was proportional to solar reflectivity. Most typical first-time comets have a greater increase. The greater proximity to the sun—"

"It's not off-gassing, then?" *Another stupid question. You knew that already.* "The brightness is strictly from greater reflectivity off a white or near-white surface?"

"The increase in brightness is directly in proportion to the amount of sunlight received. The object shows two differing surfaces, one with an albedo of point nine nine and the other with an albedo of point six five."

"Those are both high. What else?"

"The duration suggests that the differing surfaces have close to the same surface area."

"It's regularly shaped then?"

"Images suggest a crescent shape."

Crescent shaped with differing albedos on different sides? That was definitely odd, but there were potato-shaped and dumbbell-shaped small bodies. Why not a crescent? "Have you reported that to the IAU?"

"No. That requires your approval."

"You have my approval." In a way, Alayna was sad about that. If the anomaly wasn't an active comet, even a gassed-out one, it was effectively an asteroid, or a small solar system body, at least for classification purposes, and there were over a half a million of those, and that didn't count those that were small boulders or the like, as opposed to a mere five thousand or so identified and named comets. The fact that she had discovered a highly reflective asteroid, or one highly reflective on one side, might be worth something on her professional vita, but a comet would have been preferable. She smiled, faintly. If it were an alien spacecraft, on the other hand . . .

She shook her head. It couldn't be. First, it wasn't radiating heat, and anything carrying a lifeform needing support and sustenance should be, even at a minimal level. Second, it was far too large to be a spacecraft built by any technology of which she was aware—and if it had been the creation of an advanced technology, it wouldn't have been approaching on a cometary orbit with a velocity strictly consistent with that of a comet. And finally, at that velocity it would have taken more than seventy thousand years to come from any nearby stellar system. Also, she doubted that anyone would build a crescent-shaped vessel.

Enough daydreaming. She almost snorted. The words in her thoughts could have come from her all too practical father. Her mother had encouraged dreams.

She leaned toward the console and began to consider how she could adapt her approach to discovering more about the solar photosphere so that it was more productive. *You think you can discover something about the photosphere, when nothing new has appeared in almost a century, only refinements on what was already known?* She pushed that thought away. There were always new discoveries, and someone had to make them.

By midafternoon, UTC, Alayna was less than half-occupied, although there was enough going on with the optical array and the radio telescope that she needed to stay close to the control center. She just wished that Chris had messaged. Although she had always waited for Chris to reply before she messaged him again, she hadn't heard from him in over two weeks.

Is he all right? Or is he tired of a remote and not-very-interesting junior astronomer? She shook her head. *The hell with waiting.* If he wasn't interested in continuing the relationship, such as it was, she might as well find out sooner rather than later.

An hour later, she began to read over what she had written.

> Chris—
> Here's hoping that everything's going well with you. Since you've avoided details about your new duties, I can't very well comment. Even if I knew, commenting on another's specialized work isn't the best idea. Everyone has simplistic views. They

certainly do about astronomy. Some people still think we peer through a little eyepiece to look at the stars. Our array here doesn't even have an eyepiece. The light sensors are far more sensitive than the human eye, and we can filter out any wavelength we want.

I don't think I mentioned it before, but several months ago I observed a new comet—well, COFAR did, and I reported it to the International Astronomical Union. The IAU named it as a provisional comet—Comet COFAR—with my name attached as the reporting astronomer, since COFAR actually did the discovering and comets are named after the discoverer. It's not behaving like a comet should, and the reflected spectrum suggests that its surface is white and predominantly silver and silicate. Most comets are icy and dark dustballs. I'm getting the feeling that my comet is either so ancient that it's stopped off-gassing when it nears the sun or not a comet at all and some sort of misfit asteroid that must have been kicked into a strange orbit a long time ago. Since there are more than a half million asteroids, officially small solar system bodies, in the solar system, there goes my chance at notice—even if it would have been only for a short time.

That means I need to shift my approach to figure out a better way of observing and analyzing the mini-granulations. I just hope I haven't wasted too much time. I'm also worried about the fact that the sun is in a solar minimum, and that might affect the mechanisms impacting mini-granulations.

Two years seems like forever, but I've already been at Daedalus Base for six months, and all I've managed is to confirm and perhaps refine slightly what others have already done. Professor Janes would have just admonished me that I didn't waste time and that I just learned another approach that wasn't the best way.

She frowned for a moment, then smiled, if ironically. Chris would take that the right way, and if he didn't . . .

Apparently, however I handled the Noram IG team was acceptable. There's been no comment from the Foundation, and I'm certain there would have been if they'd found some glaring error. According to the news, the Noram Senate is battling over the appropriations for DOEA. Even with the threat of greater Sinese control over the outer solar system, they've cut tax subsidies for the lunar mining outfits, but not for research institutions. So far, anyway.

I hope all is well with you.

She continued to reread the message. When she finished, she sent it, then asked Marcel, "Are all systems good?"

"All systems are functioning at expected efficiencies, Dr. Wong-Grant."

"Thank you."

She turned to the console and called up her project. She really did need to get to work on a better approach to her research, and she had a day or two before she absolutely had to message her father . . . or Emma.

17

The colonel looked across the six officers seated in the sealed and ultra-secure briefing room. Of the two majors and four senior captains, one major and two captains were women. Tavoian thought the colonel's eyes lingered on him for a moment, but that was probably his own imagination. From what the others had said, all of them respected the senior officer, and not a one believed that he had any favorites . . . and no one wanted to be a favorite. Not when the colonel might expect even more from that officer.

"You're getting an oral briefing because what you are about to hear has not been committed to any database you can access . . . and will not be. You are not to write down what I'm about to tell you. You are not to discuss it with anyone once you leave this chamber. Even among your-selves. You all know why."

To Tavoian, that was obvious. Nanotechnology had reached the point where nowhere was secure, except for places and spaces where enormous and continuous effort was required to keep them cleared.

"If you have been following the media in any form, you all know, or should know, that tensions between the Sinese Federation and the India-UAAS coalition have been continuing to rise. Despite the efforts of the Noram government, it is likely that if matters escalate, Noram will be drawn into the possible conflict, if only indirectly. Space Command has learned of two developments that will impact Donovan Base . . . and you. The first is that the Indian Defense Ministry, under the guise of gravita-tional research, has been constructing a large installation at L5 for some unknown period of time. That installation is an adaptation of a largely nickel-iron asteroid. It is shielded with nonreflective and energy-absorbent dark-body. Space Command has reason to believe that the asteroid was either undiscovered and shielded years ago and/or nudged into that po-sition. It is roughly a third smaller in diameter than the largest asteroid in L4. The structure and composition of the asteroid lend themselves to a highly defensible installation." The colonel looked toward Nilsenn, the most junior captain. "You look skeptical, Captain."

"The largest asteroid in L4 is roughly three hundred meters in diameter, sir. It was discovered over a century ago. Even if this L5 body is only two hundred meters in diameter, that's a huge amount of iron . . . and mass. Maybe twenty million tons' worth. If anyone moved it, sir, if they even could, sir, the energy signature . . . Either way, sir, how did it escape notice?"

"I am not an astrophysicist or an astronomer, but I understand that the asteroid in question was an Apollo asteroid in an inferior position, which makes it more difficult to observe, and that it took several years of use of a fusion drive timed so as not to be easily observable in orbit to stabilize its orbit in an L5 position. Since there are over five thousand Apollo asteroids, one might forgive astronomers for not noticing the gradual repositioning of one of the smaller members of that group. It is also believed that work on shielding and reconfiguring the asteroid began over five years ago. It has a code name of Shiva . . ."

Tavoian managed to keep his face calm. A solid nickel-iron asteroid two hundred meters in diameter held enough iron to build almost anything. If partially hollowed out, and left with an outside shell of three or four meters, if reinforced correctly, it would probably be impervious to any weapon in any human arsenal, certainly any weapon currently in orbit or space, and at the L5 distance from Earth even a laser powered by a fusion plant wouldn't do anything except maybe offer a glimmer of illumination.

"You look amused, Captain Tavoian."

"No, sir. I was thinking that it sounds more like a combined fortress and manufacturing facility, but I can't see it being that much of a danger there. There is also the question of militarizing space . . ."

"I will not address the militarization issue, except to say that, sooner or later, human beings have militarized everything, and usually the last one to do so has suffered. As for the Indian installation, its remoteness is exactly what the Sinese fear . . . especially if India completes its space elevator. More precisely, if India successfully converts its partial space elevator to a full ocean-level elevator."

"Sir . . ." offered Major Wilkens, "wouldn't the distance from L5 preclude any ease of attack? I mean . . ."

"At nearly a hundred and fifty million kays, it would indeed. But as a near impervious manufacturing facility possibly powered by several fusion reactors, it offers a unique stand-off capability. Also, it's likely that the Indians moved it once. The more iron they use or remove . . ." The colonel smiled. "It would take power and time, of course." After the briefest of pauses, he went on. "The second factor is that the Sinese have their own initiative. It includes a large ship now approaching Jupiter with a magnetic targeted fusion drive. You might ask why MTF. It can be operated continuously at lower power, or at least with fewer breaks. It is more powerful than a vasimr drive, and more durable than a direct fusionjet, and it is designed for either deuterium-deuterium fusion or deuterium-tritium. It appears likely that there is a higher incidence of deuterium in the ice of Europa . . ."

"Sir? Was that discovered by the Sinese robotic mission to Jupiter?" asked Captain Dekins.

"That's the presumption. The Sinese reported the mission as failed and lost, but not until sometime after it should have reached Europa."

Tavoian got the picture immediately. The Space Service was concerned about the possible depletion of Hel3 sources on Luna. But the Sinese wouldn't have invested in sending a manned ship, especially one that large, if they didn't have a good idea of what to expect . . . and if they cornered a ready source of deuterium in the icy surface or in the accessible depths of Europa . . .

". . . the Sinese ship is some three hundred plus meters in length. It also contains expandable living quarters that can be rotated for artificial gravity. That suggests a crew of more than a few individuals and that the Sinese have plans for an extended stay in the Jovian environs. There are indications that it also carries a secondary fusion power plant. You can draw your own conclusions." The colonel's smile was wintry.

None of the officers being briefed ventured such conclusions.

"For these reasons, shortly all of you will begin operations designed to result in providing Space Command with more data and information on both Sinese and Indian installations and operations."

More? Given what the colonel had just said and the views he had shown Tavoian in his initial briefing, how much more data/information was necessary? And what could fusionjet pilots add that unmanned recon probes couldn't do more easily and surreptitiously? Tavoian managed to keep his expression pleasant as a second thought struck him. *Senior commanders never believe they have enough information.* Still . . . he had his doubts.

By the time the briefing was over, Tavoian had less than an hour before he had duty, but he felt that he really did need to reply to Alayna's latest message. He'd felt that way for days, and the last thing he wanted to do was to push away someone he felt he could actually talk to—or message—as the case might be. He also knew that if he didn't take the opportunity when he had a few moments, something else would come up. It always did. Besides which, the mention of her comet/asteroid was intriguing.

He immediately made his way to his quarters, small as they were, and began to compose his reply, as quickly as he could, but with a certain care.

> Alayna—
> I owe you an apology for my lack of consideration in not replying sooner, and I appreciate your thoughtfulness in messaging me again. The training here is long, often tedious, and very exacting. I suppose that applies to anything of a highly specialized and technical nature, perhaps even more to what you do than to me . . . but it is tiring.
>
> I have to say that while it may strike you as almost prosaic, and disappointing, to have discovered a new asteroid, instead of a comet, I happen to think that either one is exciting. You may think that is strange coming from a pilot, but people think of us as "seeing" asteroids and planets. We seldom see anything but planets or moons, and those almost always on screens when we're approaching an orbit installation around them, and only in passing. You probably have already seen far more different images of planets, moons, comets, and asteroids than I ever will.
>
> I'm not an astronomer or an astrophysicist. I've probably said that more than once. From my limited knowledge, I thought that a silver-silicate body of any sort would be rather rare, especially if it initially appeared on a cometary orbit. If it is, wouldn't that sort of rarity help in furthering your career? If I'm mistaken about that, my condolences. It would seem so unfair that a discovery wouldn't provide some benefit. Or is it that there are so few opportunities in your field that only discoveries considered major or important will advance you in the profession?
>
> Somehow that reminds me of the following:
>
> *Quantum AI technology allows people to juggle figures and situations beyond their understanding to arrive at results beyond their comprehension. That leads to mistakes beyond*

*their ability to correct, at which point they blame the system
or the AI. When scientists attempt to point out that it is a bad
idea to blame the tool, rather than the user, both business and
government cut their funding for everything else.*

I'm certain you know where I found that. I suspect the point
also applies to those who review the funding for what astronomers and astrophysicists do, especially in these times. You
hinted several months ago that those who fund pure research
have very different priorities from those who conduct it. That's
true in more than science.

I'd like to say more, but I'm sending this immediately because
I have another meeting scheduled, and I don't know when I'll
have another chance.

That wasn't true. Tavoian had to report to the operations center as
duty officer, but saying that might have triggered the censoring system,
and he didn't want to have his belated reply delayed further. Especially
when he tended to overfocus on what was happening at Donovan Base.
　He sent the message, then rose and headed for the ops center.

THE TIMES OF ISRAEL
3 OCTOBER 2114

TAKING THE WRONG ELEVATOR

(SHIRAZ) Back off trying to stop India's completion of a full space elevator! It wasn't that direct, but that was the message sent to Sinese Head of State Jiang Qining in a joint communique signed by Iranian President Saam Achmed Narsi, Israeli Prime Minister Merav Meir, and Nigerian First Minister Ngozi Darego. The three acted on behalf of the Unity of African and Allied States, following consultations last week in Johannesburg.

Meir noted that almost half the world's population has no easy access to space, and that the Dyaus space elevator would serve not only India but all the nations of the UAAS under the Memorandum of Understanding between India and the UAAS. "For a power that has always opposed colonialism, the Sinobloc stance of opposing access to space for those victimized most by colonialism reeks of hypocrisy."

Both Darego and Narsi agreed that the current monopoly on access to the threshold of space—geostationary orbit—by either Noram or the Sinese Federation—places great constraints on the rest of the world . . .

Predictably, Noram President Yates praised the "spirit of cooperation" behind the Memorandum of Understanding . . .

19

Monday morning after breakfast found Alayna where she was every morning—in the COFAR control center, checking the message queue, where she found nothing of interest, and nothing that required an immediate response. So, as she finished scanning the last of the messages, she asked Marcel, "Where do we stand today with mini-granulation multi-fractals?" As soon as the words were out of her mouth, she smiled wryly, because there were always mini-granular multi-fractals, and none of the regular granulations ever appeared as fractals.

"There are currently 111 instances of fractal patterns in the instances of mini-granulations in the selected solar latitude image."

"Display them." Alayna doubted that they would reveal any more than those she had been studying for the last eight months, but there was always a chance.

Marcel flashed the images before Alayna, the fractal patterns overlaid in green.

There was something about them . . . something, again, that wasn't there.

She took a deep breath. What else could she do? She'd had Marcel remove everything but the fractal patterns, and that hadn't shown anything. She'd had him put just the fractal patterns in sequential order, and that hadn't revealed anything. She'd even had him attempt to sort through to see if there were matches or near matches in any display. There hadn't been.

She had one more idea. With nearly nine months of observations, piecemeal as they had been, she might have enough data. "Can you match the fractal patterns observed to the same surface area on the sun . . . with calculation and regression?"

"That will take time."

"How much?"

"Using available processing time, more than ten years for the full width of those bands."

Alayna swallowed, then realized. She shouldn't have been surprised, given the number of mini-granulations, and the fact that the sun's photosphere rotated at differing speeds according to latitude. Marcel would have to calculate the movements by fractions of a degree of latitude, and with granulations lasting only eight to ten minutes, and multifractal mini-granulations averaging close to five minutes, the number of mini-granulations . . .

She shook her head. "Limit the area to one small enough that you can do the calculations in a month. Include those cases where you find close similarities as well."

"That is a very small area, Dr. Wong-Grant. That may be too small to show results of statistical significance."

"I know. Do what you can under those constraints." Alayna had to leave the dimensions up to Marcel. Roughly speaking each square of one degree would contain, on average, roughly sixteen "normal" granules and a larger number of mini-granules at any one time . . . but averages were only approximations, and approximations wouldn't give her anything close to even a hint of something new. And given the variables, she'd have spent hours, if not years that she didn't have . . . and wouldn't have done as good a job as Marcel. "Only work on this when it will not interfere with anything else."

"Beginning processing."

Most likely yet another idea that will turn out to be nonsense, showing nothing . . . the man or the data that wasn't there—again. She'd be fortunate if what Marcel could do would provide a hint of what she felt was there—some sort of underlying order rather than elaborate plasma convection.

She felt, just felt, that she was on the edge of something, and yet, she couldn't even define it. Was that perseverance . . . or just self-delusion?

A faint buzz intruded on her thoughts. When she did not respond immediately, Marcel spoke. "Dr. Wong-Grant, there is a malfunction in the electrostatic dust prevention system for the main optical mirror."

Alayna sighed. "Diagnostics, please. With image."

"The malfunction appears to be in the waveguide controller," offered Marcel.

She could see that, but she refrained from saying so. The dust prevention systems for all the optical mirrors and lenses were based on long-tested electrostatic traveling wave technology, since actual cleaning would only degrade the surfaces. While she *might* be able to repair the controller, given the relatively sophisticated technical shop and Marcel's expertise, the first thing to do was to remove the existing controller and replace it with a functioning one, and then bring the malfunctioning unit back to the shop, for repair, if possible, and, one way or another, notify Far-side Foundation operations.

"Is there a spare in inventory?"

"According to the records, there are three spares. The same controller is used with the lens cleaning system for the solar mirror."

"When was the controller for the main mirror last replaced?"

"Eleven years ago. There was a previous replacement the year after the present main mirror and system was installed."

"Do you have a location for the spare units?"

"Echo Charlie one three."

"Echo Charlie one three." Alayna repeated the location to herself, then rose from the console and headed for the lower level and the higher tech equipment supply room.

Finding Echo Charlie one three took several minutes longer than Alayna had anticipated, partly because it was at the end of the second row in the dimness away from any direct illumination and the bin was at ankle level. The plastfilm that covered the topmost of the three small oblong controllers bore a thin layer of dust. So did the covering of the other two. Alayna took the top one and made her way back to the suit locker room, where she began her preparations for the replacement, be-ginning with swathing the controller in an insulating wrap that would allow it to cool slowly once it left the warmth and pressure of the station. Then she began suiting up.

More than thirty minutes passed before she eased the roller out of the lock and toward the main optical array. After all the effort it had taken to repair the radio telescope antenna film, she had no anticipation that the replacement of a controller, simple as it had looked on the schematic, would be easy. Necessary, yes, because despite the lack of a lunar atmo-sphere, the dust was electrically charged and, over time, had a tendency to film over anything, and even the finest coating of dust over a telescope lens was definitely not something for which the Farside Foundation cli-ents were paying.

Alayna eased the roller toward the main mirror structure, covering the last hundred meters at a pace little more than a crawl, trying to keep from raising any unnecessary dust, a particularly important aspect of the repair when the dust-prevention system was either malfunctioning or not functioning at all. She gently slowed the roller to a complete stop just short of the door to the support systems module. Since it was lunar day on Farside, she was feeling somewhat warm as she stepped off the roller.

According to the schematic, the electrostatic dust prevention system was on the upper level of the module in the middle, and accessed by a ladder up to a horizontal catwalk. In theory, all she had to do was open the access door, climb the ladder, move a few steps to her right, remove two slip brackets, and unplug the malfunctioning waveguide controller, withdraw it, and then insert the replacement.

She twisted the clip releases on the top of the access door, and then turned the handle. It moved easily enough, but when she tried to pull the door open, it didn't budge. She pulled harder. Nothing happened.

She studied where the edge of the door flanges met the metal of the module wall. Near the bottom of the door, from where it began some ten centimeters above the regolith and extending for almost a meter, it appeared to be sealed with lunar dust. She tried to rub it away with her gauntlets, but could only remove the outer layer of the dust.

She tried to open the door again. While she thought she felt some give, she decided that brute force wasn't the answer, especially since, if she damaged the access door, she'd have an even bigger repair and maintenance problem on her hands.

She pulsed Marcel.

"Yes, Dr. Wong-Grant?"

"The access door won't open. It's almost like the dust has formed an electrostatic weld. Is there any record of something like that?"

"There is no record of any problem like that."

"All right. I'm going to see if one of the screwdrivers in the tool kit has a sharp enough edge that I can cut through the packed or welded dust. Let me know if the system does something while I'm working on this."

"I will do that, Dr. Wong-Grant."

Alayna stepped back onto the roller and searched through the tool locker until she found the thinnest-bladed screwdriver. Then she climbed down and returned to the access door, where she began to scrape, gently, starting at the top of the packed or semi-welded dust. After more than ten minutes she had only cleared a little more than thirty centimeters. She was sweating, and her faceplate was beginning to fog over. She straightened and stopped working, to see if the exosuit's system could clear away some of the moisture.

After several minutes, her faceplate was clearer, and she again addressed the packed dust. She had almost cleared another thirty centimeters when the suit's warning system beeped.

Then Marcel pulsed her. "Dr. Wong-Grant, you are bending over too much and compressing the ventilation and heating lines."

Alayna straightened.

The beeping stopped.

She tried the door again. The upper half seemed as though it might be free enough to open, but the bottom section remained stuck.

She bent over again, but she couldn't reach any lower with the screwdriver. The suit beeped even louder. She straightened up, and the beeping stopped.

"What the frig am I supposed to do now?" Alayna immediately added, "Don't answer that, Marcel. I know I still have to replace the damned controller."

She tried kneeling, but the suit wouldn't let her bend her knees and legs enough to get into a kneeling position.

She looked at the bottom of the door. If she couldn't bend over . . . In the end, after an awkward struggle, she managed to lie down on the regolith, mostly on her stomach. She began to scrape away the hardened dust, almost frantically, hoping that her faceplate wouldn't fog up too much.

Five minutes passed, then more than ten. The lower she got, the harder the dust became and the longer it took to clear each centimeter. She still had several centimeters of the hardened dust to remove when Marcel announced, "Your suit temperature is dropping below advisable levels."

"Tell me when it gets dangerous. I'm almost done." *You think.*

She kept scraping.

"The abdominal sensor indicates a dangerously low temperature level, Dr. Wong-Grant."

"I'm almost done."

"You said that before, Dr. Wong-Grant."

Alayna jabbed at the last section of the stubborn dust, once, twice, and again. Abruptly, the last segment gave way, and the screwdriver skidded downward. Alayna's gauntlets hit the regolith next to the metal wall so hard that a sharp pain ran through her hand and arm, and she lost her grip on the screwdriver. It didn't go anywhere, except into the regolith. She was tempted to leave it sticking up there, but worried that retrieving it would just require even more acrobatics. It didn't, but she did have to pry it out of the lunar surface, and then half roll on her side to start to get up. By the time she was standing, she could feel that the surface of her stomach was like ice, even while sweat oozed into the corners of her eyes.

When she reached for the handle of the door, she murmured, "Please."

It did move as she tugged on it, if slowly, and she swung it completely open. Before she went to retrieve the controller, she used the screwdriver to scrape away the remaining hardened dust, at least the section that she could reach without excessive bending and contortions.

Then she climbed back onto the roller, leaving the screwdriver on the floor where she could easily reach it, if necessary, and then picked up the controller, still wrapped in the insulating blanket, which she loosened slightly, before descending and then climbing the ladder up to the catwalk.

Although she worried about whether the malfunctioning control would also be stuck or jammed, the slip brackets moved easily, and she eased the old controller out and the new one in place without difficulty. A mist rose from the new controller, and Alayna just hoped that was normal vacuum off-gassing. She repositioned the brackets, and pulsed Marcel. "The new controller is in position."

"The system indicates proper positioning. It has commenced a recycle."

Alayna waited. She didn't want to move until she knew whether the replacement had been successful. At least a minute passed before she asked, "What does the system indicate?"

"The recycle is not complete, Dr. Wong-Grant."

Alayna continued to wait. At least her abdomen felt warmer, and she'd stopped sweating.

Finally, after what seemed another ten minutes, but was only two, Marcel announced, "The electrostatic dust prevention system is operating as designed, Dr. Wong-Grant."

"Good. I'm going to seal up here and return."

Marcel did not reply, predictably, since she had not asked a question or implied one.

With the old controller in hand, Alayna climbed back down from the catwalk, then laid the old controller next to the screwdriver before turning back to the access door and slowly but firmly pushing it shut and returning the handle to the secured position. Then she twisted the upper brackets into their secured position. There were no lower brackets, for reasons she had just learned.

She climbed back onto the roller and placed the old controller and the screwdriver in the tool bin. As she settled behind the controls and eased the roller back and away from the main mirror structure, she realized what she should have done. All she would have had to do was go back to the station and attach the screwdriver to a length of something so that she could scrape away that crap while standing up. *Hindsight is so much more accurate than foresight.* She almost snorted.

Almost another hour passed while she dealt with cleaning the roller, unsuiting, cleaning up and changing out of her totally soaked undersuit, and then taking the controller to the maintenance shop.

She hadn't been back before the controls more than five minutes, sipping a mug of what passed for hot coffee, when a faint chime alerted her to an incoming message. She called up the sender, then stiffened as she saw it was from the IAU. She immediately accessed the complete message and read through it. The point of the message was contained in less than a sentence:

> . . . has determined that the object previously classified as
> C/X/2114 FT2 COFAR-SMOA is in fact a minor body under
> IAU definitions and has been reclassified as 2114 FQ5.

"Comet COFAR is no more," she murmured. "Just another minor planet or small body in an eccentric orbit." She couldn't say that she was surprised. She paused, then asked Marcel, "Can you calculate the orbit of our anomaly, once known as Comet C/X/2114 FT2?"

"From the COFAR observations, the calculations won't be completely accurate, Dr. Wong-Grant."

"Do the best you can, and then put a system and orbit plot on the screen—just from the orbit of Jupiter inward."

Almost immediately, an image appeared.

Alayna frowned. "That's definitely a cometary orbit. It's even a sun-grazing orbit. I don't see why the IAU reclassified it as a minor planet or system small body. Its aphelion is well out into the Kuiper Belt. They just could have kept the old designation and added a prefix, the way they've done for comets that have stopped off-gassing. It's definitely a cometary orbit." She paused. "Is there any way you can check whether they've re-classified comets as small bodies recently?"

"No, Dr. Wong-Grant. I do not have access to IAU databases."

"Do you have any other resources that might refer to that?"

"Such a search would exceed communications bandwidth restrictions, Dr. Wong-Grant."

"Thank you." That was a hurdle Alayna should have realized.

For several moments, she just sat before the displays. Then she added, "As much as the contract work allows, keep a running track on our for-mer comet, now known as . . ." She had to pause and look at the message again, "2114 FQ5."

"Command accepted."

Alayna had suspected from early on that "her" comet wasn't one, or not a typical one. She'd even told Chris that, but the matter-of-fact re-classification still depressed her. She also couldn't shake the feeling that there was something strange about that reclassification, but from Farside, she had no way to check that.

She forced a shrug. *No relatively easy flicker of notice for you, Alayna. Back to mini-granulations and multi-fractal patterns.* Except, by defini-tion, fractals weren't patterns.

20

Tavoian walked past Spacer3 Riske's console into the colonel's office, felt the pressure door shut behind him, and then took the seat opposite the senior officer.

"This will serve as your briefing for your mission, Captain."

"Yes, sir." The colonel didn't have to ask if Tavoian understood why he was being briefed personally, rather than receiving it through a console. Tavoian knew. The ostensible reason was for security purposes. The secondary reason was doubtless for deniability. Even the Space Service was subject to the Noram IG, as a result of rather sordid events not quite a century before involving the old American military, but the IG would have trouble finding documentary or electronic evidence if it didn't exist.

"Officially, you will be making a reconnaissance flight from here to a point slightly orbit-inferior to the Sinese elevator orbit station. Once in position, you will activate all long-range sensors in all wavelengths at full sensitivity. You will remain there for as long as possible, gathering information, but not to exceed two standard hours. You are then to move to a position slightly in advance of the Indian space facility, where you will again activate all sensors and remain for up to one hour. You will then travel to ONeill Station, where you will refuel as necessary, and wait ten hours before commencing a return to LLOS, with passengers. Once approaching LLOS, you will be redirected to L1. That's the official profile. These orders, with the precise coordinates, have already been transferred to your ship's AI. The unofficial profile is that as you depart you will release a cubesat array at both the Sinese and Indian installations. If you follow the mission profile exactly, which we will go over in detail shortly, the thermal effect of your drive thrust should conceal the dispersion of the array, which will move slowly toward the target station." The colonel paused.

"If the cubesats are moving, sir . . ."

"They should be effective for a sufficient time. I'm not about to define sufficient, Captain."

"Yes, sir."

"Now . . . let's get to the technical details, Captain."

Tavoian leaned forward slightly and listened.

Close to a half hour later, he left the colonel's office, effectively a classified briefing room, a pleasant expression on his face that belied some of what he felt as he mused over what he had learned, and what he had not. He'd understood what the colonel had said—the mission had been planned for execution close to the time of lunar perigee with Earth. That way the distance between Donovan Base and the counterweight of the Sinese space elevator—which not incidentally also contained a Sinese space force installation—would be close to a minimum. That would reduce the window of Sinese observation as well as the amount of Hel3 required, although Tavoian doubted the second was anywhere close to a major factor in anyone's mind.

The ostensible reason for the mission was to obtain detailed information about the Sinese and Indian installations, although the secondary rationale was to establish that space installations only had a ten-kay sphere of "restricted territorial rights." Theoretically, under the provisions of various treaties, some more than a century old, militarization of any facility or body in space was prohibited, but Tavoian knew that was a provision quietly flouted, although if the Sinese or the Indians used force against his "recon mission," that would bring the issue into the light. Since such light-bringing might well result in significant damage to the burner he'd be piloting, Tavoian preferred that the issue remain in the darkness of space.

In less than ten minutes, he was seated, or more accurately weightless and strapped into the control couch of Recon two, linking to the AI and beginning the pre-release checklist. Unlike on transport flights, he was wearing a skintight pressure suit, with his helmet secured under the couch. He had his doubts about the usefulness of the suit. While it would allow him to survive decompression and would provide insulation for several hours, and oxygen for roughly the same time, its usefulness was limited to instants where damage to the burner did not affect the drives, since if he could not return somewhere quickly, he doubted that anyone could rescue him in that time—or would be terribly interested in doing so.

Before long, the checklist complete, he link-transmitted, "OpsCon, Recon two, ready for release."

"Cleared to release, two. Thrusters only. Report when ready for ignition."

"Releasing this time. Will report ready for ignition." Tavoian waited until the sensors confirmed that the lock grapples had released before he pulsed the thrusters. As the burner eased away from the lock ring, he continued to monitor the separation until he had a full kay of clearance. Then he turned the ship over to the AI for orientation.

Several minutes later, he pulsed, "OpsCon, Recon two, ready for ignition."

"Two, cleared for ignition."

"Understand cleared for ignition. Commencing ignition this time." As the burner ignited and the ship began to accelerate, Tavoian was pressed down in the couch.

While he had to monitor the screens just in case he saw something that the AI did not perceive as a danger, but might be, and to make certain that the AI wasn't malfunctioning, there wasn't much to do for the hour and a quarter that the burner accelerated before turnover, and his thoughts turned to the situation in which he was figuratively a pawn, where the major powers were all jockeying for control of space, without ever really admitting it, at least publicly.

India had established a geostationary station, with an associated installation having an enormous solar power capability, not to mention an armored asteroid manufacturing facility, or worse, at L5. The UAAS was allied with India and likely providing funding for the completion of the Indian space elevator, and as a stepping stone to something. The Sinese had a huge MTF vessel now somewhere around Jupiter, most probably in orbit around Europa, trying to corner a huge deuterium supply. At the same time, India and the Sinese Federation were trading increasing threats. Although the Noram government had said little, the Space Service was arming vessels and training pilots to operate them in a combat mode.

None of that made Tavoian very happy. He couldn't exactly argue with a recon mission to make sure matters hadn't gotten worse. It was just that what he didn't know worried him even more.

He even envied Alayna, isolated as she might be on Luna's Farside. At least she was pursuing something that had a hope of being constructive. He hadn't heard from her since his last message. He laughed softly. *You're the one who was so slow in replying . . . and you worry about her not answering instantly.*

Fifteen minutes after turnover, the AI flashed, SHIP ON PARALLEL TRACK OUTBOUND.

Tavoian called up the coordinates, studying them quickly. Even so, in the instants it took, the other ship was past him, although the closest distance had been slightly less than a hundred kays. From the brief profile gathered by the sensors, the vessel was Sinese and apparently beginning decel.

The entire notice and passage had happened in less than ten seconds. Although the AI had caught the first indications of the other ship at five thousand kays, their combined relative speeds to each other had assured the brevity of their proximity.

Another example of why ship-to-ship combat in space is highly unlikely. The only kinds of weapon that might be effective would be beam or energy weapons, and given their attenuation with distance, the power required would be impractical, if not impossible, even for a burner. As the colonel's briefings had pointed out, however, simple torps, launched from an incoming burner at even higher velocity, were more than sufficient to destroy any space installation, or stationary ship, simply because there wouldn't be enough warning time. For that matter, an array of golf balls launched at that speed would likely inflict significant structural damage, except torps could make course corrections and golf balls couldn't.

"Extrapolate the course line of that ship."

Less than a second passed before the AI replied. PROBABILITY EXCEEDS POINT NINE THAT THE SHIP'S DESTINATION IS LUNAR L1.

Donovan Base? "What was its point of origin?"

PROBABILITY EXCEEDS POINT NINE FIVE THAT IT DEPARTED FROM COUNTERWEIGHT AREA OF SINESE SPACE ELEVATOR.

Tavoian immediately burst-squirted an encrypted transmission. *Ops-Con, Sinese burner on inbound L1 course.* Then he asked, "How long would it have taken them to locate us and determine our course?"

WITH MONITORING OF THE LUNAR LIBRATION POINTS, FIVE MINUTES OR LESS.

That meant one of two things. Either the Sinese knew or anticipated a burner headed for their station. And either way, they had a ship ready to go the moment they detected something headed their direction.

Tit for tat? Why now? To prove that they can do what we can? Or to be in a position to retaliate immediately if we do something? Tavoian definitely wasn't looking forward to his arrival off the Sinese upper orbit station, a term he preferred to the more formal Heavenly Jade Station.

Two, transmission received. That was the only acknowledgment he received, not that he expected much more.

As Recon two approached Earth, decelerating steadily, Tavoian thought, not quite idly, about Alayna and what she would have made of seeing two burners trading courses, except she couldn't have seen that, not from Farside.

Little more than an hour and ten minutes after turnover, he watched the monitors closely as the AI eased the burner to a halt—comparatively, since it was really holding an orbital position at a distance of twelve kays from the Sinese installation that comprised part of the elevator's counterweight.

The sensors' light-gathering ability was better than that of any human eye, but even so the smaller details of the multispoked wheel were slightly fuzzy in the display Tavoian studied. Docked at the ring above the wheel—above from Tavoian's perspective, anyway—were eight Sinese fusionjets, more squat-looking than Recon two, given their double-ended construction, with drive nozzles and what amounted to clamshell doors at each end. The Sinese burners' design was likely more maneuverable, but also more expensive and certainly more complex. All of the burners appeared to be of the same size and design.

THE SHIP HAS BEEN LASER-TAGGED.

"Is that intermittent or continuous?"

A SINGLE TAG. ONE DIRECTED PULSE.

"No searching? Or was it a ranging pulse?"

BEAM CHARACTERISTICS INDICATE RANGE PULSE.

Tavoian checked the monitors again. They indicated twelve point two kays from the closest section of the Sinese station. The sensors continued to gather information, and presumably other data, although the only motion he could see was the rotation of the enormous wheel, nearly a thousand meters across, with a rim a good hundred meters wide and two hundred from top to bottom. He'd seen more than a few images. Although what the sensors displayed was also an image, the comparative closeness and the real-time view somehow made it more impressive.

While the Sinese station had a significant array of solar panels, perhaps slightly more than ONeill Station, which was smaller, the numbers seemed modest compared to the images the colonel had displayed of the Indian station. Whether the Sinese had extra or emergency panels to deploy there was no way of telling from exterior surveillance.

For two hours, Recon two remained in position, if with occasional drive pulses to remain in position relative to the station, since Tavoian had positioned the ship farther spaceward, in order to be able to depart without excessive maneuvering or re-orientation, and without encroaching on accepted space territorial limits. During the seemingly endless monitoring period, there were three more single range pulses, as if to verify that the Noram ship had not drifted closer.

Finally, Tavoian ordered the AI, "Begin orientation for departure." The orientation was slightly more elaborate than it needed to be technically, because, during the process, just as the AI pulsed all thrusters simultaneously, as if to test them, Tavoian released the first of the two cubesat arrays that girdled the fusionjet. If . . . if he and the AI had done it correctly, the array would disperse on a vector that would gradually carry each of the tiny satellites on a path past, over, or under the Sinese station, periodically burst-squirting a signal containing information. If any actually hit the station or anything else, the fail-safe nanotech would fry the entire fragile interior system. There had to be a receiver somewhere nearer than Donovan Base, Tavoian surmised, but where that might be he had no idea.

Even in an orbit above the geostationary level, high-speed maneuvers comparatively close to Earth were limited for reasons of both safety and practicality. Despite strenuous efforts by all powers, there was still a much greater chance of encountering some form of space junk. In addition, for shorter distances the fuel costs tended to outweigh any time savings. That was why it took Tavoian almost an hour to reach a position off his second target, despite the fact that the Indian station was actually moving toward him. Before he even had an opportunity to more than glance at the display image of the statement, there was an incoming transmission on international common.

"Unidentified Noram spacecraft, this is Dyaus Operations. Do you intend to request permission to dock?" The voice was pleasant, precise, and female. "Or do you need some form of assistance?"

Tavoian had been briefed on that possibility, and he immediately responded on that comm band. "Dyaus Operations, that is a negative this time. We do not intend to dock. We do not need assistance at this time. We will maintain position clear of your evolutions."

"Unidentified craft, request you remain beyond ten kilometers."

The Indians remained with the old-style "kilometers" and also referred to space time as GMT, rather than the UTC everyone else called it, although the clock times were identical. Tavoian smiled. "Dyaus Operations, will comply with your request."

"Thank you, Recon two."

"That didn't take them long," commented Tavoian.

THE NUMBER IS ON THE SPACECRAFT.

That suggested the Indians had an immediately accessible intelligence database . . . and that they didn't regard any Noram spacecraft as a threat, or not as an immediate one. Tavoian smiled wryly for a moment and then began to study the images, strictly for his own benefit, since the RCS and optical sensor systems would record far more than Tavoian's eyes could see.

Even so, he was impressed by the upper station, which seemed to have even more solar panels than the colonel had shown him. He could also see yet another installation, apparently still under construction . . . although there didn't appear to be anyone or any small craft working on it.

Modular, awaiting the next section? Possibly a UAAS station? Or the possible particle beam site? Tavoian had no way of knowing.

During the almost two hours that followed, Tavoian watched. The only ship that departed the station was an Indian burner, somewhat more bulbous than a Noram fusionjet, that undocked and moved away from the station before orienting itself, then accelerated on a course most probably toward L5, according to the AI, suggesting that work, or something, was continuing there.

Finally, Tavoian transmitted, "Dyaus Operations, we are departing this time. Will avoid all your subsidiary installations."

"Have a pleasant trip. Convey our felicitations to the colonel."

What do you say to that? "My superiors will appreciate your kind thoughts, Operations. The same to you."

"Bon voyage."

After a moment, Tavoian shook his head, then ordered, "Commence orientation for departure to ONeill Station."

As the AI maneuvered the ship, in the process allowing Tavoian to release the second cubesat array, he couldn't help but think how strange it was that the Operations officer or director on the Indian geostationary satellite knew about the colonel when Tavoian himself hadn't even known of the colonel's existence until he'd reported. He also couldn't help but wonder what awaited him at ONeill Station.

21

DAEDALUS BASE
14 OCTOBER 2114

Sunday was like every other "lunar night" day on Farside, at least for Alayna, where she was up early and halfway on edge, fretting that something else might go wrong, even as she knew how unlikely that was. Her present continuing worry was the mirror dust prevention system on the main optical mirror, because if anything went wrong, especially soon, all the blame would fall on her. The system monitors indicated that the controller she had replaced continued to operate without a hitch or glitch. She'd reported the repair, and received a routine acknowledgment from Director Wrae, almost a week later. Both the delay and the routineness of the acknowledgment had irritated Alayna, even though she knew that such repairs were considered a part of the job, but while replacing the controller had certainly been routine, getting to where she could replace it had definitely been anything other than routine.

She checked the message queue, but there was nothing of personal interest. She did read the news summary, and that was as depressing as always, with one of the lead stories being the Sinese Federation decrying Noram attempts to spy on Sinese space installations, and the Indians countering by suggesting that the Sinese must have had something to hide if they were upset by mere observation. President Yates had no comment. *For once, not saying anything was probably the best response.* The thankfully image-free issue of *HotNews* was both disturbing and depressing, especially the brief snippet on the use of lawsuits to prompt internal actions by opposing parties that made snoop-hacking easier.

One of the unanticipated favorable features about COFAR, Alayna realized, was that while the observation systems could theoretically be trained on nearby human installations, there were few nearby, except the relay satellites at the L2 point—only on Phobos or Deimos or perhaps the L4 or L5 points, although she wasn't aware of any installations there. But then, perhaps that very lack was a reason why the Noram IG considered cutting funding to COFAR. She doubted that the IG would have sent a team to places where the government was satisfied with the results of government spending.

"Where is our asteroid/comet?" Alayna asked almost idly.

"One point seven five AU from the sun, with an inbound velocity of approximately thirty-two kps."

"What else have you determined about its size and shape?"

"The latest observations at best resolution indicate that it is two kilometers in length, and somewhere between 340 and 380 meters wide at its thickest point. It is shaped like it was sliced from a larger sphere. The circular cross-section has a diameter of between one point eight kilometers and two point one kilometers. The object is displayed as an enlarged image on the lower screen. If it was once part of a larger sphere, the object represents less than ten percent of the larger object."

Alayna studied the image on the lower screen for several moments. "That's no off-gassed comet, and it's certainly not an asteroid." She almost asked, "Are you certain?" She did ask, "Why didn't you notify me?"

"You did not request a verbal update, Dr. Wong-Grant."

"What about its albedo? What does that show?"

"The curved side has an albedo in excess of point nine nine. The flat side has an albedo of point six."

Alayna froze. The object *couldn't* be a natural asteroid. "Can you estimate the density?"

"It is a carbon silicate, containing silver on one side, with a probable range of from four point four grams per cubic centimeter to possibly as high as six point five grams per cubic centimeter."

"Compose a report to the IAU and let me see it. Immediately."

A report immediately appeared. Alayna studied it. As was usually the case, she could find no faults. "Send that to the IAU and a copy to both Farside Operations and to Director-Generale Braun. And a copy to my personal directory."

"All three reports have been dispatched."

"Thank you."

Alayna sat there, stunned. She didn't know what else the object could be but something created by technology. But whose? And when? And why was a huge piece of it in a cometary orbit? And what technology or force could have sliced through a sphere almost three kilometers in diameter so relatively cleanly?

A thought struck her. *Shouldn't the Space Service know?* She ought to report the possibility that the object might be more than a chunk of rock to someone, just in case it was. Yet, the problem with sending off a blind report was that it was likely to be buried or disregarded, and she had no idea to whom it should go. Then she nodded. It wouldn't hurt to send a copy to the Space Service and one to Chris as well, along with a message. She began to write.

When she finished, the message to the Director of the Space Service was direct, the key lines simply being:

> ... the object described in the attached report filed with the IAU is so unusual that it might represent an artificial construction, or possibly an alien artifact. At the least, you should know of this possibility.

The message to Chris took just a little longer.

> Chris—
> I never thought we'd be corresponding on what might be officially related business, but I feel this is important. As you can see from the attached messages, my "not-a-comet" asteroid might just be something far more important. There's nothing like it in the current catalogue of small solar system bodies. That absence indicates to me its absolute uniqueness. If it does happen to be a technological artifact, then I felt the Space Service should know of it. Although I did send the message to the Director, I have no way of knowing if it will reach him, or how soon. Because I think the matter just might be too important to be left to chance, I thought you might have a way of getting the information where it should go.

Alayna sent it off, wondering if she was being too dramatic. Yet ... *one way or another, whatever that object is, it's unique enough that it shouldn't be buried ... or allowed to be singed, if not destroyed, by the sun.*

For several minutes after she sent off the message to Chris, she sat there, trying not to second-guess herself.

You need to get back to work. Alayna knew she needed to get back to her own research, to see what else she might try and come up with a plan before it became lunar day on Farside. The trouble was ... she couldn't help but think about the comet/asteroid/possible alien object.

Perhaps if she answered Emma's latest message, that would help. She called it up and let her eyes scan the text, her eyes taking in the key sections.

... hate the fact that we can't do face-to-face real-time. You'd think we were back in the early twentieth century, as far as off-Earth comm goes. Data everywhere. Personal comm? Forget it!

Sure you must have heard, or read, since you don't get full spectrum news on Farside, but we're shut down for repairs—fairly major repairs. I'd always thought that hurricanes or tropical cyclones didn't do that much damage at altitude. Wrong on that. We had winds over 300 kph here on top of Mauna Kea ... The ITRF Facility was one of the few that didn't suffer much damage ... but it was built not to budge. It hasn't, in more than a century. Us ... everything's out of calibration and, like everyone, we're short of funds. I just hope the Sinese charges about militarizing space are wrong. The last thing we need is missiles and weapons in space. We can't even get a decent road up to the astronomy park, and DOEA turned us down flat for any help with repairs ...

Times like these, I almost wish things had worked out between Carlina and me, but two headstrong bitches in the same time and place isn't a formula for stability, even if sometimes the fire's spectacular. Did you hear about Joe Dupree? He's a junior science adviser to one of the senators from Alberta. Must be through someone he or his family knew because the position was for an ecologist, not an astrophysicist.

At that, Alayna shook her head. Not that she was surprised. She'd walked away from Joe ten minutes after they met and never looked back. *And never wanted to.* Brains and looks weren't worth much if they only supported a solipsistic ego. With a faint smile, she once more began to write.

Emma—
I'm sorry to hear about the damage on Mauna Kea. I must have missed that. I knew about Hurricane Josephina and all the damage at Hilo and especially at Kawaihae, but the reports I got here didn't mention the devastation at the astronomy park ...

Should she mention her thoughts about the possible alien artifact? Alayna shook her head. *Not now.*

For a time, I thought I might have discovered a comet. I reported it, but the IAU finally decided that it was just an asteroid in an odd orbit so that it's now just a minor planet/small body with a number—2114 FQ5 . . .

She continued to write.

22

Tavoian woke early on Sunday morning. He'd not slept well the night before, especially after he'd been greeted by a Marine captain who had politely informed him that he would need to be debriefed on Sunday and that, until that time, all his comm privileges had been suspended . . . and that he was limited to the officers' quarters and mess on ONeill Station until he was debriefed. Tavoian, being the skeptical sort, had attempted to access the comm network . . . and had been denied.

All that had meant seeing almost no one on Saturday evening, except the captain and two first lieutenants who ate in a corner of the mess. On Sunday morning Tavoian ate almost alone again, except for the two lieutenants, and a pair of captains who kept to themselves.

By 0900 UTC, Tavoian was more than restless. He had to refrain from frowning when the same Marine captain who had met him the afternoon before appeared at his quarters cubicle.

"Captain Tavoian, the major is here to debrief you. If you'd accompany me."

"Of course." Tavoian didn't see that he had much choice, especially if he wanted to leave ONeill Station, which he was coming to dislike more with each passing minute. The suspension of comm access combined with the effective isolation had resulted in a situation where he had no idea of what was happening anywhere in the solar system. For all he knew, his surveillance mission had triggered all-out war . . . or had been totally ignored. The latter was far more likely, but he didn't like not knowing.

The captain, who wore no name badge, escorted Tavoian to the upper level of ONeill Station, the one just below the shaft leading to the docking ring, and then to an unmarked pressure door. "Just go in, sir. He's expecting you."

The small chamber held little more than two chairs and a console against the bulkhead. The major stood briefly and gestured to the empty chair as he again seated himself. "Major Ernest Kohler, Captain. I'm here to debrief you."

Tavoian took in the major, not caring particularly for what he saw, a round face above a chiseled body likely kept in shape by hours exercising in the full-gee centrifuge and a friendly smile not matched by the cold blue eyes. "Then we should get started."

"Did you notice anything abnormal or any other spacecraft near you when you left Donovan Base?"

"No. Not during the checklist, release, or orientation."

"Nothing?"

"I saw nothing. The monitors and screens showed nothing, and the AI noted nothing abnormal."

The major nodded. "A Sinese fusionjet passed fairly close, in space distances, to your spacecraft shortly after turnover. What did you observe?"

"I observed very little. The relative velocities were such that we were close to each other for less than fifteen seconds. I did compute the ship's course, which appeared parallel to mine, suggesting that it began its flight somewhere close to the Sinese space elevator and would end up passing close to the L1 station. I relayed that information to L1 Operations."

"Were there any other ships that approached you after that, either en route or after you took up station off the Sinese counterweight installation?"

"No."

The major offered an inquiring glance.

Tavoian waited.

"What about after you took up station? What happened then?"

"The ship was laser-tagged with a single range pulse. That happened three other times. Those were the only contacts during the entire time I was in position observing the Sinese station."

"How many spacecraft were docked there?"

"I counted eight. All were of Sinese burner design."

The major continued to ask questions about the Sinese installation, the answers to all of which would have been revealed by the data gathered by the ship itself. He did not ask about the cubesat array. That suggested that the Marines were not exactly privy to that data.

Tavoian answered all the observational questions directly, because any optical system trained on the Sinese station would have revealed that. His most frequent reply to the other questions was, "That data along those lines went directly into the ship's data system. I wouldn't know, sir."

Finally, the major said, "Then you went to observe the Indian upper station. What did you see there?"

"A large solar-powered station, and another installation that was not complete. No work was being done on the incomplete installation while I was there."

"Was there any communication?"

"The Indian station hailed me as an unidentified spacecraft. The controller asked if I was going to request permission to dock or if I needed assistance. I replied, without giving identification, that I was not seeking permission to dock and that I did not need assistance. The station did not initiate further communication."

"You proceeded from there to ONeill Station directly?"

"I did. Those were my orders."

"Were you told what would happen once you got here?"

"I was told that I would dock, get some rest, and return to L1 with whatever passengers or cargo needed transport."

The major spent another half hour going back over what Tavoian had said before finally declaring, "That should do it." He rose. "Your comm privileges will be reinstated once you leave ONeill Station, but all your comms will be rerouted through the colonel's office before they are sent or received."

"I take it I won't know about messages someone thinks I'm not supposed to get, then?"

"Oh, no. You'll get anything that's sent to you. And if anything is classified in what you send, the message will be returned unsent with a notice of what should not be discussed."

Tavoian managed not to look puzzled. He didn't see that anything was different—unless the major was saying that all his comms from everywhere would be rerouted, and not just those made from Donovan Base.

"Your ship's ready for your return hop. You'll be carrying cargo back to Donovan Base. Quite a bit of it. They've been loading it ever since you locked in yesterday." The major rose. "Your gear's all onboard. I'll see you off."

Tavoian understood. For whatever reason, someone wanted to make certain that no one in civilian status saw him on ONeill Station, and that he was leaving without any comm going through the station's net. That was clear. The reason why wasn't, but it likely had to do with his "reconnaissance" mission. Had it caused that big an uproar? Or was the colonel trying to keep the "militarization" of Space Service pilots secret for as long as possible? Or did the major have his own agenda and did not want it revealed until Tavoian reported back to Donovan Base?

The two took lift chairs to the transfer car near the center of the station, then used it to transition into the null-grav shaft that led up to the docking ring. The major motioned for Tavoian to lead the way. Tavoian did, moving hand over hand up or along the ladder—which was merely a matter of perspective—until he reached the docking ring, then used the corridor railing to propel himself to the lock where he had docked

Recon two. He had to wait for the major there, because the inner lock door was sealed.

The major tapped in a security code, and the lock opened. "Have a good trip, Captain."

"Thank you." Tavoian inclined his head, but did not add the "sir" before closing the lock and then checking the seals and pressure before opening the outer door and the ship's outer lock.

Once he was inside Recon two, he immediately saw what the major had meant. Both the forward and rear passenger spaces were filled with plastfilm-sealed containers, strapped in position, with only a narrow passage to the ladder up to the control deck.

The trip back to Donovan Base was uneventful. Tavoian still wondered what the major had been up to, and what part of DOEA he represented, or whether he also reported to the Noram planet-based Defense Forces.

Once Recon two was grappled in at the docking ring, and Tavoian had finished his shutdown check, he gathered his kit and left the ship. The same hard-faced tech2 who had first greeted him at Donovan Base was waiting just inside the lock.

"The colonel wants to see me?" asked Tavoian.

"Yes, sir. You're to report to the colonel immediately, sir." The tech's face offered an inquiring look.

"If he hadn't asked, I would have requested."

"Yes, sir." The inquiring look was replaced by one of curiosity.

"He needs to know about certain matters."

Spacer3 Riske nodded as Tavoian stepped into the colonel's outer office. "He's expecting you, Captain." She still pointed to the biometric ID attached to the wall.

Tavoian placed both hands in the gauntlets.

"Thank you, sir. Go on in."

He nodded, set his kit against the bulkhead, then moved around the console and through the pressure hatch that opened for him and then closed immediately behind him. As before, the display screen was blacked out.

The colonel remained seated beside his console. He gestured to the single vacant seat. "I assume, Captain, there was a reason why you didn't report after reaching ONeill Station?" The colonel's voice was level, without anger.

"Yes, sir. I was precluded from any comm access . . ." Tavoian went on to explain exactly what had happened, including all the questions asked by Major Kohler. Then he gave a brief summary of what happened on his mission. When he finished, he added, "I would have been here immediately even if you hadn't requested my presence."

"Why?"

"Because the major wanted to know more than he should have. As I told you, I didn't lie to him, but I also avoided answering with anything he didn't already know."

"That was still too much."

"Exactly how was I supposed to not offer some answers to a senior officer with enough control to keep me from accessing the comm system or leaving the station?"

"I'm not faulting you. You did the best you could under the circumstances." For a moment, the colonel looked as if he might say more.

"There have been other instances, then?"

"I'll leave that unanswered. Is there anything else you want to add before I start really debriefing you?"

"There was one thing. When I was ready to depart the Indian station, I transmitted that I was departing. I received a strange reply. The controller said, 'Give our best to the colonel.' I replied that I would convey the message to my superiors."

"That's not surprising, unfortunately. We do our best. Your ship is being debugged, but with nanotechnology . . . There are some officers, often very senior officers, who have never understood that there are matters they really do not need to know . . . and should not. We will leave that point undiscussed at present." The colonel cleared his throat. "Why did you report the Sinese ship? It could have been sent just to get you to make that transmission."

"To gain a clue to the encryption system, sir? I understand that, sir." Tavoian hadn't considered that at the time, but wasn't about to admit it. "I also thought that there was the possibility that the ship might not have been crewed and might not decelerate."

"Do you really think the Sinese would risk that?"

"They could have easily claimed that it was a malfunction, that the pilot suffered a seizure . . . and that the destruction of Donovan Base was a regrettable accident . . . and apologized profusely. I only stated that the ship was headed for L1." Tavoian paused only briefly, then added, "I'm assuming that the pilot mirrored what I did."

"Not completely, we hope. Our systems haven't detected independent surveillance, but they might have come up with something new. One never knows. As for you, at least you thought it through to a degree. I'll grant that. And you kept the message short. Also good. Why did you give the Sinese an extra two kays in standoff distance?"

"Because, if I ended up getting incinerated or exploded or holed by them, I wanted the margin to be large enough that they couldn't claim I'd provoked them unduly . . ." Tavoian was getting the feeling that he was in for a long grilling.

The colonel's questions continued for another hour. Then, abruptly, he nodded. "That's all for now. Check the watch board before you do anything else."

"Yes, sir."

Once he was back in the outer office, he asked Riske, "Could I use the screen to check the watch board?"

"I'll call it up for you, sir."

"Thank you."

The watch board had been changed since he'd last been able to look, and he was scheduled for operations duty officer at 0400 UTC on Tuesday—tomorrow. He studied it, just to make sure there were no other changes, then said again, "Thank you."

"My pleasure, sir."

Tavoian doubted that, but the colonel had said "before anything else," and Riske had been pleasant about it. He picked up his kit and headed for his quarters. He unpacked the few items from his kit, then sat down and accessed his messages. Besides the various news summaries, and two periodicals, there were three personal messages, one notifying him of the change in duty officer watch schedules, one from Kit, and one from Alayna.

The message from Kit was short, but troubling.

> Chris—
>
> Haven't heard from you in days. At first, I thought I'd wait for another message from you. Dad is hiding something. I can't tell what, and I can't travel to Utah right now. I'm on call for testimony before the Noram Senate on the North Atlantic fisheries. I know you can't come Earthside, either. It's not the wildfires near Brian Head. I checked on that. They're nowhere close to their place. He says Mom is fine. I have my doubts. Please . . . if you hear anything, let me know. I'll do the same for you.
>
> Kit

Tavoian shook his head. What could he do? After several moments, he began to read the message from Alayna, intrigued and concerned when he saw that it had two attachments. He smiled wryly as he read aloud one of the key sentences: "If it does happen to be a technological artifact, then I felt the Space Service should know of it . . ." So understated. She just might have made the greatest discovery in human history, and she felt the Space Service should know of it?

And so should the colonel. Although Tavoian suspected the colonel already knew, there was no doubt of what he had to do next. With a sigh of resignation, he turned and made his way back to the colonel's office.

Spacer3 Riske smiled as Tavoian stepped into the outer office. "He said you'd be back. Go on in."

The colonel smiled, if briefly, after the pressure door closed and Tavoian seated himself. "Yes?"

"I assume that you've read the message I received from Dr. Alayna Wong-Grant and just read? If not—"

"I've read it. I'm glad it only took you a few minutes to appreciate its import . . ."

Tavoian managed not to bridle at the not-quite-veiled irony in the colonel's voice.

"I don't like the fact that your astronomer or astrophysicist friend has reported this to as many people as she did. On the other hand, since the Sinese are co-discoverers, they may have already come to the same conclusions. She followed procedures. She did think . . . somewhat. At least, she had enough sense to notify the Space Service. I would have preferred Space Command, but she wouldn't know the difference. I'm also glad she let you know. She was right about that. I doubt if CinCSpace would have seen that message for another twenty-four hours . . . if then. He's thinking it over now. I also appreciate the fact that you immediately came to notify me personally."

"Might I ask . . ."

The colonel offered a tired smile. "If she's right, we have a problem. It's a problem that has to be addressed on the highest level. I've made a recommendation. We'll see if it's accepted. Send your friend a polite and thoughtful thank you, and ask her to keep you informed of anything new that she discovers about the object. A very warm thank you."

"Yes, sir." Tavoian would have anyway.

"Now go and get some grub and rest." The colonel gestured toward the pressure door.

"Yes, sir." Tavoian rose and inclined his head.

Riske actually gave Tavoian a sympathetic smile when he left the colonel's office the second time.

PEOPLE'S DAILY
15 OCTOBER 2114

[BEIJING] "For the past century, the Sinese peoples have made their goals in space open and known to all," declared Head of State Jiang Qining. "We have been proud of our successes. We have built upon efforts that were less successful, just as we are now with our follow-up mission to the moons of Jupiter. We have nothing to hide. For all that, others have continued to harass and spy upon our peaceful space activities. Less than friendly observation is the first step toward indirect hostilities. Others would be wise not to continue such efforts."

While Head of State Jiang did not offer names, sources close to him have hinted that the head of state is less than pleased with covert operations by both Noram and India in an effort to obtain Sinese space technology.

Noram officials, predictably, denied any such effort.

"What is most disturbing about the comments attributed to Head of State Jiang," said Noram Defense Secretary Olassen Trudeau, "is that he is far more moderate than senior officers in the Sinese military." Trudeau's remarks were termed "excessive" by party sources because of his long-time critical attitude toward the Federation. Others indicated Trudeau's words were "worrisome" because they indicated Noram was actively considering efforts to militarize outer space in the solar system.

"If Noram takes such a step, it will be a step it will regret bitterly," declared Sinese Minister for Space Wong Mengyi.

A spokesman for the Indian government, who declined to be named publicly, stated that observation by itself was harmless and suggested that the Sinese over-reaction might indicate that the Federation was the guilty party and already showing "military-like" efforts with its latest Europa mission and the ongoing diversion of an ice asteroid toward the inner solar system.

Monday morning, after Alayna finished the immediate chores, and of course once more checked the dust prevention system on the main optical mirror, she went to the message queue—and was surprised, almost stunned, to find a reply from Chris. In over a year, he'd never replied so quickly. *There has to be a first time.*

She opened it quickly, almost holding her breath, and began to read.

> Dear Alayna—
> You'll likely be shocked to receive such a rapid reply from me. It's not in character, I know, but I just received your message after I returned. Yes, I'm still piloting, if less frequently and on a far less regular schedule. One of the reasons I replied so soon was that I've often been remiss, partly because the training here has been intense, and partly because I have the bad habit of not getting back to things for a time if I put them off. I'll try to be better.

Alayna paused. *One of the reasons? There are two, and he's just getting started, it sounds like.* Another thought crossed her mind. Chris was an experienced pilot. Yet he was still piloting and undergoing intense training. What exactly was he doing? Could there be some truth in the rumors that Noram, the Sinese, and the Indians were militarizing space? Was Chris part of that? She forced her eyes back to the message.

> No matter what you said, I know you had to be initially disappointed when you thought your comet was only an asteroid. From your reports, it's pretty clear you discovered something a great deal more exciting. As you requested, I immediately met with my superior, and he forwarded your report to the head of the Space Service. He didn't say it exactly, but I think he either talked to him or to someone near the top. I'm not

anywhere close to an astrophysicist, as you know, but your discovery is special one way or another. If you could keep me posted on anything else you find out about it, he and I would be most grateful.

He and I? Alayna swallowed. But Chris was saying to keep him posted. Why him and not the head of the Space Service? Or even Chris's superior? That seemed strange . . . unless . . . *Unless it was less likely to come to anyone else's attention when a report was just part of a message from a junior astrophysicist in a one-off position to her male friend that she'd been messaging for months?* But why keep it secret in such a roundabout way, unless they really thought it could be an alien object or artifact?

I don't know about you, but I'm worried about all the angry words and charges flying back and forth between the Indians and Sinese. Now even the Noram Defense Minister is getting into the act, and President Yates hasn't said a word. I don't see the Indians as the troublemakers here, but that may not matter if the Sinese insist.

He's not talking about what Noram is doing . . . or what he's doing. It was clear to Alayna that Chris knew a great deal more than he was saying, but what, she could only speculate.

How is your other project going, the solar research? You haven't said much in your last few messages. A while ago, you said that what you were trying to find was a long shot. All I can say is that you're quite a lady, and that long shots are hard work, but sometimes they pay off far more than conventional projects. Keep at it, and you might have a chance for two long shots to pay off. That doesn't happen often.

As I've written too often, most of the time here is training and routine . . . and late night supervisory duties. Every Noram off-planet installation requires round-the-clock monitoring, and tomorrow, probably actually after you read this, I'll be up at 0400 UTC, bleary-eyed and looking at screens.

I keep meaning to mention it, but my sister Kit—Katherine, officially—is a marine biologist with the Noram Department of Environmental Affairs. She's in Ottawa now, trying to explain to the politicians why the collapse of the Gulf Stream current can't be reversed. Not anytime soon, that is. They want to think that just slowing the rise in atmospheric CO2 will solve everything, including warming the British Isles. They also don't understand that North Atlantic fisheries won't recover completely, maybe ever. They say a little knowledge is danger-ous. That's especially true with politicians. We've seen it with DOEA, and I can't imagine it would be much different in your field if we faced some possible great change in astronomy and astrophysics.

Alayna smiled. She had at least one answer as to why Chris wanted her to send copies of reports to him, and she couldn't fault it. She paused and then checked the rest of the message queue. There wasn't a reply from either the IAU or from the Foundation. She wouldn't have expected a quick reply, or any immediate reply from the IAU. In a way, the lack of im-mediate response from her own organization validated Chris's concerns— although she suspected the concerns were as much his superior's as his own.

Was she being fair about the Farside Foundation? Still, it had been twenty-four hours since she'd sent off the report . . .

Then she shook her head. *No one was working.* She'd sent the report early on Sunday, and it was still early on Monday, well before anyone came to work, since Daedalus was on UTC, and the Foundation on Eastern WestHem time, some five hours later. Of course, they hadn't replied. *Now . . . if there's no response by this afternoon or tomorrow . . .*

She returned her attention to the rest of the message.

> I can't resist calling your attention to another passage from *Observations on Politics.*

> *Liberals always want to save the world on principle and worry about the costs later. Conservatives worry about the cost-accounting so much that they can never decide whether any-thing's worth saving, except for every single worthless project in their own district, including, especially, the bases and weap-ons the military says it doesn't need.*

> I wonder what Exton Land was like. There's very little about him, except he was a political appointee in the old U.S. govern-ment, and later a consultant of some sort. Gently cynical, and sometimes not even gentle. But what he wrote is as true today as it was then. People don't change, I guess.

Oh . . . you owe me a quote. Now, I need to close and get a good night's sleep. Until later.

Chris

Owe you a quote? Then she realized that she'd been so concerned about the possible alien artifact that, for the first time in months, she had not included a quote in her last message.

Alayna couldn't help but smile, if momentarily, as she closed his message, thinking over the implications and meanings semihidden within his words. She quickly ran through the rest of the message queue. Once she made sure there was nothing else urgent, she settled herself to reply to Chris, at least as indirectly as he had messaged her.

The most frightening aspect of it all, she realized, although the tenseness within her had meant her subconscious had already made that conclusion, was the possibility that she had in fact discovered—or co-discovered—an alien artifact . . . and that the Sinese likely knew that it could be an artifact as well. And with the spectre of the possible militarization of space . . .

Tavoian was still considering the possible implications of Alayna's discovery when he settled into a seat at the officers' mess on Tuesday morning and took a slow sip of tea through the wide nipplestraw, necessary on a station where gravity was provided by rotation, a variety of tea that passed, if poorly, for English Breakfast. He especially wondered where it would all lead after the veiled references to his surveillance mission had turned up in most of the major news summaries. He carefully squirted syrup over the French toast and the protein strips that passed for bacon. He took one bite, and then another.

Moments later, Liendra Duvall sat down across from him. "You have a very serious expression for so early in the morning, Chris."

Tavoian managed a rueful smile at the other captain, who had roughly the same seniority as he did, and who was always pleasantly low-key. She also tended to be almost shy, or at least retiring, which made her comment slightly surprising. "Just thinking. I probably shouldn't start before I have something to eat."

"You were the one, weren't you?"

"The one what?"

"The one that the Sinese are making a fuss about. Every single pilot in . . . advanced training was here on Saturday and Sunday. Except you. Who else could it have been?"

"I'm certain I haven't been the first. Last week . . . you were gone. I doubt it was a transport run."

"Behind that casual façade, you don't miss much."

Tavoian grinned at her nonadmission admission in response to his ambiguous acquiescence to her assumption. "Nor you. What do you think of the current situation between us, the Indians, and the Sinese?"

Her amused smile vanished. "Tense . . . and getting tenser. The Sinese won't back down. The Indians certainly won't, and they've got enough Indra scramjets to take out most of the Sinese government."

"The government won't be where the scramjets can reach them."

"Unless the Indians strike first. Both of them know that."

"Know what?" asked Major Martinez as he sat down beside Duvall.

"That the Indians have to strike first if their scramjets are to be effective," replied Tavoian.

"Everyone has to strike first." Martinez sipped his coffee, strong enough that Tavoian could smell it from across the table. "That's the problem. We're at a time in history and weapons when offense beats defense. It'll change. It always does."

"Provided we all survive long enough for that to happen," Duvall pointed out.

"We've done it before. The early atomic age and the Cold War."

"That was different," Tavoian said. "There were only two contending forces. Now there are three, and three's not a stable number in great power confrontations."

"You've definitely got a pessimistic streak there, Chris," replied Martinez. "It's not as though we can do anything about it."

"Except show force to match force and hope that no one presses the issue," said Duvall quietly.

"Isn't that what we've had to do for generations?" Martinez set his mug on the table, and began to eat the French toast, without syrup.

"Every advance in weapons technology raises the costs if someone makes a mistake." Tavoian took another long sip of tea, then added, "Or just believes that God is on their side. Like the Taliban in Pakistan seventy years ago."

"They deserved what they got," Martinez said.

"They may have, but what about the Afghans, those few who survived? Or the Indians in Kashmir." *Or the coast and the marshlands bordering the Arabian Sea.* Tavoian didn't voice the last because he doubted the others would know or care about the immense damage to the marine ecosystem there, not that the pollution from the Indus hadn't already created havoc before that.

"There are always casualties. All we can do is make sure the other side takes them."

"Which other side?" asked Duvall. "Is either trustworthy? Do we want to pick sides?"

"If we don't they will, and it might be us against both of them."

"That seems unlikely."

"How likely did it seem that the Iranians and the Israelis ended up on the same side in the Middle East Meltdown?" Martinez smiled sardonically. "You can't count anything out."

Even the possibility of an alien artifact? Tavoian mused. *With the rem-*

nants of technology . . . or would that be expecting far too much? Far too much, he decided. That was definitely wistful thinking.

Martinez said something, but Tavoian didn't really hear it. "I'm sorry. I was thinking about the next simulator session."

"It wasn't important. I just wanted to know what you thought about the President."

Tavoian wasn't about to offer an opinion there. "She's the commander-in-chief. What else should I think?"

"Anything but nothing." Martinez shook his head. "You're too junior to talk like the political officers."

"I'm too junior not to," countered Tavoian. *Especially when every word is heard by someone you don't know.*

"Playing it safe is the most dangerous course, you know."

"You're suggesting that playing it dangerous is the safest course. I'm not sure about that logic." Tavoian caught the glint in Duvall's eyes and the hint of amusement, as if she were watching two big-horned sheep position themselves. He immediately laughed self-deprecatingly and added, "I'm not sure about most logic. Could be because strong logic is necessary to overcome poor assumptions or insufficient facts, and insufficient facts are usually all the facts that junior officers have access to." He smiled, then eased his chair back. "I need to do some prep."

As he left the mess, Tavoian couldn't help contrasting Liendra Duvall with Alayna. Somehow, he couldn't imagine Alayna acting the way the other captain had. *You only talked to Alayna for less than an hour—once, ten months ago.* He shrugged ruefully. That might be, but he had the feeling he knew more about her than the people with whom he spent far more of his time. *Because you really don't have that much in common with the other pilots? Or because piloting is a solitary experience? Or because that's what you want to believe?*

He wasn't certain he could answer his own questions honestly. He was certain that he wasn't prepared as well as he should be for his next session in the simulator. *That's something you can do something about, unlike determining what the Sinese or Indians will do or whether Alayna's comet or asteroid is really something more.* Except they both knew it was something more. They just didn't know how much more.

Almost a week after receiving a reply from Farside Foundation Director-Generale Braun, Alayna was still irritated. The Director-Generale had politely thanked her for an interesting report, congratulated her on discovering such a unique asteroid, and suggested that any further reports go directly to Operations Director Wrae. Director Wrae had sent an acknowledgment of the reclassification without comment, with the bulk of her message consisting of an inquiry about whether Alayna had been able to persuade the IAU to grant partial credit for the discovery to the Williams Consortium. Alayna's very polite reply had stated that she had made the effort and that the final decision rested with the IAU.

She'd heard nothing further from the IAU, but had received another message from Chris, to which she had replied. He had not yet responded, but since she'd only sent her message on Sunday night, and it was only Tuesday morning, she didn't exactly feel ignored, besides which, she was still working on trying to find another approach to discovering how she could discover more about the solar multi-fractal mini-granulations.

What about the last idea? Alayna consulted her calendar. It had in fact been a month, or maybe a day less than a month, since she'd tasked Marcel with seeking out mini-granulation multi-fractal pattern matches. "Marcel . . . it's been a month. Have you been able to match any of those mini-fractal patterns?"

"There are similarities in quite a few instances, but there are no exact matches."

"Let's see what you have, one at a time."

The first set of images appeared before her. Alayna studied them. As the AI had said, there was definitely a similarity between the two. *But what?* She kept looking. Finally, she asked, "Marcel, could you rotate one of the highlighted multi-fractal images, as if it were a cylinder, just slightly, to see if that increases or decreases the similarity?"

"The multi-fractal only appears as a flat image, Dr. Wong-Grant. Any rotation of the multi-fractal would require extrapolation that would not necessarily have any relation to the actual shape of the multi-fractal mini-granulation."

In short, that might or might not increase the similarity, but it wouldn't prove anything. "There's nothing that might give even the faintest indication of what lies directly beneath? Besides the observed convective patterns?"

"No, Dr. Wong-Grant."

Alayna went through the other pairs that represented instances where Marcel had found similarities. There were more than a hundred, of which perhaps thirty seemed to show remarkably close similarities, at least to Alayna's eyes. Given the distance, the size and scale, and the number of multi-fractal mini-granulations, those comparatively few similarities, even at the same positions on the sun's surface, could just as easily represent chance occurrences. At least, most astrophysicists and astronomers would want to know what proof there was that they weren't. *Correlation doesn't prove causation, especially when you have absolutely no idea why solar convection would result in the phenomenon of multi-fractals. Except the fact that the larger granulations are essentially regular and distributed in a Gaussian field. Why not the mini-granulations?* Except that had been the question for a century . . . one without an answer.

"Keep observing and continuing the process, but only when it doesn't interfere with other observations and processing."

"Yes, Dr. Wong-Grant."

Just to get one thing done and off her mind, she quickly began a message to her father, knowing that, if she didn't, before long, most likely in the next day, she'd have to write a much longer one.

> Dad—
> Nothing new here since the IAU decided my comet was an asteroid. It's unusual enough that I've been requested to supply updates. So far, it's not unusual enough . . .

She paused. She hadn't asked Marcel about her discovery in over a week because of the combination of the object's position, COFAR's position, and the commitment of the main optical mirror to other projects, but in the last day or two, there might have been a window . . .

"Marcel, what additional data do we have right now, on our anomalous asteroid with the dual nature?"

"The object is approximately one point six AU from the sun. It is not off-gassing. That would confirm that it is a solid body. The only heat signature is that of re-radiated sunlight. The intensity off the white side indicates a reflectivity of point nine nine."

"What does the spectrometer analysis show?"

"Rayleigh scattering and Raman shift indicate a mixture of silver, silicate, and carbon."

"What about the dark side?"

"The spectroscopy is indicative of carbon."

"Carbon nanorod or nanotubes with diamond nanorods?"

"It is close, but not identical."

All that **has** *to be artificial. The white side might as well be a mirror.* "You need to make up a report for transmission. I'll look at it in a moment." She went back to the message to her father, changing part of what she had written.

> So far, while it appears unusual to me, those to whom I report have not yet found it remarkable, although a friend who is a pilot finds it very exciting. I think I'm glad he does, but I hope my discovery doesn't outshine me in his eyes . . .

She smiled wryly, realizing that she actually meant the words and wondering if she should change them. She shook her head.

> Anyway, except for clearing a minor obstruction in the water recycling system the other day, there's not much else to say. I'm doing well, and I hope to make some progress in my solar research, but you can never tell, although I'd really like to develop a better methodology for what I'm doing . . .

She finished off the message and sent it. After reviewing the report Marcel had generated, and altering the language slightly, she began the next message, the one that had to offer more than reassurance.

> Chris—
> Everything here remains largely routine. It's busier now that it's night here. It always is. I haven't had any major repairs, not with the observation systems, but I did have to do some intensive maintenance on the base water recycling system this past Sunday.
>
> The latest analyses of solar multi-fractal mini-granulations are suggestive of something, but "suggestive" in a way that doesn't constitute proof or even hope of proof in the strictest astronomical or astrophysical context. I'm convinced that there's something there, but it could be that others have seen the same

phenomena over the century since multi-fractals were discovered and been unable to discover anything more, either. Am I banging my head against a wall? I hope not, but even if I'm not the one to discover the reason or cause or solar mechanism behind the multi-fractals, I do believe that there's something more than massive convection.

I've enclosed the latest information on the "abnormal asteroid." It's definitely not a typical small solar system body and might possibly be what I suspect we both feel. Over the next few months we should get much better information, at least until it gets too close to the sun, which appears will be in January.

Now, for the near-obligatory quotation, once more from *The Passion of Science:*

How can you not be passionate when you discover that the Earth's plasmasphere reacts to coronal mass ejections in a way that protects the planet? Whether it's a systemic reaction or something more, the plasmasphere is protecting, or trying to protect, the planet.

As always, my best to you.

She took a deep breath and sent the message. What the Space Service could do, or would do, she had no idea, but it was all too clear that the Foundation didn't care that much, nor, apparently, the IAU. *Unless they're only pretending not to care because the Sinese have leaned on them, or on IAU members or staff.* That was all too possible, given that SINOP had been a co-discoverer of the mysterious object . . . or alien artifact.

Then she dispatched copies of the report to the IAU and to Director Wrae, who likely would take days to get around to reading it. She still had very mixed feelings about sending copies to Chris, even though she felt that if she didn't, especially if the object turned out to be an alien or out-system artifact, the Sinese might well find something to their advantage . . . and that couldn't be good, not the way the great powers were acting.

Not at all.

It was 0258 UTC, and Tavoian continued to study the screens at the duty officer's console. They showed nothing out of the ordinary—the Lunar L1 Station little more than ten kays away, the other drum-shaped storage facility ten beyond that, a shape that matched Donovan Base in all particulars. At that moment, there were no fusionjets docking anywhere, and the only motion outside any of the facilities was the continual arrival and departure of the elevator climbers coming up from the lunar polar base and then returning. The screens showed no incoming vessels or anything else. The only sounds were faint hums, and the hissing of the air being circulated into the duty center.

Tavoian was standing watch from 0000 to 0400—what the surface ocean navies called the midwatch—which seemed pointless in a way on a station that never saw darkness in its corridors, but which still made sense in terms of maintaining security while most of the station slept in order to maintain biological circadian rhythms. While he certainly had free time, reading or composing nonofficial messages was strictly frowned upon. That left a lot of time for thinking.

He'd passed on the attachment from Alayna's message, but not the message itself, to the colonel, although the colonel could have read it himself, and probably had. The colonel hadn't acknowledged the transmittal, and likely never would. From Alayna's report, the object was either an incredible astronomical phenomenon or an artifact. Yet how had it ended up in a cometary orbit? From the reports Tavoian had seen, the artifact was only part of a larger structure, and that raised other questions. What sort of force had been used to slice it apart? Had there been a war somewhere? Or had the larger body collided with something? What sort of technology had built the object? Were there any traces of it left?

All those questions had swirled around in his mind, along with several others. What was Space Command going to do about it, if anything? The Sinese were already trying to exploit something on Europa. Would they attempt to send an expedition to the object? Why wasn't Space Command? Or were they, but keeping it secret from everyone? That was certainly the most likely prospect, but these days . . . who would know, except those involved?

He'd sent a reply to Alayna, but one that expressed appreciation and congratulations without being specific, along with a brief quote from *Observations*. He smiled as he recalled it.

> *Political science came into being as alchemy was being discredited, although history has since proved that alchemy had a better record.*

The screen bleeped, but Tavoian had already noticed that the detectors had registered a Noram fusionjet inbound for either L1 or Donovan Base, although the ETA suggested that he would be off watch by the time that it locked at whichever was its destination. The timing suggested urgency of some sort, because all Noram space installations operated on UTC.

"Log possible incoming FusEx," ordered Tavoian.

"Logging FusEx."

Tavoian then checked the official message log, but there were no station-alert messages or warnings, except for the notice from the previous day to restrict EFAs and to shutter sensitive equipment until 1800 the previous evening from the effects of a strong CME. The news summaries didn't hint at anything that hadn't already been occurring, except the UAAS charged the Sinese with an attempt to steal sensitive energy research project data. The Sinese predictably had denied any such activity.

Energy research project? Particle beam research? Was that the purpose of the unfinished station near the Indian installation he'd observed? But the Indians hadn't said anything at all publicly about his "observation."

He shook his head. As even a moderately senior captain, he wasn't going to find out the answers to his questions until the entire human solar system did. Then there was the problem with his parents. His father had replied to his last message, when his mother was usually the correspondent. *Kit was right about that.* At the moment, though, he didn't know what else he could do except message them frequently . . . and hope Kit could find out more, since she could visit them, and even when she couldn't, she could do real-time face-to-face, which he couldn't.

HOTNEWS!
30 OCTOBER 2114

[Image Deleted For Off-Earth Transmission]

A Sinese coup! That's right. They have a permanent base on Europa. They're not saying why, but it might have to do with deuterium, the magic stuff that makes fusion easier and cheaper. They've just locked up one of the sources. Might make them the energy czars of this century. They're serious. By the way, the code name is Jade Spear. That tell you something?

[Image Deleted]

Sleazal Easel! Neidreich Nazi, the slash parodist . . . did he go too far with his nude satire piece on Pres Yates? CP-ers in Ottawa are fuming, and it's not hash-haze or Elerium dust. Beyond the pale? Who knows? Could be dear Dyana's really a sexy prexy beneath all that somber garb?

[Image Deleted]

Three Indra scramjet missiles are missing. Or maybe five. Yes, indeedy. An official audit says three of the armed missiles have vanished. Our sources say five. Gone, just like that. Sinese Defense Minister Wu Gong screams that it's a plot to foist off blame on benighted Bhutanese terrorists inadvertently acting as Indian agents. Or maybe Kyrgyzstani terrorists. He's not mentioning Mongolia First! Got to be the Bhutanese. That's what he says, HotNews fans. Wonder why?

[Image Deleted]

Brit pop-opera diva Mamselle insists on current realtalk for her role in *Hillary*. She claims fans won't identify with the period language a century old. Why would they care, with all the sex and power? Especially given Mamselle's talent for, shall we say, exposure . . .

DONOVAN BASE
31 OCTOBER 2114

Wednesday morning at 0755 UTC found Tavoian walking into the colonel's outer office, and nodding to Spacer3 Riske. She smiled slightly more than politely and gestured for him to go through the pressure door.

"Thank you."

"You're welcome, Captain."

Tavoian managed not to smile at the pleasant use of his rank as a polite reminder of the Service's discouragement of fraternization between officers and techs. He thought Riske was an attractive woman, but appearance wasn't everything. After meeting Alayna, he'd come to realize that—not that Alayna wasn't attractive. She was. She just wasn't physically stunning. Mentally however . . . and that was far more appealing to him, he realized. *If belatedly.*

He stepped into the colonel's inner sanctum where he took the chair offered and waited to hear what the colonel wanted.

"I understand you have some past experience in building AIs." The matter-of-fact tone the colonel used suggested he was in no way asking a question.

What does that have to do with anything we've been doing? Tavoian hoped he concealed his surprise as he replied, "Very small and modest ones, sir." His words were cautious. "That's how I helped pay for university."

"You programmed them as well?"

"Yes, sir. In AdMek."

"Yourself or with a compiler?"

"I had to learn it myself. I couldn't afford the kind of compiler that would do that."

The colonel nodded. "What do you think of your training and mission?"

"I like the challenge and learning new techniques. I hope they're not necessary."

"So do I, believe it or not." A slight frown appeared and vanished. "Would you be interested in an even more challenging mission?"

"I'd be interested, sir." *How interested depends on the mission.*

"A little caution. Good." An amused smile appeared. "What do you think of your friend the astrophysicist's discovery?"

"I think it's possible it might represent an alien artifact. If not, it's certainly the most unusual asteroid I've ever heard of. That's just an opinion, sir."

The room darkened and an image filled the wall. Most of it was shimmering silver-white and curved. The demarcation between the silver part and the smaller darker section was sharp, like a knife edge. The object appeared as though it had once been a small section of a huge silver ball with a black interior.

"That's the best image we've been able to obtain of your friend's discovery. It's slightly fuzzy because we enlarged it beyond clear resolution. What does it look like to you, Captain?"

"Like it's a piece of a much larger sphere, almost as if this part got sliced off. Or maybe what was left after most of the sphere was destroyed."

"The astronomers tell me that the odds of a natural body being formed with a curvature like that combined with a perfectly flat side are so high that it's preposterous. And it's far too regular. It's a piece of a perfect sphere. It's hard to tell, but the dark portion has holes or indentations in a flat surface. There's no visible pitting or indentations on the silver-white side."

"As if it were an impenetrable hull."

"Your words, not mine. But I'd tend to agree." The colonel paused. "How would you like to go take a look at it?"

"You want an armed FusEx ship . . . because of the Sinese? What about scientists?" Tavoian's eyes went back to the screen.

"First, we have to get someone there, to make certain they don't monopolize it. We aren't sure what it is, and it's hard to get that large a commitment of resources without that. The other problem is that there's no ship immediately available with sufficient habitability to support a team and all they need for more than a week or so. Possibly a month. We also have to gather a team and get them together. All that takes time that we don't have."

"So . . . a ship with one man and an array of AI devices that can investigate and probe immediately. With enough arms to keep the artifact open to us."

"Precisely."

"With a pilot who has no significant other and a talent for AI."

"That would be useful."

"It sounds like a minimal resources mission," ventured Tavoian.

"Not quite minimal, but close. We're not skimping on fuel, drives, or habitability. We've also beefed up the radiation shielding because of the time you'll be out there, but there's not enough time to develop specialized equipment, not if we want to look at the object before it grazes the sun."

"You're gambling that there's something of value there."

"Wouldn't you, Captain?"

Rather than comment verbally, Tavoian let a wry smile appear. "What if the Sinese reach it before we do?"

"That's unlikely, but the pilot's mission is not to forbid their exploration, but to allow ours when a team arrives, and to set out as many AI devices to discover what those devices can determine in the meantime."

"What about communications?"

"We won't restrict your comm. The pilot will have full comm, through targeted encrypted burst."

"Including personal messages?"

"After review . . . yes."

"When would this . . . mission begin?"

"Tomorrow morning. We're awaiting additional AI equipment. Are you interested?"

"How could I not be?"

"There's a definite element of danger. You'll have to match inbound velocity, and you may have to stay with the object for quite some time, depending on what you discover."

"Weeks?"

The colonel barked a laugh. "More like two months, if necessary. Theoretically, if any FusEx had the fuel capacity, it could reach the object in four days of constant one-gee acceleration and then constant decel. The ship is having additional Hel3 tanks installed, but not that kind of capacity, and the drives can't maintain that acceleration near long enough. There are also habitability concerns . . ."

"No one has spent months in a FusEx, only a few weeks."

"Five weeks at most with three people. The systems weren't strained."

Tavoian understood the unspoken concern. No one knew how long the systems would remain unstrained. They weren't designed the way lunar or satellite systems were.

"The other aspect is that if you stay with the object until it nears the orbit of Mercury, perhaps somewhat longer, you'll have enough fuel to depart, but there would be no way for any ship to reach you if matters turned black."

Tavoian frowned. That didn't make sense.

"Think about it. What's the maximum safe continuous thrust at one gee."

"Two hours. Two and a half under optimal conditions."

"That thrust will give you a terminal velocity just over seventy kays per second . . . I can't do all the math in my head, and I'm not about to ask the AI to calculate for reasons I trust you understand, but even with an acceleration and drive rest cycle, and given fuel limitations, it would take a FusEx nearly seven days at speed to reach where you *were*. But by the time this object nears Mercury, it will be traveling at somewhere in the range of sixty kays per second, accelerating to as high as 250 by the time it reaches perihelion . . . a real solar express."

"I get the picture, sir. I'd be at perihelion with the object before any ship could get close."

"There's also the small problem that the solar escape velocity much inside the orbit of Mercury would test the capability of any of our burners, except on an elliptical flyby, and that doesn't provide the best odds for a rendezvous."

Tavoian understood that as well. A tangential course from the object might be possible, even halfway between Mercury's orbit and the sun . . . but it wasn't something he'd want to bet his life on, and an elliptical orbit around the sun was likely too close for the shielding, besides which, it would add to the ship's speed, and any rescue attempt after perihelion would face an even greater initial exit velocity.

"Would you be willing to take on this mission? This is not a perfunctory request, or the kind where failure to accept would damage your career. I want a committed and interested volunteer. If you're uncertain, I will understand, and not a word of this meeting will ever appear anywhere."

Tavoian didn't think of hesitating. "I'd very much like to do it, sir. Very much."

"Good. I thought you would. You'll have a formal briefing early tomorrow. We're aiming for a 0700 departure. You'll have to hold off informing your astrophysicist friend for several days. After that, it won't matter." The colonel's smile turned wintry. "It might not matter anyway, but there's always the chance that it might."

"There's not a problem with what I tell her when I can message her?"

"Not about your undertaking the mission. Some details should remain undisclosed, but you know what those are."

The colonel's matter-of-fact attitude about Tavoian's messaging froze him for a moment, before he asked, "And messages from her?"

"You'll get all incoming messages. Burst sent all at once."

"Encrypted, of course." Tavoian managed a smile.

"Of course. We wouldn't want to make it any easier for the Sinese."

As he left the colonel's office, Tavoian had the feeling that making it hard on the Sinese to intercept communications would be the easiest aspect of the mission. He also began to question how such a mission would be even possible with a conventional FusEx or even with the reconfigured Recon burners. The object was somewhere beyond Mars, and Mars was about as far as burners could travel with passengers, under current fuel and habitability considerations. Going months? Even with a crew of one . . . ?

Yet . . . for a possible alien artifact . . . a onetime solar express? How many pilots would have a shot at something like that?

30

Late on Wednesday afternoon, Tavoian received word that his departure time had been shifted to 1100 UTC and that his briefing would begin at 0800 the next morning. That didn't exactly help his thoughts, especially the more he considered the mission, exciting as it had seemed initially. At 0755 on Thursday, he stepped into the colonel's inner office. His mouth was dry.

Unlike most times, the colonel stood. He also wore the dark blue uniform shipsuit of the Space Service. He handed Tavoian a flat package.

"Sir?"

"At ease, Major. Those are your new rank patches. There needs to be some reward for what you're about to do."

After that indirect reminder that he was about to undertake a dangerous mission with less than optimum resources, Tavoian thought, only momentarily, about replying in Latin—with the old phrase "morituri te salutant," but instead said, "Thank you."

"I know what you're thinking. You're right. It's dangerous, but no more so that the other mission you've been training for . . . and it might even be less so. Especially for you."

Tavoian didn't miss the double meaning behind the colonel's words, but just nodded.

The colonel gestured to the vacant chair and seated himself. "First, some preliminary explanations. The basic problem we have is that almost everything in the solar system is in the wrong position for an easy and quick approach to the target object. The object's already in-system of Jupiter, even of the asteroid belt, and still well above the ecliptic. Mars is nowhere close to where you could use it as a gravitational fulcrum to kill your outbound velocity and change course. Given the Earth's position, you'll get a boost from its orbital velocity after separation. We also can't get you to rendezvous with the object with enough remaining fuel or habitability, not with a conventional burner. That's why we had to come up with another approach. We've stripped another burner down to the basics, and turned it into the equivalent of a booster. It's little more than engines, directional thrusters, and fuel. The flight profile is simple enough. The booster will accelerate your Recon bird for two hours at one gee, rest for two hours, accelerate for two hours at one gee, using the same pattern for the first sixteen hours. Then you do an early turnover and coast for a bit less than a week before beginning decel . . ."

Early turnover?

Even before Tavoian could verbalize the thought, the major replied to the unspoken question.

"That allows you to lead with the booster fusionjet. The way the connector structure is designed, if you do encounter something that you can't detect fast enough to avoid and too large for the Whipple shields to handle, the entire booster will absorb it. You're going to be moving about as fast as any piloted craft has ever gone." The colonel continued without even commenting on the velocity required for the mission, as if it were obvious.

Tavoian supposed he should have realized the reason for the early turnover.

". . . The booster should last long enough to kill your outbound velocity. Then you'll separate, unless there's fuel remaining. You'll need about an hour of acceleration to match speeds with the object and close on it. The target is calculated to reach an inbound speed of thirty-six kays per second at the time it crosses the orbit of Mars. You will intercept it inside the orbit of Mars at a solar distance of approximately one point two AU on November eighth. You will deploy all cubesats and other recon equipment as expeditiously as possible, and then follow with exploratory AIs, depending on what initial reconnaissance discovers."

Tavoian nodded. "How did you manage the booster conversion so quickly?"

"We didn't. It was something we'd already tried for other reasons."

"Since it was there and no one had another use for it?"

"There are other uses for it, but nothing as pressing as your mission."

"Aren't the Sinese going to do the same thing? Or the Indians? Even the EC?"

"It's a matter of fuel and timing. By sending a single-pilot ship, we get more time on station because of habitability. Even so, for safety's sake you'll need to break off near or just inside the orbit of Mercury. For purposes of the mission, we're calculating that distance at an average of fifty million kays."

Tavoian managed not to frown. Mercury's orbit was the most eccentric of all the true planets in the solar system, ranging from roughly forty-five million kays from the sun to seventy million. Selecting an orbital figure slightly larger than the orbit at perihelion gave a greater impression of a safety margin, while allowing several more days of dealing with the artifact. *But it's only an impression.*

"At that point, you'll have a closure rate with the sun in excess of fifty kps. With a solar escape velocity of close to seventy kps at that point . . ."

Tavoian got the picture. The longer he stayed with the target, the longer the fusionjet would have to fire, and he would need roughly four hours of acceleration to reach escape velocity, except that was an oversimplification because he couldn't risk more than two hours of continuous acceleration without overstraining the drive. Then, once he canceled the solar closure rate, each hour of acceleration would move him farther away where the escape velocity was lower. Even so, getting close to the sun was pushing it, given that fusionjets weren't designed for long stretches of continuous use, even at power settings of less than one gee. If he had time, then there were other options, but since sustaining habitability for more than two and a half months would also be a problem, he likely wouldn't have that much margin in terms of time.

"Did anyone consider a totally robotic mission?"

The colonel looked unhappy at the question. "Let us just say that there are issues of both equipment and security involved."

Like the fact that it might be far more difficult for the Sinese to deny involvement with an "unfortunate" accident to a manned mission? Or even that requesting certain equipment might scuttle the mission? "I take it any data or information sharing will be handled by Space Command? And to say that if anyone commlinks and asks me to share anything?"

"Exactly. We'll immediately release any spectacular visuals . . . for a number of reasons."

But not any that might reveal tech secrets.

"Also, no comms for forty-eight hours. Except in case of an absolute emergency. After that, standard commlink procedures. As I said earlier, personal comm messages are allowable, but they'll be checked and relayed."

"Yes, sir."

"There's another aspect of this you need to remember. The booster linkage isn't feasible for an attack or anything but straight-line constant acceleration or deceleration. You can't make rapid shifts in acceleration or deceleration, or you could break the linkage."

And that would abort the mission and maybe worse.

"You will carry two torps, but they won't be usable until after you separate the booster. You shouldn't need them until after separation in any case."

Because there won't be conflict or danger until you near the target, and then, only if it is an alien artifact.

"We need to go over the basics of your cargo, mainly AI components with a variety of body types and propulsive systems, some with grabbers, saws, that sort of thing."

"What about a diamond nanorod drill or a drill or sampler like it? An artifact with that kind of albedo and no marks on its surface might be incredibly difficult to obtain pry samples from."

"Silvered silicon . . ." The colonel paused. "I'll see what I can do. Just a moment." Whatever the colonel did was near-instantaneous, most likely through an implant. "Back to the AIs and the associated equipment . . ."

Tavoian listened.

After fifteen minutes, the colonel smiled. "You'll have a week en route to go over all of this. There are complete schematics in the ship's database, two sets, one in the AI and one in your personal infobank. There's also a print manual as backup."

After that, Tavoian got a briefing on the mission profile, from the timing, the possible corrections necessary, and if the object turned out to be alien, what Space Command would like, and if it did not, all the astrophysical and other data the scientific types would like. In the event of the second case, the mission would be much shorter, but it was clear that Space Command believed strongly that the object was more than a unique asteroid. It was also clear that time was of the essence, especially in getting a Noram spacecraft to the object, and that the colonel had been ordered to get the most suitable pilot from those available at Donovan Base.

Carrying his kit, Tavoian reached the lock for Recon three at 1030 UTC, meaning that he had little time to waste. *But any delay was the colonel's, and a few minutes won't change much for something that's been there a long time, especially since this isn't a preprogrammed mission where every second changes every calculation.*

Except every second did change every calculation. It was just that Recon three's AI could make those adjustments so that a few minutes or seconds didn't change much, especially since Tavoian wasn't getting any help from any other planet's gravity field, beside Earth's.

He cycled the locks and lock doors to enter the spacecraft and, once aboard, made an interior inspection, noting that Recon three had been converted from a standard fusionjet, with a tiny galley in the passenger space and an extensive food supply, extensive for a fusionjet.

He stowed his kit before making his way to the controls, where he strapped in and activated the control system. "Commence booster checklist."

Tavoian went through the booster checklist with the AI, because he wasn't familiar with it, although it was effectively a second, if shorter, FusEx checklist. Then came the checklist for Recon three.

When he finished, he commlinked Operations. "OpsCon, Recon three, ready for release."

"Recon three, you are cleared for ungrappling and release this time. Cleared for use of thrusters. Notify when you have full separation before ignition."

Those weren't precisely standard release instructions, but clearly Operations did not wish to broadcast that the boosted Recon three needed greater clearance from the docking link and Donovan Base . . . or that it might be boosted or otherwise different.

"OpsCon, will notify readiness for ignition." Tavoian watched and monitored the AI as it eased the overlong booster and ship combination away from Donovan Base.

"Begin orientation."

Tavoian had to wait several minutes before the AI reported, ORIENTATION COMPLETE.

"OpsCon, Recon three, ready for ignition."

"Recon three, you're cleared for ignition this time."

"OpsCon, commencing ignition. Request departure clearance."

"Recon three, you are cleared to depart."

"Activate drive."

DRIVE ACTIVATED.

The gentle pressure began to build, pushing Tavoian into his couch as it gradually approached a full gee of acceleration. It had to be his imagination, but he felt that the Recon three booster combination was somehow slow and sluggish. Yet a one-gee acceleration was a one-gee acceleration. It just took more power to accelerate more mass. *And much more Hel3 . . .*

He just hoped that the Space Command mission planners had calculated that correctly, and with a hefty safety margin.

He watched the monitors and screens as Recon three continued to accelerate away from Donovan Base on a course that would gradually rise above the plane of the ecliptic toward an unknown object discovered by the only astrophysicist he knew.

31

Daedalus Base
2 November 2114

At 1001 UTC, almost precisely midmorning on Friday, assuming a work day began at 0800, which it didn't on days that fell during the lunar night when Alayna was usually in the COFAR control center by 0700, Marcel announced, "All outgoing communications have ceased."

"For what reason?" she asked.

"There has been a failure in the pretransmittal process. No signals are being received by the transmitter. The streaming compression system is inoperative."

Alayna gulped. "What about the data from both the radio telescope array and the optical systems?"

"The data is being saved in the backup databanks for transmittal."

At least the data's not gone. But the delay would generate complaints, and that was something she didn't need. She paused. "Shouldn't a failure have switched the data stream to the backup compression server?"

"That did not occur."

"Why not?"

"The failure mode was not activated."

"Then activate it."

"That requires a supervisory override, Dr. Wong-Grant."

Sometimes! Alayna turned and entered the codes, with her password and thumbprint.

"Communications have resumed, Dr. Wong-Grant."

"What about the data that was stored?"

"It was sent first. The system will be three minutes late for the next nineteen minutes, two minutes late for the next seventeen, and one minute late for the next fourteen."

Assuming we don't have another foul-up. "Is the problem in the system codes or routines?"

"No, Dr. Wong-Grant."

"Where, then?"

"The server monitoring system malfunctioned."

"Is that the result of a hardware failure?"

"Until the relay override box is replaced, that is impossible to determine."

"Where in the storeroom is the replacement?"

"Delta Zulu six seven."

"Delta Zulu six seven." Alayna shook her head at the location codes, revealing the old United States military origin of COFAR's developers and builders. She called up the compression server schematic and a diagrammatic map of its location in the main information processing center. "Is your link to the information processing center working?" The question was not a formality because several of Marcel's links did not work, such as the one in the suiting/unsuiting locker room, but since repairing them would have required drilling into the walls of the base, or installing hardware that the base did not presently have, and since those locations were not considered critical, the Foundation had deferred those repairs. Alayna certainly wasn't about to drill into base walls, not knowing just how accurate the base specifications were and not as the sole inhabitant of a base set on an airless moon.

"The link in the information processing center is operative."

"Is the screen there operative?"

"It is."

"Good." Alayna immediately stood and made her way down to the lower level equipment supply room.

Delta Zulu six seven was in a stack of bins almost adjacent to the door, something she never would have guessed from the numerical identifier. Thankfully, the stack and bin numbers were large. There were six of the server relay override boxes, all identical oblongs of black composite ten centimeters long and roughly three wide, with large white letters— SRO-2(a)—on the top. *Definitely black boxes.* She took two, just in case, and walked down the long corridor to the main information processing center.

When she entered, she asked, "Marcel?"

"Yes, Dr. Wong-Grant?"

"Display the system plan that shows where the server relay override box goes."

"System plan is on the screen."

Alayna studied the map/diagram, then walked over to the racked electronics. She didn't see what she was looking for. She walked back to the diagram and studied it more closely, realizing that the diagram was oriented to lunar north, and that she'd been looking at it wrong. The second time, she quickly located the relay, its upper surface covered with a thin film of fine dust, suggesting that it had not been touched or moved in some time. As with most of the other components, it was a plug-in, and she eased it out, replacing it with the new relay.

"Marcel, the new relay is in place."

"The replacement relay is not functioning."

"Frig!" Alayna eased the supposed replacement out and tried the second. "Now?"

"The replacement relay is not functioning."

Two out of two not working? Alayna studied the flat panel under the relay, finally noticing a stud or button that had likely once been white but was a dark gray. She pressed it.

"The replacement server override relay is functioning. The streaming compression system is inoperative."

"Why?"

"The coding integration module has also failed."

Alayna went back to the screen. "Display the location of the coding integration module."

This time, before she went to find another part, she checked the location around the "failed" module. There were no reset studs anywhere near. With that, she turned and once more headed for the equipment supply room.

Ten minutes later she slipped out the old integration module and replaced it with a new one—yet another blackbox replacement—simply numbered LACCD 761—and that put the main data compression server back on-line.

As she walked back from the information processing center to replace the relay she had not used and then up the ramps to the COFAR control center, she was still thinking about the design. *Why a relay that could be overridden or bypassed by the main system, and one with a reset stud as well?* That didn't make sense. Either that, or there was a reason she didn't comprehend. *How many other things are there here like that?* It all brought home to her the fact that COFAR was old, very old as astronomical installations went, although the main optical mirror had been replaced comparatively recently. Still . . .

When she reached the control center, she immediately asked, "Marcel, if the main system could physically activate the failure mode and switch to the backup compression server, why is there even a relay override box?"

"The relay override box was part of the original design. The data transmission system was upgraded after the installation of the present main optical mirror. There is no information on why the relay override was retained."

"Why was there a reset stud as well? Is that information available?"

"It is both a reset and an on/off switch."

That makes at least two other ways for things to go wrong. But was that true, or was she still missing something? "Thank you." She settled back in front of the displays, going over the system indicators, and then the messages, except the only thing that had arrived was an outsystem news flash, beginning:

> "Free Mongolia!" terrorists claim to have obtained five Indra scramjet missiles, along with the coordinates of locations where top Chinese political officials are often located . . .

Alayna hadn't even heard of whoever or whatever the "Free Mongolia" terrorists or political agitators might be, but how had they obtained Indian high-level weaponry? Or had they? Who would know until it was too late, one way or the other? Since COFAR was back to operating normally, she searched the news databases, especially *HotNews!*, which for all of its racy and sexually obnoxious content, also had the most recent revelations, and with a high degree of accuracy.

She didn't find that much that wasn't old history, such as the Chinese takeover of 2081, and the infighting among the Sinese multinationals to control the resource subsidiaries. Most of the Noram corporations had agreed to cash settlements for their interests or even whole subsidiaries because the United States had been essentially bankrupt, and the whole world knew it could exert neither economic nor military pressure, and hundreds of billions of hard yuan had been more than welcome in a collapsing U.S. economy . . .

She shook her head. There was nothing about the "Free Mongolia!" movement, but she supposed that was to be expected with the effectiveness of the Sinese "media guidelines." Except . . . why had they allowed the story to be reported? Again, more questions than answers, and she didn't have access to the sources she would have had back on Earth. But there wasn't much she could do, not from Daedalus Base.

She was also concerned about Chris. He'd avoided saying what he was doing, and he'd been very clear about his piloting duties between the Noram space elevator and the lunar stations, either L1 or the Low Lunar Orbit Station. Since he'd been transferred, he hadn't written a word about his new duties, except about training and doing supervisory duties in the middle of the night—she stiffened in the chair. An officer supervising in the middle of the night at 0400? *That's watch-standing. He's on what amounts to a military installation!*

Alayna swallowed. If Noram had a de facto military base, then so did the Sinese and the Indians most likely . . . and everyone was right to be worried. *How could you not have seen that?*

He'd never said he was an officer, except when she had noted his uniform on the trip to the LLOS. He'd passed it off as a requirement imposed by DOEA for all Noram pilots. She'd wondered about that and looked it up. It was a requirement with the rationale that Noram wanted to assure pilot loyalty. *But that requirement allows rapid militarization and control of Noram fusionjet spacecraft.*

She tried to think matters through. The last message she'd received from Chris had been on October twenty-fifth. While he'd expressed his "appreciation" for keeping him informed and congratulations on the uniqueness of her discovery, that had been all he had written about. At first, she'd been upset, almost hurt, before considering that the way in which he had replied might well have signified how important it was. At least, that was what she hoped, especially after the prosaic responses from Director Wrae and the total lack of response from the IAU. Then again, after two centuries of seeking evidence of other intelligent life in the universe, maybe no one wanted to commit to saying much of anything until there was absolute proof.

But why hadn't he replied to her last message? It had been over a week, hadn't it? And he hadn't taken that long in replying in some time. Was he in trouble? Or was he on some military mission, something dark and secret?

THE TIMES OF ISRAEL
3 NOVEMBER 2114

(BEIJING) "Government operatives have seized one of the Indra missiles reportedly missing from the Indian military," Sinese Defense Minister Wu Gong announced late yesterday. According to sources close to the ministry, the missile was located in an undisclosed location in Mongolia, close to being ready to launch, and was of Indian manufacture. The official announcement did not name the group possessing the missile, presumed to be Mongolia First!, but indicated that further antiterrorist operations were ongoing in Mongolia. Other sources reported sporadic outbreaks of violence outside Ulaanbaatar and Choibalsan.

Local observers have also reported the movement of close to a division of Sinese troops into the northern sector of Arunachal Pradesh, an area China has claimed for well over a century, but which India has held since 1914.

Indian Prime Minister Narahaj Ravindra denounced the movement of troops and declared that the "so-called Indra missile is a fabrication by the Sinese government to justify aggressive action against India to prevent its completion of the Dyaus space elevator, which is designed only for the peaceful use of space."

Noram Secretary of Defense Olassen Trudeau cautioned the Sinese Federation against "overreacting" and inaccurately linking a homegrown independence movement within the Sinese Federation to legitimate and reasonable aspirations to improve access to space by India and the UAAS.

Israeli Prime Minister Meir spoke briefly with Indian Prime Minister Ravindra, but did not disclose the substance of the conversation. Israeli military experts downplayed the ability of a terrorist group to program and launch such a sophisticated weapon, especially with the need for either a rocket-assisted or high-speed air launch. One suggested that the Sinese had obtained a prototype mock-up that had disappeared five years ago and were using the mock-up for political and military purposes . . .

RECON THREE
5 NOVEMBER 2114

Although Tavoian was trying to keep to a schedule, if only in an effort to hold his biological rhythms close to regular, he woke close to 0500 UTC on Monday morning, climbed out of the sleeping bag strapped to the control couch, stowed it, and checked all the monitors and screens. There was no sign of any hull damage, certainly less of a possibility now that he was largely above the system ecliptic, not that there was that large a probability, but as the old saying went, an extremely low probability high speed impact could kill him just as dead. He could only hope that he didn't run into anything that the Whipple shields and the graphene aerogel couldn't handle. He also really didn't want the booster to shred on him before at least some deceleration, since there was no way he'd have enough fuel to kill his outbound speed, let alone attain enough inbound velocity that he could return to the inner solar system before his habitability collapsed. The problem of traveling at the velocity Recon three had achieved, well over 315 kps, was that even the most sensitive scanning systems couldn't detect small objects still large enough to turn the fusionjet into fragments exploding everywhere early enough that even the nano-quick reactions of the AI could move Recon three to avoid such a collision. If they were to encounter something larger, the systems would detect that soon enough.

Far from the first time, he tried not to think about that as he strapped himself into the body-exercise suit and went at it for an hour. Then he cleaned up and returned his attention to his mission. He called up yet one more set of technical and operating details on another of the specialized AIs stowed in the cargo section of Recon three. After more than an hour, he shook his head and closed his eyes, trying not to think about anything for several minutes, but that was difficult with the only sound being the faint hissing of the ventilation system. He could have asked the AI for music from the tracks he'd loaded, but most of the time, except when he was trying to sleep, he preferred hissing to music. As for realies . . . although he'd loaded a few, he wasn't desperate enough yet to sample the technically sophisticated production of so-called entertainment that, if the viewer was lucky, actually had a plot, if basic, on which subliminal emoticons, suggestive rhythms, and four-note background music from a synth orchestra had been piled.

Finally, he called up one of the books he'd loaded into his personal system—*The Economics of Failure*—on his screen to read and continued from where he had left off, although he had certain misgivings already.

> ... *one of the worst miscalculations by both American financiers and politicians was the equation of liquidity to the availability of capital for both mid-and-lower income home-owners and for small businesses. In point of fact, the excessive liquidity created by speed-trading and lax regulation of the U.S. securities industry merely subsidized increasing speculation and led inexorably to the second and then to the final collapse of the old American economy. The growing misallocation of capital starved small and regional businesses and overemphasized service and media-oriented enterprises relying on comparatively few employees and capital-and-technology intensive infrastructures* ...

Tavoian paged ahead. He'd *thought* the book would be more interesting than it was turning out to be. It had been advertised as a tell-all about the Great Collapse.

> ... *the final bulwark against encroaching financial anarchy collapsed with the decision in* Goldman Sachs v. U.S. ...

He kept paging.

> ... *the first sign of unrest occurred when the Grads WithOut Work [GWOW] simultaneously severed major high-speed fiber-optic cables serving the major securities trading networks of U.S. financial institutions, then deployed sophisticated self-replicating malware that transferred the assets of the institutions randomly to individuals and small businesses across not only the United States but Canada and Mexico before destroying a significant percentage of financial records* ... *The unsolved sniper shootings of David Jindal, the president of Wells-Fargo, and Robert L. Sullivan, the chairman of Goldman-Sachs, created greater consternation* ... *followed by the imposition of martial law*—

At that moment, slightly after 0700 UTC, the ship's AI informed Tavoian, MAJOR, YOU HAVE A MESSAGE.

Tavoian frowned. "Display, please."

The pages of *Economics of Failure* vanished.

> Tavoian, Christopher A.
> Major, NSC
> NSS-21/Recon Three
>
> Communications block is hereby lifted. All communications will be burst-sent to Donovan Base, including personal transmissions, no more often than once every twelve standard hours, with the exception of those of an urgent or emergency nature.
>
> Official and personal messages follow.

The first message was official, as well as short and without any identification. As soon as he began to read it, he understood why.

> Sinese fusionjet recently docked at Sinese counterweight orbit station. Receiving supplies. Crew size unknown. Armament, if any, unknown. Ship type: Twin-drive longliner, Jiang class.

The newest class Sinese longliner, when longliners almost never docked at the counterweight station? *Their quick conversion to an alien-artifact chaser?* Tavoian nodded, then looked for others that might be official. There weren't any, which surprised him. The next message was the official Space Service news summary. The only entry that was of great interest was the summary on the continuing developments surrounding rising tensions between the Sinese Federation, the Indian-UAAS alliance, and Noram.

> President Yates called for a three-party conference to discuss the issues surrounding the space elevator issues. Sinese Head of State Jiang agreed "in principle," but reiterated that a necessary precondition for any such talks was a multination inspection of Indian space installations to assure that no militarization of those facilities was occurring. Prime Minister Ravindra countered by indicating that no such inspection would be allowed until and unless a similar inspection of

Sinese installations occurred concurrently. None of the three
have made further statements.

Since there wasn't much he could do about any of that, when he finished reading the news summary, Tavoian called up the first personal
message—from his sister Kit.

> Chris—
> I don't want to bother you. Not now, with all the problems
> with comms and the Sinese, but I haven't heard from you. As
> soon as I could get away from Ottawa after the hearings, I flew
> to Cedar, and drove to Brian Head.

Tavoian winced. Even with her salary, the cost of flying would have
cost half a month's pay.

> Dad didn't expect me. He didn't want us to worry, he said. How
> could we not worry when he's been hiding something? I know
> you're on some kind of training for something, but is there any
> possibility at all you could come home, for even a day? I wouldn't
> ask, but I thought you should know. Mom's got T3.

Tuberculosis three? Tavoian felt like he'd been punched in the gut. T3
was resistant to every known treatment. It didn't kill immediately, but
most people who contracted it had only a few months. A few might last
a year, but their mother was already frail. He kept reading.

> Is it at all possible for you to get emergency leave or some-
> thing, sometime, before too long? I'm sorry to send a message
> like this, but I knew you'd want to know, even if you can't get
> home. She made me promise not to tell you. So I lied and said
> I wouldn't. I hope you can come home. If you can't, and even
> if you can, PLEASE don't let her know I told you. She doesn't
> want you to worry when you could be in danger with Noram,
> the Sinese, and the Indians all threatening each other. I hope
> I'm not wrong, but I did think you'd want to know, rather than
> be kept in the dark . . .

She was right about that. Tavoian had been worrying anyway. *But . . .*
T3? How had she even come in contact with anyone? Then, the reports
were that it was far more contagious than previous versions of TB. He
continued to read.

I hate testifying before legislative committees, or even advising anyone involved. Almost none of the politicians want anything objective. They barely listen until some fact comes up
that they can use, distort, or turn into a campaign issue. I suppose it's always been that way, but it doesn't make me feel
any better . . .

Tavoian read through the rest of the message, mostly about her
expensive and tedious flight to Cedar City, and how their father was
handling matters, then immediately began to compose a reply, even if he
wouldn't send it until later, with everything else he needed to write and
include.

Dear Kit,
Thank you for letting me know about Mom. I'd worried that
she was having some sort of trouble, but I never imagined it
was as terrible as T3. Something like that makes any of my
problems seem trivial. Compared to what she's facing, I don't
have any real problems . . .

Not any that you can mention or would want to.

There's no possible way I can get home for some time. I wish
I could. You know that I'd come if there were any way possible, but with what's happening right now, I doubt that anyone in the Space Services is going anywhere at the moment . . .

All that's true, but misleading. What else can you say?

. . . I hope the politicians can resolve this mess peacefully,
but the Sinese seem determined to find a way to dominate the
solar system, one way or another, and the Indians and the
UAAS seem equally determined not to let them. Our official
position seems to be . . .

He paused and then deleted the last sentence. He really had no idea
what the Noram official position was, and there was little point in
speculating, because that might be censored and that would delay the
message.

Until matters settle down, and probably for some time after
that, I'm stuck where I am. I can't tell you how glad I am that

you can see them both. I also can't tell you how much I appreciate what you're doing. I'll never be able to make that up to you, and it's so unfair, but life isn't always fair. We can only try our best to make it that way when we can. Sometimes, we don't get even that chance. My love, and more appreciation, to you.

After putting his reply to Kit in the "send" queue, he checked all the screens and indicators, not that the AI wasn't faster and more accurate, then asked, "Are there any objects anywhere close to our immediate course line?"

THERE ARE NO OBJECTS NEAR THE COURSE LINE WITHIN DETECTION RANGE.

Compared to the more than a million large and small objects already detected in the solar system, there were only a comparative few that had either supra-ecliptic orbits or orbits inclined more than twenty degrees to the plane of the ecliptic, most of which were comets or cometary remnants. Of those few asteroids with such orbits, the largest was Hildago, with an inclination of forty-two degrees, and for an asteroid with such an irregular orbit, it was huge, with a diameter of twenty kilometers.

Tavoian smiled. If he hadn't looked all that up, as a result of both the mission and his message correspondence with Alayna, he would never have known that. A million objects sounded like a lot, but with time to spare, he'd worked it out . . . and come up with the rough estimate that within twenty degrees above and below the plane of the ecliptic, on average there was just one object in for every five million cubic kilometers—and almost none for that part of the solar system where he was presently traveling. Of course, those numbers didn't include very small chunks of matter that could still wreak havoc.

After several minutes, he turned his thoughts back to the next message, a moderately long and cheerful message to his parents, saying very little, except that the training and what piloting he had been doing were both very challenging, but rewarding in the sense that he was continuing to learn. He also mentioned learning in another sense, with what he'd picked up from an astrophysicist he'd ferried to the Moon months before, but with whom he'd maintained a message contact.

He felt almost dishonest in not saying anything, but he did add a few lines at the end, which he likely would have written anyway if Kit hadn't told him.

I haven't heard much about how either of you are doing personally, and that worries me. I suppose Kit and I are now reaching the stage where we worry about you, rather than you about us, although I also have the feeling that you've never stopped worrying about us. Once the current uneasiness subsides, I'm looking forward to coming home, but at present, I don't think anyone here is going anywhere soon.

When he finished that message he just sat, loosely strapped to the control couch, thinking about how surreal the situation was. He was hurtling at incredible speed through the darkness toward a strange object that was at the least unique and at most might well be the evidence of alien intelligence that humanity had been seeking for over a century. Back around Earth three powers were positioning themselves for a conflict that could effectively cripple, if not destroy, most of civilization. And he was composing messages as if nothing at all was happening. But there was little else that he could do. *Not yet.*

Had it always been that way? He supposed so. Alexander's soldiers had done far more walking than fighting, even when they had been in the process of conquering much of what they thought of as the known world.

After checking with the AI again and going over all the systems, he got back to composing another message, this time to Alayna. He really owed her as much of an explanation as he could provide. He frowned. The colonel had said that he could tell her once the comm block had been lifted. He wasn't certain that he exactly wanted to blurt it out, though. He began the message.

Dear Alayna—

I must apologize for being incommunicado for the past week, but I've been in a situation where communications were not possible. I'm still on an extended assignment, one closely associated with your discovery, and will be for a while, although I don't know yet exactly how long it will last, certainly past the end of the year. It appears as though I'll be able to send and receive messages for a time, provided, of course, that matters between the Sinese and everyone else don't deteriorate too much.

Is there anything new on your asteroid/possible artifact? I've not seen anything in the news. In a way, that surprises me, because it is definitely unusual, at least from what you've let me know. Sooner or later, I suppose, something will appear somewhere in the media. In the meantime, I'm looking forward to whatever can be discovered. Also, have you made any progress in discovering more about the solar multi-fractal minigranulations? [I hope I got the terminology correct.] It seems so strange that we really know so little about what lies beneath the surface of the sun, except for the massive processes that produce light and energy. The more we investigate other bodies in the solar system, the more we discover. It's like the sun's surface is a flexible, but impenetrable barrier to greater discovery. Or maybe there have been more discoveries over the past century than I'm aware of. I'm certainly no astronomer or astrophysicist.

Going to less grand and glorious subjects, how about this? I thought about this because I've been reading a book called *Economics of Failure,* which is about the economic and political collapse of the United States. You don't even have to guess from where I got it.

An economist has an advanced degree and years of study and experience in order to be able to predict less accurately than a coin flip. And most economic explanations after the fact only make sense if certain facts are omitted, which they usually are.

Then again, we all would prefer not to deal with unpleasant facts. Maybe honesty is defined by how many of those we'll face and accept.

That's all for now. Until later.

When he reread the message and decided he had no more changes to make, he put it in the dispatch queue, paused, and then, because there really wasn't anyone else he wanted to contact, he took a deep breath and sent the entire batch.

You might as well get on with your technical refresher on the AI equipment.

And he didn't even know, yet, whether he'd be using it to explore a unique asteroid or an alien artifact of some sort.

34

Daedalus Base
5 November 2114

The night line had crept past Daedalus Base sometime in the last twelve hours, but Alayna hadn't actually taken note, not totally surprisingly, because COFAR workloads dipped during the transition hours, although, with the lack of atmosphere and what was in an atmosphere, Earth's anyway, especially associated water vapor and particulate matter, there really wasn't much of a "transition" on the Moon. One moment there was sunlight; the next there wasn't.

The message queue wasn't that long. It never was early on Mondays, because few people on Earth, even astronomers, worked over the weekend, and the astronomers who did weren't the ones who sent messages to COFAR. The messages came from administrators and bureaucrats, and they'd arrive later in the day, usually after 1200 UTC. Those messages were seldom welcome and usually required more essentially nonproductive work, something that was a growing irritation for Alayna, especially as she realized how ambitious her own research was and how much observational time it was likely to take.

There was a perfunctory message from the IAU thanking her for continued reports on "her" asteroid, except it was always referred to officially as "2114 FQ5," and requesting that she continue providing updates. Then there was a message from the director of personnel at the Farside Foundation, dated the previous Friday, advising all employees, permanent and contract, that any changes in elective additional health insurance needed to be registered before the first of December in order to have coverage beginning the new calendar year.

As if you could afford additional elective health insurance beyond the government minimum.

Then there was a message from Emma, which, since there didn't seem to be anything exceptionally pressing, Alayna immediately read.

> I can't believe you didn't say more about your discovery! Just plain old 2114 FQ5? An asteroid in a cometary sun-grazing

orbit . . . with an albedo brighter than ice with an odd silicon spectrum? Sonya was dancing when she found it . . . until she realized someone had discovered it earlier. It's either the greatest outer system oddity in more than a century or something even rarer. You know exactly what I mean, but I won't say/ write more. Why no media or joyburst? Nothing from the IAU. Nothing from Farside Foundation.

Is someone squashing this? How could this happen? Everyone knows everything about anything. Or is everyone afraid it won't pan out? There's not even any word or plan about someone sending at least an uncrewed probe to look. Somebody has to be doing something about this, don't they?

Someone is. Noram Space Service. Alayna had no doubts about that. She just didn't know what.

Can't imagine that this will be secret much longer. They've probably managed it so far just because everyone's worried about what the Sinese and Indians are going to do . . . and whether our so-called President will do anything at all. I can't believe I actually voted for her. I wish I could blame Carlina, or someone, but I did it all on my own . . .

Alayna smiled at that and kept reading. Once she finished, she asked, "Marcel . . . where is our strange asteroid or object?"

"The object is approximately twenty-five million kilometers inside the orbit of Mars."

"Can you calculate its speed?"

"Thirty-six kilometers per second."

"That's faster than we'd calculated earlier."

"The data baseline is better, Dr. Wong-Grant."

Alayna tried not to wince. She hated being corrected, even by an AI. "Do the calculations continue to support a sun-grazing orbit?"

"They do. 2114 FQ5 has a calculated perihelion of two point four million kilometers on eighteen December 2114."

Two point four million kilometers? The number seemed familiar, but she couldn't place it for an instant, until she realized it was the sun's Roche Limit, if for fluid bodies. "That's close." Still . . . the asteroid or artifact was a solid object, unlike most comets, few of which had survived that close an encounter with the sun. Compared to those that had survived, however, it was much smaller, and its shape, especially at two kilometers long, likely made it more vulnerable. *And more likely to be artificial than natural.* Except . . . there were more than a few "unnatural" natural shapes in the solar system. Still . . .

The corner of her personal screen showed an incoming message. She checked immediately. It was from Chris. Her smile was more one of relief than pleasure. She *had* been worried about him. As she read what he had written, that worry returned in full. Even if there hadn't been anything in the news, his words confirmed that he'd been sent out to scout her discovery. Why else would he have said that he would be on extended duty past the end of the year . . . and linked to her discovery?

When she finished, she checked the timestamp. His message had been sent four hours earlier, UTC. It had just arrived. Why the delay? Were his messages being reviewed and censored? By whom and why? She shook her head. Of course. He'd been in some at least semimilitary installation, and the way he had written it didn't give much indication of where he was or what he was doing. Yet he had written, *In a situation where communications were not possible.* Just what had he been doing? Had it been anything to do with the surveillance that the Sinese had complained about? Or something even worse?

How could it have been worse without something appearing in the media?

She worried her upper lip with her teeth. While she was relieved that he was safe, for the moment, it appeared, the evasiveness of his message suggested that he was still in danger or had been and might be again. Because the Sinese might send another ship after him? Or even try to attack his ship? *And for what?* Hostilities between the major powers would only devastate everyone, and no one seemed to understand that. The struggling countries of the UAAS would only be worse off, and Noram was still struggling financially, as she knew directly from the IG visit to COFAR and all the concerns expressed by Director Wrae. The Indians would certainly lose their partial space elevator. For that matter most likely everyone would lose effective access to space. And how long could the various lunar installations last without replacement equipment and technology? Months, certainly, possibly years, but definitely not forever.

Then again, with the Sinese spread across the solar system, they might end up with a monopoly on space travel—except, with all the Indian scramjet missiles, there might not be a great deal of central China left intact.

Could the politicians be that stupid?

Considering that over a fifth of the old Middle East remained uninhabitable, that the Crimean peninsula was essentially black glass, and that there were radioactive ocean floors where Tel Aviv and Alexandria used to be, Alayna thought her question was largely rhetorical.

Still . . . she could hope . . . and send cheerful messages back to her father, Emma, and Chris, especially Chris—right after she read his message. She had the feeling that he might need some cheer. And then, she'd continue to struggle with the seemingly unsolvable puzzle of the solar multi-fractal mini-granulations, as well as keep tracking her artifact. She hadn't yet given in to using the official identification numbers, at least in her own references to it.

35

RECON THREE
7 NOVEMBER 2114

Wednesday morning Tavoian spent programming and setting up small AI sampling units, designed with various forms of grappling and grasping capabilities. Which one he'd deploy he'd decide after an initial scan of the target. Then he set up a string of signal repeaters so that a rover AI could immediately relay its findings from within caves, crevasses, or passageways. At 1200 UTC, while he was still working on the AI with the diamond nanorod drill, the message indicator lit.

"Our daily ration of comms," observed Tavoian, knowing that he was largely talking to himself, since the ship's AI didn't respond, except to questions. He set aside the miniature AI unit and began to read the first message.

> Tavoian, Christopher A.
> Major, NSC
> NSS-21/Recon Three
>
> This is to inform you that the Sinese longliner *Jiang* class, departed Sinese counterweight station yesterday at 0400 UTC. Indications are that the ship maintained a 1.5 gee acceleration for two hours, then resumed drive use two hours later for another two-hour period. This pattern was maintained for sixteen hours.

How could they do that? Tavoian fed the figures into the AI. As he'd guessed, the Sinese longliner was moving almost twice as fast as he was. *A hundred and seventy-five percent, roughly.*

"How soon before they catch us?" he asked the AI. "Or how long will we have at the target destination before they arrive?"

WITHOUT ADDITIONAL DATA, PROJECTION IS IMPOSSIBLE.

"Assume a one-gee deceleration for us, and a deceleration pattern for the Sinese ship that matches the acceleration pattern outbound from Earth. Assume both ships are within one hundred fifty thousand kays of the target at the end of deceleration."

THE SINESE VESSEL WILL ARRIVE AT THE OBJECT BETWEEN FIFTY AND FIFTY-TWO HOURS AFTER RECON THREE.

Belatedly, Tavoian turned to read the remainder of the message from Donovan Base.

> Ship and acceleration parameters strongly suggest that Sinese longliner is uncrewed and AI-directed. Preparations of a second and larger craft suggest crewed vessel to follow once the target is farther in-system and the uncrewed longliner is in position close to the target.

That answered his question about the acceleration and fuel requirements. Without habitability concerns, the Sinese could pack more fuel into the hull . . . and they had a larger platform to begin with. They also had better drives—or at least more durable ones—and that was another worry, both for him and for Space Command. He continued reading.

> Do not make contact with Sinese vessels unless contacted first or unless such vessels act in a fashion hazardous to you or your vessel.

> Request daily reports, commencing immediately.

That would be easy enough to do, considering he'd done little except watch screens, exercise, study AI documentation, and send a few messages. In roughly eighteen hours that would all change once Recon three began its decel and approach to the asteroid or artifact.

Then he read the Space Service news summary. His own summary of that was that matters were slowly degrading, but no one was shooting, launching missiles, or moving troops. *Yet.* He was much more interested in the message from Alayna.

> Chris—
> I know you can't tell me precisely where you are and what you're doing, but I'm fairly certain I know what it is. It sounds like it could be hazardous, especially if others get involved. Maybe I'm reading too much into how you said what you did and what you didn't say, but I'm concerned. Now that I've said that . . . I am glad to hear from you, and I hope you'll be

able to send messages on a more frequent basis, for more than the selfish reason that I like hearing from you.

There's not been that much progress on the multi-fractal mini-granulations. I feel that I'm on the edge of something, that if I could only see just a shade—or a fraction of another layer deeper—into the sun I might find a hint of what I'm looking for. I can't believe that the fact that the smaller areas of convection have multi-fractal properties while the larger granulations are essentially regular and Gaussian in distribution and field pattern is merely an affect of deeper solar mechanics. At the same time, the history of science shows how misguided belief can be. Einstein insisted that God did not play dice with the universe. We know what quantum mechanics and subsequent developments did to that belief.

Tavoian smiled at those words. They called up his image of Alayna, both incredibly earnest and focused, yet with a wry cynicism beyond her years—or his, he realized. *Aren't you the one who never thought that the military nature of being a pilot would ever be exploited? That people would learn?* He paused. *No one's fired any missiles yet. It's not too late.* Rather than dwell on that, he went back to reading what Alayna had written.

I can also hear, in my mind, Professor Janes saying something like, "*Merely* an affect of solar mechanics, Miss Wong-Grant?" That might be like saying Newton's apple's falling was merely an affect of gravity.

The unique asteroid that's behaving like a comet and is possibly neither remains on course for a sun-grazing pass in late December. One of my colleagues at another well-known observatory can't believe that there's been *no* media or obvious government interest. She wonders if someone is keeping it quiet. I'm getting that feeling myself, but now that it's in range of amateurs with telescopes with enough resolution to determine some of its unique features, I don't think it can be kept hidden much longer . . .

What Alayna was saying, as much to the colonel as to Tavoian, was that her discovery appeared likely to explode through the media at any moment, if it hadn't already, since he was getting messages but not media, except for the Space Service news summary, which hadn't reported anything about it.

> . . . we've done some recalculations based on better data and more observations. It looks like the "asteroid" has an extremely long period, somewhere in the vicinity of eleven thousand years since the last time it made a pass at the sun, which I think, although I can't prove it, might have been its first pass.

Tavoian frowned. That meant, if it were an alien artifact, whatever was there was *old*. On the other hand, things didn't deteriorate that much in conditions of cold and vacuum, at least not after the initial decompression, assuming that it had been an artifact and pressurized.

> . . . From the time the object passes Mars's orbit to reach Earth's orbit will take about three weeks, and from there to Venus's orbit will take less than two weeks, and from there to the averaged orbit of Mercury will be six days, possibly less. That's not much time for something this unique, and our projections show it's going to pass close to the Roche Limit. If it does, it may not survive perihelion, and that would be a great loss to science . . .

Seven weeks from now, and she's sending a not-so-veiled warning to me and the colonel not to stay around too long. Tavoian wanted to tell her that matters were under control, but he wasn't in a position to do so, and even if he did, the colonel or whoever was reviewing his messages would not allow anything that definite to go through.

> I've attached the latest data and observations. We're getting some clearly defined images. I don't know how it could be, but I'd say that the silver-white side might be as polished as a mirror. How that could have occurred, considering that there are no visible craters, scarring, or abrasion, leaves me speechless. That's a poor statement of fact. As you know, I'm seldom speechless.

> Responding in kind to your last quote, I have another from *The Passion of Science:*

> *As an astronomer, you'd better be passionate; a billion stars aren't even a significant faction of our own galaxy, let alone*

the visible universe. Most people can't comprehend what a million of anything means, except in devalued currencies. They toss around millions and billions as if they understood. A scientist has to understand what numbers mean, what they represent, and how to use them accurately and not dishonestly. In our ever-more complex world, the only thing that can fuel such dedication is the passion for knowledge, in and of itself, and not in pursuit of material gain.

Passion for what we do takes us to the strangest places. Why else am I on Farside, hundreds of kilometers from the nearest other human, and hundreds of thousands from friends and family—except you, and at the closest, you're still thousands of kilometers away? Because I can't do what I love doing without being here. While I'm speaking for you, and that's always dangerous and often self-deceiving, I would think you must feel the same way.

Do you? Do you feel as passionate as she does about what you do? Tavoian had his doubts. He liked piloting. He liked being good at it, and he especially liked it when he could actually handle the ship, rather than oversee the AI. He also realized that he hadn't hesitated in the slightest to take on a mission that could easily go wrong and kill him when he'd found out that he would be the first to see and explore, even if only through cubesats and remote AIs, what might be an alien artifact.

He sat for a time, loosely strapped in the control couch, thinking, *Why are you here?* It certainly wasn't for duty. Or patriotism. Who could feel that patriotic about a nation cobbled together from necessity and for survival some forty years earlier? *You're going to have to think about that.*

A sardonic smile crossed his lips as he considered that he and Alayna were roughly the same age. He might be several years older chronologically, but she was far older in every other way.

I look forward to hearing from you as you're able to message.

After several moments, he accessed the next message—from Kit. It was short.

Dear Chris,
I was afraid that you wouldn't be able to get back here, especially with what the media news is spouting. It's frightening. Neither the Sinese nor the Indians want to back down, and

President Yates appears to be totally ineffectual at calming the situation. I want to ask if they're all idiots, but after working with politicians for the last year, I'm afraid I already know the answer to that question.

Mom and Dad did get your message. They were happy to hear you're fine, but they worry. So do I. I know you can't say much. That's obvious. We just hope that you'll come through whatever you're doing.

All my love, little brother!

He half grinned, knowing how much love was contained in the words "little brother."

Then he checked the monitors. There was no sign of the Sinese longliner, but then, given the limits of the ship's detection systems, the first time he should be able to detect it would be once he reached the target, possibly not until it was almost there.

At least he had three messages to respond to . . . and there was always the AI programming and documentation. But first . . . Alayna.

36

HOTNEWS!
6 November 2114

[Image Deleted For Off-Earth Transmission]

A space race! For real. A Noram FusEx burner is blasting outsystem. A Sinese fu-sionjet's two days behind. There's nothing where they're headed except a recently discovered asteroid. Word is it *might* not be an asteroid at all, but something old and alien. Sinese Space Minister Wong—all he'll say is that the Sinese space program is proceeding according to plan. Noram DOEA Director Luvalle won't comment at all. He must be imitating Prexy Yates. As for EC Chancellor Rumikov, he's demanding sharesies from Noram and the Sinobloc. That man-dexer wants shares of everything, especially women. Does he think there's an alien beauty out there?

[Image Deleted]

Don't miss *Seduced and Screwed* . . . most tre-awesome realie of the fall, the true story of Vikson Brady's seduction of former Noram Pres Robby Sawyer, and what hap-pened at the Top of Ottawa the night before Sawyer sent Army spec-ops against the Idaho Libertarians.

[Image Deleted]

Double, no triple, brace yourself for the spectacle of fall, *Patsy!* The docu-realie about the sexyist enviro ever to assassinate a politician and get away with it. Loosely based on Patrice Kennedy-Harper's involvement with Senator Steven Bush during the last days of the sovereign USA.

[Image Deleted]

One big chill's going to boil India's Mars plans! India's Prime Minister Ravindra claims that the ice asteroid the Sinese have sent careening toward the Red Planet will impact the meridian lowlands. That's where India has just finished its multi-dome geo-forming project. Sinese Space Minister Wong claims Ravindra's all wet. That's left Ravindra steaming.

[Image Deleted]

Noram Border Security agents patrolling the New Orleans wetlands made a really big find yesterday—crocodile style—and almost didn't live to tell about it. The eight-meter-long saltwater crocodile nearly upended their hovercraft as they patrolled the abandoned sections of the submerged city. No one could explain how the monster croc—native to Southeast Asia—ended up in the ruins of New Orleans unless it was a survivor of a southern water park destroyed decades ago.

37

RECON THREE
8 NOVEMBER 2114

At 0743 UTC, the AI began deceleration, following the same pattern used to accelerate Recon three to the greatest real velocity Tavoian had ever experienced, not that he had experienced much of anything at all. With vacuum beyond the ship, unless something pinged the shields hard enough for the vibration to get through the graphene and shields to the inner hull, the only sounds were those generated inside, and the screens gave no indication of the speed. *Over a million kays per hour, and there's no real indication of it at all.*

After two hours of deceleration and two of waiting for the drives to recover, Tavoian was relieved when, shortly after the AI resumed decel, it also announced, TARGET LOCATED ON PLOTTED COURSE. CURRENT DISTANCE IS FIVE POINT FOUR MILLION KAYS.

The AI didn't have to say more, but Tavoian knew that even after two hours of decel Recon was still headed outward at more than 245 kps, and with the inbound speed of the asteroid/alien object, the distance between the two was shrinking by something like 280 kps.

He also wasn't looking forward to thirteen more hours of alternating decel and zero gee, while wondering the entire time how long the FusEx "booster" would last.

Some twenty minutes into the second two-hour stint of deceleration, the day's messages arrived. The first, as always, was official.

> Tavoian, Christopher A.
> Major, NSC
> NSS-21/Recon Three
> Request immediate update on status and position of target when acquired. Also request you report when Sinese longliner appears in vicinity of Recon three.
>
> At any sign of hostile action by any Sinese vessel, you are authorized to use requisite force as necessary.

Requisite force? Two torps? Tavoian supposed two torps were better than nothing.

> Astronomical data suggests possible artifact may be of great age. Recommend initial survey with care.

So that you don't damage anything that might be useful, especially technology, as if anything there is going to be laid out for the taking . . . if it even is an alien creation.

> Report all events immediate real-time once on station.

Tavoian did not bother with an immediate acknowledgment message, since he was not on station and the acquisition of the target was at such distance that he could not report on its status. Somewhat surprisingly, there was a second official message, except it wasn't addressed to him specifically, but to all Noram Space Service installations and spacecraft. The text was simple:

> At 0200 UTC, 7 November 2014, the Sinese Federation closed all Sinese borders with India, Bhutan, Nepal, and Myanmar, and ordered the mobilization of all Sinese Federation reserve forces. The mobilization order was described as strictly precautionary, in response to threats to Sinese security. The nature of such threats was not disclosed in the mobilization order.

> In response, all Noram installations are hereby placed on Security Threat Level 3 [SecThreat3].

> No Sinese vessels or personnel are to be granted access to any WestHem or Noram space elevator or space installations or vessels. Exceptions may be made only in emergency conditions and only by an installation commander or higher authority.

Tavoian hadn't seen anything about the Sinese action in the last news summary; so he immediately looked to see if the latest Space Service news summary was included in his message dump. It was, and he began to read.

> Sinese Head of State Jiang placed all Sinese forces on high alert and closed China's southern borders. Subsequent statements from the Ministry of Defense stated that "Indian-affiliated" in-

surgents had infiltrated the Sinese Federation with weapons of "targeted and mass destruction." A ministry spokesman warned India that the Federation would retaliate with necessary force against any violence . . .

The rest of the summary wasn't any better. Tavoian couldn't see that there was much evidence of all the Indian hostility toward the Sinese . . . and that there hadn't been all along. Was it all a pretext to force the Indians to back down on completing their space elevator? Or was the uncompleted installation in orbit truly the particle beam weapon that the colonel had implied?

At times, he did wish that he could receive the vidloids, even the lurid ones like *HotNews!* and *InsideOut.* Sometimes, if infrequently, they revealed more hard news that the so-called reputable news sources, and definitely more than the Space Service news summaries.

The third message was from Kit.

> Dear Chris,
> Is everyone crazy? Does it really matter whether the Indians complete their space elevator? What do terrorists inside the Sinese Federation have to do with that? Or much of anything else.

Tavoian nodded. Logically speaking, Kit was right. But it wasn't about that. The other obvious difficulty was that the Sinese hadn't asked the Indians to do anything that they could do or were likely to do. And if the Indians couldn't or wouldn't . . . the Sinese would lose face if they didn't do *something* . . . and likely something that the rest of Earth would find disturbing . . . and possibly requiring a response.

> Mom and Dad appreciated your last messages. All your messages, in fact. They think you've always been good about that. Amazing how much guilt can be instilled before you leave home. Maybe it didn't hit you quite so hard, but if more than a few days go by . . .

An involuntary chuckle escaped Tavoian. *Obviously, we got the same treatment.*

> Mom's getting frailer by the day, but so far she's not in any pain . . .

By the time he finished the message, he was shaking his head. *If Kit's right, there's no way I'll see Mom again.* And about those sorts of things, his sister was seldom wrong. And there was nothing he could do about it . . . now. If he hadn't agreed to the mission . . .

He shook his head. First, while he'd worried, he hadn't known. Second, under the current circumstances, even if he'd declined the mission, he still wouldn't have been able to go Earthside until the standoff between the great powers had been resolved one way or the other.

Still . . . He shook his head again. *Thinking like that will drive you mad.*

He finally turned back to the message queue. The last message was from Alayna. As he read it, it was more than clear that she understood what he was doing, but that she wasn't about to make it too obvious for anyone who might intercept the message, and that was fine with him. He smiled briefly . . . and then again near the end when she described just how close the target was going to come to the sun. Although the colonel had instructed Tavoian not to go much inside the orbit of Mercury, Tavoian was warmed by Alayna's effort to make the danger clear to the colonel as well.

Since he wasn't sleepy at the moment, he decided to answer all his messages and send one to his parents, although keeping that upbeat and cheerful without sounding totally false would take a great deal of time and care. The time he had. He began by drafting a position report on the target for Donovan Base, followed by the messages to Kit and his parents, and ending with the one to Alayna. Once all his messages were ready, he sent them.

Then he studied more AI documentation, just long enough to feel sleepy, when he dimmed the cabin lights, flattened the control couch, and stretched out. He had the feeling he wouldn't be getting that much sleep in the hours after Recon three reached the target.

At 2146, decel ended, and Tavoian woke up with the loss of decel-pseudo-gravity. At 2152, the AI announced, THE TARGET IS THREE HUNDRED SEVENTY-SIX THOUSAND KAYS OUT-SYSTEM OF RECON THREE.

About as far from you as the Moon is from Earth. That distance was necessary because the drive couldn't be used again for two hours after decel, and during that time the asteroid or artifact would close that gap by a quarter of a million kays. If the AI's calculations were correct, and they usually were, that is, if the data supplied by Donovan Base and updated daily happened to be accurate enough, by the time Recon three was traveling at the same in-system speed as the target, they would be close enough for fine maneuvering. *A few hundred kays would be acceptable, less than that even better.*

"What's the status of the booster?"

ESTIMATED FUEL REMAINING IN BOOSTER IS FOURTEEN MINUTES.

Tavoian nodded. It could have been worse.

Because it would be almost another two hours before the drives could be used and close to forty minutes after that before Recon three was anywhere close to the asteroid/alien object, Tavoian dimmed the control area lights once again and closed his eyes, hoping he could sleep or at least doze for some of that time.

The resumption of acceleration immediately woke Tavoian. Except it didn't last for more than two or three minutes. His eyes went to the status board. It was blank.

"Interrogative status!" he snapped.

BOOSTER FAILED. FUEL EXHAUSTED. BEGINNING SEPARATION. With the words from the AI, the monitors all reappeared.

Belatedly, Tavoian realized that everything had gone blank for the time it had taken for the AI to switch from booster power to the Recon three system. *But there shouldn't have been that great a lag.* "Report on separation."

AUTOMATIC SEPARATION FAILED. EXPLOSIVE BOLTS TRIGGERED. RECON THREE IS NOW CLEAR OF BOOSTER. MINIMAL DRIVE OPERATION REQUIRED UNTIL SAFETY CLEARANCE ACHIEVED.

Tavoian watched the monitors and the readouts as Recon three crept— that was the way it seemed to him—away from the spent FusEx booster. He understood the need for that minimal acceleration, since there was a definite, if small, possibility that higher power on the drives might reflect from the booster back onto Recon three. Small as that probability was, he couldn't risk it, not where he was, especially if the result damaged the drive.

Finally, the AI announced, CLEARANCE ACHIEVED. COMMENCING ACCELERATION. CURRENT ACCELERATION WILL RESULT IN TARGET OVER-TAKING US BEFORE WE REACH VELOCITY SUFFICIENT FOR MAINTAINING STATION.

Had the manual separation taken that long? He checked the time. Twenty-five minutes since the booster had failed. That delay couldn't have caused that much of a discrepancy, could it? It could, he realized. Twenty-five minutes at the target's inbound speed of thirty-six kps meant it had covered almost fifty-five thousand kays. That wasn't an insoluble problem, but it would mean having to accelerate above the target's speed in order to catch up, and then decelerate to match speeds and rendezvous. And all that took extra fuel. *You should have ditched the booster after decel. But how were you to know that the fuel calculations were wrong and that the uncoupling would take so long?* He also had another thought. *How accurate are the fuel calculations for Recon three?* "Distance to target?"

TARGET IS FIFTY-NINE THOUSAND THREE HUNDRED KAYS OUT-SYSTEM OF RECON THREE.

On and off, Tavoian watched the screens, concentrating on the plot showing the relative distances, with the actual separation in kays reading out at the bottom of the plot. It was fascinating, in a way, to see how the distance between the target and Recon three shrank, even as Recon three increased speed, although the rate of closure shrank with each passing moment.

Then, just about forty-five minutes after Recon three had commenced acceleration, the AI announced, TARGET IS NOW IN-SYSTEM OF RECON THREE.

Tavoian had been watching the optical screens as well as the position plot and hadn't seen a thing on the optical view. "What was CPA?"

CLOSEST POINT OF APPROACH WAS FIFTEEN KAYS THIRTY-ONE SECONDS AGO.

Recon three's in-system speed was slightly over twenty kps and accelerating, while the target was steady at thirty-six kps. In less than a minute, the target that Tavoian had only seen as a dot on a screen was well over a hundred kays insystem of Recon three. Another twenty-four minutes passed before the AI had initiated turnover and a brief decel.

Almost an hour and a half of extra acceleration because you thought you could save Hel3. Tavoian winced inwardly.

IN-SYSTEM VELOCITIES MATCHED. BEGINNING APPROACH MANEUVERING.

As Recon three neared the target, Tavoian concentrated on the visual screen. Even at ten kays, all he could see was a thin sliver of white. Abruptly, he realized that when he only saw darkness—and no stars on one side of the white line—he was looking at what appeared to be a dark circle viewed at an angle. He could also see that it was rotating slowly, which explained the variability in brightness mentioned in Alayna's reports.

The AI eased Recon three closer. Over the time of the gradual approach, Tavoian just stared at the enhanced image in the screen—from one angle it looked like a perfect circle that had been sliced from the side of a far larger sphere. From another, from what he would have called a side view, it looked flat on one side and slightly curved on the other. "What are its dimensions?"

ITS CIRCUMFERENCE IS A PERFECT CIRCLE WITH A DIAMETER OF 1,989 METERS. THE THICKNESS AT THE EDGES IS FIVE METERS. THE THICKNESS IN THE CENTER IS 359 METERS.

Almost two kays across or long, but only a fifth of a kay at its thickest point. "Calculate the diameter of the sphere from which it came."

ASSUMING THAT THE CURVATURE OF THE ORGINAL SPHERE WAS UNIFORM, THE SPHERE'S DIAMETER WOULD BE FIVE POINT FIVE KAYS.

Who or what could possibly have created a sphere that large? And if there had been a sphere that large, what had happened to it? Had it been destroyed . . . and by what? Or was it orbiting somewhere in the solar system . . . or had the artifact drifted in from out-system?

He turned his attention back to the artifact. Since the white side was likely merely a polished shield, the first part that Tavoian wanted detailed images of was the darker side. "Maneuver so that we can get images of both sides in full sunlight. Far enough out that we can get a complete image of the entire object." After that and after Tavoian studied the images, he could move Recon three closer.

COMMENCING MANEUVERS.

"Is there any heat radiation besides reflected sunlight?"

NEGATIVE.

That confirmed that the object was either old or totally insulated.

Almost ten minutes passed before Recon three was in position sunward and slightly "below" the object. At a distance of five kays, it loomed over Recon three, as well it might, considering the difference in size. The object rotated, the curved side slowly turning toward the sun. In the light, the reflective side appeared to be a brilliant silver-white, with no visible marks, gouges, or impact markings. *After eleven thousand years, it's unmarked?* Tavoian found that hard to believe, yet the lack of heat and the orbit suggested great age. And if someone or something had created the object more recently and placed it in such an orbit—that was even less believable. He continued to study the image, knowing that there was something about it that nagged at him. "A composite image of the reflective side, with false color shading for anything different."

Another screen appeared on the monitor wall, showing the entire domed circle, which shimmered, then shifted, revealing smaller circles spaced regularly across the two-kay expanse. Tavoian counted. There were thirty-two of the circles. "What is the diameter of those off-color circles?"

EACH IS TWENTY-THREE POINT EIGHT METERS ACROSS.

"What is the difference between them and the rest of the surface?"

THE COMPOSITION OF THE MATERIAL, BASED ON THE REFLECTION AND RETURN OF THE PROBE RADIATION, IS THE SAME. THERE IS A SLIGHT DIFFERENTIAL IN THE SPECULAR REFLECTIVITY.

"Which is?"

THE CIRCLES DO NOT REFLECT LIGHT AT THE WAVELENGTH OF 379 AND 380 NANOMETERS.

"Can you determine the reason for that differential?"

POSSIBILITIES INCLUDE THERMAL STRESS, RADIATION, OR DELIBERATE COLORATION.

In short, there wasn't enough information. "As the dark side rotates toward us, display a composite image of the nonreflective side." Tavoian definitely wanted to see the dark side, the one that telescopes hadn't captured except as a dark blur.

He caught his breath as the first detailed images of the dark side began to appear, with patterns filling the entire circle, which now showed up as a deep and dark shade of green. The patterns were definitely regular rectangles, and the shorter sides of the rectangles had a space between them and the next rectangle. All the rectangles were the same width, roughly five meters, but the longer ones were huge, some almost fifty meters in length, according to the AI. The smaller ones were likely twenty-five in length. The rectangles formed polygons approximating circles, with a trapezoidal space between the ends. Each polygon contained fewer rectangles, until the last polygon, which was a hexagon around an open space too deep for Tavoian to see whether it extended all the way to the back side of the shimmering hull.

The majority of the rectangular chambers had had their overheads removed. *Sheared off by whatever force separated this section from the original sphere.* And that had to have occurred almost instantaneously by a force that hadn't crushed, fragmented, or crumpled the severed material. *Like a gigantic knife only molecules thick that separated two sections . . . or a particle beam or the like with an edge so finely defined that the material not destroyed was scarcely affected.*

At first glance, the edges of the rectangles appeared regular but when Tavoian increased the magnification he could see that the tops of the walls around them seemed slightly rounded. *By intense heat?* The rounding suggested the interior of the artifact had been constructed of materials less indestructible than the outer hull. Except that didn't seem right to Tavoian. The interior—the walls and structure, at least—couldn't have been too much less hardy than the shining outer hull, since there were no obvious scars, pits, or craters on the dark green side, either.

He could have watched and studied for far longer, but he knew he was getting too tired to think as clearly as he should be, and he did have his orders. That meant composing an immediate message. When finished, he read it through.

Robert Anson, Colonel
Noram Space Command
Donovan Base

1. Recon three on station.
2. Target object appears to fit all parameters of technologically created object.

3. Object appears to be remnant of far larger object, likely a sphere with an estimated diameter of five point five kays.

4. Initial scans, measurements, and images follow.

Tavoian paused. *What else can you say?* He really felt like shouting, "Yes, it's a frigging alien spacecraft!" *Part of it anyway.* Instead, he ordered the AI, "Attach all data and images we have so far and send the message."

MESSAGE, DATA, AND IMAGES SENT.

Next came the grunt work. Tavoian had decided to deploy a single array of cubesats around the alien artifact, along with a repeater that would automatically send the data to Donovan Base if anything happened to Recon three. Then he'd begin with close-up scans of the "dark" side of the alien craft/object to determine if there were points of entry, since there didn't appear to be any on the silver-white side that had likely been the outer hull of the larger craft.

"Deploy outer ring cubesats in optimal pattern."

BEGINNING CUBESAT DEPLOYMENT.

Tavoian watched intently as the ISV, the independent space vehicle, slipped away from Recon three and began to release the cubesats in a pattern designed to cover all parts of the artifact simultaneously. That took over an hour, but after the first few minutes, Tavoian was preparing the first AI rover for the ISV to ferry over to the artifact once the cubesat deployment was complete.

Once the ISV had returned, picked up the AI rover, deposited it on top of one of the larger rectangles, and returned to Recon three, Tavoian began to deploy and unshutter the solar panels designed to power Recon three while on station. By the time he was finished, he could barely keep his eyes open.

"If the rover gets dislodged, have the ISV recover it and hold until I wake up." With that, Tavoian dimmed the control area lights, hoping he hadn't forgotten anything, but he'd only slept, really slept, something like four hours in the last thirty-six, and he didn't want to do something stupid because he was too tired to think straight.

Before his eyes closed, he had a disturbing thought. *It looks too new to be as old as Alayna thinks it must be.*

THE TIMES OF INDIA
9 NOVEMBER 2114

(DELHI) "At the first offensive movement against India, we will retaliate in massive force. We will not be intimidated by Sinese threats," declared Prime Minister Narahaj Ravindra, immediately after the Sinese Federation closed all its borders in South Asia.

No comment was forthcoming from Sinese Head of State Jiang. Requests for elaboration were referred to the Sinese Defence Ministry.

In a related development, the Indian Defense Ministry announced that both Noram and the Sinese Federation have dispatched high-speed fusion-powered spacecraft to investigate a mysterious object heading toward the sun. "Noram and the Sinese both seek to monopolize whatever discoveries may await them," stated the ministry in a prepared statement. "They have not offered to share any benefits. India has suffered enough of what has become a one-way avenue to the future, where we have supplied expertise to both nations and received little in return. The Sinese attempt to bully India into halting its near-Earth and deep space initiatives is nothing more than twenty-second-century colonialism." A high-ranking ministry official confirmed that all of India's Indra scramjet missiles were on high alert and ready to launch at a nanosecond's notice.

The Indra has a range of over fifteen thousand kilometers at a speed of between Mach 10 and Mach 16, approximately twenty thousand kilometers per hour, depending on altitude, and can be programmed to strike within a ten-meter square. India is presumed to have more than two hundred such missiles. Some experts claim that number is closer to five hundred.

Sources within the Noram government conceded that there was an "element of truth" in the news stories claiming that both the Noram and the Sinese Federation have dispatched exploratory craft to investigate an object approaching the sun that is rumored to be of possible extra-solar origin.

Noram President Dyana Yates was unavailable for comment on either matter. Sources close to the President indicated that Yates was giving both issues "immediate and serious attention" and was deciding among possible options to deal with the situation. They refused to elaborate on what those options might be . . .

On Friday, Alayna was up early, not because she had to be, but because she had slept fitfully, her mind and dreams racing from one subject to another. Over the past ten days, she had tried a number of variations on the screening system that she had developed for Marcel to apply to the solar observations she'd been able to make in between or concurrently with observations contracted for by various Earthside astronomical entities. None of the variations were markedly any more satisfactory than the initial screens had been, although several revealed more multi-fractals . . . but not any more near-matches. Nor had any of the screens revealed anything different about solar convection, flares, or prominences . . . or anything else that might shed light on what lay beneath the solar surface. With more than nine months of her twenty-four gone and only relatively minor progress, she couldn't help but admit she was getting worried. Maybe a solar minimum wasn't the best time for her research.

She'd also heard nothing from the Foundation, and that was troublesome, and there had been no further communication from the IAU, although that wasn't exactly surprising. 2114 FQ5 had been classified, and now it was up to her and others to discover what it was . . . or was not.

When a message from Chris finally did arrive, she immediately called it up and began to read.

Alayna—
I've been busy, but wanted you to know that I'm well and on station, so to speak, where I'll be for the next several months. By now, even the news summaries I receive mention your discovery. I wouldn't be surprised if every media outlet is rumoring it might just be the first indisputable evidence of alien life discovered by humanity, but since I don't get any of the vidloids, I'm only guessing. They're also probably speculating on the fact that both Noram and the Sinese have sent expeditions

out to investigate. Before long, if your main optical array is trained on the object now . . . well, you'll likely see.

Main optical array? To see something as small as a spacecraft? He's going to be there? "Marcel, when will we be able to get new observations on 2114 FQ5?" Alayna could have figured it out, but asking Marcel was faster.

"November twenty-second."

"We'll need observations then. Work the time in on every day when it's observable." She went back to the message.

I'll have to say that periods of alternating decel and weight-lessness don't do much for my sleep patterns, and it will be good to get back to a more regular routine, not that any routine off-Earth is ever exactly regular. For the next few months, I won't be doing much piloting, more like station-keeping and programming various AI units. That's what's planned, anyway, but that could change. I'll know more in a while.

Alayna nodded. Another indication that Chris was where she thought he was.

There's not much else I can say at the moment so I'll ask how things are coming on your solar multi-fractals. I hope you've either found more information or another approach that will prove more productive.

I'm not as creative as I might otherwise be, but here's another quote from *Observations*:

Most politicians fall into two categories—those already bought, in one way or another, and those not worth the price. That truism, unhappily, also applies to all those in other occupations who achieved their positions through political expertise as opposed to subject matter or technical expertise.

Alayna would have laughed, except that the quote was all too true. She'd already seen that in grad school and again in the Farside Foundation.

I'd have to wonder if all intelligent species run a race between technical and scientific advances and the corresponding increase in political self-interest that becomes indistinguishable from species stupidity. That's certainly been true of human beings. I suppose at some point, if we survive long enough, we'll find out.

There's not much else to say at the moment, and since I can't do anything else right now, I'm going to try to get some sleep before I do something stupid induced by fatigue.

Until later.

She reread the message, then frowned. He couldn't have reached the object, not yet, not the way he had phrased his words, but the implication was that he was close. If he were closer when he'd sent the message, and it was just an asteroid, he would have said so, or at least hinted more strongly. And if it were more than that . . . there would have been hints.

Are you reading too much into his messages?

There was always that possibility, just as there was the very real and growing possibility that she would be unable to discover anything more about the source or mechanics of the solar multi-fractal mini-granulations. In the meantime, she needed to think about yet another way to deal with her own problem, since there wasn't anything she could do to help Chris. *And likely never had been.*

40

RECON THREE
9 NOVEMBER 2114

Exhausted as he was, Tavoian didn't sleep all that well—or long—waking at 0610 UTC, worrying about whether the AI rover and the cubesats were still functioning. He immediately asked, "Interrogative status of rover and cubesats."

ALL UNITS FUNCTIONING. DATA BEING RECEIVED.

All that meant was that nothing had happened to the equipment, not whether the data and observations were useful or even related to the alien artifact. Tavoian took a squeezebottle of water and drank almost half of it before focusing on, first, the input from the solar panels. He nodded. They'd managed to meet Recon three's needs and to recharge the aux power system's energy storage units slightly. If he didn't draw on the system too heavily for the next few days, that would work out, since each day would bring the artifact and the ship three million kays closer to the sun. *More than that, since our inbound speed will increase second by second.*

He frowned, then asked the AI, "Have you had to use the drive to maintain station on the object?"

AFFIRMATIVE.

"We should be affected by the same gravitational forces as the object. Can you calculate our inbound speed?"

SUCH CALCULATION WILL NOT BE COMPLETELY ACCURATE. CURRENT IN-BOUND VELOCITY IS APPROXIMATELY THIRTY-EIGHT KAYS PER SECOND.

Even if the AI was off by a kay or two, the artifact was moving faster than the colonel's experts had calculated. "Keep us in position as necessary." Tavoian paused. "Can we orbit the object?"

ORBITING IS NOT FEASIBLE. A STABLE ORBIT WOULD FALL WITHIN THE SWEEP OF THE OBJECT'S ROTATION.

Tethering the ship to the object definitely wasn't even theoretically possible because of the rotation. Tavoian decided to postpone that problem, and check on the rover and the cubesats.

He began reviewing images—except the current view from the AI rover showed nothing. The last view displayed a slowly changing panorama of stars, with occasional sweeps across the alien artifact and, less often, views of Recon three. He quickly ran backward through the images, and gradually each view showed the artifact as larger, as if had left the surface of the object soon after the ISV had placed it there. "What's the location of the rover?"

ROVER IS ABOARD ISV. ISV IS DOCKED OUTSIDE MAIN LOCK.

"What happened?"

ROVER COULD NOT MAINTAIN POSITION ON ARTIFACT. ARTIFACT'S ROTATION PROPELLED IT TO A POSITION 803 METERS FROM THE CENTERLINE OF THE ARTIFACT. ISV WAS DISPATCHED TO RETRIEVE AND RECOVER ROVER.

Rather than ask more questions, Tavoian went back to the beginning of the data and images gathered by the rover and began to watch. At first, nothing seemed to happen. The rover's sensors just showed the flat green surface stretching away from it. Then, abruptly, it appeared to be floating across one of the open passageways, all of which appeared to be the same "height" as the rectangles, but only about three and a half meters wide, before hovering over the flat green surface of another. After a time, the rover moved again, this time away from the green side of the artifact, slowly moving increasingly farther from it as the artifact rotated. Tavoian studied the initial images once more . . . and then again.

From what he could observe, the rover had simply slid off the top of the large rectangle on which the ISV had deposited it and then just been pushed away into space. The other thing was that there were gaps in the signals. A little more study revealed that the artifact blocked all transmissions that weren't line of sight, and since it rotated, half the time, at least for the first several hours, there were gaps in reception, although the rover's buffering capability meant that images and data had not been lost.

Neither of those should have happened. The rover's tracks were edged, yet it was as if the rover had been on polished ice, and Recon three had been close enough that the remotes should have relayed the data in real-time. *You'll need more remote repeaters all the way around the artifact.* They'd also have to be repositioned frequently, Tavoian suspected.

He went back over the images again, slowly, seeing more clearly the slightly rounded edges of the top of the dark green "walls" over which the AI rover had passed. On the other hand, the outer corners of the rectangles bordering the "passageways" looked to be knife-sharp, except at the very top, where they were also rounded.

Tavoian called up the data to see if the rover's sensors had registered anything about the material on which it had been placed. They didn't.

Apparently, the dark green material was hard, impermeable to electro-magnetic waves, and possibly nonconducting. *And very slippery . . . possibly even almost frictionless.*

Next, he called up the images from the cubesats. They revealed nothing except images of the artifact slowly rotating, the silver side glowing like it was almost independently illuminated and the dark green side black where not struck by the sun's light.

He immediately drafted a brief report and sent it off, then ate what passed for breakfast and cleaned up. The food did help, removing the last traces of a faint headache that he hadn't realized that he'd even had. Then he checked his messages. There was only one. It was official, and the text wasn't even remotely a surprise

> Tavoian, Christopher A.
> Major, NSC
> NSS-21/Recon Three
> OP-IMMEDIATE
> Sinese research probe/longliner ETA less than forty-eight hours. Begin immediate remote exploration of artifact if you have not already done so.
>
> Report all significant discoveries immediately.

Tavoian sent a brief acknowledgment that he had begun remote exploration and that he would report any significant discoveries. There were no other messages. That wasn't because there weren't any, Tavoian thought, but because the colonel didn't want him receiving anything that might distract him.

Next he checked and opened the main lock and had the ISV enter. While the lock was pressurized and the ISV and rover warmed up, he began to program the small spy-eyes. When he finished that, he unpacked more remote signal repeaters and had the AI calculate optimum positioning for what he planned.

Finally, he opened the inner lock. Even after an hour, the chill from the ISV blasted into the former passenger space where he had gathered the remote repeaters and ten smaller spy-eyes with their miniature thrusters, lights, and transmitters.

Arranging the repeaters and the spy-eyes and then launching the ISV took another half hour. It was 0911 UTC by the time Tavoian had used the ISV to place the remote repeaters and then guided the ISV to a point along the top end of one of the green rectangles. Once there, he shifted his attention to the bottom sensor to study more closely the chamber beneath. He blinked and concentrated again on the images from all sources, then asked the AI, "Are the sides slanting away?"

THE SPACE IS A HEXAGON.

Tavoian looked again. It was indeed, except from the viewpoint of the ISV, it was a hexagon on its side. Then, abruptly, he understood. If the artifact had been part of a sphere, and the sphere had been rotated to obtain artificial gravity, then the section of the chamber through which he viewed the hexagon would have been a side wall, except during acceleration or deceleration. *Unless they used some other form of propulsion.* He studied the chamber once again. It was empty.

For a moment, he couldn't figure that out. Then he realized why. If the artifact had been pressurized, and it would have been for any life form, pressurized with *something*, then any chamber suddenly opened to space would have depressurized, releasing at least the majority of its contents. And given that the artifact was still rotating, and given the shape of the chamber, almost anything loose would have eventually worked its way out into space over time, and the artifact had been in space a long time.

After all the time the artifact had been in space since whatever happened, Tavoian doubted that any room or chamber held atmosphere or the equivalent, but others might well hold objects, technological equipment . . . something. All he had to do was find a way into them.

He also noted that the image wasn't as sharp as it should be. "Why isn't the image sharper?"

THE IR COMPONENT IS LESS EFFECTIVE WHEN SCANNING THE GREEN MATERIAL.

"Why?"

THAT CANNOT BE DETERMINED.

Tavoian thought for a moment. The ISV was using both a light beam and an IR beam. The light was obviously being reflected, but the IR beam was either being reflected uniformly or not at all. One way or another, there was no detectable differential. At least, the optics worked with visible light.

He guided the ISV to the next open chamber, which was twice as large at the open end, but half as deep, essentially half a hexagon, one that had been cut in two. The next beyond that was like the first. A good hour later, Tavoian halted, realizing that he'd barely scratched the surface.

He asked the AI, "Interrogative estimate of the number of rectangular objects visible on dark side of object."

NINE THOUSAND THREE HUNDRED TWENTY-ONE.

His initial thought was that number was far too high, but the object

194 L. E. MODESITT, JR.

was almost two thousand meters across, and that meant a surface area
of more than three point one million square meters, and if each hexagon
showed a rectangle on the end, the average area of each would be almost
two hundred square meters . . . that would amount to fifteen thousand,
allowing no space for passageways or whatever the separations between
each hexagon might be.

"Thank you," he replied after a moment.

He considered what he'd seen. All of the chambers whose sides had
been sheared open were empty hexagons or, rather, parts of hexagons.
The spaces between the ends of the hexagons were shafts, except that
when the artifact had been part of a sphere—*assuming it had been*—those
shafts would have been passageways. *Again, assuming that it had been
rotating to maintain artificial gravity.* Several of the hexagonal chambers
were separated by large brackets anchoring or supporting or maintaining
separation between decks. The supports were elongated hexagons, also of
the dark green material with hexagonal cutouts, rather than being solid.

Tavoian stretched and found himself moving away from the control
couch for a moment, until the loosely fastened restraint straps halted his
motion. He took another swallow of water from the squeezebottle,
squared himself before the controls, and guided the ISV back to the center of the dark side and eased it down the hexagonal shaft that measured
fifty-eight point seven meters across. While the ISV lights could reach the
sides of the shaft, Tavoian could not make out where it ended, although
the instruments indicated that the bottom was less than a hundred meters away. The massive hexagons touched at their vertices but left open
spaces above and below. Tavoian could make out what appeared to be
more of the hexagonal supports in those spaces, again with hexagonal
spaces cut out of the supports, but not what lay beyond.

The bottom of the shaft was just that—a smooth hexagon of the dark
green material, with no openings whatsoever. In addition, for the last fifty
meters, there were no openings between the hexagons, just more of the
solid green material, although to Tavoian, the filler material looked to be
just a shade lighter.

For a moment, Tavoian also wondered, *Why hexagons?* The obvious
answer was that hexagons and squares were among the few polygons that
fit together without wasted space, and hexagons fit even better within a
sphere. But that was also an assumption.

He returned the ISV to the top of the hexagonal center shaft, and then
eased it over to the nearest "vertical" shaft, which he was convinced
would have been a horizontal passageway. Then he gave the command
for the first spy-eye and sent it down the angled shaft. While he had a
smaller backup ISV, he wasn't about to hazard either the main ISV or the

backup, although it seemed like the most likely problems were either signal loss or thruster failure, rather than any threat from the artifact. *But
then, anything that built something this massive that has endured so long
without obvious damage just might have a few surprises.*

The relayed image gave Tavoian the impression of walking down a
wide and dimly lit corridor. After several moments, he had the spy-eye
check one side of the passage and then the other. "Is there a difference in
reflectivity or color in the sides?"

EACH SIDE REFLECTS WHITE LIGHT IN A SLIGHTLY DIFFERENT WAVE-
LENGTH. ALL ARE VISUALLY GREEN.

"Are the passageway wavelengths different from the outside wavelengths?"

SURFACES WITH THE SAME ORIENTATIONS HAVE THE SAME REFLECTIVE
PATTERNS.

After about twenty meters the passageway split, with one shaft heading parallel to the outer dark surface of the artifact, and the other heading
back, essentially reversing the angle of the first length. Tavoian halted the
spy-eye. The intertwined passageways could go on forever. He hadn't seen
anything even hinting at entries to the hexagonal chambers. Then he shook
his head. He'd been looking in the wrong place. What he'd thought of as
the bulkheads or walls would have been the deck or overhead when the
sphere rotated. He reversed the spy-eye and had it scan "above" and
"below," then told the AI, "Halt the spy-eye when there's a change in color
reflectivity."

The spy-eye traveled a little over ten meters and stopped.

Tavoian studied all sides of the passageway. He didn't see anything
different. "Where is the color change?"

AT NINETY DEGREES AND 180 DEGREES FROM THE CENTERLINE OF THE
SPY-EYE.

Effectively directly overhead and directly below. Tavoian repositioned
the light and looked. He still couldn't see anything. "Show the difference
in false color on another display screen."

Another screen immediately appeared on the control wall, showing
two images, each of which had a hexagonal light green shape, one directly overhead from the spy-eye, and another below it. Tavoian could
not see any difference in the smoothness or the texture of the material,
even when he positioned the spy-eye within centimeters of the surface.
Nor was there any sign of a control mechanism.

Tavoian had the spy-eye touch every section of the possible entry, then
did the same around the edge of the entry. He didn't expect anything to
happen, and it didn't. He tried aiming the spy-eye's light at every point
that might trigger a response, but that didn't elicit any response.

At that point, he recalled the spy-eye to the ISV and then turned the rest of the recovery over to the AI.

Because transmission was strictly line-of-sight within the alien artifact, if he wanted to do any exploring of any depth, at least through the equipment, he needed to establish a hardwired connection. So while the AI was recovering the ISV and the spy-eyes, he made his way back to the cargo section, where he found the spool of enhanced fiber-optic line, and then laid it out in the former passenger section, which was rapidly becoming his workshop. Then he began work on modifying the AI rover, by attaching a thruster pack to it, and then adding, just in case, the nanorod drill assembly and a laser cutter, not that the small laser had anywhere near the power necessary to cut through the depth of the hexagon walls, but Tavoian wanted to know if a laser would have any effect at all.

He decided against sending a report to Donovan Base and the colonel, at least until he had more information.

Almost an hour later, at 1113 UTC, Tavoian began the second exploration by sending the ISV back to the artifact and down the center hexagonal shaft to the lowest openings. That had required using the lock again. Then he sent the AI rover, trailing fiber-optic line, from the ISV into one of the six lowest openings, chosen at random, since there was no indication either he or the ship's AI could discern that any opening was any different from any other.

The rover did need to use both thrusters and treads, but it did seem to gain some traction on the surface that would have been the "deck" during rotation, possibly confirming Tavoian's suspicions that the artifact had been a sphere rotated to create artificial gravity. He guided the rover along one stretch to the next junction, then on to another passage sixty degrees to the left and along another side of a hexagon, and then left another sixty degrees and straight "down," at which point the rover entered a trapezoidal space blocked another twenty-odd meters ahead by a solid wall of the dark green—seemingly identical to the wall that had blocked the bottom of the hexagonal shaft. If Tavoian had calculated correctly, it was in fact the same wall.

He had guessed that what lay beyond the wall might be either a drive or control section, based simply on the pattern of discoloration detected on the curved outer hull by the AI. That was fine, but exactly how was he going to get through the wall to see what might be beyond it?

"Can you detect any variations in reflectivity or color from the rover data?"

AFFIRMATIVE.

"Display in false color."

What Tavoian saw on the control wall screen was the hexagonal coloration of what apparently was an opening into the section beyond, except there was a large circle that touched two sides of the passageway, and within the circle was a symbol that appeared to be a backward "Z." *Entrance forbidden?*

"Copy that false color image and save it for transmission."

IMAGE SAVED.

Now what?

Tavoian eased the rover forward until it touched the presumed entry. After repeating touching the entry, using lights, Tavoian then had the AI attempt to drill into the dark green material. The drill made no impression on the entry. Neither did the small laser. Nothing.

Tavoian didn't have much hope, but decided to see if the silvery curved side of the artifact afforded any better possibilities. It took almost an hour to return the rover to the hexagonal shaft, then have the ISV carry the rover to the other side of the artifact, where he set the rover down beside one of the discolored circles that only the ship's AI could discern.

Another hour's worth of effort brought no result, and Tavoian recalled the ISV to Recon three, docking it to receiving and refueling assembly on the outer hull, then asked the ship's AI, "Scan all of the rectangles on the dark side of the artifact. Determine if there are any that look to have contents of some sort or narrow openings."

COMMENCING SEARCH.

While the AI combed through past images, and refueled the ISV, Tavoian tried to figure out what he had actually learned. The false color images suggested two possibilities, that either the aliens could easily discern colors too close in shading for human eyes, or that there had been a system of internal illumination that would have made those distinctions clear, or even of radically different colors or shades when powered. That seemed more likely, but he couldn't discount the first possibility. If the sizes of the chambers and the putative entries were any indication, either the long-gone aliens had been larger than humans or they needed more space. *Or all the hexagons you investigated were for storage of some sort.*

At 1407 UTC, the AI announced, YOU HAVE EIGHT MESSAGES.

"They just arrived?"

AFFIRMATIVE.

The first message was from Colonel Anson. The operative section was simple enough.

Interrogative any evidence of advanced technology.

Tavoian skimmed through the headings on the rest of the messages. Two were news summaries; one was a notice to all Space Service personnel, and two were personal, one from Kit and one from Alayna. He opened the allpers notice. He smiled sardonically at the notification that all Earthside leaves had been canceled pending the resolution of current political and military "uncertainties."

He decided to answer the colonel's message immediately, since he didn't have any immediate and good ideas for learning more about the alien artifact that, it was clear to him, definitely represented an artifact of advanced technology, possibly an artifact so advanced that no Earth technology could even get into it.

Tavoian saw no point in sugarcoating what he had determined and began with a straightforward statement:

> In response to your inquiry, there is overwhelming evidence that the artifact was manufactured or created with advanced technology, but initial exploration has failed to reveal any evidence of what that technology was or how it operated . . .

He went on to explain what he had learned and accomplished so far, mainly that the artifact was incredibly durable, so tough that even a nanorod diamond drill could not scratch it, nor could a laser cut it, and that whoever or whatever had used it had left no obvious traces. He also noted the present apparent inaccessibility of sealed chambers, then had the ship's AI assemble information and images on the interior and exterior of the artifact.

After Tavoian finished his reply and sent it, he smiled wryly. Given the positions of Recon three and Donovan Base, the one-way time lag was around thirteen minutes, which made any sort of real-time communications effectively impossible, and gave him twenty-six minutes before the colonel came up with another question or potentially impossible demand.

Next he read Kit's letter.

> Dear Chris,
> I've just learned that no Space Service personnel are being allowed to return to Earth. You already suggested that would happen. Why now? I know that the universe and politics don't accommodate to personal needs, but do they have to be so perverse in when they affect us? That's taking the indifference of the universe personally, I know. But life is *personal* . . .

Tavoian smiled as he read the last words. They were so like Kit, who could be so analytical in talking science and so intense on a personal level.

... and I miss you so much at times like these. I feel so emotional, but I can't be cold and rational when it's our mother who's failing and probably won't see you again, and you can't do anything at all about it. You're better balanced than I am, or maybe you just hide what you feel better. Sometimes, I think you even hide it from yourself.

I don't understand all this threatening and fighting. Not personally and not even intellectually. There's what everyone claims is an alien artifact headed toward the sun. If that's true, there is or was another civilization that could do more than we have. There might be so much to learn from whatever it is. But the Sinese seem to want to destroy India and the rest of the world with the Indians because India wants to be independent in getting into space. What's that all about? More power-politics blackmail, and our own weak-kneed President won't even call it what it is. It makes me furious. No . . . I don't want a war, especially with you in the middle of it. If she said more, the Sinese might reconsider . . .

Then they might not.

. . . but she's probably afraid to say too much, with all the Noram bonds and notes that the Sinese hold. Talk about being damned one way or the other . . .

I've ranted long enough, but who else can I tell?

Besides all my senior officers?

All I can say is to please take care, little brother, and come home safe when you can.

When he finished reading the message, Tavoian wondered when he should let Kit know what he was doing and where he was. *Not yet.* That would just worry her more and not accomplish much of anything.

Because he wasn't certain how he wanted to answer Kit, he called up Alayna's message and began to read.

Chris—
The silence from the Foundation has been deafening. Not a word from either Director Wrae or from the Director-Generale.

I have a feeling about that. Rather, two ambivalent ones. Either my explanation was completely accepted . . . or I've lost all shot at ever having a career as an astrophysicist.

Or they could be waiting to see how things turn out before deciding which way to go. One thing Tavoian had learned was that people often failed to recognize which decisions had to be made immediately and which did not. *Should you suggest that?* Tavoian decided to finish reading the message before deciding. *Or maybe longer.*

When he finished Alayna's message, he decided that he would have to wait to reply to her . . . and to Kit. He also realized he couldn't put off trying to figure out what he should do next, then realized he hadn't gotten an answer from the AI on the question he'd asked. "Have you discovered any smaller openings into any of the rectangles on the darker side of the artifact?"

AFFIRMATIVE.

With the AI's response, Tavoian realized he'd ordered an action, but not told the AI to report back on the results. "How many?"

EIGHTEEN.

"Display the locations."

Tavoian didn't even have to look hard to see the pattern. All of the eighteen rectangles—which were in all probability the sides of hexagons— were on one side of the artifact, all adjoining each other. "Can you determine if there is anything inside them?"

THERE IS NOTHING IN THE OPENINGS THAT HAVE BEEN SCANNED. IN-DEPTH DETERMINATION IS NOT POSSIBLE. THE OPENINGS ARE ANGLED WITH REGARD TO SOLAR ILLUMINATION.

"How big are the openings?"

ALL ARE LESS THAN TWO METERS BY FIVE METERS.

Knowing that time was running out before the Sinese probe arrived, Tavoian couldn't put off sending the ISV back for a look into the partly open hexagons. At least, he hoped they were only partly open. With a half sigh, he unstrapped himself from the control seat and half rose, half floated toward the back of the ship. He needed to restock the ISV with slightly different equipment.

Almost an hour later, Tavoian was back before the controls watching as he guided the ISV back toward the artifact. The choice was whether to start at one end or in the middle of the line of hexagons. He decided on the middle and brought the ISV to a relative halt above the rectangle that was close to being in the middle of those the ship's AI had indicated only had small openings, rather than being sealed or totally sliced open.

The opening was as the AI had described it, roughly except it was little more than a meter wide and extended some three meters from top to bottom. "Show the opening and the area around it in false color."

Another screen appeared on the control wall. Tavoian nodded. The opening was exactly in the center of the slightly different colored area that he thought of as a "door." It also appeared as if something had blocked or diverted, just slightly, the force that had sliced the artifact from the sphere. He moved the ISV closer. A ridge less than ten centimeters high ran across what he assumed was the bottom of the hexagonal opening, as if the material had melted and flowed into the functional equivalent of a doorway, keeping it from fully sealing.

Why here? He had the ISV scan the area, turning it toward the curved outer edge of the artifact, then asked the AI, "Is there any color differentiation near where the silver hull ends?"

AFFIRMATIVE.

"Please display the differentiation in false color."

Tavoian switched his attention from the ISV screen to the one displayed by the AI, which showed in false lighter green, a thin arc that followed the hull line. All of the eighteen semi-open hexagons were inboard of the arc, itself just behind what looked to have been three adjoining sections of hexagons whose main part had vanished in whatever had sheared away the remaining artifact. That didn't tell Tavoian anything about what the arc was, only that it likely had something to do with whatever had kept the few hexagons from having their ends completely sheared off. He just hoped that he could discover *something* in or through those eighteen hexagons.

Tavoian didn't bother with a spy-eye. Instead, he sent the AI rover, using its thrusters and trailing fiber-optic line from the ISV, through the meter-wide space and into the hexagon, hoping he would find something.

He did. There were large lumps of material, as if stone or the same kind of material that the hexagons were made of had been heated and instantly fused with sections of metal, both dark and light. The lumps ranged in size from a meter square to several more than five meters long and a meter wide. They all jutted out from the surface closest to the edge of the artifact, but no more than a meter, again suggesting that they were what remained of equipment fastened in place and that, under normal circumstances, the massive craft had been rotated and that the outboard surface had been the "floor."

"Does the reflected light indicate the materials or elements in that melted mass?" Tavoian asked the AI.

THERE ARE TRACES OF IRON, BORON, RHENIUM, CARBON, SILICA, COPPER, AND SILVER.

Rhenium? It was heat resistant, but why rhenium?

Tavoian concentrated on following the gentle sweep of the rover's lights, but so far as he could tell, and the AI's sensors confirmed it, the only objects in the hexagonal chamber were the fused masses of material heat-welded to the "floor." There were also no other objects, equipment, or protrusions. And the image still wasn't as sharp as it might have been.

"Still no IR?"

NOT WITHIN THE ARTIFACT.

Tavoian guided the ISV to the adjoining hexagon, which had similar fused protruding lumps, as did the two chambers flanking the first two.

The "door" to the fifth chamber had been frozen in a position that left an entry space of little more than half a meter. Tavoian found himself holding his breath as the rover's lights penetrated the dimness. He couldn't help but smile as he saw an unmelted shape affixed to the outboard bulkhead/deck. He guided the rover closer, noting that the shape was an elongated hexagon that extended roughly seventy centimeters from where it melded seamlessly with the bulkhead/deck. The surface was green, but a lighter green than that of the rest of the chamber . . . and absolutely featureless. There were no signs of the metals that were swirled through the melted and fused masses in the first four hexagons.

Tavoian had the rover scan the entire chamber, but it was empty, except for the extruded/protruded hexagon. What he did discover at the far or lower end of the hexagon was another "door," also jammed open the same amount as the one through which the rover had entered. When the rover went through that opening, the view was identical to the passages through which Tavoian had guided the spy-eyes earlier. Further exploration of the maze of corridors could wait until the rover had investigated the remaining "open" hexagons, Tavoian decided.

Sending the rover into the remaining thirteen hexagons identified by the ship's AI took another three hours, and discovered no other protrusions, either fused or intact, by which time Tavoian's head ached, and his eyes burned. Absently, he checked the time. It was 1937 UTC.

No wonder you can hardly see straight.

At that, he had the rover clamp itself to the ISV, then turned control over to the ship's AI. "Return ISV to the lock. Refuel the ISV and the rover."

COMMENCING RETURN.

When he checked the message queue, Tavoian found another message from the colonel, whose arrival he had not even noticed when he had been directing the exploration of the alien artifact. The gist of the colonel's communication was contained in one sentence: "Request immediate update on your progress and findings."

Do they think that there's wonderful technology laid out with a manual for them to follow? Tavoian wasn't feeling terribly sympathetic to the colonel's urgency. After almost three hours of following the rover in and out of hexagons, and only four to six hours sleep out of the past thirty-six or so, Tavoian's eyes were so heavy he could barely keep them open, and his vision was blurring if he didn't concentrate on focusing.

The body of his response was short and simple.

> Have spent almost thirteen straight hours investigating arti-
> fact. To date, have found great evidence of technological
> prowess but no immediately identifiable and replicable tech-
> nological artifacts. More information attached. No longer able
> to concentrate. Will resume efforts after getting some sleep.

Regardless of what the colonel thought and wanted, Tavoian couldn't do anything more without some sleep.

He didn't even have to dim the control area lighting before his eyes closed.

41

THE NEW YORK TIMES
10 NOVEMBER 2114

[OTTAWA] "Getting involved in a fight between the Sinese and the Indians is total idiocy." That was Senator Castenada's opening statement in the debate over emergency funds for the Department of Off-Earth Activities. Castenada (CP-NY) called DOEA Secretary Luvalle's report of a "potential" alien artifact a "blatant ploy" to funnel more money into the military functions of DOEA, adding that Luvalle's middle name ought to be "Serendipity if he thinks the Senate is gullible enough to swallow the idea of the sudden appearance of an alien spacecraft just when DOEA needs money to embark on deep space military adventures at a time of overwhelming national needs that are far more pressing." The Senator also dismissed as "pure propaganda" the news reports that the Sinese Federation has already dispatched a probe to investigate the mysterious body that is now halfway between the orbits of the Earth and Mars.

Castenada is currently under investigation by the Noram Inspector-General's office in regard to charges that he revealed classified DOEA material to the media after the Administration failed to provide additional disaster relief to New York City.

Senator Kim Greywinter (D-ALB), chairman of the DOEA oversight committee, just finished holding hearings on the Administration's request. Greywinter suggested that failing to take advantage of the "startling information" provided by the Space Service would be a grievous mistake. He also noted that Castenada had a "perfect record of deliberate misinformation."

Castenada could not be reached for further comment.

EC Chancellor Rumikov chided both Noram and the Sinese Federation for failing to inform other nations about the potential alien spacecraft, and stated that it would set "a terrible precedent" if either failed to share fully any scientific information recovered from missions to investigate the object.

DOEA Secretary Luvalle declined comment on whether the Noram probe was manned and whether it had actually reached the mysterious object, despite reports from various astronomical facilities that a small body has been sighted orbiting the mysterious object that rotates slowly, showing alternatively a shimmering brilliant white side and a dark side.

Sinese Minister for Space Wong Mengyi let it be known through ministry officials that no comment would be forthcoming until the Sinese probe reached the object and relayed preliminary information to ministry scientists. A Sinese official who declined to be named also stated that any interference with Sinese space operations and research would be considered "hostile military action" and would invalidate all nonmilitarization of space treaties and agreements . . .

RECON THREE
10 NOVEMBER 2114

Tavoian slept longer than usual, at least longer than he had been, but that made sense given how he'd collapsed the night before and given the fact that he was sleeping in weightless conditions. It was still comparatively early—0537 UTC—when he woke and checked the time, but after some initial grogginess, he felt much better. He felt even more refreshed after eating, prepared foods or not, largely from squeeze type containers, which indicated that whoever had stocked Recon three had known that most of the provisions would have to be consumed in weightless conditions, rather than under acceleration or decel. The orange juice even tasted remotely fresh.

He cleaned up quickly, then settled in front of the controls. There were no messages, either from the colonel or anyone else, and he wanted to get started before there were any. The next step was to run a systems check on the AI rover, before sending it down to the artifact on the ISV and then through the open doors of the hexagon to see where the passages might lead. Because he believed in backups, he'd decided to have the rover go as far as it could under his direction. Then when it reached the end of the fiber-optic line—or if the line snarled or broke—it could proceed on its own. Tavoian intended to use direct control and linkage as far as he could so that he had real-time visuals, even though he knew that to get into the depths of the alien artifact he'd have to set the rover loose on its own. He only had two rovers. He could likely cobble together a third if necessary, but he certainly didn't want to hazard the rovers unnecessarily or quickly, not when he was likely to be on station for more than two months, although he had the feeling he probably wouldn't be the only Noram ship around the artifact before that long, not after the colonel transmitted images and data to the head of Space Command.

Then again . . . With all the possible hostilities between the great powers and the position of the artifact on the far side of the sun from Earth, even the colonel might have trouble gathering the necessary resources for a full scientific team, especially doing so quickly enough to allow them sufficient time and resources. *But that's not your problem, and you've got enough to deal with without worrying about his difficulties.*

Getting the systems check done, and then transmitting the programmed instructions and guidelines inputted to the rover's AI took close to an hour, and close to another hour passed before the ISV hovered above the half-open door to the hexagonal chamber that had held the unmarked equipment still anchored to the floor. Tavoian eased the AI rover, using its fully charged thruster pack and trailing the fiber-optic line, through the opening, past the protrusion that might be some form of equipment or technology—or might not—and then through the second opening. The idea was to guide the rover in the direction of the outer hull, hoping to find another passage there leading "down," the idea being to see if there might be a way close to the hull that led around the barrier at the bottom of the central hexagonal shaft.

If that failed, Tavoian could look for other "doors" that had been left open, but in his estimation, there were over twenty thousand hexagons in the artifact, assuming the places where he hadn't yet explored were like the others. Trying to send the rover through all those passages would exhaust all the thruster propellant before even a fraction of the hexagons were investigated. The next possibility was remote, but he could try beaming various lights and electromagnetic wavelengths at the doors to see if that created any reaction . . .

One thing at a time. He pulled his thoughts back to the rover. Once through the second opening, the one out of the first hexagon, because he could only go parallel to the outer hull, he guided the rover to the left. Some twelve meters farther on he came to a four-way junction—left or right, each at sixty-degree angles, or toward the rim and where the silvery hull ended or away from it, at a ninety-degree angle. He guided the rover toward the hull, for all of about eight meters, when it reached the layer of hexagonal chambers closer to the hull. The next junction was a stretch of twenty-five meters away, but the short passageway "out" toward the hull ended in a blank wall of the dark green material.

"Are there any color differentiations?" he asked the ship's AI.

NEGATIVE.

"Are there any other differentiations not visible to the human eye?"

THE SURFACE PARALLEL TO THE FLAT SIDES OF THE HEXAGON AND CLOSEST TO THE OUTER ARC OF THE ARTIFACT IS FRACTIONALLY ROUGHER. WITHOUT IR CAPABILITIES, MORE DISTINCTION IS NOT POSSIBLE.

Another indication that they did spin the larger sphere.

Tavoian supposed that was progress. After quick inspection of the blank wall, he headed the rover back to the last passage split, and turned the rover farther along a passageway parallel to the rim of the artifact, looking for another passage leading back out toward the rim, but when he guided the rover outward once more, passage was blocked by another blank wall.

Once more he guided the rover back to the last junction and went parallel along another twenty-plus-meter stretch . . . and, abruptly, the image from the rover vanished.

"What happened?"

THE SIGNAL WAS LOST. MOST PROBABLE CAUSE WAS TENSION ON THE LINE. SECOND MOST PROBABLE CAUSE WAS PRESSURE ON THE LINE AGAINST A SHARP EDGE OR OBJECT.

Tavoian mentally calculated. The ISV carried five hundred meters of line on a largely frictionless spool. According to the ISV readouts, a little less than 140 meters of line had paid out. He had a good general idea where the rover was, but no way to track it where it might go. He could only hope that the AI guidance would enable it to get farther along, perhaps even to find a way past or through the barriers seemingly built into the artifact everywhere to restrict access to whatever lay immediately under the outer silvery hull. Because that hull was so strong that human technology that could be transported to the artifact was unlikely to break through it, the only real hope was to find ways into that section of the ship without using force. Of course, doing that was essentially useless if the AI couldn't also direct the rover back to the ISV.

Thinking of that, he focused on the images from the ISV. Nothing had changed. It remained over the open door, occasionally using its thrusters to hold its position. As he studied the image, Tavoian wondered if there was any way he could figure out to simply attach the ISV in position . . .

Then he shook his head. He could simply put it inside one of the hexagons against one of the walls where the rotation would hold it—except he couldn't do that and maintain control without a fiber-optic line to a repeater outside the hexagon. Nothing was simple, given what the massive artifact was, including being totally opaque to any transmissions. Belatedly, he had the ISV retrieve the severed line. He'd take a look at it once the ISV returned to Recon three. *Assuming it does.*

For the moment, he had to hope for the best.

His thoughts went back to the alien artifact. *How did they communicate within the original sphere?* There had to be a comm system built into the walls of the structure. Would the areas around the "doors" respond to electronic signals? Light or laser pulses? Various levels of electromagnetic radiation?

Tavoian heard his stomach growl. He did feel hungry, and a little lightheaded. He checked the time—0957 UTC. That late already?

"Notify me if there's any sign of the rover . . . or anything else, including any other spacecraft that might be approaching." Tavoian didn't expect the Sinese longliner for another day, but relying on expectations wasn't a good idea, especially given the situation between Noram and the Sinese. Since there was little point in sitting and waiting, he decided he might as well check to see if any new messages had arrived and then take a break and eat something, especially since it had been hours since breakfast.

There was a message from the colonel, requesting a report on any new developments as they occurred. Tavoian replied that there were no new developments, but that he had dispatched an AI-guided unit on another search of an area of the artifact in an effort to discover a way into apparently sealed areas.

Once that message was dispatched, he took several long swallows of tea from one of his squeezebottles, ate a few crackers, trying to do so without spraying crumbs anywhere, since they'd eventually end up in the ventilation system, and turned to the problem at hand. What other ways might there be to discover more about the artifact? The light reflected from the green surfaces varied minutely, but precisely, with a definitely engineered wavelength differential. *What would happen if you replicated those exact wavelengths?* The first step was to determine if that were possible with the resources he had on board Recon three. It only took moments to verify that he did indeed have a tunable broadband laser that covered wavelengths from longer than the infrared up through the UV spectrum, and it had enough power to generate a continuous light that would meet his specifications. Best of all, it could be recharged from the deployed solar panels, and it had been adapted to be mounted on the ISV.

Tavoian had no idea who had been intelligent or farsighted enough to include that piece of equipment, but he was glad of it. Without it, it would have been hard to pursue that line of inquiry. Then he took a deep breath and called up the "Investigatory Methods" document that suggested various tests. It didn't take much reading for him to see that some of the suggested "inquiries" weren't going to be much help. How could he sample various materials when he didn't have anything that could cut or break the material of the artifact? Then he read the line beneath:

> *Any loose material, detritus, or even dust might prove useful . . .*

He hadn't even thought of that. He continued reading, nodding occasionally. When he finished, he had to admit that the colonel either knew a great deal more than military and space matters, or he had access to a wide range of expertise. Either way . . .

While he waited for the return of the AI rover—and kept hoping that it would return—he made his way to the equipment hold, the one aft of the passenger area, where he located the tunable broadband laser and brought it forward to the passenger area, now serving as a de facto work-room, where he readied it, as much as he could, for mounting on the ISV. He had taken out the small extruder/nanotube formulator, just in case he needed additional supports for mounting, but it turned out those weren't needed.

When he finished and returned to the control area, he asked the ship's AI, "Is there any signal from the AI rover?"

NEGATIVE.

With a headshake, Tavoian made his way forward to the control area, where he used the system to find the location of the sampling gear. While he hadn't looked for dust or loose material in corners of the artifact, surely there had to be some . . . somewhere in all those chambers and pas-sageways.

He was just about to go aft once more for the sampling gear when the ship's AI announced, SIGNAL RECEIVED FROM AI ROVER.

Simultaneously, an image appeared on the control wall—that of the ISV as seen from the hexagonal opening.

"YES!" Tavoian couldn't help shouting, but that was tempered by the AI.

THE ROVER IS IN A LOW POWER STATE.

Immediately Tavoian took control of the ISV and the rover, and began the recovery of the AI. He didn't breathe easily until the ISV was safely in the main lock of Recon three, a good half hour later. While the lock was being pressurized and the temperature slowly raised, he had the rover's images uploaded to the ship's AI.

Then he began to watch them, from the beginning, so that he had some idea where the AI had guided the rover. The first views were what he had already seen before the fiber-optic line had separated. After that, the AI followed the general guidelines he'd set up, and worked itself "down" another set of hexagons, then out into another blank wall, then back and down, and into what looked to be another dead end . . . but wasn't, because in the corner of what initially appeared to be a corner, there was an open hexagonal "door," except narrower than those open above, perhaps a little less than a meter across at its widest point. The passage-way ran straight onward beyond the door, if roughly paralleling the outer hull.

The rover continued through the opening and along the passageway for less than twenty meters before coming to another narrow hexagonal door on the outboard side of the passageway. The rover entered and scanned the chamber beyond—the first actual semirectangular space in the artifact—some thirty meters wide and thirty high, it extended at least 150 meters in length, and the side away from the rover curved slightly, suggesting that it might lie directly beneath the outer hull. There were also ridges protruding less than half a meter from the hull-side surface, forming a rectangle slightly smaller than the surface itself. From what Tavoian could tell from the rover's scanning light, the surfaces were all green, possibly slightly lighter in color than those on the outside.

A *cargo or launching lock?* While that was Tavoian's first thought, outside of the suggestion of lock doors created by the protrusions, there was nothing else obvious in the chamber.

The AI completed its scan, returned to the narrow passage, and continued onward for another fifty meters to where the passage turned left and ended at another hexagonal opening. The "door" was fully open, assuming that the false color images the ship's AI had created for Tavoian earlier corresponded to full opening, but what the rover's image revealed for the first time was that a section of the interior edges of the opening were not regular. The corners of the opening that would have been at the base, assuming the artifact had been rotating for artificial gravity, were surrounded by uneven rounded masses of the same green material as the walls, as if someone or something had deliberately done so to keep the opening from closing. There was no sign of melting or other materials any higher.

As the rover moved through the defaced doorway and began to scan the immense chamber beyond, Tavoian swallowed even at the initial images. It took him a moment to place what he saw in perspective, especially with the limited beam width of the rover's light. What appeared to be an immense pillar or small tower jutted out in front of him, except that it was more than twenty meters away and extended toward what had to be the underside of the outer hull. The towerlike column, which also looked to be hexagonal, did not quite reach that underside, but stopped a few meters short of one end of what looked to be hexagonal funnel-like devices, possibly energy-focusing equipment, apparently just beneath the inside of the outer hull of the artifact. Unlike anything else Tavoian had seen in the artifact, that hexagonal pillar or tower was a pale gray.

As the rover moved farther into the huge chamber, Tavoian checked the other images. Standard radar showed nothing, but the laser scanner showed other columns protruding from the wall or barrier that separated the chamber from the remainder of the artifact. How many, he couldn't tell, but his gut instinct was that there were thirty-two—the same number as the slightly discolored circles revealed by Recon three's scanners. The rover slowly turned, and its scanners took in the area around it, but revealed nothing but bulkheads and decks, and the towerlike pillars. There were no fused masses, no other protrusions, and not even any debris, from what Tavoian could determine.

After moving to a point close to and beneath the first pillar, the rover again scanned the chamber, revealing more towers, then turned and began the return to the ISV. Tavoian checked the timing, then nodded. The rover was down to a little more than half power, and the AI had cut off the exploration. As the rover reentered the passageway paralleling the outer hull, Tavoian had the AI create programming for the route the rover had taken, so that it could be used again. Then he returned his attention to the screens showing the area around Recon three.

"Are there any other craft in detection range?"

NEGATIVE THIS TIME.

Tavoian considered what the AI rover had discovered. Although he had no way to prove it, his instincts told him that the columns were the discharge points of something, most likely the drives or engines that had propelled the original sphere.

"Can you determine where that drive or engine chamber is from the rover's track and data?"

AFFIRMATIVE.

"Display it."

An image of the silver side of the artifact appeared. After an instant, the false color image of the thirty-two circles appeared. Then a red dot appeared midway beside one of the circles closest to the edge of the silver circle, although that slightly discolored circle was a good fifty meters inboard of the long-severed edge.

It had been hard to judge the distance between the outboard end of the hexagonal pillar—or drive/engine shaft—and those massive hexagonal clamshell nozzle-doors or energy-focusing devices, or whatever they were, apparently just beneath the hull of the artifact, but it appeared to Tavoian that the barrier wall between the drive or engine output devices was more than fifty meters thick.

That can't all be wall. Are the drive systems or controls within that space? He didn't have an answer for his own question.

While he waited for the ISV and rover to warm up so that he could prepare them for the next investigation, he began to compose a message to the colonel, informing him of the latest findings. After he dispatched it, he noted that he still had no messages. That suggested not that he had none, but that any he did have were being delayed.

The colonel doesn't want you distracted.

With that thought, he went to find something to eat and drink.

He'd barely finished what passed for a sandwich—a chicken spread squeezed onto half a bagel, topped with a cheese spread, and captured by the top half of the bagel—when the message system chimed and a horn squawked loudly enough that Tavoian almost spit out the last bite. He had no doubt that the urgent message was from the colonel.

It was.

> Tavoian, Christopher A.
> Major, NSC
> NSS-21/Recon Three
> Re: Last Report
>
> Last report received, along with data and images.
>
> More detailed information absolutely necessary. Request greater investigation of technological capabilities embodied in artifact.
>
> Estimate arrival of Sinese longliner at artifact at approximately 0814 UTC on 11 November 2114. Sinese Federation readying full exploratory expedition. Timetable currently unknown.

More detailed information absolutely necessary? Tavoian shook his head. *Hasn't anyone read or understood what you've sent?* More likely, no one believed what he'd sent. *After all, how could anything manufactured or created be so strong that no human tool could penetrate it?*

Tavoian realized that he was being excessively cynical. The colonel was likely under great pressure to produce results. He immediately began to compose a reply.

> While all of the passageways connecting the hexagons in the section of the artifact entered from the dark green side appear to be open, so far investigations have revealed no objects at all in any passageways. The section of the artifact below the dark-entered side appears to be separated from the section beneath it by a bulkhead barrier extending across the entire artifact. Beyond the barrier is a space ranging in "height" from fifty to approximately 150 meters, as calculated along the center hexagonal shaft. Neither the laser nor the diamond nanorod drill will even scratch any of the material. To make matters more challenging . . .

Tavoian smiled wryly. Challenging was an understatement.

> ... all the surfaces of the object, interior and exterior, are so smooth that nothing adheres to them. With the rotation of the artifact no device can maintain position without power and thrusters.
>
> In addition, there are over ten thousand separate hexagonal compartments. The smallest measure twenty-five meters on a side and are five meters in height/width. So far, as noted in previous reports, searches have only found eighteen intact that also were left open, either deliberately or as a result of the event that apparently severed the artifact from a much larger craft. Of the hexagons that could be entered, the only objects found were those protrusions in five of the partly open intact hexagons. Since each hexagon is surrounded by passageways, it appears unlikely that all passageways can be explored within the time and resources set for the mission.
>
> While the rover and ISV are being repowered, another investigation is being prepared to probe other possibilities for obtaining entrance to sealed areas. Will report on the results when that probe has returned.

What else can you say?

Tavoian sent the message, then headed to the main lock to mount the tunable laser and the sampling module on the ISV.

Positioning and mounting the tunable laser on the ISV took Tavoian more than half an hour. Surprisingly, setting up the sampling gear took slightly less time, but he also had to load two signal repeaters. When he closed the airlock and returned to the control section, he immediately checked for another message from the colonel. Thankfully, there wasn't one. In fact, there were no messages.

Still wanting to keep you undistracted and on task.

A scan of all screens and inputs from the cubesats revealed nothing new about or around the artifact. There was also no sign of the Sinese longliner. After satisfying himself that there was nothing requiring his immediate attention, Tavoian did a last check to make certain the ISV was fully repowered, then opened the outer door of the main lock and dispatched the ISV to return to the artifact.

Once it neared the artifact, he guided it back to a position less than a meter from the first opening that the rover had investigated.

"Tune the laser to the same wavelength reflected by the surface imme-diately adjacent to the opening," Tavoian ordered the ship's AI.

LASER TUNED.

"Direct the beam across the surface adjacent to the opening. Monitor results at all wavelengths."

THERE IS NO REACTION.

"Have the laser run the test and reaction pattern."

PROCEEDING WITH TEST.

The test pattern was merely a preprogrammed series of wavelength pulses.

Less than two minutes later, the AI reported, THERE WAS NO REACTION.

"What about reflected light? Did the amount of light reflected vary at any wavelength from the amount expected?"

THERE WAS A DECREASE IN EXPECTED REFLECTIVITY WHEN THE LASER BEAM MATCHED THE COLOR OF THE SURFACE BESIDE THE OPENING. THAT DECREASE WAS LESS THAN ONE PERCENT.

A slight decrease in reflectivity? "Was that the result of scattering from a rougher surface?"

THE SURFACE DOES NOT VARY NEAR THE OPENING.

"What about absorption and retention as heat?"

THE SURFACE TEMPERATURE REMAINS UNCHANGED.

"Conduct the same test on the surface three meters farther away from the opening."

After several moments, the AI replied, COMMENCING TEST.

Tavoian waited.

THERE WAS NO REACTION. THERE WAS NO DECREASE IN EXPECTED RE-FLECTIVITY WHEN THE LASER BEAM MATCHED THE COLOR OF THE SUR-FACE OR THE COLOR OF THE SURFACE BESIDE THE OPENING.

"Try the tests on the openings to the next chamber."

The AI directed the ISV to the opening of the adjoining hexagonal chamber. The results were the same. While Tavoian had hoped for a more definitive reaction, he wasn't surprised. Even if his hypothesis happened to be correct, the odds were that all the "doorways" on the exposed sec-tion of the former interior of the original sphere had been extensively damaged by the force that had severed the artifact from the larger sphere. If so, chambers farther from the severing might exhibit a different re-sponse. But then, his hypothesis could be wrong . . . or the damage could have affected the entire artifact.

"Move the ISV to the center shaft."

MOVING ISV.

Tavoian had the ISV deploy a repeater just inside the shaft so that it should remain for a time despite the artifact's rotation. Then he directed the ISV down two levels where he deployed the second repeater before moving the ISV down the passageway to the nearest "doorway," as indicated by the false color image overlay provided by the ship's AI.

"Direct the laser beam across the surface adjacent to the opening. Monitor results at all wavelengths."

THERE IS NO REACTION.

"Have the laser run the test and reaction pattern. Then report on reflected light."

THERE WAS A DECREASE IN EXPECTED REFLECTIVITY WHEN THE LASER BEAM MATCHED THE COLOR OF THE SURFACE. THAT DECREASE WAS FIVE POINT FOUR PERCENT. THERE WAS NO CHANGE IN SURFACE TEMPERATURE OF THE AREA WHERE THE LASER FOCUSED.

Five point four percent? Compared to one percent at the first two openings? "Repeat the test at twice the focus time and report."

REPEATING TEST.

Once more, Tavoian waited.

DECREASE IN EXPECTED REFLECTIVITY WAS SEVEN POINT SIX PERCENT.

"Was there any increased scattering?"

NEGATIVE. LACK OF RETAINED HEAT AND LACK OF SCATTERING INDICATES QUANTA TRANSFER BENEATH SURFACE.

What Tavoian would have called the door-frame section was actually absorbing some of the light. *After how many years in deep space?* He definitely had something . . . but what? From what he recalled of his physics, generally only metals exhibited the photoelectric effect . . . *But that's increased reflectivity, not decreased.* He frowned. If the greenish material absorbed the light, then it was photoconductive . . . but how could it absorb just part of a single wavelength light? From what Tavoian knew, that was contrary to physical laws of reflectivity, or certainly not normal. All those photons had to be going somewhere, but they weren't heating the material. What was the material doing with the light? Where was it going?

Since only the "door frames" exhibited that apparent photoconductivity, at least so far, they had to have been engineered that way, especially since the longer the exposure, the greater the decrease in reflectivity, and presumably, the greater the absorption. Greater absorption would have made sense for a solar cell gathering sunlight, but how could the material only accept part of the photons at a given wavelength? How did that make sense on what would have been the interior of the spacecraft? And the artifact had to have been part of a spacecraft, Tavoian was convinced.

Because he worried about maintaining signal contact with the ISV, given the rotation of the artifact, Tavoian immediately moved the ISV down the shaft to the barrier bulkhead, where he again searched the openings directly off the shaft until he found one that showed the false color hexagon suggesting a doorway, this one displaying the large backward "Z." When he focused the laser on it, though, and began to run the tests on it, the "Z" flared a color that Tavoian could only have described as fluorescent headache purple, a color that certainly conveyed, at least to Tavoian, that proceeding was unwise, if not forbidden. It certainly made him not want to proceed.

SIGNAL STRENGTH WEAKENING.

Tavoian immediately recalled the ISV, instructing it to recover the repeaters on the way back. He'd barely issued the commands before the images from the ISV vanished. Then he worried. Ten minutes passed before the images resumed, as the ISV cleared the center shaft on the dark side of the artifact.

At that moment, he realized he'd done nothing to gather samples, or even look for them. He checked the power remaining to the ISV, then decided to investigate the possibility of debris, detritus, or small fragments of anything, first, around the partly open hexagons where he'd begun the laser testing, and then, if the first locale proved fruitless, around the edges of the dark green material, where the silvered hull ended.

The ISV's scanners and even enhanced images revealed nothing in either place.

The entire day's events, along with the loss of IR capabilities, suggested that the green material was not only incredibly smooth and hard, but also nonconducting. *Except how can a material that's photoconductive, even selectively so, be so nonconductive that it doesn't even generate static electricity after all these years of being bombarded by various forms of electromagnetic radiation?*

Tavoian had the ISV attempt sampling in other areas, but it fared no better. There didn't appear to be any loose material anyplace where the ISV could reach it. That meant rigging up the rover with fiber-optic line and looking in the corners of the open and more accessible hexagonal chamber. With the ISV's power running out, he recalled it to Recon three.

By the time the ISV was back in the lock, it was well after 1900 UTC, and it would be another standard hour before Tavoian could even begin to ready it for another reconnaissance foray. That would give him time to send another report to the colonel. But how could he word what he had discovered in a way that made sense but that was neither sensationalistic nor excessively understated?

With a long breath that was not quite a sigh, Tavoian settled himself in the control couch and considered how to word his report. Then he began to compose it. When he finished, he displayed it on one of the screens and began to read it over, concentrating on the key sections.

... Certain surfaces appear to be entry points. They are identifiable, as noted previously, by a minute and barely detectable
difference in coloration. When a laser tuned to the frequency
of the reflected light is focused on those surfaces a portion of
the directed light, but only a portion, appears to be absorbed,
rather than reflected or scattered. This suggests some form of
photoconductivity. One "doorway" exhibited a bright purple
symbol similar to a reversed "Z" when the laser focused on it
at the selected wavelength ... Further investigation of this will
be undertaken, but a more complete examination may require
high-powered and intensive light sources greater than those
used in the initial investigations ... also, the green material
shows no differentiation under IR scans ... renders IR useless to date inside the artifact ... So far no loose material of
any sort that could be sampled and analyzed has been discovered. Searches for material that can be sampled will be
continued ... All images and records since the last update
are attached ...

After reading the message again, Tavoian thought about changing it,
decided there was no need to, and sent it. Next came a message to Alayna.
He'd decided that she might be able to offer some insights—assuming
the colonel agreed and would allow Tavoian's message and attachments
to go through—and possibly even some suggestions. *Since you're going
to need all the intelligence and help you can get.*

Alayna—
As you must know by now, I'm part of the Noram effort to
investigate your discovery. It is definitely an artifact, and does
not appear to be anything created by any known human civilization. So far, no tool I have will make an impression on
any surface, and there are no obvious artifacts or technological objects, except for the entire artifact itself. Certain surfaces seem to exhibit photoconductivity, since the total of
reflected and scattered light from a laser focused on them at
certain wavelengths shows a decrease in energy from that reaching the surface, and there is no corresponding increase in surface temperature ...

Should you go into more details? He decided against it, not in the body
of the message.

My initial feeling is that any technology that exists is subsumed within the interior bulkheads and decks, although that could be wishful thinking . . .

When he finished the message, he attached some, but far from all, of the images and data he had sent to the colonel, and then dispatched it. He had no idea whether the colonel or the Donovan Base censorship would allow its retransmittal, but hoped they would.

Then he pulled himself down to the passenger section and the main lock, where he began to reprogram and reequip the AI rover and repair the fiber-optic line system in order to allow the rover to view and scout corners in the upper-level hexagons. By the time he finished, the ISV had warmed enough for him to open the inner lock door and to begin to reconfigure the ISV. Since the ISV had not finished recharging when he finished, which included reprogramming the AI rover and repairing the fiber-optic line, he fixed a sandwich of various substances, ate it, which amounted to washing it down with water from the squeezebottle, and then tidied up the air of the control space with a sticky pad.

By the time Tavoian got the ISV ready for another sortie and sent it off, it was well past 2130 UTC. He sat, as much as floating half-strapped to the control couch could be considered sitting, in front of the screen displays and ate what passed for cheese-flavored crackers and sipped water from the squeezebottle while he watched the artifact grow larger in the image relayed from the ISV. The sampling module mounted on the ISV contained a gas chromatograph, a mass spectrometer, and a tunable laser spectrometer, all of which focused on a sampling drawer that, when material was placed in it by the rover, could supply a wide enough range of heat to enable the analyzer to identify a wide range of chemical compounds and determine the ratios of different isotopes of key elements.

Once the ISV was in position just above the opening into the hexagon that contained the apparently undamaged protrusions, Tavoian turned the controls over to the AI. "Investigate the corners. Have the rover gather any debris or particles possible."

The rover, again trailing fiber-optic line and guided by the AI, used its thrusters to maneuver through the meter-wide opening, then turned toward the corner closest to Recon three of the two that were nearest to the opening. Needless to say, there wasn't a trace of anything large enough to be picked up by the rover's scoop or sticky pad, and the ship's AI guided the rover to the other upper corner.

MATERIALS DISCOVERED. FIRST SAMPLE PLACED IN DRAWER.

While the sampler heated, Tavoian checked the screens and long-range radar. There was still no sign of the Sinese longliner, not that he expected it before the following morning. He kept waiting until the data stream began.

"Summarize the results from the first sample."

SAMPLING ANALYSIS INDICATES THE PRESENCE OF SILICON CARBIDE, WATER ICE, POLYCYCLIC AROMATIC HYDOCARBONS, CARBON GRAINS, AND SILICATE PARTICLES.

"That's just standard circumstellar dust, isn't it?"

AFFIRMATIVE.

"Nothing else?"

NEGATIVE.

"Try the second sample."

SAMPLER CYCLING.

Tavoian waited.

SAMPLING ANALYSIS INDICATES THE PRESENCE OF SILICATE PARTICLES, WATER ICE, POLYCYCLIC AROMATIC HYDOCARBONS, NITROGEN, CARBON GRAINS, PALLADIUM, AND SILVER.

Palladium and silver? The silver and silica he understood. Alayna had indicated that both were present . . . but palladium? "Is there anything else?"

THE ANALYSIS REVEALS NO OTHER ELEMENTS.

"Are there other samples waiting for analysis?"

THERE ARE NO OTHERS.

"Have the rover gather more samples from the chamber."

Tavoian was having great difficulty keeping his eyes open by the time the rover finished scouring the hexagonal chamber. Only two of the remaining four corners contained material, and probably, from what he could determine, only a few grams worth. Still . . . he waited for the results.

The results were essentially the same as those for the last sample.

With that, Tavoian recalled the rover and the ISV. Once they were safely inside the main lock, he managed a deep breath. Any reports would have to wait. He dimmed the ship's lights. Almost immediately, his eyes closed.

43

HOTNEWS!
11 November 2114

[Image Deleted For Off-Earth Transmission]

Sinese Minister for Space Wong Mengyi—he's demanding that Noram and India share all their deep space discoveries! And without any Sinese sharing of theirs? Who could believe it? Maybe better said . . . who couldn't? Have to admire the man for his effrontery! The Sinese Minister for Space wants to be everyone's minister for space . . . and then some. Noram Prexy Dyana Yates is not amused.

[Image Deleted]

The latest realie of the year? That's—dare we say it—the full-bodied exposé *The Falwell Fiasco*. Producer Kuomo Allen-Farrow claims that every word is absolutely true. That may be true of the words, but what's full-bodied and exposed is anything but true. Too bad. Might have been interesting to see how the politician granddaughter of an evangelical colossus actually looked when she took Wall Street underwater, figuratively and literally.

[Image Deleted]

You want to read a book? Once this year? You could do worse than *Throne of Gamesters*. A bracing retelling of how one man united publishing and media by stooping to literary depths everyone thought were heights. Call it inverted perspective. Delightful, if horribly dated.

[Image Deleted]

Noram Secretary of Defense Olassen Trudeau has another rebellion to worry about. And it's not in Mongolia. This one's on his home territory. Rumor is that his military chief of staff is so exercised that DOEA's supposed nonmilitary fusionjets are getting refits—is that another word for militarized?—that he's gone straight to President Yates. Much good that's likely to do him.

[Image Deleted]

Here's one for you tree-cuddlers and squid-lovers! So much of Utah's Great Salt Lake has evaporated that the water's now too briny for even brine shrimp. In another fifteen years, all that will be left will be salt flats. It definitely won't be the place...if it ever was.

44

Sunday morning, Tavoian woke early, slaked his thirst with water from the squeezebottle, which he then had to refill, and immediately composed a message to the colonel, reporting the findings of the night before, essentially the fact that the small samples of free material inside the artifact seemed to represent some of the elements indicated by spectrographic analysis of light reflected from the object and possibly some elements that *might* indicate carbon-based life, but mostly represented an accumulation of circumstellar dust. He also attached all the analyses.

There were no messages, not that Tavoian had expected any, given the effective, if *de facto,* censorship and message management exercised over his communications by Donovan Base.

Since he hadn't done any exercises for the past four days, he ran through half an hour's worth, knowing that was far from sufficient, then ate while he considered what explorations might be most fruitful. With that in mind, once he finished eating he decided to take an inventory of resources. The efficiency of the solar cells had increased with the ever-decreasing distance to the sun, and that increase was even slightly more than projected. That had resulted in not having to use the auxiliary power unit, in turn meaning that the ship hadn't drawn down fuel supplies for shipkeeping.

The big surprise—except it really shouldn't have been one, Tavoian realized—was that the ISV and the rover had already gone through seven point three percent of the total thruster propellant stocks. *Because of the need to continually reposition themselves with relation to the artifact as it rotated.* Even so, going through seven percent of thruster propellant in the first three days of a mission projected to last almost another seven weeks . . . *At least.*

Was there any way to anchor the ISV to a spot above the artifact, given the smoothness of every surface? Abruptly, he shook his head. There certainly was a means to anchor the ISV, if only over the partly "open" hexagons, one he should have thought of earlier.

He made his way back to the cargo section and the extruder. There he programmed it to produce three lengths of heavy-duty carbon/nanorod tubing, each rod three meters long, close to the maximum length possible with the formulator aboard Recon three, which was why he needed three lengths. Then he programmed in five meters of carbon cable. Leaving the extruder to do its job, he returned to the control area.

SHIP APPROACHING. ETA ESTIMATED AT 0709 UTC.

"Is that the Sinese longliner?"

THE SHIP FITS THE PROFILE FOR SINESE LONGLINER.

More than an hour earlier than the colonel had expected. Tavoian immediately composed a short message to the colonel, noting the anticipated arrival, sent it, and then thought about what he should do next. "Focus scanners and optical imagers on incoming ship once it's in range for clear identification. Relay those images to Donovan Base."

COMMENCING TRANSMISSION.

Tavoian checked his two torps, making sure both were ready, if necessary. He wasn't about to undertake any immediate explorations, not with the Sinese approaching and not until he had his makeshift "space anchor" in place. As he waited for the Sinese vessel, he considered where else he might be able to position the ISV, besides over the hexagonal chambers whose "doors" had frozen in partly open positions. Finally, he asked the ship's AI, "How many openings has the rover encountered in the artifact that have widths of about a meter? Where are they?"

NINETEEN OPENINGS MEET THAT CRITERION. EIGHTEEN ARE IN THE HEXAGONAL CHAMBERS ADJOINING THOSE WHERE THE ROVER TOOK SAMPLES. ONE IS AT THE ENTRANCE TO THE LARGE CHAMBER ON ONE SIDE OF THE HULL THAT YOU SPECULATED MIGHT BE A LAUNCHING BAY FOR SOME FORM OF SPACECRAFT.

Tavoian wanted to shake his head. The only places where he could really anchor the ISV were near the chambers he had already investigated. *No one said this was going to be easy.* At the same time, he doubted any of those who had prepared Recon three had had any idea just how advanced the technology and materials seemingly used by the builders of the artifact really appeared to be.

Still . . . he might be able to investigate the photosensitivity to a greater extent. The "door frames" off the center shaft that had not been directly exposed to the force of whatever had sheared away the artifact showed greater photosensitivity than those that had. But the "doors" on the inner levels he had been able to reach were sealed closed. Before he tried there, given how much thruster propellant it would take, it might be better to test the idea on the partly open lower doors of the eighteen hexagonal chambers. The most obvious problem was that only the ISV was large enough to carry the tunable laser, but it was too large to enter any of the largely intact hexagons with open doors to get to the doors on the lower side. Going around the hexagon through the passageways bordering the hexagons was possible, but not without losing contact. He'd only been able to maintain contact with the ISV using two repeaters for a short time when he'd investigated the chamber doors right off the central shaft. Trying to go around the outside of those hexagons would take much longer, long enough that using the repeaters as he had before would result in losing contact long before he could do a test. *Unless you do some creative engineering and programming.*

As he headed back down to the crew area to make some changes and additions, he smiled wryly. He should have thought about reverse engineering sooner. *You've been thinking like a pilot, not a problem solver.* That brought up another thought. Wasn't there anyone more suited at Donovan Base? He shook his head. They'd all been trained for every possible set of problems dealing with fusionjets and space installations, not alien artifacts and high-technology archaeology.

The first thing he needed was three more of the long rods and almost fifty meters of the carbon cable, the fabricating of which would take a good hour more, if not longer. He programmed the additional items into the fabricator, and then set to work reprogramming, if slightly, one of the signal repeaters. Then he set up contingency programming for the ISV, largely along the lines of returning the way it had come until it reached a signal, or Recon three. Finally, he assembled the first "space anchor" by fastening the three rods already completed by the extruding fabricator together at their midpoints and with each set at sixty degrees from the next. Then he sealed the rods in position to form a spindly-looking starburst shape.

By that time, the second set of carbon rods was ready, and he fastened them into the second anchor. When he finished, with nothing more he could do to implement his preparations until more of the cable was fabricated and extruded, he returned to the controls, watching the monitors that showed the approach of the Sinese craft.

He couldn't see it on the visual screen until it was almost opposite Recon three, on the far side of the alien artifact. The Sinese longliner was a good two hundred meters in length, almost twice the size of Recon three. Tavoian watched for a moment longer, then dispatched a short message to the colonel announcing the arrival of the Sinese ship. There were no attempts at communication, and the other vessel appeared inert, although Recon three's systems detected scattered light, radiation, and other indicators that the Sinese unscrewed probe, if that was what it was, was busy scanning and trying to analyze the artifact.

THE SINESE SHIP HAS LAUNCHED HUNDREDS OF TINY PROBES. ALL ARE DIRECTED AT THE ARTIFACT.

Tavoian couldn't make out any of them visually even as he looked at an enlarged view of the longliner. "Let me know if it launches anything else, moves toward us, or does anything but sit there and monitor matters."

He went back to the passenger/work area to check on the cabling, but had barely reached it when the AI pulsed him.

YOU HAVE AN URGENT MESSAGE.

"From whom?"

COLONEL ANSON.

Tavoian hurried back to the controls and called up the transmittal, skipping over the headings and addresses to the body of the message.

> Continue investigations with deliberate haste. Do not attempt contact with Sinese craft, believed to be uncrewed. Do not initiate any maneuvers or actions that could be construed as hostile or provocative.

> Do stand ready to retaliate with all means at your disposal if the Sinese craft or any other vessel initiates measures against you or your equipment . . .

Any other vessel?

> . . . At present, we have no knowledge of other nations undertaking investigations of the alien artifact. That does not mean that others may not be doing so.

> The Sinese are preparing a much larger vessel, sixty percent larger than the standard longliner, which appears to be a crewed mission. Should Noram decide to follow up with such a mission, it would be helpful to have your recommendations for what equipment might be most important . . .

A super laser or particle beam that can cut through something harder than anything human beings have ever created . . . Tavoian couldn't put it quite that way, he knew.

> . . . speed in supplying such recommendations would be appreciated . . . Report all observed activity relative to Sinese craft . . .

When he finished reading the message, he looked up at the screens, but the longliner still appeared inert. "Has the fabricating extruder finished?"

IT IS FABRICATING CARBON CABLE. IT WILL FINISH IN TWENTY-TWO MINUTES.

"Thank you," Tavoian said dryly.

He might as well try to write up his recommendations in polite officialese while he was waiting. The first thing was to report the release of the hundreds of minute objects. The second was his evaluation of necessary equipment.

> . . . the laser employed in the initial evaluation of the artifact triggered a limited photosensitivity in what appeared to be mechanisms surrounding openings functioning as doors, the amount of that sensitivity apparently proportional to some degree to the intensity of the light, as reported earlier. Given the limited power of the tunable laser sent with Recon three, a far more powerful laser might better probe that photo-response . . .

> . . . the extraordinary durability of all surfaces of the artifact has presented another problem, since no equipment aboard Recon three has been able to scratch, much less penetrate, sealed spaces in the artifact . . .

> . . . the artifact appears, at least in terms of exteriors of surfaces, to be opaque to all electromagnetic radiation and may well, as part of its photosensitivity, actually absorb free radiation. Thus, any exploration within the artifact has required fiber-optic line as a means of control and conveyance of information on a real-time basis . . .

In the end, it took Tavoian more than forty minutes to craft and dispatch his observations and recommendations. During the entire time, the Sinese ship remained on the opposite side of the alien artifact, apparently scanning the artifact and receiving information from its miniatures.

"Can you detect what is being sent from the miniatures to the Sinese ship?"

THE SIGNALS ARE SO LOW-POWERED AND DIRECT-BEAMED THAT NOT ALL ARE DETECTABLE. RECORDING AND TRANSMITTING THOSE THAT ARE IS NOT POSSIBLE BECAUSE RESOLVING THE ENCRYPTION WOULD EXCEED SYSTEM PARAMETERS.

"You can't do that?"

THAT LEVEL OF ENCRYPTION WOULD DIVERT ESSENTIAL RESOURCES FROM THE MISSION.

Tavoian decided to get on with his next attempts at finding something else new about the artifact. He went back to the passenger/work space and continued preparing the ISV, which included removing the sampler gear, in order to have enough space for the AI rover, so that it could position the starbursts in place inside the two of the meter-wide openings in two of the adjoining hexagons that had traces of what was most likely fused equipment of some sort. Then he loaded the rover, the starburst assemblies he had constructed, with the heavier carbon cord.

What he'd rigged up was almost the reverse of what he'd had in mind originally. The two space anchors wouldn't anchor the ISV in place, but the heavy line between them would, in the middle of which was a signal repeater, to which one end of the fiber-optic line was connected leading to the spooling mechanism on the ISV. That arrangement would, if Tavoian had calculated correctly, allow him and the ship's AI to direct the ISV, with the tunable laser, down the larger outer passageway to the lower partly open doors and to run a series of photosensitivity tests on "door frames" that might not be quite as damaged as those more exposed.

Once the ISV was reequipped, he sealed the inner lock door, returned to the controls, where he opened the outer lock door and dispatched the ISV toward the artifact, watching the longliner closely to see if it responded in any way to the small craft. So far as Tavoian could tell, there was no response.

USE OF LOCK FOR REPAIRS AND DISPATCH HAS NOW USED TEN PERCENT OF RESERVE AIR SUPPLY.

The AI's calm announcement stunned Tavoian. *You've only been here three days and you've gone through that much?* Did they expect that he'd launch the ISV and never add equipment to it or repair it? *Another thing to consider.*

It took more than an hour for the rover to position the two tubing starbursts inside the openings and then return to the ISV. Almost another hour passed before the rover had positioned the signal repeater in the middle of the cable and the ship's AI could begin to direct the ISV down the "outside" passageway between the two hexagonal chambers.

A slim chance, but what else can you do with what you have?

Once the ISV was in position so that the tunable laser could focus on the side of the partly open door—the one directly below where one of the starbursts was positioned—Tavoian said, "Tune the laser to the same wavelength reflected by the surface immediately adjacent to the opening and direct the beam across the surface adjacent to the opening. Monitor results at all wavelengths."

THERE IS NO REACTION.

Based on what had happened before, that didn't surprise Tavoian, but he wanted to use the same steps as before. "Have the laser run the test and reaction pattern. Report on the reflected light."

PROCEEDING WITH TEST.

The AI reported after the test finished, THERE WAS A DECREASE IN EX-PECTED REFLECTIVITY WHEN THE LASER BEAM MATCHED THE COLOR OF THE SURFACE BESIDE THE OPENING. THAT DECREASE WAS SEVEN POINT THREE PERCENT.

Encouraging, it still doesn't tell you what's happening to that energy. "What about absorption and retention as heat?"

THE SURFACE TEMPERATURE REMAINS UNCHANGED.

"Try the tests on the openings to the next chamber."

The AI directed the ISV to the lower opening of the adjoining hexagonal chamber. The results were the same, down to the percentage points. While that tended to confirm the photosensitivity of the "door frames," and the fact that the doorways exposed to whatever force had severed the artifact from the larger sphere had less photosensitivity suggested damage . . . *But that could also be because they've spent thousands of years more directly exposed to solar and other radiation.*

"Focus the laser on the door frame at maximum intensity for the maximum time that will optimize the intensity and not damage the laser, its power supply, or any other part of the equipment or ISV. Not more than two minutes." Tavoian wasn't quite certain why he'd put in a time limit, but it felt right. "Report on the results."

FOCUSING.

Tavoian waited.

THE DECREASE IN EXPECTED REFLECTIVITY WHEN THE LASER BEAM MATCHED THE COLOR OF THE SURFACE BESIDE THE OPENING WAS ELEVEN POINT FOUR PERCENT. SURFACE TEMPERATURE REMAINS UNCHANGED. THERE IS NO RADIATION OR HEAT.

More than eleven percent? Where are those photons going?

"Is there enough fiber-optic line to reach the next lower opening?"

THE REMAINING LINE IS ADEQUATE IN LENGTH.

"Then direct the ISV there."

The ISV moved down another of the passageways set at sixty degrees from the junction . . . and the image went black.

"Frig!" Tavoian immediately checked the screens displaying the Sinese longliner. "What happened?"

THE SIGNAL WAS LOST. THE FIBER-OPTIC LINE INTO THE ARTIFACT REMAINS INTACT. OBSERVATION INDICATES IT HAS LOST TENSION.

"Cut off by another sharp edge."

THAT IS THE MOST LIKELY PROBABILITY.

Tavoian just hoped that the ISV followed its programming. He kept watching the monitors.

Eighteen minutes later, the image from the ISV resumed, showing a view of the signal repeater as the ISV approached it.

"Have the ISV and rover pick up the signal repeater and then return to Recon three."

RECOVERY UNDER WAY.

As the ship's AI handled the recovery, Tavoian drafted another message to Donovan Base, reporting the latest results, and the apparent lack of anything but miniature probe scouting by the Sinese longliner. Once he'd dispatched it, he wondered why he'd received no messages, especially from Alayna, but if the colonel hadn't relayed his message to Alayna, there was no way he was going to get a reply. He would have liked her insights. He would have liked insights from anyone. The way things were going, the colonel wanted results, but he wasn't exactly a font of suggestions, and so far, Tavoian wasn't getting any help in addressing the problems he faced.

One thing he did know. He needed more carbon cable if he wanted to do more explorations, even of the eighteen partly open hexagons. So he pulled and maneuvered his way down to the fabricator and set it to extruding more cable. He could reclaim the space anchors and reuse them.

With that done, he decided to get back to exercising, something that he'd skipped far too much for a pilot going to be in weightless conditions for far too long. It wasn't his favorite occupation, unlike some Space Service types, who gloried in it, but he definitely didn't want to pay the deferred price for not exercising.

He checked the message queue a last time.

Still no messages.

45

Sunday morning hadn't found Alayna any closer to discovering anything more about the multi-fractals. Although Marcel had recorded and classified more than fifty additional near-matches, not a single pair showed enough similarity that she could have claimed, or even indirectly hinted, that the repeated closeness of matches suggested something beyond coincidence. During the last lunar day, she'd had the AI take sample image comparisons and detailed measurements at higher solar latitudes as well, but the results were what any astronomer would have expected—that the convection activity tended to slow at higher latitudes, and that there were fewer examples of the multi-fractals. The only change was the slightly higher number of sunspots over the past few days, although sunspot numbers did vary considerably, even during a solar minimum.

When she checked the messages that morning immediately after getting to the control center, she'd noted only the news summaries, *HotNews!*, and a single personal message—from her father. She didn't expect anything from the Foundation on a Sunday, and if anyone there had sent a message on a weekend, the odds were high that the contents wouldn't be good. The news summaries were routinely ominous. *HotNews!* was worse, with the story about brine shrimp not surviving in what remained of the Great Salt Lake being the least foreboding. She still hadn't heard anything recently from either Chris or the Foundation, and she wasn't sure which silence was more worrisome.

She'd waited to read the message from her father until she'd checked all the systems and made certain that all the arrays were operating as they should be, which was especially important now that Farside was full dark. She didn't need anything else to go wrong, not with both Director Wrae and the Director-Generale apparently less than pleased with her performance . . . and her failure to act as politically astutely as they thought they would have. In addition, although her father responded quickly most of the time, getting a reply from him in little more than a day after her last message worried her.

Dearest Alayna,

I was extraordinarily relieved when I received your latest missive, especially after learning that the Sinese Federation has threatened to retaliate against all Noram space facilities if any weaponry is used by anyone against Sinese territory or facilities anywhere in the solar system . . .

Where did he get that idea? It had to have come from one of his friends in the Justice Department or somewhere in government. Except, Alayna realized, it wasn't an idea. It was a warning. She hadn't seen a word about that kind of threat in the news summaries over the last week, and she'd been perusing them down to the last word, mainly to see what news might have shown up about her discovery and to see when anyone reported Chris's ship. Were the Sinese that deluded? Or were they deluded at all? Did they really think the rest of the world would back down? *Except everyone else has, except for the Indians.* Yet, from Chris's messages, it didn't sound like the Noram Space Service was backing down.

. . . with what sounds like an attempt to establish a military installation on Europa, as well as an attempt to corner another source of deuterium, the Sinese are acting in a fashion congruent to the first Chinese empires. They have decided, it would seem, that their attempts to develop a commerce-based world hegemony will continue to be thwarted by the Indian-UAAS trade and technology alliance and by the residual inventiveness of Noram, not to mention Noram's unparalleled skills in financial chicanery and manipulation. They have avoided the worst effects of their twenty-first-century population decline by absorbing almost all of east and south Asia, but the comparative prosperity they created is leaving them, again, with a declining population. Thus, it is and has been with most empires, whether they have styled themselves as such or not . . .

Alayna smiled. She remembered all too many impromptu lectures on the lessons of history.

. . . One can only hope that saner minds will prevail, as they often have, but there have been enough times when few listened to the dry words of sanity. One way or another, you may be in one of the better locales as this scenario plays out, although I cannot imagine anyone wasting weapons on Lincoln, Nebraska, either. Even more I cannot imagine the Sinese spending resources on an isolated research installation on the far side of the Moon when there are other military and pseudo-military targets whose destruction and/or impairment would serve what they believe to be their ends more effectively.

You were always destined for discoveries, and although you downplay your efforts, it appears that you have discovered something very special, either an astronomical oddity or a potential alien artifact. I know I'm pontificating, but there are always new discoveries if you persevere, and not persevering would be a waste of your abilities . . .

She'd certainly heard those words before.

. . . The Court of Appeals still has not set a hearing date on the case dealing with the residual groundwater rights in the Ogallala Aquifer. It may be a most pedestrian suit in these times of high drama and potential alien artifacts, but most of life is pedestrian indeed, and should be addressed with as much care and industry as the most exciting and entertaining events flogged into oblivion by the media, not that I, or most truly thoughtful individuals, find much of what is flogged to be either useful or entertaining . . .

Alayna smiled again, despite the scores of times that she had heard various phrasings of those words.

. . . and for all of my pedantries, you must know that they are among the few ways I can express my concerns, my love, and my support for you and for your dreams . . . and you should know that in these parlous times.

Her father hadn't offered an effusive closing. He hadn't needed to. She swallowed several times, then blotted eyes that she hadn't realized, at first, were watering.

He's worried. Truly worried. She'd never gotten a message quite like that from him.

After several moments, she blew her nose and checked her messages. Still nothing from the Foundation or from Chris, and it would be almost two weeks before the Moon and the optical array would be in position for her to confirm for herself that her alien object had company. There had been enough media reports about both Noram and Sinese probes, with no denials, that she was fairly certain of what she'd see. There might even have been images in the Earthside media, but without a change in comm systems and protocols, the only image comm traffic from COFAR was one-way—back to Earth. But since there were no references to images, she had doubts that any had yet appeared.

In the meantime . . . Her lips quirked. For all of her father's often heavy-handed advice, he was right about continuing to seek new discoveries, and that meant coming up with either another approach to her solar conundrum, or a new way of looking at or interpreting the images and data that she already had.

At that moment, the comm chimed, indicating an incoming message. She immediately called it up, smiling as much in relief as with pleasure when she saw the sender.

She immediately began to read.

> Alayna—
> As you must know by now, I'm part of the Noram effort to investigate your discovery. It is definitely an artifact, and does not appear to be anything created by any known human civilization . . .

Despite her speculations, her mouth opened. It was one thing to think that he was there. It was another to have it confirmed by him. She kept reading. Then she got to the attachments—or rather the statement that prefaced them in bold lettering.

> **THE ATTACHED FILES ARE CLASSIFIED MATERIALS INTENDED FOR THE RECIPIENT SOLELY FOR PROFESSIONAL USE. THEY ARE NOT TO BE RETRANSMITTED OR COPIED. NOR ARE THEY TO REMAIN IN PERMANENT STORAGE. FAILURE TO OBSERVE THESE PRECAUTIONS COULD RESULT IN PROSECUTION UNDER THE NORTH AMERICAN SECURITY ACT OF 2109.**

Alayna immediately created a special temporary directory in her own personal directory and shifted the files there, rather than copied them, although technically she knew she'd actually copied and then destroyed.

She was speechless as she read the report Chris had sent, as well as the images. *A fragment, just a section, of an immense spacecraft . . . and who knows how long . . .* She stopped.

"Marcel . . . what do your calculations show now for the probable orbital period of 2114 FQ5?"

"Thirteen thousand fifty-three years."

"I thought you had calculated eleven thousand . . ."

"There is more observational data. The object's speed is also faster than originally calculated."

Alayna frowned. "There shouldn't be that much difference. Even if the object is more massive, gravitational acceleration doesn't vary. Albedo might . . ." She shook her head. Reflecting shouldn't matter with the number of observations they had.

The AI usually wasn't that far off in calculations. Then again, neither she nor the AI had ever run across an alien artifact before. No one had.

After her first quick reading of the attachments and another reading of Chris's message, she had even more questions. His message to her had been delayed almost a full day, and the preface to the attachments was official, and in a different type style, suggesting that either someone else had added it . . . or that Chris had done so in a way to suggest that. She had her doubts that he would have done that, but the delay did indicate to her that his messages were being scanned before being transmitted, and that suggested they had been initially sent by a more secure means.

So why are they letting you see this material? Alayna feared very much that it was because the Space Service didn't have any good suggestions for Chris. The problem was that, at least at first, and second, reading she didn't either. Materials so hard lasers couldn't leave a mark on them, but materials doped or modified so sections exhibited selective photosensitivity, linked to a wavelength differential of perhaps as little as a nanometer? After more than fourteen thousand years?

Who or what built something like that? And who or what was so much more powerful than those builders that it could slice through such materials? Alayna shivered, very conscious of just how insignificant she felt after considering those questions.

She also had no answers for Chris—or for whoever had let her see all the documentation, an indication of how worried and desperate the Space Service had to be. Yet . . . she had to see if she could come up with something . . . somehow.

46

HOTNEWS!
12 NOVEMBER 2114

[Image Deleted For Off-Earth Transmission]

There's an alien spaceship headed our way. Does it have real aliens? That glittering white object you see is what's left of an ancient spacecraft. You heard it here first! It's just a piece, and it's two kilometers across! The Sinese and Noram exploratory ships are both circling the remnant. No one's saying anything. Maybe they can't. Meanwhile, it's headed toward our sun at more than one hundred forty thousand kilometers per hour and accelerating. Might better be called the Solar Express. Did we say that before? It's worth repeating...

[Image Deleted]

T'Yara Dya claims she's the first Mongolian of the realies. The first most highly exposed diva from Mongolia—that she can claim. With what she shows, anyone can see why she's a refugee. She's also said that there is no such thing as Mongolia First! She wants to expose that as a Sinese fabrication to justify killing successful Mongolian businesspeople and blaming the Indians. Did we mention that Dya has had her own tiffs with the execs in Bollywood...over exposure, no less?

[Image Deleted]

The Nielsen-Kelly Religious Freedom Foundation has been sued by a woman claiming to be the great-grandniece of one of the women for whom the Foundation was named. Seraphina Nielsen sought damages for defamation of her family name— or did until *Hot Phoenix* outed her, for the simplest of reasons. The original Nielsen was a scarlet woman—that is, she was a redhead—but she repudiated the LDS faith early in life. That's religious freedom. No one's heard of Seraphina since the court summarily dismissed her suit as frivolous, and won't, unless she wants to make a personal exposé. She might not be up for that kind of freedom.

[Image Deleted]

Indian Prime Minister Narahaj Ravindra isn't saying much. No one in New Delhi is. But the preparation of hardened command centers across India says enough. Did we mention a deep space impregnable fortress armed with doomsday missiles? Perhaps Sinese Head of State Jiang Qining should reconsider? Except he keeps saying that he's only protecting Sinese interests and property. Could it be he thinks the entire solar system is Sinese property?

[Image Deleted]

Those oily slicks seen in the middle of the North Pacific? They're the work of a rogue GMO outfit called Clean Earth. Seems that they've successfully engineered microbes that feed on plastic, especially on tiny grains. The only problem is that they break down the plastics into a version of the petrochemicals from which they were initially made. No more plastics, it appears, just natural oil slicks. But what happens if they reach Ottawa? No problem, claims Clean Earth. Those little bugs can only survive in salt water . . . for now, anyway.

RECON THREE
12 NOVEMBER 2114

When he woke up, for several moments, Tavoian had no idea what day of the week or month it was, and for a moment, as he found himself weightless, he even wondered what had stopped Donovan Base from rotating—before his memories dropped into place and he recalled that he was aboard Recon three, struggling to find a way to discover something meaningful about the alien artifact. Before he did much of anything, he fumbled with the pressurized heating tube that substituted for a kettle and made a strong batch of tea. After the third long swallow from the squeezebottle, when he felt as though his thoughts were slightly more focused, he checked all the monitors and systems, even though he knew the ship's AI would have alerted him if anything had been seriously amiss. Still, he was thinking fuzzily, and he immediately checked the CO_2 level. According to the monitors, the level was point five percent, below the long-term Spacecraft Maximum Allowable Concentration standard of point seven percent. So his problem wasn't CO_2. That, at least, was good.

There were no new messages, and the Sinese longliner remained in the same position as it had been relative to the artifact and to Recon three.

"Report on anything that the Sinese ship has done."

AT 0140 UTC, THE SINESE SHIP LAUNCHED A SMALL CRAFT SIMILAR TO THE ISV. IT HAS BEEN METHODICALLY SCANNING EVERY EXPOSED SURFACE OF THE ARTIFACT. AT THE PRESENT RATE OF COVERAGE, IT WILL TAKE 206 HOURS TO SCAN THE ENTIRE EXTERIOR.

"That long?"

IT COVERS THIRTY THOUSAND SQUARE METERS AN HOUR. THE EXTERIOR SURFACE OF THE FLAT SIDE EXCEEDS THREE MILLION SQUARE METERS, WITH THE CURVATURE—

"Enough. I trust your calculations." Again, Tavoian hadn't been alert enough to recall just how huge the artifact was, especially for being just a part of a spacecraft. "What else?"

THE SINESE LAUNCHED SMALL EXPLORATORY MODULES. THEY ATTEMPTED TO SETTLE ON THE ARTIFACT. THEY WERE NOT SUCCESSFUL.

"What happened?"

THE ARTIFACT ROTATED OUT FROM UNDER THEM. SOME WERE STRUCK
BY THE SURFACES AND WERE PROPELLED AWAY FROM THE ARTIFACT.
OTHERS REMAIN IN ORBIT AROUND THE ARTIFACT.

Tavoian couldn't help but smile, recalling what had happened with the
AI rover's first attempted excursion. *The artifact might show the Sinese
that they don't know as much as they think they do.* Tavoian had already
been made well aware of his own shortcomings—and that of the technology he was using—in dealing with the artifact. "How many did they
launch?"

FIFTEEN.

"That's all the Sinese have done so far?"

IT IS.

"They're waiting for instructions. Have you detected any communications?"

RECON THREE IS NOT IN A POSITION TO IDENTIFY OR ATTEMPT TO
INTERCEPT TIGHT BEAM BURST TRANSMISSIONS. NO OTHER KIND OF COM-
MUNICATION HAS BEEN DETECTED.

"Has anything else changed?"

THE INBOUND SPEED HAS INCREASED MORE QUICKLY THAN PROFILED.
RECON THREE AND THE ARTIFACT NOW HAVE A VELOCITY OF ALMOST
FORTY KAYS PER SECOND.

"Has additional power been required to maintain position?"

NO.

"Good." Tavoian nodded. He'd been briefed on the fact that the closer
they got to the sun the greater the speed that both Recon three and the
artifact would attain. Apparently, the calculations had been a little off.
That happened, no matter what anyone thought. He went on with preparing his makeshift breakfast, something called an egg croissant that
tasted like it had a nodding acquaintance with yeast and fowl. It did stop
his stomach from growling. Then he cleaned up, as much as he could,
and went aft to his work spaces where he used the special splicing tool
to rejoin the fiber-optic line severed by the previous day's exploration.
He wished the fabricator had been designed so that he could make more
of the line, but that was beyond its capabilities. He had five hundred meters of fiber-optic line, but that wasn't sufficient to go very far into the
artifact, even if he used it all. Who would have thought that five hundred
meters would be woefully insufficient?

Then, everything's turning out to be insufficient in one way or another.
He went back to work, modifying his space anchor system.

Two hours later, he was watching as the ship's AI guided the ISV through
the set of passages that bordered another of the partly opened hexagons.

The ISV encountered nothing new, and the test results were identical to the ones of the day before. By 1900 UTC, the ISV had tested the open doors on another five hexagons, and Tavoian's eyes were bleary, especially when he thought about the eleven with open doors remaining . . . and the thousands of sealed hexagons. The ISV had discovered nothing new, and the laser photosensitivity tests remained maddeningly identical.

He had just ordered the ship's AI to recall the ISV and recover the signal repeater when a chime announced an incoming message. Tavoian called it up. The body text was direct and to the point.

> Your report from yesterday received. Suggestions noted and appreciated.
>
> Please report soonest on Sinese expedition and any additional findings.
>
> Oversized and heavily shielded Sinese spacecraft departed high Earth orbit 2100 UTC yesterday, presumed to be crewed expedition to the artifact. ETA not yet determined.

Trying not to grit his teeth, Tavoian began to fix more tea before replying to the colonel. *He either doesn't understand what's out here or doesn't care.* Except that there was more to it than that, even if Tavoian couldn't verbalize it. And now he'd have to deal with a crewed Sinese expedition before long.

A chime announced another message, this one from Kit, but Tavoian decided not to read it until he replied to the colonel. He couldn't do anything about whatever Kit might say, and if it held bad news, he didn't want to deal with it before dealing with the colonel's "request," and if it held better news, he'd enjoy it more later.

His reply to the colonel, when he completed it a half hour later, was not that much longer than the colonel's initial message.

> Sinese expedition has sent fifteen [15] miniature rovers to artifact. All failed to maintain physical contact. Some propelled away by contact with the artifact's surface as it rotates, others in orbit for now. Sinese remote vehicle scanning all surfaces of artifact. AI calculates scanning will take eight more days [206 hours total].
>
> Additional investigations of other doorways to hexagonal chambers reveal no contents within and photosensitivity iden-

tical to that determined by previous tests of other doorways. Detailed results attached.

Only after dispatching the reply and finishing his tea did he open and begin to read the message from his sister.

> Dear Chris—
> Father and I were glad to hear that you are fine, wherever you are. Mother sends her best, but she thinks you're still piloting FusEx ships between Noram station and the Moon. Father and I tried to tell her you had a different duty, but she was insistent. She's increasingly frail, and we decided not to argue or persist. I do wish you were here, but I know that's not something you can change.

Tavoian nodded. Even if he had turned down the alien mission, he'd still have been stuck on Donovan Base . . . or worse.

> One of the more sensational media outlets—that's *HotNews!*—has announced that the asteroid your friend discovered is an alien spacecraft. They've even taken to calling it the Solar Express, and all the other media outlets are using the term. The whole idea of an alien spacecraft, or the remnant of one, is too ridiculous to consider. We live on a nondescript planet circling an unremarkable star in a galaxy that has over 200 billion other stars. Even if aliens did develop a means of propulsion that would attain a speed that made travel between solar systems vaguely practical—years instead of decades or generations— why would anyone want to come here? If I had to guess, I'd say that both the politicians and the media types are looking for a deus ex machina to rescue us from our own incompetence and paranoid selfishness. At least you're not involved in that foolishness.

Tavoian smiled wryly. *Just like Kit . . . so practical that there was sometimes no room for dreams.*

> The foolishness here is close to reaching insanity. I won't recap what you must get in the news summaries, but . . . there aren't any words to express my anger and frustration. Our collective grandparents didn't do enough to stave off environmental disasters, that's true, but they didn't actively act to destroy most of

the human race if they didn't get their way. There is a difference between stupidity and total insanity . . .

Is there? Doesn't willful stupidity border on insanity?

I just wish you had enough rank and position to influence matters . . .

Tavoian chuckled sardonically. Reason didn't matter when you dealt with people who wanted things their way, no matter what happened, and he doubted he'd do much better than many of those in office. *You can't even figure out a way into a big dumb object.* Except it was a big dumb object built and operated by long-dead and scientifically brilliant aliens.

He finished his sister's letter and immediately began a reply.

Dear Kit,
I wish I could be there, but where I am now is where I'll be stationed for at least another month, possibly two, no matter what happens. I'm so glad you can be with Dad and Mother. I cannot tell you how much I appreciate that . . .

When Tavoian finished the message and sent it, he decided to try another tack in dealing with the artifact—just listing what he had discovered about it, as well as a few speculations he thought were accurate, but could not prove. The listing took more than an hour, and his eyes burned even more by the time he put down the last words. It was also painfully short for such a discovery and momentous event in human history.

Every chamber but two is a flat hexagon, regardless of size, and most come in one of two sizes, rather unusual for a craft of such immense dimensions.

One of the two different chambers appears to have been an airlock, large enough to hold a spacecraft as large as Recon three, but there is no sign of double lock doors.

The other different chamber is filled with thirty-two hexagonal gray columns that might be a part of some drive system.

The only excessively large open spaces are those two chambers and the central shaft.

There is no indication of any provision for parks, natural environmental systems. Either the aliens did not need them or such spaces were contained in the larger missing part of the sphere.

All functional technology has to be within the impermeable bulkhead/deck structures or the few giant projections in the large chamber under the hull.

There do not appear to be pressure doors sealing various sections of the artifact, unless those two are concealed within the bulkheads/decks. Would they be necessary, given that the materials of the artifact are impermeable and impregnable?

In an odd fashion, all of the hexagons reminded Tavoian of a honeycomb, but no honeybee could have built and operated the artifact that rotated slowly, as it had for thousands of years, a few hundred meters from Recon three. What were the aliens? Incredibly high-tech analogues to honeybees, or "just" aliens who liked hexagons? *Both . . . or neither?*

He saved the list, then looked for something to eat. He was too tired to think or to do any more, even though he knew the colonel would have more questions by Tuesday. *Tomorrow is Tuesday, isn't it?*

48

Tuesday afternoon Alayna was still struggling with Chris's message and the information he had sent. She was also marveling at the images of the alien artifact. It was one thing to speculate on something's origin based on light patterns and spectrographic analysis; it was another to see detailed images showing the brightness of that silvered hull, and the incredible regularity of the former interior with the spaced rectangles that actually represented the sides of thousands of hexagons.

For all of that, it was clear to her that there was great risk—like legal prosecution and possibly even time in prison—for her to share that information with anyone, especially the Foundation, yet the Foundation was her employer, and she had, in effect, broken the agreement by sending the images from COFAR to Chris. *Isn't there a higher duty than just an employment contract?* Her lips twisted. She knew what her father the attorney would likely have said, words to the effect that the law seldom recognized higher duty because anyone could claim they were acting in accord with higher principles. He'd also said more than once that the legal profession was about law, not justice, and that fewer people worried about principles than their pocketbook, notwithstanding the fact that almost no one had a pocketbook anymore, just a personal asset balance.

The other problem was the implied obligation she had incurred by accepting the data and images from Chris, an obligation to attempt to offer Chris—and the Noram Space Service—some sort of advice or insight. And that was something she certainly wasn't about to tell the Foundation. It also bothered her that, because of the Moon's current position, she wouldn't be able to use the optical array to see 2114 FQ5—calling it an alien artifact still felt strange to her—for another ten days.

In the meantime, the only messages she had gotten from the Foundation involved time-sharing on both the solar observatory and the radio telescope. She was beginning to suspect that those were going to be the only kinds of messages she would get, unless there was a truly unavoidable reason that Director Wrae had to contact her.

At that moment, she saw that another message had arrived, and rather than wonder who had sent it while she tried to work on her own solar project, she called it up and began to read.

> Alayna—
> You win! Not in the way anyone wants to. I thought what happened to me at DAO was near the top for minimizing and undercutting, and I've seen enough how the more-ethical-than-you nonprofits really operate. Like what the Farside Foundation did to you this morning in this morning's *Times* story. Claiming that the Farside Foundation's lunar array was the first to discover 2114 FQ5 and bring the "Solar Express" to light . . . and not a word about you.

Alayna couldn't keep from wincing. *Not a word?* And the story hadn't even made any of the off-Earth news summaries?

> The most momentous astronomical discovery of the century, and they couldn't even mention your name. Those people aren't small. They're nanosized! I've already started a whispering campaign with all the people I know. Your friends at the Farside Foundation only thought they had fundraising problems.

Great! You'll get relieved before you even have a shot at discovering more about the multi-fractals.

Except it wouldn't happen that way. The Foundation couldn't afford the extra funds to search for another qualified academic grunt and then send someone to Daedalus a year earlier than planned, and the Basic Science Foundation would likely object as well. Much as Alayna liked Emma personally, she could see why the older woman had been through a few positions, despite her winning the Heineman Prize and the Eddington Medal.

> Just keep working on your other project. Remember that every negative reveals something about the positive.

That was so like Emma. *Every negative reveals something about the positive.* For a moment, Alayna smiled. Then she began to think . . . especially about Chris's problem with the alien artifact. How could he investigate something that large . . . what could he do that might reveal more about something almost impregnable and impermeable? She also couldn't help but wonder about the different values of Marcel's two calculations of the artifact's orbital period. Part of that might well have been because the assumptions made on the basis of the light reflected from the artifact did not match standard mass and density assumptions, and initially she had assumed it was a comet, and not a solid body . . . *Except it's not a solid body, not with all those empty hexagonal chambers.* She began to calculate.

Ten minutes later, she was frowning. Then she recalculated. Finally, she gave her estimated figures to Marcel and asked, "Assuming that the walls of each hexagon are five meters thick and that each hexagon is surrounded by a passageway three point five meters wide, what percentage of 2114 FQ5 is composed of solid material . . ."

She broke off the question. She had no way of knowing if the walls were solid, and if they weren't, which was more likely, what percentage was vacant and what was solid. Nor was there any way to determine density, not immediately, since without the ability to sample and measure the materials from which the artifact was constructed, only longer term observation of gravitational effects/impacts could provide mass data. The increase in velocity above what Marcel had initially calculated did suggest that the artifact had initially entered the inner solar system at a velocity considerably higher than that of either Oort Cloud or Kuiper Belt objects. But the artifact could have been constructed of impregnable lower density material or higher density matter, for all that she, or anyone else, could tell. There were ways to use spectrographic analysis to determine density, but all the ones she could think of required, in effect, something like a spark electrode or laser gasification, and the material of the artifact wouldn't react to either.

In the end, she didn't feel as though what she wrote was all that helpful.

> Dear Chris,
> From the information you sent, it appears that a certain percentage of single frequency light is absorbed by certain surfaces of the artifact for purposes or reasons that are not obvious . . .

Is that an understatement!

> . . . You might consider determining if that surface reflects full spectrum light, or sunlight in the same fashion. I cannot say what that might indicate, except that it would confirm that the properties might definitely be engineered and possibly to

what end. A comparative analysis on the silvered hull section and around the "circles" on the hull that you mentioned also might offer some information. Such measurements also might reveal why the artifact has an albedo higher than can be accounted for so far.

I'm not a materials scientist, but from what you've written, I think someone ought to consider, if they haven't already, that whoever built the artifact had the ability and technology to construct materials up from the most basic of forces. Nothing else I can think of would explain what you've discovered . . . unless I'm overlooking something, which is always possible. I once read that a twentieth-century politician quipped something to the effect that all problems offer opportunities, and that he faced what appeared to be insurmountable opportunities. I hope our "opportunities" are more opportune and surmountable.

I have my doubts as to whether these suggestions will prove helpful, but I do feel that they will at least remove possibilities and narrow the focus of where further inquiries might proceed. In thinking about the difficulties you face, I was reminded of a few words from my current favorite quote source:

Oceanic coastlines are fractal. Down to the tiniest level, they're fractal. How amazing is that? Except, when you say something like that as a scientist, no one except a fraction of the population, any population, knows what you mean, and those who do are all scientists, and half of them want to dispute it or qualify it, while the politicians deny it or ignore it out of habit and unwillingness to expand their horizons beyond the next election.

I couldn't find a quote like that, well, not exactly, about astrophysics and space, although I recall there is one, somewhere, but I must be remembering it wrong, because even searches don't show it. Your sister Kit might appreciate this quote as well.

My very best to you, and my hopes that you don't encounter any more of such special opportunities.

After finishing the message to Chris and sending it, Alayna was almost relieved to get back to working on her own seemingly intractable problem of trying to discover something—anything!—new about the mechanism of multi-fractal mini-granulations.

49

RECON THREE
14 NOVEMBER 2114

Wednesday morning came with the piercing sound of an alarm. Tavoian jolted into a semi-upright position, kept from floating around the control spaces by his sleeping bag and the loosely fastened restraint straps.

"Report!" Tavoian's words came out half hoarsely, half squeaked.

THREE REMOTE UNITS ARE APPROACHING.

Tavoian coughed and cleared his throat. "From the Sinese longliner? Full display."

THE UNITS DEPARTED THE SINESE LONGLINER FORTY-TWO MINUTES AGO.

Simultaneously with the words, an image appeared on the control display, showing three widely separated objects, each with a squat cylinder mounted on a rectangular box with miniature thruster ports on all surfaces, essentially spy-eyes, or the equivalent, attached to a thruster pack of some sort.

THE UNITS ARE THRUST-BRAKING.

"How far away are they?"

TWO HUNDRED TEN METERS.

"Are they still closing?"

NEGATIVE. THEY ARE MAINTAINING SEPARATION AT 205 METERS.

"Notify me immediately if they change position." Given just the time it had taken the small devices to cover the distance between the Sinese spacecraft and Recon three, Tavoian was relatively confident that they were just what they seemed to be. The slow speed meant they didn't have to use much propellant. He also suspected that at least one of the spy-eyes was focused on Recon three's main lock. Their most likely purpose was to give the Sinese warning if Recon three attempted anything that appeared hostile. "Is the Sinese scanning of the artifact continuing?"

SCANNING CONTINUING.

"Are there any other detectable activities being undertaken by the Sinese?"

ONE SMALL REMOTE ISV ENTERED THE CENTRAL SHAFT OF THE ARTIFACT

FOUR HOURS AND ELEVEN MINUTES AGO. IT RETURNED TO THE SINESE
CRAFT TWENTY-SEVEN MINUTES AGO. DELAY WAS PROBABLE SIGNAL LOSS
WHEN ARTIFACT ROTATED. RETURN OCCURRED WHEN CENTRAL SHAFT
FACED SINESE SPACECRAFT.

So it's not just our signals. Except Tavoian had never thought that, but
he was perversely gratified to know that the Sinese had apparently not had
any better fortune than he had with transmitting signals inside the artifact
and had also not thought about the total opacity of the alien artifact. He
did wonder why the Sinese hadn't observed what he had done the day
before with the signal repeater as he had finally finished investigating the
last of the eighteen hexagons . . . except maybe their AIs weren't that bright
or whoever was monitoring things from wherever hadn't seen what he'd
done, or hadn't understood what it meant. He had found some more
detritus and debris, and analyzed it, but the results were discouragingly
similar to the earlier analyses. He just hoped that someone—Alayna or a
DOEA scientist at Donovan Base, if there was one there—would offer a
suggestion. That assumed that the colonel had let his message to Alayna
go through . . . and that she had a viable suggestion.

So far, he'd had no response to the report he'd sent the night before,
but since the colonel had ordered him to report Sinese activities, he immediately began to compose a message.

> Recon three under close surveillance by three remote spy-eyes.
> Spy-eyes do not appear to be armed. Images attached.
>
> From observation, Sinese longliner has experienced difficulty
> in maintaining direct control of probes when lines of trans-
> mission are blocked. They also cannot maintain physical con-
> tact with outer surfaces of artifact.
>
> Recon three was initially required periodically to use drives
> to maintain station on alien artifact, but not in the last few
> days . . .

That bothered Tavoian. According to his basic pilot training, gravity
had the same force of attraction for any object, regardless of mass. *So
why had the artifact seemingly been attracted slightly more strongly than
Recon three? And what had changed?* Because he just might have missed
or forgotten something, he wasn't about to ask those questions, just send
the observation.

Once he finished the message he dispatched it immediately, and then
fixed himself a squeezebottle of hot tea, hot meaning that it didn't im-

mediately cool to sickeningly lukewarm, followed by preparing and eating a pseudo-ham and cheese omelet on a passable bagel. Then he exercised, both because he knew he needed to and because none of the remaining tests or explorations that had been suggested and sent with Recon three by the DOEA science types were possible because of the artifact's properties. He also thought the exercise might get his blood flowing and metabolism speeded up, which just might help with his own creative processes.

One thing was certain. He wasn't about to waste thruster propellant in attempting to gather more samples of material. Going back for materials observed in trying other tests was one thing, but given how little loose material there was, just looking blindly for it didn't seem to make much sense. He also hoped he could keep use of the lock for repairs and equipment changes to a minimum, since he'd already used almost twenty percent of reserve air supplies.

He had finished a solid hour of exercise and had done his best to cool down and clean up by the time he received a response from the colonel, along with a message from Alayna. Tavoian read the one from the colonel first.

> Sinese Space Ministry lodged a complaint with DOEA two hours ago, declaring that you were jamming their transmissions to their research probes. DOEA replied at 0714 UTC that the artifact is opaque to all electromagnetic signals. DOEA also made complaint and reply public. No response yet from Sinese.

> Be advised that Sinese are seeking any pretext to use force or to declare that DOEA and/or Space Service have militarized space beyond Earth.

> Sinese expedition likely to arrive by 16 November 2114. Report arrival soonest.

By the sixteenth? How are they managing that? Part of the shorter travel time was that the artifact had traveled in-system and Earth had moved closer to it, but that time was still less than a Noram fusionjet would have taken.

> DOEA science board requests more sampling be attempted, and suggests using laser at full power on narrow surface near severed edge of hull to obtain minimal sample . . .

*That **might** work.* It was at least worth a try.

... board also suggests inspecting rim-interior interface as potential location for loose or trapped material . . .

When Tavoian finished with the colonel's message, he immediately
composed and sent a short acknowledgment that also asked the colonel
to convey his appreciation to the DOEA science board. Then he began
to read the message from Alayna. He found himself nodding at her suggestions, although he wondered if the laser measurements would actually reveal anything new about the material factors behind the silvered
side of the artifact having a higher albedo. Yet, whatever the results might
be, if enough brilliant minds studied them, there just might be someone
who might tease something meaningful from data that, to Tavoian, was
just too often inscrutable numbers and patterns. The fact that the colonel had let his messages go through to Alayna was an indication that
he thought she might be one of those brilliant minds . . . and that the
DOEA science types were almost as perplexed by the artifact as Tavoian
himself.

He couldn't help but smile at her quotation about the fractal nature
of ocean coastlines, and he saved the quote to his personal storage so that
he could send it on to Kit. She'd appreciate it.

Then he stretched and headed aft. Between the DOEA science board
and Alayna, he had a good day's work cut out for him . . . and maybe a
lot more, given the circumference of the artifact where the shimmering
silvery hull ended, well over six kays, that the ISV would have to inspect
to see if there were any sampling possibilities. It would take some work
to reconfigure the ISV so that it could handle the laser, the sampling array, and the AI rover needed to recover any scraps for sampling. But once
he changed the configuration, the ISV wouldn't need any additional re-
working for a time. *You hope.*

Reconfiguring the ISV so that the sampler and the tunable laser array
were on the same side took another hour's doing and some ingenious fas-
tenings, but by a little after 0900, the ISV was once more on its way over
to the artifact, on a course that avoided coming too close to the Sinese
spy-eyes. Tavoian could only hope that whoever or whatever was monitoring the feeds from the Sinese spy-eyes would be able to understand
that the ISV was not making hostile moves toward the spy-eyes or the
longliner.

Initially, as the ISV neared the rim of the alien artifact, the image from
the ISV's optical system showed what appeared to be a clear and sharp
demarcation. On one side was the dark green material of the interior. On
the other was the silvery, metallic-looking, and seamless hull. But as the
ISV's scanner came even closer to that edge, Tavoian could see that it was

just slightly rounded, as he had earlier determined for the edges of the hexagonal chambers that had been sliced open. Still, if the AI guided the ISV all the way around the circumference there was a chance, just a chance, that there might be a sliver hanging loose . . . somewhere.

Another hour passed as the AI monitored the optical and infrared scans of the seam where the green and silver had been sheared side by side and as Tavoian intermittently considered whether to stop the methodical approach to scanning the artifact, while also watching the latest efforts by the Sinese probe. Those consisted of a good thirty small and self-guided spy-eyes descending into the artifact, heading down various passageways . . . and vanishing.

The brute force approach. Most of those won't make it back, and they can't transmit anything they find from inside the artifact.

Tavoian had twenty similar probes remaining, but he had been reluctant to send more out, at least until he had a better idea of where they might prove most useful, especially after the difficulties experienced by the AI rover. The only problem was that he still had no real idea just where they might prove the most useful.

You have to try something, especially before a full-fledged Sinese exploration team appears. With that thought, he called up the route taken by the rover to the "drive" section of the artifact, and began running calculations based on the distance and the thruster propellant carried by each of the two classes of spy-eyes he had available.

Finally, he asked the ship's AI to calculate the most propellant-efficient route for the larger spy-eyes, not from Recon three, but from the farthest point into the artifact that the ISV could go using the anchors Tavoian had developed.

MOST DISTANT POINT THEORETICALLY POSSIBLE IS FIVE HUNDRED METERS BEYOND THE POSITION REACHED BY THE ROVER.

Five hundred meters beyond what the rover had seen was better than anything else Tavoian had come up with. He went back to the cargo area and unpacked five of the ten larger spy-eyes, then had the ship's AI program each with a different direction once they reached the defaced entry to the artifact's "drive" chamber. Then he began to ready the second ISV.

ISV HAS DISCOVERED A POSSIBLE SAMPLING SITE.

"I'll be right there." Tavoian could have let the AI handle the sampling, but he wanted to be watching, especially given just how difficult it had been to find any material at all to sample. He just hoped that the AI was right.

When he reached the control area, the largest display screen showed a close-up from the ISV, a thin threadlike strand trailing from the edge of the dark green material, at the end of which was a small lump of the same dark green matter. The thread was so fine that Tavoian couldn't make it out without visual enhancement. "How large is the lump?"

THIRTY-EIGHT MILLIMETERS AT ITS GREATEST DIMENSION.

"What about the strand attaching it to the rest of the green material?"

IT IS NOT POSSIBLE TO DETERMINE THAT EXACTLY THROUGH THE SCANNING IMAGE. THE THICKNESS IS BETWEEN FIFTY AND NINETY MICROMETERS.

"See if the rover's clamp can cut the lump free."

Tavoian watched as the rover used its thrusters to position itself, then extended a sharp-edged clamp, which closed around the dark green strand that was likely the thickness of a human hair. The lump vibrated, but did not break free.

THE CLAMP CANNOT CUT THROUGH THE STRAND.

Tavoian wasn't surprised in the slightest. "Bring the laser to bear and tune it to cutting at the shortest UV wavelength possible for the laser."

TUNING AND CUTTING.

The screen went black for several moments.

RETRIEVING IMAGE USING ROVER'S OPTICS.

From what Tavoian could make out from the image that appeared on the screen, the front of the tunable laser assembly was a fused mass and what looked to be wisps of vapor surrounded it, most likely particles of what had been part of the laser.

"What happened?"

THE CAUSE OF THE EXPLOSION IS UNKNOWN. THE ROVER HAS RECLAIMED THE SAMPLE WITH ITS GRASPER. ITS CLAMP ARM HAS BEEN DESTROYED.

"Display stored view from Recon three's opticals. Maximum magnification." Tavoian watched the view of the ISV, but there was really nothing to see. One moment, the ISV was poised above the circumference of the artifact. The next, there was a flash that blotted out any image of the ISV, and after that, the ISV was still poised where it had been, with the faint haze around the damaged laser.

"Return the ISV to Recon three. Is the sampler functioning?"

IT IS NOT.

"Can you determine whether it is repairable?"

NEGATIVE.

"Note the location where the sample was found."

LOCATION NOTED.

Tavoian left the controls and returned to working on the second ISV. Then, almost half an hour later, after the ship's AI had locked in the damaged ISV, and the ISV and its equipment were warming in the lock, he unpacked the second rover and the backup tunable laser. Before continuing a search for another sample along the rim of the artifact, he wanted to test Alayna's suggestion for spectrographic analysis, especially of the hull section and the off-colored "circles."

By the time he had the second ISV ready to go, with the second AI rover and the laser fastened in position, the first ISV had warmed enough for him to open the inner lock and pull the damaged equipment into the former passenger compartment. The sampler didn't look that damaged, and the rover seemed intact, except for the grabber arm, which was totally gone. *You might have a spare for that.* There wasn't much left intact of the front part of the laser.

He checked the parts and supply list. There was a small case of rover parts, including two grabber arms. The spare parts for the tunable lasers consisted of replacement laser modules, a replacement fore-optics chamber, and two replacement sensors. That looked promising, but when he went back and looked at the damaged laser spectroscope/analyzer, he just shook his head. Shreds of metal, possibly from the missing grabber arm, had penetrated the assembly behind the sensor and shattered the analytics module, despite the shielding that looked thick enough to stop what had happened—and hadn't.

And you don't have a replacement for that.

Next, he looked at the sampler. A small bit of flexible conduit, from the grabber arm, had wedged into the door assembly, preventing a clean seal. That, he could fix . . . after he finished preparing the second ISV.

After another forty minutes, the second ISV was on its way toward the artifact, and Tavoian was setting up the larger materials analyzer that had been installed on one side of the cargo section of Recon three. Larger was relative, because the equipment used with the ISV was little more than sixty centimeters by twenty-five and twenty centimeters high. The one in Recon three was eighty by forty by thirty, and much of the extra size was accounted for by a larger sampling bay.

Tavoian debated whether he should even attempt analyzing the lump of material recovered from the artifact. Still he had to try . . . but after what had occurred with the laser being used as a cutter, he wasn't about to apply high power to anything. Even so, he had his doubts as to whether even the more sophisticated and high-powered sampling equipment onboard Recon three would be any more effective in revealing anything about the silver or green material comprising the structure of the artifact. The only place where spectrographic analysis had worked thus far was on the melted and damaged protrusions in the handful of hexagons with partly opened doors . . . and in revealing the silicon and silver in the outer hull, but even Tavoian knew that silver and silicon couldn't make a hull as durable as that of the artifact—not with any technology known on Earth.

Finally, he decided he'd attempt an analysis at low power. Less than a minute after he closed the bay door, the display panel showed its results.

No gasification at current power settings.

Spectrographic reflection analysis reveals the following elements: carbon, silicon, silver.

Material impervious to electromagnetic penetration beyond surface.

Impervious? How could that be? What looked to be the same material in the door-frame area of the hexagons showed a photosensitivity. Was the photosensitivity confined to the surface of the material? Tavoian had to think that over. The perceived color of an object or material was determined by the wavelengths reflected. Yet the door frames had selectively accepted photons in the wavelength that was being reflected, in addition to all other wavelengths of visible light, as well as UV and IR. Was there something about that material that changed its composition when exposed to light? Or when it became the surface? The lump presumably had come from the interior, and the majority of interior surfaces were the dark green.

He needed to report on the sampling results, but the report could wait until he had at least some preliminary results from attempting what Alayna had suggested. He made his way back to the controls.

"Interrogative status of ISV?"

ISV IS IN POSITION RELATIVE TO THE OUTERMOST HEXAGON YOU SELECTED.

"Conduct spectrographic analysis on hull area outside the circle." Tavoian doubted that he'd find anything differing much, but sometimes things didn't.

ANALYSIS REVEALS CARBON, SILICON, AND SILVER.

"Nothing else?"

NO OTHER ELEMENTS DETECTED.

Even though he'd expected that, it still bothered him. How had the aliens managed to create such a hard and durable material from just those three elements? *Finding that out isn't your job. Your job is to get as much information as possible to those people who can.* Except Tavoian was finding his job far harder than he—or anyone else, he suspected—had thought it would be.

"Commence reflectivity tests on the hull area beyond the circle and report results."

COMMENCING REFLECTIVITY TESTS.

Tavoian waited.

REFLECTIVITY IS NINETY-NINE POINT EIGHT ACROSS ALL WAVELENGTHS. RANGES FROM ULTRAVIOLET TO INFRARED.

That level of reflectivity seemed extraordinarily high for a ship's hull. From his messages and his initial conversations with Alayna, Tavoian knew that optical telescopes came close to perfect reflectivity . . . but for a white hull that didn't seem polished, that didn't seem possible. "How can that be?"

IN THEORY, NANOLEVEL DIFFRACTION GRATINGS COULD ACHIEVE THAT REFLECTIVITY.

"With a surface so hard that lasers can't scratch it?"

AT PRESENT, THERE IS NO RECORD OF SUCH A MATERIAL HAVING BEEN FABRICATED.

But the aliens managed that, it appears. "Move the laser to the center of the circle. Repeat the tests and report."

A few seconds after the two minutes had passed, the AI reported, RE-FLECTIVITY IS NINETY-EIGHT POINT THREE ACROSS ALL WAVELENGTHS. RANGES FROM ULTRAVIOLET TO INFRARED, EXCEPT FOR WAVELENGTHS OF 379 AND 380 NANOMETERS.

Absorbing two wavelengths and one and a half percent drop off . . . but why there? "Is there any detectable difference in the hull surface inside the circle?"

ANY DIFFERENCE IS BEYOND THE SENSITIVITY OF THE EQUIPMENT.

Tavoian thought about another high-power test, then shook his head. With near perfect reflectivity of the hull surface, about the only thing that could happen was to damage his own equipment. "Repeat the tests on eight other circles, two on this side of the curved section of the hull, three in the middle, and three on the far side. Then test two other open sections of hull. Report the results when the tests are done." He had a good idea what those results would be, but he'd need at least that many confirmations to report back to the colonel and the DOEA scientists.

At the same time, he realized that there was . . . something . . . about the hull and the measurements, something that nagged at him. But he couldn't recall exactly what it was, except that he'd fleetingly thought it was unusual.

You're tired. You'll think of it later.

He hoped so. In the meantime, he began to write up the results of the tests and investigations conducted over the course of a very long day, knowing that he'd have to be careful about exactly how he wrote up the results before he sent them off to the colonel. He'd likely have to rewrite them at least once, knowing that he tended to be sloppy when he was tired, but if he didn't take care of it immediately, he'd worry about it instead of sleeping.

He also needed to eat.

After that, if his eyes could still focus, he'd see about writing a message to Alayna . . . and maybe to Kit and his parents.

50

The New York Times
15 November 2114

[OTTAWA] "The North American Union has not placed remote explosive devices anywhere in space," declared President Dyana Yates late yesterday. "We remain fully
open to peaceful cooperation in matters of space research and development." Her
statement was in response to a charge by Sinese Minister for Space Wong Mengyi
that a small laser-triggered explosion in space was absolute proof that the Noram
Space Ministry had already begun to militarize space in violation of the Outer Space
Treaty of 1967 and the Joint Space Agreement of 2051.

The explosion occurred near the possible alien artifact many have termed
the Solar Express. DOEA Secretary Luvalle declared that the "minuscule explosion" was the result of the energy reflected from the surface of the artifact back
into a laser measuring unit that caused a power overload in the remote sampling
device.

Senator Riccardo Castenada (CP-NY) charged Luvalle with a "blatant coverup"
and declared that if Luvalle thought reflected light was explosive, he had no business
serving as DOEA Secretary. Castenada went on to charge the entire Yates Administration with malfeasance in subsidizing a bloated military-industrial space combine,
whose only priority was profit, while ignoring the "real and pressing needs of the
people of New York and other states" of the North American Union.

In response, a joint statement from Senator Kim Greywinter (D-ALB) and Tanya
Patton (D-SASK) noted that Castenada had yet to retract his erroneous statement
about the so-called Solar Express being a hoax and a fabrication, a failure that
demonstrated Castenada's total ignorance about DOEA affairs. Castenada remains
under investigation by the Noram Inspector-General's office in regard to charges that
he disclosed classified DOEA material, and a government source indicates that an
indictment is "possible" in the near future.

Acting EC Chancellor Alceste Ciorni, serving while Erek Rumikov recovers from
injuries incurred from the failed assassination attempt by Scottish separatists, repeated
the EC's disappointment with both Noram and the Sinese Federation for failing to
inform other nations about the potential alien spacecraft.

One of the top authorities on space law, Kacia Elspeth, noted that while military installations and weapons of mass destruction are prohibited under existing treaties, there is no prohibition on conventional weapons. In addition, the distinction between a warship in space and a ship carrying conventional weapons has never been precisely defined . . .

51

Daedalus Base
15 November 2114

Thursday morning Alayna woke up early with the words she'd thought had vanished, at least for a while, going through her head:

> Yesterday, upon the stair,
> I met a man who wasn't there.
> He wasn't there again today.
> I wish, I wish he'd go away.

She didn't even try to push them away as she hurried and got dressed. Since it was day on Farside, and there was actually a free block of time on the solar optical array, she didn't waste any time in gulping down coffee and checking the coordinates she'd set up for her latest observing plan, once "her" block of time became available at 0830 UTC. *Maybe today will be the day when you discover the little solar man who's there again today, but isn't.*

After she had more coffee and ate, she went over all the systems, looking especially at the indicators for the aeroponics and the water feeds, but those were doing well, now that she'd adjusted the system to take into account the higher calcium load. The only messages she received were news summaries, one of which reported that a large Sinese spacecraft, almost twice the size of the standard longliner, had left high Earth orbit four days earlier, by which Alayna assumed an orbit well beyond geostationary, in the direction of the artifact dubbed the Solar Express. The Sinese refused to comment, beyond saying that it was an unarmed research craft.

Something that size as a research ship and poor Chris is out there in something like a hurriedly converted fusionjet? Alayna forced her thoughts back to the next step in her research, which was an attempt to correlate the appearance of the multi-fractal mini-granulations with either the duration or the intensity of the "regular" granulations in the same latitude bands. She would even have been happy if a correlation of a negative sort appeared, that the multi-fractal mini-granulations appeared some time either before or after either greater convection activity or less, although there had been some limited research in the past that could not find such a correlation, but the observation periods had been too short to be conclusive.

While Marcel carried out the observations, Alayna called up the message she'd received late on Wednesday from Emma, reading over the key parts before she dashed off a quick reply.

> . . . your Solar Express is definitely acting alien! We've seen an increase in its inbound velocity. Several percent more than can be accounted for by standard mass/gravitational force. I don't want to put figures on an open communication. We're not the only facility that's noted this. John Dorcaster at Yerkes has also. If he has, so has most of the astronomical world . . .

Emma never did like Dorcaster. With good reason, from what Alayna had overheard, but Yerkes needed an astronomer who was as much mediaslut as astronomer, and Dorcaster was certainly both.

Alayna shunted Emma's message to the side, considering again that it really hadn't been an error in Marcel's calculations. In one way, that definitely relieved Alayna. In another, it was a real concern. There was absolutely no indication of a propulsion system, and Chris had consistently referred to the alien creation as an artifact. The physical parameters indicated that it was old, but the images he'd shared with her definitely didn't show that. The lines were crisp. There were no craters, scrapes or scratches, or anything that revealed wear and age . . . and that was another worry. What if it was all a colossal hoax? But who or what could have engineered that? The Sinese had a base on Europa, farther out from where the artifact had first been observed . . . but to create something that massive? With all the reported properties?

Unless Noram and the Sinese were cooperating . . .

Alayna shook her head. That was most improbable, even more improbable than an actual ancient alien artifact.

She had already replied to Emma, most carefully, trying not to be curt but without revealing too much and noting that COFAR had observed the mass/velocity discrepancy, but that, because of the location of Daedalus Base, did not have recent observations that would confirm the magnitude of that discrepancy. Alayna definitely needed to be careful. The way things were going, she'd need every contact and every possible supporter once she left COFAR and the Farside Foundation . . . assuming that the growing hostilities between the three major powers didn't escalate into all-out warfare.

She checked the message queue again. Nothing there.

Since she did have time while Marcel actually carried out the observations, and she wouldn't later, when she'd have to pore over them and suggest analytical patterns, she decided to reply to Chris. After what he'd sent her, she definitely owed him, although in some ways, she also envied him.

> Chris,
> The images are stunning, and I wish I could send you some from a distance, for comparison, but COFAR won't be in position to view you and the artifact for another week. There are disadvantages to observing from a body whose full day-night cycle is twenty-eight days. Sometimes, we have to wait a long time, unlike deep space observatories or even those on Earth. On the other hand, it's all relative, because we have advantages they don't.
>
> I have to admit that the artifact doesn't look as old as all our observations suggest. Whoever or whatever constructed it designed for it to last eons . . . or longer . . . That's clear. I can only hope you're able to find out as much as you can in the comparatively limited time you have there.

She paused. "Marcel . . . do you have any better data on 2114 FQ5? Perihelion time and distance?"

"No, Dr. Wong-Grant. Until COFAR can observe the object again, more accurate calculations are not possible."

"Thank you." Alayna went back to the message.

> . . . According to our present calculations, sometime last Sunday you and the Solar Express [officially known as 2114 FQ5] crossed Earth's orbit, not that Earth is all that close to where you are. For what it's worth, the artifact isn't behaving like a normal small body. Unless our calculations are wrong, and that is always possible, it has been speeding up more than can be accounted for by the sun's gravity as it moves in-system. We won't be able to calculate better speed and approach data for another week, but I thought you'd like to know, because you may not have as much time there as initially calculated.

The following quote struck me as intriguing because while it mentions passion in passing, it also deals with the issue of time. We think of what happens in the here and now as so vital. To us, it is, but . . . was it to whoever built the artifact? I have to wonder. Any beings that built something to last tens of thousands of years must have had a different perspective . . . or am I missing something?

Don't ever debate anything with a geologist. They're passionate enough, and they care, deeply, about good science, but for them, a million years is a short time, and so many of them really don't think that anything that can happen in mere decades or centuries can matter all that much, but it can, as witness the recent global warming. Astronomers who study galactic dynamics are similar, but haven't had their various applecarts upset yet . . .

Yet, here I am trying to upset applecarts, and you're dealing with one. Sorry to distort the metaphors totally out of proportion.

Anyway, I hope my poor suggestions have helped in some way.

Do take care.

She sent the message immediately, but wondered, not for the first time, if and when he might receive it.

Two hours later, Alayna's observation time came to an end, and she immediately asked Marcel, "Have you found anything interesting?"

"The granulations in the latitude belt being studied appear to be somewhat more violent. Based on past observations, that would indicate they are shorter-termed. There is also a higher number of multi-fractal mini-granulations. It will take several more days of observation to determine whether multi-fractal mini-granulations are also shorter-termed."

"Thank you." Alayna had been squeezing in minutes and fractions of hours on the optical array for the past several days, but this was the first indication of increased solar convection, and such an increase did not exactly fit the long-term observed pattern. But then, over the years, that pattern had been interrupted, changed, even reversed upon occasion, and supposed period of solar minimums and maximums had been anything but that.

After reviewing the images selected by Marcel, Alayna had to admit that the AI was on to something. Not only was there a five percent increase over the mean in the numbers of multi-fractal mini-granulations, but the definition appeared to be more distinct. *But why would that be?*

"Marcel, are there any usable images from the Lick contract yesterday? Ones we could use as a baseline."

"Those were for a high latitude study, Dr. Wong-Grant."

"Wasn't that a multi-day study? How many days? Could you scan their images to see if there are any multi-fractals over the course of their observations?"

"That is possible."

"Make the comparison scans, please. Let me know what you find."

"Yes, Dr. Wong-Grant."

While she waited for what Marcel might or might not discover, she wondered if she might be the first to be observing the multi-fractals at such a time. She shook her head. That was highly unlikely. *But you can hope.*

Less than ten minutes later, Marcel reported, "There is a slight increase in convection activity in the higher latitude bands, but it is well within normal parameters."

"As possible, keep track of that."

"Yes, Dr. Wong-Grant."

Alayna realized that her mouth was dry, and she had a headache . . . and that she hadn't had anything to drink in almost four hours. With a wry expression, she headed for the galley, still wondering if the slight uptick in convection might reveal her solar man who wasn't there.

So far.

RECON THREE
15 NOVEMBER 2114

Tavoian woke with a throbbing headache on Thursday morning, and his eyes burned. Wondering if something had gone wrong with the environmental systems, he immediately checked the oxygen and CO2 levels, and the internal atmosphere analysis. Oxygen and CO2 were fine, and there were no worrisome levels of contaminants in the air, especially not of ammonia, carbon monoxide, or formaldehyde. With the possibility that he might be somewhat dehydrated, Tavoian drank half a squeezebottle of water before starting in on his tea. While he drank, he checked his messages, but all that had arrived while he was sleeping were news summaries. That suggested that whoever vetted his messages at Donovan Base hadn't gotten to them, or that the colonel hadn't signed off on them.

He would have liked to use both ISVs at once, especially before the manned Sinese expedition arrived, but he couldn't use the first one for his spy-eye expedition until he repaired the AI rover so that it could place the space anchors.

So he had the ship's AI dispatch the second ISV to inspect the circumference where dark green and silvery white joined, and while the AI was monitoring that, he forced himself through an hour of heavy exercise, after which he cleaned up. By then, his headache had slowly dissipated, and he began on the repairs to the first rover AI.

The hardest part was removing the damaged grabber arm without disabling the connections that had been splashed with globs of instantly melted materials that had, in turn, immediately solidified upon striking the connector. That alone took more than an hour of painstaking work. Then he had to clean the connections before he attached the new grabber arm. Once the repaired AI rover was back together and tested, he set up the first ISV with the spy-eyes, the rover, and the space anchors, ready to launch from the lock.

Then he headed back to the controls, where he checked on the progress of the circumference inspection. So far, no other traces of material from the artifact that could be retrieved or sampled had been discovered.

Even if the ISV did discover another "thread," Tavoian had absolutely no intention of using his remaining laser to try to cut anything loose. He did want to be able to report that he'd covered the entire rim, especially since it was indeed possible that something might be caught or attached where the hull and interior were exposed side by side.

"What have the Sinese been doing?"

ANOTHER TEN SPY-EYES ARE INVESTIGATING SURFACE AREAS OF THE ARTIFACT. THOSE AREAS ARE BEING NOTED. THEIR ISV CONTINUES TO SWEEP THE SURFACE OF THE ARTIFACT.

"How much thruster propellant do they have?"

THAT INFORMATION IS NOT AVAILABLE. WITHOUT HABITABILITY REQUIREMENTS, ASSUMING SIMILAR INTERIOR PARAMETERS, THE SINESE CRAFT COULD CARRY A MINIMUM OF THREE TIMES THE PROPELLANT ABOARD RECON THREE.

"More like five or ten times," murmured Tavoian.

THAT IS POSSIBLE.

"Keep searching with the same pattern and parameters."

SEARCH CONTINUING.

At 0917 Tavoian decided to dispatch the second ISV. He watched as it neared the passageway between the two hexagons he had selected as providing the closest access to the route the rover had taken to the hull chambers he thought might contain drives or engines or some sort of propulsive system. The rover set up the anchors and the cable between them, then attached the signal repeater and the fiber-optic line to it, before returning to the ISV, which then eased into the passageway.

It was well past 1100 when the first of the five programmed spy-eyes left the ISV on the way through the passageways toward their objective.

With little more to do than wait, Tavoian began to draft a report to the colonel. He could at least outline what he had programmed the ISVs, rovers, and spy-eyes to do, and it wouldn't hurt to mention that he'd repaired the one rover.

He'd almost finished drafting what he could when the ship's AI announced, A SINESE SPY-EYE IS MONITORING THE SIGNAL REPEATER POSITIONED BETWEEN THE TWO ANCHORS AND OVER THE ENTRY PASSAGEWAY.

"How far away is it from the repeater?"

TEN METERS.

"Can you tell what it's doing?"

IT IS LIKELY ATTEMPTING TO INTERCEPT ANY SIGNALS SENT FROM THE REPEATER.

"What's the probability that it can?"

THAT IS UNKNOWN.

In one sense, the attempted signal theft didn't bother Tavoian, because the only signal Recon three was receiving was an image from the ISV that showed a featureless passageway some five hundred meters inside the artifact. In another way, the effrontery angered him. But he really didn't want to take out the Sinese spy-eye because, first, it was clear that the Sinese had far more of those than he did, and if they retaliated, he'd be the one who came up short. Second, that would give the Sinese a pretext to claim Noram was behaving militaristically. And third, with a crewed Sinese vessel due to arrive in another five days, he'd be outnumbered and likely outpowered, as well as outequipped. "Let me know if it moves any closer."

Tavoian had no sooner shifted his attention back to finishing what he could of his next report when the faint chime of an incoming message surprised him. He was even more surprised to see that it came from Alayna, but he immediately began to read it.

> Dear Chris,
> The images are stunning, and I wish I could send you some of our images taken from a distance, but COFAR won't be in position to view you and the artifact for another week . . .

Won't be in position? He felt stupid when he read the next words. He hadn't thought about the fact that a Farside observatory really wasn't optimal for real-time intelligence or observation of the entire sky or of parts of it for weeks, no matter how ideal it might be for astronomy or astrophysics.

He did enjoy her words, even if the observation about the artifact's increased speed worried him as well, although he'd noted that earlier, but he hadn't checked in the past few days. He immediately asked the ship's AI, "How much farther in-system are we than projected by the mission profile?"

TWENTY POINT THREE MILLION KAYS.

Tavoian immediately checked the mission profile. He moistened his lips when he saw the date the colonel had projected for his return—December thirteenth. If Alayna was correct, and he had no doubt about that, he and Recon three would be charred to ashes if he waited that long. *And she's implying that the alien artifact may reach perihelion even sooner than that.* He had realized that they were traveling slightly faster than projected, but he'd also known that their inbound velocity increased daily. He just hadn't made the connection. Alayna had, and he very much appreciated the early warning. He also realized two other things. First, he had less time than planned, and second, if the artifact and Recon three were also traveling faster, that likely meant that he might have to break off the mission even before crossing the orbit of Mercury or, rather, the figure for the orbit used for mission purposes. He couldn't imagine that was something the colonel would like, either.

How could everyone have been that wrong?

He shook his head. In so many ways, they'd all been wrong. No one had expected the materials and construction of the alien artifact, or the difficulties involved in finding out anything meaningful about it—

A wry smile crossed his lips. He'd found out a great deal that was meaningful in more ways than one. What he hadn't discovered was a single thing that was useful to Noram or the human race. Not a single recognizable tool or element of technology, just impossibly hard and durable materials and an inscrutable or hidden science behind the creation and operation of the artifact . . . and the hint that the strange dark green material, or its surface, was photoconductive, and most likely also had been selectively plastic in being able to shape itself to the needs of the structure or its users. Another thought struck him.

"Have you detected any radiation or any activity showing energy, heat, or the like from the artifact or anywhere nearby?"

THE ONLY SOURCES OF RADIATION OR ANY FORM OF ENERGY WITHIN A MILLION KAYS ARE RECON THREE AND THE SINESE LONGLINER.

That was good . . . and bad. Whatever was causing the acceleration wasn't coming from the artifact. *Or it's something we can't detect.* But that didn't make sense. How could something, particularly something without any energy signature, come from an artifact that was tens of thousands of years old? And an artifact that was only a piece of something much larger?

All he could do was to inform the colonel that Recon three could not detect any cause for the increased inbound velocity, but there was no point to sending him a special message, not when there were three weeks or so before they neared the orbit of Mercury, even at their higher speed. He'd just address the issue and what he hadn't found—like so many other things he hadn't found—in the next report.

He lingered over Alayna's last words, then realized another message had arrived. It was from Kit. That gave him a chill, because he'd only sent off his last message to her the night before, and a quick turnaround didn't mean anything good. He immediately began to read.

Chris,
I wish I knew where you are. You've been so vague. I know.
With all the problems the Sinese are causing, you can't tell me.
But we all worry, especially after the border attacks near Korba
and Bruini . . .

Border attacks? Tavoian had only seen mentions of rising tensions along the Sinese/Indian borders. He stopped reading and checked the latest news summary, only to find a mention that Sinese and Indian forces had traded weapons fire at several locations along the northern and eastern borders of Arunachal Pradesh.

> . . . isolated as those places are, when the Sinese start attacking and the Indians get their backs up . . . You know what I mean. I worry. We all worry.

> I wish you were here. Mom keeps insisting that you'll be here soon. We can't tell her otherwise. She coughs all the time, and we've had to move her into what amounts to home isolation. I know otherwise, but I still can't believe no one can find a treatment for T3. It's like it's almost a cross between the old Ebola virus and tuberculosis, except that can't be because one's a virus and the other's a bacterium. There are still times I wish I'd opted for med school, and this is one of them.

> Oh . . . I forgot to mention it. I did enjoy the quote about ocean coastlines, especially the part about how politicians react. Just from that, I think I'd like your astrophysicist friend. I take it she's just a friend from your mentions. Too bad, but maybe someday, little brother.

How could Alayna be anything else? He'd only spent something like three hours anywhere close to her, and they'd only talked for an hour. The rest of the time he'd been piloting the FusEx. He had definitely enjoyed her messages, but . . . He couldn't help but smile. Kit definitely wanted a partner for him.

Should he let Kit know exactly where he was? Even assuming that the colonel would let that go through, he wasn't sure it was the best idea. While he might actually be safer, at least more removed from possible direct military action, no deep space mission, with no immediate backup available, was exactly safe, and Kit would certainly know that.

You volunteered. That was true enough, but he hadn't expected his mother to be dying, or the three major powers squabbling on the brink of war. And he had to admit that he had liked the idea of exploring Alayna's artifact far more than loosing torps at Sinese installations or ships . . . if it even came to that. *Which it might the way things continue to deteriorate.*

He finished reading her message and then immediately replied, thankful that the requirements to burst send messages only once a day had been lifted.

> Dear Kit—
> I'm so sorry. I really can't say where I am at present, except that I'm certainly not in the direct line of fire if matters worsen. Even if I were still piloting FusEx ships between Earth and the lunar facilities, I wouldn't be able to go Earthside.
>
> I wish you didn't have to deal with it all. That's not something I'd wish on anyone, and especially not on you, and especially not now . . .
>
> As for Alayna, I've found her interesting and intriguing, but I'd like to point out that we've spent all of an hour in person talking, and she'll be at Daedalus Crater for another year. Who even knows where I'll be in a month, let alone in a year? I will admit, willingly, that I look forward to her messages and that I enjoy reading them and sharing thoughts with her. For now, that's all that's possible.
>
> How is Dad doing under all this strain? And you? You're both taking every precaution, I hope? I know T3 isn't wildly contagious, but please don't take any chances . . .

He still wondered where his mother had caught T3, but she'd never had great resistance to illness, even when he and Kit had been children, and modern technology and travel meant that diseases traveled just as easily and quickly as people did.

After he sent the message to Kit, he checked on the progress of the circumference survey, but the ISV had discovered nothing that could be sampled.

As time passed, Tavoian tried to think of other possible avenues of exploration and other approaches. The one possibility was a more thorough exploration of the space that might have been hangar for a spacecraft using the spy-eyes in the same way as they were currently operating. If the spy-eyes located any material that looked loose, then he could send one of the rovers after it.

By 1245, he was beginning to worry that he might have lost five spy-eyes for nothing. By 1300 he was definitely concerned. *What's taking so long? Did you miscalculate the thruster fuel requirements?* Except he'd had the ship's AI check his calculations.

The first of the spy-eyes returned to the ISV waiting in the passage-way beneath the hexagons at 1307 UTC, and Tavoian began to breathe more easily. The last one returned to the ISV at 1317, and the ISV eased its way back out of the passageways and above the hexagons, where the rover recovered the anchors and line. It was almost 1500 by the time the ISV and spy-eyes were in Recon three's main lock.

Tavoian could still download what the spy-eyes had recorded while the ISV and equipment warmed, and he began reviewing the images, in order of the devices' return to the ISV. The first spy-eye followed the an-gled passageways roughly perpendicular to the "drive" chamber. Even though he froze the image when the spy-eye reached the open aperture to the large chamber he still considered as a possible ship lock he could not make out anything in the darkness beyond. The spy-eye continued in a direction he thought of as downward, although it would have been sideways if the sphere had rotated on an axis perpendicular to the drive chamber. When the last passageway turned inward and continued toward the drive chamber, Tavoian waited until the image feed showed the partly melted doorway, when he again froze the image, studying the evenly slumped ridge of dark material at what he thought was the base of the opening, but could easily have been the side. There was no indication of change in coloration or other materials, as had been the case in the half-melted protrusions in the partly opened hexagons earlier explored.

Once inside the huge "drive" chamber, the spy-eye proceeded along the bulkhead from which the massive gray hexagonal columns extended. As with the earlier images from the AI rover, Tavoian could not deter-mine exactly the size of the columns, but he could make out that they tapered slightly from the bulkhead. He judged that they were twenty me-ters across, but that was as much guess as estimate. Although the bulk-head was the dark green and the hexagonal column gray, there was no visible joint where they met, just a change of color. That suggested to Tavoian that the hexagon extended into or through the bulkhead.

But you don't know.

The spy-eye continued past three more of the hexagons before turn-ing and heading back toward the passageway that would take it back to the ISV. Tavoian went back over the images and froze the picture just be-fore the spy-eye turned. He could see the vague outline of another hex-agonal column. If the columns matched the slightly discolored circles on the hull, there would be one or two beyond the one barely visible. The images of the return showed Tavoian nothing he had not seen before.

The next spy-eye dropped "lower" compared to the first, but also hugged the base bulkhead . . . and passed three hexagonal columns, spaced so that they were lower and midway between the ones scouted by the first spy-eye, before turning back. Tavoian stopped the image feed several times, trying to see if there was any loose material or any objects that might bear closer investigation. He saw neither, nor did he find anything on the return.

The third spy-eye, following Tavoian's programming, made straight for the nearest of the hexagonal funnel-like devices, possibly energy-focusing equipment, attached to and apparently just beneath or in back of the inside of the outer hull. While Tavoian had thought that the funnels, or energy nozzles, were the same dark green shade as the other decks and bulkheads, as the spy-eye drew closer, he could see that the funnel was a lighter green.

Lighter green and gray . . . While the difference in color for both likely had significance, he could only guess that the color difference was because both columns and funnels/nozzles handled or channeled some sort of energy. The fact that both were fixed, rather than extruded as needed, also strengthened his hypothesis. *Unless they were all in use when the artifact was severed from the rest of the sphere.*

And that, mused Tavoian, was also a definite possibility. *So many possibilities and so few certainties.*

The fourth spy-eye went straight to the surface between the two nearest hexagonal funnels. As the device neared that surface, Tavoian could make out the very gentle curve, strengthening his belief—and the calculations already made by the ship's AI—that whatever the columns and funnel-nozzles did, it was close to the hull and designed to project beyond the artifact. The most likely possibility, to Tavoian, was a propulsion system, especially given that the thirty-two circles on the hull were set in a balanced pattern, and that there was no indication of anything similar elsewhere . . . *although there might have been on the missing part of the artifact.*

The last spy-eye immediately turned right after coming out of the passageway and scanned the bulkhead from beside the damaged entry all the way to the barely curved surface backing the hull. It found nothing except smooth green surface. Nor did it discover anything loose or which might reveal more about the artifact, either in the large chamber or on its return to the ISV.

After studying the feeds, Tavoian linked them to the artifact database, then said, "When not otherwise occupied, scan the feeds from the spy-eyes and report anything that might reveal information about the artifact or its builders."

THAT WILL REQUIRE WAITING UNTIL AFTER THE SECOND ISV RETURNS.

"That's acceptable." Tavoian remained before the controls, thinking, noticing that, even by 1641 UTC, the other ISV had only completed inspecting another third of the circumference . . . and had found nothing unattached or even another "thread."

After making sure that the ISV with the spy-eyes was securely docked to Recon three, Tavoian fixed himself what might have passed for a cheese and salami wrap and slowly ate it, or washed it down with cool tea, definitely not the same as truly iced tea.

The next thing was to finish his daily report to the colonel, which he sent off immediately, along with selected images from the spy-eyes feeds, since trying to send the full feeds would have taken far too long, and left the entire transmission open to interception. Because the manned Sinese expedition was scheduled to arrive the next day, he left the ISV to continue its study of the circumference, and decided to reply to Alayna. She might have some other suggestions. Before he did, he reread her message. One passage caught his attention—again.

> Any beings that built something to last tens of thousands of years must have had a different perspective . . . or am I missing something?
>
> *Don't ever debate anything with a geologist. They're passionate enough, and they care, deeply, about good science, but for them, a million years is a short time, and so many of them really don't think that anything that can happen in mere decades or centuries can matter all that much, but it can, as witness the recent global warming. Astronomers who study galactic dynamics are similar, but haven't had their various applecarts upset yet . . . not in a decade or so.*

Tens of thousands of years . . . and not in a decade? What a juxtaposition! He shook his head at the incongruity and began his reply.

> Alayna,
> Thank you so much for the updated calculations about the artifact's increase in velocity. The impact wasn't something that was immediately obvious, or not to me, because while I was aware of the increase in inbound velocity, I didn't immediately realize the magnitude of the cumulative effect on timing. I should have, but I've been so focused on trying to decipher the enigma that is the artifact that it didn't register immediately. Part of that might have been because there's no indication here as to what is causing that, either. According to what little

I know about gravitation, we shouldn't be speeding up as much as we are, but there's no detectable radiation of any sort from the artifact, and my ship hasn't used its drive. Nor has the un-crewed Sinese craft. Another part of the enigma puzzle. Have you any ideas along those lines?

By the way, I did forward your quote about ocean coastlines to Kit, and she enjoyed and appreciated it.

What quote should he use in return? He came across one that appealed to him: "Military technology is that marvel that allows a person too tenderhearted to slaughter a sheep to annihilate half the world with the touch of a button." While he smiled, he wasn't about to put that into something read by a high-ranking military officer. He kept looking until he found another.

It's been a long day, but I did come up with a quote. It's not precisely on target, but it reminds me of the Sinese rhetoric, and their continual protestations of being fair and open-minded in the use of space.

Any ideologue who rallies his supporters with cries for "economic justice" neither has justice in mind nor understands economics.

I'd say that any leader who says he opposes the militarization of space and theoretically wants space free to all nations while building a base on Europa and threatening India for building its own space elevator neither has nonmilitarization in mind nor understands the concept of open access to space . . .

When Tavoian finished, he attached selections from what he had sent to the colonel and sent it off, wondering, again, if Donovan Base would let it go through.

Then he checked the ISV once more, but it continued to scan the circumference, unsuccessfully, so far.

He'd remain awake as long as he could, then have the AI wake him if the ISV detected anything . . . or if anything else went amiss. He still couldn't believe that he'd missed the fact that the increased speed of the artifact and Recon three meant that they'd near the sun that much sooner.

And why hadn't someone at Donovan Base caught it? Or were they all so overworked and overstressed about the Sinese-Indian-Noram power-play triangle that it had slipped past them? Or had everyone thought someone else had let Tavoian know? He wondered if he'd ever find out . . . or if, like so many things in the Space Service, there just wouldn't be any record of the slipup.

Cogito
15 November 2114

Solar Express: Fate

Lonely orb, artifact of dark,
Spinning slowly, alien spark
Of ancient flame or distant mind,
Could we now mourn a queerer kind?

Silent song, stilled by space and time,
Of unknown rhythm, cryptic rhyme,
Green confined in silvered shimmer
Sunward bound in growing glimmer.

Down relativity's deep well
Toward an incandescent hell
Or through perihelion's fierce flames
In parabolic flight from fleeting names?

No choice for artifact or sun,
No altering the orbit's run,
For mass draws mass, from dark to light.
The question left? Flamed day? Dark night?

54

RECON THREE
16 NOVEMBER 2114

When Tavoian woke on Friday morning, he wondered by how much they were inside Earth's orbit, and he asked the ship's AI.

ACCORDING TO ALL INFORMATION, RECON THREE IS WITHIN THE EARTH'S ORBIT BY SLIGHTLY OVER TWENTY MILLION KAYS.

"Did the ISV discover any material that could be removed for sampling?"

NO SAMPLES WERE DISCOVERED.

"Status of ISV?"

ISV IS IN MAIN LOCK. IT IS WARM ENOUGH TO BE SERVICED OR REMOVED.

"Reserve air supply status?" Tavoian hated to ask, but he needed to know.

SIXTY PERCENT REMAINING.

That amounted to about one and a third total replacements of the atmosphere in Recon three. "What about the Sinese ship?"

SPY-EYES AND REMOTE EQUIPMENT HAVE BEEN DISPATCHED TO AREA OF CENTRAL SHAFT. REMOTE SCANNING OF ARTIFACT CONTINUES.

"Is there any sign of another vessel?"

NO VESSELS WITHIN DETECTION RANGE.

"Notify me immediately when there is any sign of one."

WILL COMPLY.

Tavoian checked the systems and monitors and then looked for messages. There were none, except for the standard Noram Space Command news summary. It was getting so that he didn't expect meaningful messages the first thing in the morning, but then he was waking earlier than most officers at Donovan Base. He scanned the news summary, noting that both the Indians and the Sinese had mobilized more forces, while the Israelis and the Iranians had offered military support to India. Noram President Yates and DOEA Secretary Luvalle offered no comment. *Matters are definitely going in the wrong direction.*

After eating and drinking hot tea, Tavoian immediately began to reprogram the spy-eyes for a survey of the large space that he thought might be the equivalent of a ship launching bay. From the images returned by the AI rover, it had looked large enough to accommodate Recon three and possibly even a bigger vessel.

Even though you don't know whether they even had such ships. Except whoever had built the artifact had to have had some way of getting to and from the artifact, since it was far too large to enter a planetary atmosphere and did not appear designed for landing on even smaller bodies such as moons or asteroids.

What if it was totally self-contained? That was theoretically a possibility, but the hexagonal chambers the rover and spy-eyes had been able to enter had been empty, and there didn't seem to be enough space inside the material between the chambers to support a complex system. But then, he didn't know what might be inside all the sealed hexagons. Could they still hold devices, materials, information?

Tavoian had no way of knowing, but after little more than a week, he had his doubts about the ability of human technology to enter those sealed chambers with anything short of weapons that would likely destroy anything remaining there, assuming that anything at all did. *But what was all that space for?* It couldn't have been just for structural support, not with all the passageways outside the hexagonal spaces, and not with what were clearly entry and exit points.

Tavoian returned to the reprogramming. When he finished, he made his way down to the lock and moved the ISV there out into the passenger area, and then eased the first ISV into the lock, along with the AI rover, the spy-eyes, and the space anchors. Once he returned to the control area, he watched as the ISV moved back toward the artifact. Less than an hour later, the first of the spy-eyes departed on their preprogrammed routes to investigate the possible "launching bay." When all the spy-eyes were on their way, Tavoian turned over monitoring to the ship's AI and began his exercise routine.

He actually finished and was cleaning up when a message from the colonel arrived—a very formal-looking message.

Tavoian, Christopher A.
Major, NSC
NSS-21/Recon Three
Latest reports and attachments received. Continue explorations and analyses to the greatest degree possible commensurate with resources and safety. Request you do not leave ship except for emergency situations.

Interrogative frozen traces of possible atmosphere?

That was a good question. Tavoian would have to consider how he might gather such traces. Any gases from an atmosphere that were frozen on the outer surfaces would likely have long since sublimed, and if not, given the almost frictionless green material, would have slipped away centuries ago. Theoretically, if there had been gas crystals—oxygen and the like—they would be deep inside the artifact, yet, so far, none of the images had shown any indications of such, but perhaps he hadn't been looking closely enough.

> Understand difficulty of obtaining samples. Continue to seek new ways to obtain materials.

Exactly how?

> Time and resource limitations now preclude any other Noram mission to alien artifact. Lack of optimum Earth/artifact positioning also a factor. This underscores the importance of gathering all information and data possible.

As if you hadn't gotten that message already.

> Report arrival of Sinese research vessel immediately. Report any discrepancies of any sort.

Discrepancies of any sort? Sabotage? The immediate appearance of monsters out of the sealed hexagonal chambers? Attacks by the Sinese?

As he floated just above the control couch, Tavoian wondered if the colonel understood, emotionally as well as intellectually, that there just might be civilizations or beings whose technology humans could not yet understand. *Will our descendants, if we have any, be able to?* Tavoian knew he had to hope for both descendants and enlightenment, but . . . at the moment, he wasn't all that hopeful.

He turned his attention back to the message, but there was only one section left.

> Do not hesitate to risk duplicate equipment if necessary to obtain data or anything else of value . . .

Tavoian already knew that. As soon as he finished reading the message, he said to the ship's AI, "Scan all feeds from rovers, ISV, and spy-eyes for small crystals, especially blue crystals. Start from the first feeds."

BEGINNING SCANNING.

Tavoian looked for other messages, but there weren't any.

SCANNING OF ALL RECORDED FEEDS COMPLETE. THREE POSSIBLE AREAS EXIST WHERE LIGHT REFLECTIONS SUGGEST MATERIAL OTHER THAN THAT OF THE ARTIFACT'S CONSTRUCTION.

"Display images."

Tavoian couldn't see anything in any of the images. "Enhance the location where the reflections suggest material."

The ship's AI immediately did so, but Tavoian still had to strain to recognize the tiny pinpoints of light. The first image was one that Tavoian didn't recognize at first, but then realized was one of the dead-end areas first explored. The second was another dead end off the central shaft of the artifact. The third was in the hexagonal chamber with the fused and melted protrusion, near the base of the half-melted mass.

Interestingly enough, the ship's AI hadn't found traces of possible frozen atmosphere or materials in the "drive" chamber, but that didn't mean there weren't traces there, only that none had appeared within the limited range of the lights used by the rover or the spy-eyes.

He was about to make his way from the controls aft when the AI announced, ISV AND FOUR SPY-EYES RETURNING TO RECON THREE.

So soon? Except it had been over two hours. "What happened to the fifth?"

IT MALFUNCTIONED. REASON UNKNOWN. FEED FROM THIRD SPY-EYE SHOWED IT WINDING THROUGH PASSAGES AWAY FROM TARGET.

"I'll review the feeds after I finish with the sampling mission."

Once the ISV with the spy-eyes neared the ship, Tavoian held it outside the lock while he continued readying the other ISV to seek out the AI-identified locations for atmospheric remnants. Given the limitations of Recon three, and the fact he had no way to keep any possible frozen atmosphere that cold, the analysis would have to be handled by the repaired sampler on the ISV.

Because all of his fiber-optic line was with the other ISV, and he didn't want to spend more time letting the first ISV warm up and then re-rigging things, he'd set up three programs for the AI rover, each able to be triggered separately through the ISV. He decided to begin with the hexagonal chamber containing the fused mass, since that was the simplest one to reach. An hour or so later, once he'd finished his preparations, he sent off the second ISV and recovered the first.

Some twenty minutes later, the rover was entering the opening. When it was some five meters into the chamber, Tavoian lost the signal. Once again, he hoped that the rover could find what the AI had indicated was there. Some ten minutes later, the rover, propelled by its miniature thrusters, reappeared, as did its signal and the images from its sensors, and headed toward the ISV.

Tavoian accessed its memory, and discovered that there had indeed been something there, a bluish crystal-like object perhaps the size of his fingernail, which had been lodged in a slight declivity on the side of the fused protrusion farthest from either of the partly open doors. He held his breath as the rover maneuvered into position opposite the sampler drawer. As the grabber arm placed the crystal in the drawer and it began to close, a large part of the crystal broke and slowly drifted out of the sensors' view.

A flash crossed the sensors.

"What was that? A Sinese device?"

A SINESE COLLECTOR-BOT. A NUMBER OF THEM HAVE BEEN MAKING PASSES OVER THE ARTIFACT.

"What is it doing?"

IT IS HEADED BACK TO THE LONGLINER.

Stealing our sample. Even though Tavoian couldn't have immediately recovered the larger fragment of the gas crystal, not with the positioning of the ISV and the AI rover, somehow the "theft" irritated him, especially since he wondered if there was enough in the sampler to analyze. And how representative might it be? He waited, and finally the analysis data appeared on the screen in front of Tavoian. According to the sampler, the small crystal contained nitrogen, oxygen, and argon, in that relative order of abundance, with about twice as much nitrogen as oxygen, and only trace of argon.

No carbon or carbon dioxide? That was interesting, but Tavoian didn't know what to make of it.

Before moving the ISV to the central shaft, Tavoian had the ISV sweep the area around it, but there did not seem to be any other Sinese spy-eyes that close. Less fortuitously, there was one monitoring the central shaft, but it remained in position as the ISV moved into the opening and headed "down" it. Nor did it advance toward the signal repeaters that Tavoian had the rover deploy.

The wait for the rover to return seemed endless to Tavoian, and it was almost an hour before the rover emerged from the passageway and moved to the ISV. But it held a crystal twice the size of the first. This time, the entire crystal went into the sampler. Although the second crystal appeared to look like the first, the analysis showed three times the nitrogen as oxygen and a great deal more argon, almost ten percent. *Could that have been because you got a larger sample?* Tavoian had no idea.

That thought vanished as the ship's AI announced, CLEAR SIGNAL WILL FADE IN THREE MINUTES.

Tavoian used more thruster propellant than he wanted hurrying the ISV up the shaft, picking up the lower signal repeater on the way, and moving the ISV into the center of the shaft. There was a moment where the images vanished, but only a moment. Then the ISV was headed back toward the first side passages that Tavoian had explored.

The rover headed off. An hour later it returned, its grabber and sticky pad both empty. A quick check of its sensor feed revealed that when the grabber arm touched the crystal, it fragmented into tiny pieces that sprayed everywhere.

Two out of three samples wasn't bad, and there were likely more tiny crystals here and there, but there was no way that Tavoian or even all the tiny Sinese devices were going to be able to find any appreciable fraction of them in the time that they had.

And you thought a month or two would allow plenty of time. Tavoian smiled crookedly. He hadn't really understood just how big the artifact was until he'd started trying to explore it.

Belatedly, he realized that his eyes were blurring and burning. He checked the time. More than seven hours since he'd had anything to eat . . . and not much to drink either. Those would have to wait a few minutes longer. He turned the ISV over to the ship's AI with instructions to return it to the ship and dock it outside the lock.

Then he gulped down a bag-bowl of mushroom risotto, along with cool tea. He was so hungry he didn't even mind the fact that the tea was cool, neither hot nor cold. As he ate, he monitored the Sinese craft, and the occasional small device appearing out of or disappearing into the artifact. He had noticed that those devices did not interfere with the equipment he had deployed—except for stealing part of the one sample. *So far, anyway.*

With each day that passed, Tavoian had found himself feeling more and more helpless, and that he just didn't know enough to find as much as he should be discovering. The sampling incidents had just reinforced that feeling. *You're a pilot, not a scientist.* But he'd thought he knew something about science, yet with each day around the artifact, he felt like he knew less and less.

When he finished eating, he immediately called up the feeds from the spy-eyes.

The first spy-eye followed the programmed route from beneath the hexagons out to a point paralleling the hull and then toward the "drive" chambers before slowing at the narrow hexagonal opening on the outboard side of the passageway. The spy-eye rotated slightly and entered the chamber. Once again, Tavoian was struck by the fact that the space was essentially rectangular.

The spy-eye immediately moved to the slightly curved bulkhead opposite the entry, where it scanned the ridges projecting a third of a meter from the bulkhead, ridges a third of a meter thick, situated a third of a meter from the deck and the overhead, suggesting to Tavoian that they did indeed form the outline of an enormous lock. The spy-eye followed the ridges the entire length of the space to where they ended—a third of a meter from the end of the bulkhead. The two ridges at the top and bottom, some thirty meters apart, were joined seamlessly by another ridge, indicating that the same ridge formed a huge rectangle. The spy-eye's light revealed more clearly that the material framed by the ridges was also a lighter green, possibly matching the shade of the hexagonal energy funnels in the drive chamber. *That's all supposition on your part.* There was little enough to support that supposition, Tavoian knew, and it was also based on what might well be excessive anthropomorphism, but the two areas that seemed to be possible openings directly to space were a different shade, and that was at least suggestive, and there was also no trace of any gray coloration, pointing to different functions for the two spaces.

From the first spy-eye's examination Tavoian could also find no trace of debris, frozen atmosphere, or anything else. He had the ship's AI examine the feed as well, but the AI could find no traces, either.

The missing spy-eye had actually been the second one, because the second feed that Tavoian watched showed a spy-eye ahead in the passageway, with intermittent thruster pulses causing it to waver from side to side. Then at a junction where the passageways between hexagons separated, the second spy-eye took the passageway not on its programmed route and began to accelerate into the darkness, its point of light soon vanishing.

Some mechanical failure, or did you somehow misprogram it? Unless the spy-eye turned up somewhere on its own or another device from Recon three encountered it somewhere, Tavoian doubted that he'd ever see it again. All the devices had micro-locator beacons, but since the interior of the artifact didn't allow any signal transmission except line of sight, trying to track down the errant spy-eye would be a waste of time and thruster propellant. *Speaking of which . . .*

"How much thruster propellant is left?"

SIXTY-NINE POINT TWO PERCENT.

That was assuming that the measuring systems were perfectly accurate and that Tavoian could draw everything that was in the tanks. Neither was a hundred percent likely; ninety-five percent was a far safer assumption of working propellant stocks. *Thirty percent used in eight days, with four weeks to go.*

While he could explain and explain why he was going through the propellant stocks—for starters, the rotation of the artifact, the need for line-of-sight signal transmission, the sheer size of the artifact—the plain fact was that he couldn't keep operating the way he was.

That was emphasized by the fact that none of the last three spy-eyes found anything new or of import.

LARGE UNIDENTIFIED SHIP APPROACHING AND MATCHING SPEED TO THAT OF ARTIFACT.

"Ship characteristics?"

SHIP EXHIBITS DOUBLE-ENDED DRIVE CLAMSHELLS. SIZE IS APPROXIMATELY 295 METERS. ENERGY RADIATION INDICATES IT IS CREWED. EXTERIOR SHIELDING RESEMBLES ARMOR.

"Display what you have." As another screen on the display bulkhead opened, Tavoian shifted his attention, watching as the vessel drew nearer and the image grew larger, clearly heading for the uncrewed Sinese craft. As it came to rest, relatively, anyway, beside the other Sinese craft, the disparity in size was more than apparent. Not only was the new arrival almost a hundred meters longer than the longliner, but it appeared to be half again as large in diameter. Tavoian didn't see anything resembling weapons bays, but a pair of circular exterior hatches strongly suggested torp ports. Given the size and mass of the ship, and the comparative speed of its arrival, Tavoian's first thought was that the Sinese had to have developed a better drive system. Then he realized that wasn't necessarily so. All that they had to do was add a second drive, and do turnover, letting one drive cool while using the other. Hel3 fuel constraints—they could only carry so much—limited how many hours they could accelerate or decelerate, but they could accelerate for longer and achieve higher speeds sooner.

And if they have achieved even modest drive improvements as well . . .

Tavoian kept his message to the colonel short.

> Two hundred-ninety-five-meter ship taking station on artifact this time [1511 UTC] beside Sinese remote longliner. No visible identity, but has double-ended clamshell drive nozzles. Appears to have two torp ports. Radiated energy suggests crew aboard. No exterior activity yet.

He was certain he'd have to send more information before long, but his orders were to report the Sinese arrival immediately.

55

Saturday morning Alayna woke up early, very early—and on purpose, not that she was all that enthused, but she had received a message from Director Wrae the day before noting that the Williams consortium had booked three straight hours of both the optical and radar arrays for a special galactic coordinated study, dealing with a recently discovered active galactic nucleus. That was all that the director had indicated. While Alayna was well aware of the schedule, the director's mention of the Williams consortium was just another indication to Alayna of the fact that nothing should go wrong, particularly after her "failure" to give credit to the consortium for the use of their time in discovering 2114 FQ5 . . . the alien artifact that the world now knew as the Solar Express. Considering that almost no one outside of astronomical circles had even mentioned her name or COFAR in talking about the artifact, she had her doubts about how much the consortium had lost. She did know how much she was likely to lose if *anything* went wrong with the Williams observations. So, even though there was very little more she could do in advance, she wanted to be ready in case something occurred at the last moment.

That was why she was up checking everything well before the consortium's observation program began. She could find no problems, but she sat with her coffee in the COFAR control center as the consortium observations started, ready to react if she had to, but her thoughts were actually on active galactic nuclei. Early on in her grad work, she'd thought about working on AGNs, and the mysterious way in which the massive black holes at the center of such galaxies balanced gas and energy outbursts over millions if not billions of years, regulating the energy radiated from that galaxy. She'd read something else about AGNs recently, not in any professional publication, but somewhere else. She just couldn't remember where. She began to search, and before long, she found what she was looking for—in her personal directory—from *The Passion of Science:*

It's more than merely interesting that AGNs regulate their galaxies. That's like saying superheated steam is warm, or liquid oxygen is slightly cool.

In considering the words, she couldn't help but think about the artifact. While it had been following its orbit since before humans had been using metal tools, and possibly far longer, even that time span was nothing compared to the timespan on which galaxies and all the suns that humans observed as stars operated. *Does it all really just happen through the interaction of the mechanics of physics that we still don't understand fully?*

She smiled ironically. Was that why she kept pursuing the idea that there had to be something behind—literally underneath—the multi-fractal mini-granulations? *Because you need more meaning in the universe, and if there isn't, you at least need to understand more of how it operates?*

Was there really any question about that?

That was another reason why she had been working on—and had almost finished—a multiple correlation-regression-link program that analyzed the appearance and frequency of multi-fractal mini-granulations, high-powered ultra-thin coronal loops, inter-granular magnetic fluctuations, and the convective activity of "normal" granulations.

Alayna tried not to check the systems too often, but the tightness in her abdomen didn't go away until the three-hour window reserved by the consortium ended, and an hour block for the University of Nevada began.

She stretched and started toward the aeroponics section.

"There is an incoming message," Marcel announced.

Her abdomen tightened again, almost painfully, as she sat down and accessed the message.

Just a word of thanks for the excellent service and support for the project. We appreciate it.

Alayna frowned. The message was from Jay Mehlin, the Director of the Williams Observatory, with a copy to Director Wrae. She'd never gotten a single message of thanks in the time she'd been at COFAR. She'd never heard of a postdoc getting something like the message she'd received, not directly and personally.

Where had that come from? Emma's doing? Or did Director Mehlin have something else in mind? How could he? She'd heard of him, but never met him. In fact, she doubted that she'd ever been within a hundred kilometers of him.

She had to respond, but what exactly could she say? Too formal a reply, and she'd come off cold and uncaring. Too effusive, and she'd come off as an ambitious young postdoc. *Which is exactly what you are.* She just didn't want to show that to the entire solar system.

Almost an hour later and after who knew how many attempts discarded, she sent her acknowledgment.

> Dear Dr. Mehlin:
> Thank you for your kind words.
>
> Director Wrae has always insisted that any of us at COFAR do our best to provide optimal services, and it is good to know that we could help in your project, especially since there is still so much to be learned about AGNs.
>
> With much appreciation.

She just hoped she had struck the right balance, but without knowing Dr. Mehlin and having heard nothing about his character or habits, that was the best that she could do . . . and not to reply would definitely be a mistake.

Still wondering about why Mehlin had sent the message, and since there was little else she could or had to do for the moment, she hurried down to the lower level to finish the laundry she'd neglected for too long, which, thankfully, didn't require that much time to fold and put away.

With that done, she returned to the control center, where she sat down and reread Chris's latest message, again. She smiled as she read his self-deprecating comments about how, according to what little he knew about gravitation, the artifact shouldn't be speeding up as much as it was. Somehow that pleased her, as did the information he passed to her about there being no detectable reason for that acceleration. *But what could be causing that in an inert body?*

Another thought struck, one that she should have considered earlier—much earlier. If the artifact was accelerating, was Chris having to accelerate to keep position on it? Because, if the increased speed was a result of something associated with the artifact, it shouldn't have affected his ship because the artifact certainly didn't have enough mass to bring the ship along with it.

She wished she'd thought to ask Chris that, and much earlier.

Either way, the logical answers boiled down to two. Either some outside force, beyond gravity, was acting on the artifact, or the artifact wasn't as inert as it appeared to be. The problem was that, according to what she knew, both answers were impossible. The next most obvious conclusion was that the object wasn't speeding up and that the calculations were somehow flawed, but she couldn't check those with observations from COFAR for another four days, possibly five, depending on the exact positions of the object and COFAR.

What if the impossible is happening? Who can you contact—Emma!
Alayna immediately composed a message, then read through it.

> Emma—
> I don't know if you've recovered enough from the cyclone/hurricane damage to determine this, but we've done some tracking on 2114 FQ5—yes, my Solar Express—and we either don't have enough data points or . . . it appears to be accelerating more than can be accounted for by gravitational forces. Because of COFAR's current position, we won't be able to check positions until the 22nd.
>
> I thought you might be interested.
>
> Oh . . . by the way, I received a very nice message from Dr. Mehlin.

If Emma responded to the last line, that might also tell Alayna something else.

After checking all the COFAR monitors, she headed off to make sure the aeroponics system was operating as optimally as possible.

Less than two hours later, when she returned from her at least daily check of the aeroponics system, a longer time than she'd anticipated because she'd had to replace two of the sprayers, and locating the spares had taken more time, because they hadn't been stored where the system indicated, Alayna discovered another message—from Emma.

> Alayna—
> We've been tracking 2114 FQ5. Same results. Details attached. Would appreciate your updated information when available.
>
> Dr. Mehlin can be very thoughtful.

The line about Mehlin was suggestive, but not conclusive in any way, but the very terseness of Emma's response confirmed Alayna's feelings about the alien artifact. The more worried the older astronomer became, the less voluble she was. The data definitely suggested that the artifact was speeding up more than could be accounted for by solar gravitation. In turn, that meant Alayna needed to reply to Chris immediately.

Chris—
COFAR is still not in position to confirm the increase in inbound speed that you've reported. I've checked with one other astronomy facility, and that facility's observations tend to confirm what you've reported.

Your observation about the effect of gravity is largely correct, in observed practice. Although gravitational attraction between two bodies is proportional to their masses and inversely proportional to the square of the distance between them, the sun's mass is so much greater than that of any small bodies in the solar system that, for practical purposes, the speed of attraction to the sun is effectively equal for such bodies and the result of the sun's mass. In effect, all small bodies should move with equal acceleration under gravity toward the sun, but that obviously isn't the case with regard to the artifact, which is why it just might deserve the name of Solar Express, unless the calculations of at least three reliable sources are all wrong.

This brings up another question, one which I should have asked earlier. Have you had to accelerate in order to maintain position? That would be helpful to know.

Whether you have or not, that still leaves us, and you, in particular, with three possibilities. (1) All our calculations are wrong. (2) The artifact has some form of yet undetected propulsion. (3) The artifact is far more massive than its size indicates. The third possibility seems unlikely because if the artifact has as much mass as would affect its inbound speed, it would also have enough surface gravity to attract your ship and squash you flat. At the same time, I'm dubious about two facilities and your AI all making miscalculations of the magnitude represented by the increased inbound velocity over what it "should" be. At this point, all the possibilities seem impossible. What makes them "impossible"? In the first case, it seems unlikely that speed calculations could be so misconstrued, but it has happened. In the second case, it is certainly possible, at least theoretically, that an alien technology might develop a propulsion system undetectable to us, but the odds seem long that such a technology would still be operable after thousands of years in only a fragment of the original sphere or craft when there is no sign of heat or energy as far insystem as you now are. In the third case, the only way the artifact could be that massive is if some technology restricted the effect of gravity around the artifact, and if that were the case, then the effect of that mass would seem to be nullified.

In short, at this point, I don't have any answers. I do have a very strong feeling that it would be far better to make plans to depart the area of the artifact much sooner than whatever date you had originally anticipated. Right now, I can't justify that through calculations, but I will as soon as I can after the twenty-first of the month.

As for your quotation, I would agree. Human beings talk about sharing knowledge while doing their best to hide it or get it first. Open space for the Sinese seems to mean open to them and open to others on their terms, but from what I've read of history that wasn't much different when the British Empire ruled Earth's oceans.

I don't have a quote this time, and I want to get this off.

Please take care.

Alayna immediately dispatched the message. She sat looking at the COFAR monitors, her thoughts on the impossibility that her discovery had become . . . and on the fact that so few, so far, seemed to know, or care, about what it might represent.

56

ASTRONEWS
17 November 2114

On 24 March 2114, two observatories reported within minutes of each other an object tentatively identified as a comet [C/X/2114 FT2 COFAR-SMOA]. The first report came from the Combined Farside Array at Daedalus Crater on the far side of the Moon, the second from the Sinese Main Optical Array. At first, there was nothing to distinguish Comet COFAR/SMOA from any other long-period comet with a high inclination, typical of comets originating in the Oort Cloud. Then, by the beginning of April, several observers discovered that the object's albedo varied dramatically, suggesting that the object rotated and had two sides with different characteristics. By mid-April, the comet brightened as it passed the orbit of Jupiter, but not as much as might have been expected, and early spectrographic analysis suggested the presence of silicon and silver, rather than the ice and dust composing most comets.

By September, the International Astronomical Union reclassified Comet COFAR/SMOA as a minor body [2114 FQ5], most probably an ice-covered heavy silica-based asteroid in a cometary orbit. More observations determined that 2114 FQ5 was far smaller than initially assumed, less than two kilometers at its greatest dimension, with one side having an albedo of point nine nine, and the other comparatively dark side still with an albedo of point five four.

Reports indicate that sometime on 1 November 2114, Noram Space Service launched a modified fusionjet on a trajectory aimed at a rendezvous with the so-called asteroid. Within several days of that, likely on November third, the Sinese Federation launched an uncrewed modified longliner. Observations made by the DOA facility in Victoria have verified that two smaller objects are positioned close to 2114 FQ5. Those observations also indicate that one half of the object has a shimmering surface containing silver and silicates.

Unverified reports suggest that 2114 FQ5 may be an artifact that has been orbiting the sun since approximately 12,900 B.C. More than a score of amateur observers have also noted that the object is moving toward the sun significantly faster than can be accounted for. Neither DOEA authorities nor the Sinese Space Ministry have replied to requests for information or comments.

A noted astronomer, who requested anonymity, noted that it is "almost certain" that the object is an alien artifact of some sort...

RECON THREE
18 NOVEMBER 2114

By midday on Saturday, Tavoian was even more frustrated and concerned. The second Sinese vessel had avoided Recon three and its ISVs, even while it disgorged independent monitors that seemed to swarm everywhere. More worrying was the manned space tug/sled that carried space-suited figures and equipment to various parts of the artifact, particularly to the partly open hexagonal chambers with extruded protrusions. He hadn't seen any signs that the Sinese had found or explored the side chambers and passageway to the "drive" chamber, unless they had found an entry on the far side, which was certainly possible. All of this he had dutifully reported to the colonel, including the fact that the Sinese had made no attempt to contact him, as if carrying on a charade that they believed Recon three was an uncrewed mission like their longliner was. Following his own orders, in turn, he had not attempted communications with the Sinese, although he had attempted, unsuccessfully, to intercept their communications.

He had continued to use the ISVs, the spy-eyes, and the rovers to investigate passageways, concentrating on those bordering the hull, but after two more days had little to show for those efforts, except a few assorted frozen atmosphere crystals that were similar to the earlier crystals analyzed and a handful of what analysis revealed to be circumstellar dust. The first ISV was doing more laser studies of the barely discolored circles on the hull, for comparison, if nothing else, and he had just dispatched the second ISV to look into a passageway that had reflected sunlight slightly differently, at least to his eyes, when another message from the colonel arrived. The key point was simple:

> The increased speed of the artifact toward the sun requires
> more rapid completion of investigatory tasks and discovery of
> replicable technology, materials, or insights into the advanced
> technology represented by the artifact.

In short, produce some results.

Tavoian's problem was that he really didn't know what else he could do besides what he was already doing. He was looking into every passageway and hexagon into which he could send the rovers or the spy-eyes. He was sampling all the loose material he could find. He was using the laser to investigate material composition and possible properties, and he had the ship's AI watching the artifact continuously. But the fact remained. There were at least ten thousand of the hexagonal chambers, most of which were the smaller ones, and while the majority of those that his remotes had investigated were sealed, there was always the possibility that one with something of value in some way might not be. So he kept sending the remotes out.

You might as well find out now just how you're coming. "How far inside Earth's orbit are we now?"

RECON THREE IS INSIDE THE EARTH'S ORBIT BY THIRTY-SIX MILLION KAYS.

It didn't feel like he and Recon three were hurtling toward the sun, but he didn't doubt the fact that it was happening, and that he was slowly, but inexorably, running out of time.

While he was thinking over what else he might be able to do, since he wasn't getting much in the way of useful suggestions from the colonel or his advisers, another message arrived from Alayna. He immediately noticed that it had been delayed almost eighteen hours. When he finished reading it, he thought he knew why it had been delayed—because more than a few people had looked at it—and why it had finally been sent on—because the colonel was hoping something that she had said might inspire Tavoian.

He read the message again, slowly.

While what she had sent made sense, it also pointed out the quiet impossibility of the situation and the artifact itself. She'd outlined the options clearly. Either human calculations were wrong, or the seemingly inert alien technology was incredibly advanced, advanced enough to have an impact in a way that was undetectable except by its effect. He also realized something else, after the first day or so, the ship's AI had not had to use the drive to keep position. *But what did that mean? That the artifact was carrying them along as it increased its speed?* How was that possible without being detected?

It might not be that undetectable if we could only get into those sealed chambers. But what if they were like all the ones he had been able to investigate?

Almost absently, and because he was out of ideas, he asked the ship's AI, "Is there anything new or different about the artifact?"

THERE IS. THE ARTIFACT'S OUTER HULL NO LONGER REFLECTS ULTRA-VIOLET RADIATION FOR WAVELENGTHS SHORTER THAN 370 NANOMETERS.

"When did this happen?"

AT 0947 UTC.

"Display the hull optically. Maximum resolution." Tavoian studied the image. Although it was probably his imagination, somehow the hull appeared duller. "That either means the hull isn't receiving UV or it's suddenly absorbing it. Have the Sinese done something to screen the object?"

THERE IS NOTHING BETWEEN THE ARTIFACT AND THE SUN WITHIN RANGE OF RECON THREE'S DETECTION CAPABILITIES.

"Is the artifact radiating energy, other than by reflection, in any fashion?"

NEGATIVE.

"Is there any possible external reason for the change in the reflectivity of the hull?"

NONE HAS BEEN DETECTED.

"Has the artifact changed in any other way?"

NO CHANGES HAVE BEEN DETECTED, EXCEPT FOR THE PRESENCE OF INVESTIGATORY REMOTES AND SINESE PERSONNEL.

Somehow Tavoian didn't think that the Sinese had anything to do with the change in reflectivity.

While he watched the monitors, and waited for the return of both ISVs and the results of their latest investigations, he decided to reply to the colonel's last message . . . and if he didn't come up with more ideas after that, then he'd write a long message to Alayna . . . and answer her question. She might have an idea about why the artifact's hull suddenly had stopped reflecting UV and shorter wavelengths. She also seemed to be more helpful than all of Donovan Base.

That's not true.

Not totally, anyway, but it was still how he felt at the moment.

Despite it being lunar day, on Tuesday, Alayna rose early to take advantage of a half hour block of unbooked time on the main optical array. The position of the sun was such that she could finally focus the main telescope on the alien artifact and have Marcel make the necessary observations and measurements.

When she saw the first image, with the three objects around a bigger disc, she frowned for a moment, until she recalled Chris's mention of the arrival of the second Sinese ship in his last message, the one that had also mentioned that he had not had to accelerate his ship to keep station on the artifact. And that brought up the question of how and why the artifact could apparently carry the ships with it as it accelerated—when it apparently didn't have a mass sufficient to do that—under any form of astrophysics she knew.

"What's the position of the artifact with regard to the orbit of Venus?"

"2114 FQ5 crossed the orbit of Venus last night at 2133 UTC."

"That's even earlier than you calculated from the Mauna Kea data, isn't it?"

"Twelve hours earlier."

"It shouldn't be doing that."

Marcel did not respond to that, obviously, because Alayna had offered an opinion and not asked a question.

She did need to find out if the optical array saw what Chris had reported.

"Marcel, are there any changes in the image of 2114 FQ5?"

"There are now no reflected wavelengths shorter than 370 nanometers."

That certainly confirmed Chris's observation. "Are you certain?" *Dumb question!* The AI was connected to all the monitoring systems. "Is there any indication of what might have caused that change?"

"There is not, Dr. Wong-Grant."

First the inbound speed issue, and now this! Chris was right beside the artifact, and none of his instruments recorded anything but an inert object. Yet what was occurring with the alien artifact was impossible, according to present theory. *Not necessarily theory,* she corrected herself. Since something was happening, it had to be undetected or undetectable by any instruments or equipment trained on the object. In turn, that meant it was concealed within the object by the impermeability . . . *Except we don't know of any way that could work without some external evidence— heat, radiation, energy flows . . . something.* In turn, that suggested some aspect of current theory wasn't either inclusive enough, overlooked a possibility, or was wrong. *Or the theory is right, and the builders of the artifact found a way around the theory.*

Alayna didn't like any of the possibilities, but there wasn't anything she could do about it at the moment. "Please calculate the probable position of 2114 FQ5 at 1200 UTC each day for the next month, with the projected distance from the sun at that time. Put a copy in my incoming."

"Yes, Dr. Wong-Grant."

Alayna forced her attention from the alien artifact, the Solar Express that was living up to its name, and to the other matter at hand—the issue of the man who wasn't there, but was—the question of how to get a better insight on the sun's multi-fractal mini-granulations. And she needed to get on with finalizing her own observations when she got her block of time on the solar array later that afternoon—an unexpected cancellation—because she hadn't anticipated having the extra time.

After that, she had more repairs to make, this time in the cargo lock, and she really needed to replace an entire section of seals before the arrival of the "pack train" from Lunara Mining on Thursday.

The little repairs were continual, and they added up. *But that's really why you're here, so far as the Foundation's concerned.* And she needed to reply to Chris, but she could do that later, after her own work . . . and the repairs.

Yet somehow the alien artifact was working, or so it seemed, after thousands of years, and Daedalus Base needs constant attention after less than thirty-five years?

She forced her thoughts back to what other variables might have a regressive correlation . . .

HOTNEWS!
19 November 2114

[Image Deleted For Off-Earth Transmission]

Chancellor Erek Rumikov's back in bed . . . we mean back on the job . . . rumor has it that the so-called Scottish separatists who wounded him two weeks ago were separatists in a different sense—separated spouses of Scots who didn't take kindly to Rumikov's attention to their exes. You'll notice we didn't mention gender, either. Rumikov's not talking about it, either, and no one's been able to find the attackers. Could be that no one wants to.

[Image Deleted]

It's getting crowded out there in space! Around that alien artifact, anyway. Word is that a Sinese "research" ship reached the Solar Express. No one's talking, not publicly, about the fact that it's armored and twice the size of anything else floating around out there. Except it's not floating. The Solar Express is sprinting toward the sun. That's what the very noted John Dorcaster, head of the Yerkes Observatory at the University of Chicago, claims. We told you it was an express, right from the first. Remember that when it goes up in solar flames!

[Image Deleted]

Ramona Cunnard's not happy. Not at all. If you don't remember the name, well, she's Kitten on *Sex and the Sin-Team*, and she's anything but pleased to find out that her partner's taken up with a cougar, the female type. Worst of all, that cougar is none other than Elise Read, and she's the Kitten's agent. Lots of claws and screeches. More entertaining than *Sex and the Sin-Team*.

[Image Deleted]

Talk about takeovers! The evangelical cooperative BibleTruth has just purchased the century-old Creation Museum from the ailing Answers in Genesis Foundation for one billion dollars. That's right. That's the biblical theme park that allows visitors to experience the destruction of Sodom and Gomorrah and be chased through the Sinai desert by a tyrannosaurus rex after barely escaping the Red Sea swallowing the Egyptian army under the sinister gaze of one of the pharaohs Ramses. Must still be a lot of dollars in being a true believer!

[Image Deleted]

That school explosion in Xigase? Chinese Minister of Defense Wu Gong claims the school, holding more than a hundred children, was destroyed by an Indra missile launched from Bhutan. Indian Prime Minister Ravindra denies the charge. He claims that if India wanted to target anyone in the Sinese Federation, it would have been Minister Wu Gong. Just kidding! That's what the Prime Minister should have said. He only denied that it was a missile and said that nothing came from either Bhutan or India. Rumors abound, but one source claims it was a natural gas explosion. For the Sinese, everything is someone else's plot.

[Image Deleted]

The last free-floating section of the west Antarctic ice sheet broke free yesterday . . . The remnants of the Thwaites Glacier collapsed. A chunk of ice the size of Rhode Island is now drifting away from Antarctica. Between 2110 and 2113, the once massive ice sheet retreated almost fifty kilometers. Scientists are forecasting another ten meters of ocean level rise in the next century. What's next? Beachfront property in Philadelphia or Dallas? Swamps in California's central valley?

RECON THREE
23 NOVEMBER 2114

By Thursday Tavoian's spy-eyes had investigated another thirty-three hexagonal chambers, none of which were open, without finding anything new or different. In the process, he'd lost two more of the large spy-eyes. Exactly how, he had no idea, since neither returned. One of the other spy-eyes had captured a momentary image of one of the errant remotes, wobbling side to side for several moments before suddenly heading down a passageway not on its programmed route.

The Sinese continued to send their remotes and the crewed tug/sled to various parts of the artifact. The AI reported occasional flashes of light, reflected or scattered laser beams. Spectrographic analysis of the two flashes that reached Recon three without spreading revealed the same elements that Tavoian had discovered. Faithfully Tavoian sent daily reports to the colonel, and just as regularly received requests for any additional data or information Tavoian could muster.

The ship's AI had calculated that Recon three had crossed the orbit of Venus late on the night of the twentieth. With a continuing increase in speed over what solar gravity could account for, the artifact and Recon three were now over eight million kays farther inside the orbit of Venus.

If not farther, thought Tavoian as he readied the ISV and the four spy-eyes for their next exploration mission. At the rate he was losing spy-eyes, he just might have four of the ten large ones left by the time Recon three needed to depart the vicinity of the artifact.

By 0743, the ISV was headed to the side of the dark green expanse directly opposite where the AI rover had discovered both the possible ship launching bay and the passageway leading to the drive chamber. Given the use of hexagons by the builders of the artifact, Tavoian had decided to investigate the areas that would have formed a hexagon with one vertex located at the point of the passage already discovered. He would have made that expedition on Wednesday, but the Sinese space-sled had been hovering in the area; so Tavoian had sent the slightly larger ISV with the remaining laser to study as many of the circles as possible.

The circles had bothered him because, outside of the circle caused by the severing of the artifact from its original sphere or spacecraft, there were no other circles anywhere. The only explanation he could come up with for their explanation was that the hexagons below had projected some form of energy in a hexagonal field, but that field had spread slightly and manifested itself as a circle in whatever effect it had upon the substance of the hull. In terms of the physics he knew he wasn't sure that made sense, but he mentally termed it a working hypothesis, until he came up with a better explanation.

While the ship's AI monitored the ISV after it released the programmed spy-eyes, Tavoian positioned himself roughly on the control couch, strapped loosely in place, and began to compile, once again, what he had discovered about the artifact, a listing of the obvious, the apparently mundane, and the not-so-mundane:

> The materials of both hull and interior were impregnable, and showed no impact damage from thousands of years in space.

> Some force had sheared the artifact from a larger body of which the artifact appeared to constitute less than five percent.

> The hull was largely silicon and silver, but fabricated in a fashion that made it harder than any human-created material and a nearly perfect mirror, but finished with microscopic diffraction gratings, impossible as retaining impregnability seemed for such a finish.

> The interior was largely carbon, again fabricated in a fashion that made it harder than any human-created material.

> Attempting to sever a "thread" of the hull material, roughly some eighty micrometers thick, released enough energy in vacuum to vaporize the closest parts of the tunable laser.

> The chambers were flat hexagons, almost all of which were one of two sizes, the majority having sides of somewhat less than twenty-five meters, the larger having sides of somewhat less than fifty meters. They were arranged in a fashion with the flat sides roughly parallel to the hull, suggesting the artifact could have been rotated to provide artificial gravity.

The material comprising the hexagons was nonconductive, except at certain select wavelengths where it exhibited apparent photoconductivity.

Several days inside the orbit of Earth, the hull began to absorb electromagnetic wavelengths in the UV range and shorter. There was no discernible increase in the hull temperature and no additional radiated heat or energy.

All functional technology had to be within the impermeable wall structures, but had been able to be extruded when required.

There did not appear to be pressure doors sealing various sections of the artifact.

If the crystals were frozen atmosphere, that atmosphere was largely nitrogen and oxygen, with a larger-than-expected component of argon.

There was at least one large and empty chamber that appeared to have been an airlock, large enough to hold a spacecraft as large as Recon three.

The "drive" chambers contained thirty-two hexagonal gray columns. On the exterior hull, there were thirty-two circles that appeared to coincide with the placement of the columns beneath the hull. The circles reflected all wavelengths of visible light except one, and one of UV not visible to most human eyes, a difference of two nanometers, precisely. And the circles were one point five percent less reflective than the rest of the hull.

The only less than common elements detected, and each in only one location, were rhenium and palladium.

With no detectable radiation, or other energy, the artifact was accelerating toward the sun faster than accounted for by solar mass/gravitation.

After close to an hour, Tavoian could not think of anything else. He also knew he'd think of more in time. He hoped he would.

He also felt guilty, in a fashion, for not sending out the other ISV on some sort of investigation or mission, but his stocks of thruster propellant were now below forty percent, and he didn't want to use up any more, not immediately, unless he had a better purpose than randomly pursuing investigations. *Maybe the spy-eyes will find something new.*

THE CONCENTRATION FOR CO2 HAS REACHED ZERO POINT NINE PERCENT.

Tavoian frowned. That was two-tenths of a percent over the maximum recommended long-term SMAC level. The atmosphere maintenance system was supposed to be able to handle five weeks without strain. "Supposed to" wasn't the same as doing it, and not many fusionjets had been continuously inhabited for as long as the more than three weeks he'd been aboard Recon three. "Status of atmosphere maintenance system?"

SYSTEM IS OPERATING NORMALLY. RESERVE AIR SUPPLY IS AT FORTY-FIVE PERCENT.

"Keep me posted if the SMAC level goes up more than another tenth of a percent."

WILL COMPLY.

The rising SMAC level was a concern, but not urgent. *Not yet.*

At that moment, the message indicator flashed, showing three incomings. Tavoian glanced through the senders' names—the news summary, Kit, and Alayna. The news summary could wait.

Although he dreaded reading Kit's message, he decided to begin there.

> Dear Chris—
> As usual, I'm still worrying about you, wherever you are. The news never seems to get better. Now the Sinese are trying to blame a natural gas explosion on the Indians. That's as if the Indians would waste a missile that costs more than some countries' total environmental improvement budgets on a school in an out-of-the-way mountain town with no military significance. The Indians are suggesting they might use those missiles on personnel targets. If that means high Sinese military officials, I can understand the thought, but what happens to the world then?

If we all survived it, the survivors might remember . . . except human memories are so short . . . and everyone thinks they're different, even when they repeat the mistakes of the past.

> Mother rallied briefly the other day. She remembered you couldn't get home. She said it was better that way. That you

wouldn't remember her at her worst. She apologized for making us take care of her. Today, she thought you were still piloting fusionjets from the Earth to the Moon. Dad doesn't talk much. He hates wearing a mask and gloves even to hold Mother's hand.

Tavoian swallowed and looked away from the screen for several minutes before continuing.

I've been granted familial leave, with full pay, and I have more time banked than I'll ever use. One benefit of being a work addict. It's not as though much work is getting done anyway. The Department of the Environment's half furloughed because the Senate still hasn't passed the environmental appropriations. That idiot Castenada keeps offering amendments to transfer funds for useless remediation in and around New York. It's not the Venice of the western hemisphere there. It's the replacement for the worst of what was Florida and Louisiana . . .

When he finished Kit's message, Tavoian found a spare tissue and blew his nose. He was careful to stuff it into his pocket. He didn't need tissues floating around. Then he ate several soft rye crackers. He also had to be careful with those. Crumbs and weightlessness weren't a good combination. Finally, he started Alayna's message.

Chris—
You're always so encouraging about my work with the multifractals, and I definitely need that encouragement. I feel that they're something more than random creation as the by-product of Gaussian-distributed mechanistic convection of solar granulations, like the man upon the stair who wasn't there. (That's an allusion to an old poem; I guess it was a song as well.) But whatever it is, I haven't yet been able to find out what that something might be. I also haven't found anything that would rule it out, except for mechanistic nuclear-generated convection. It could just be that I don't want to admit that the most basic processes in the universe don't lead to more, and that could be a fatal failing on my part, at least occupationally.

Don't we all want some meaning in the universe? Meaning that transcends mechanics? Tavoian snorted. He doubted that the universe had meaning. Structure, but not meaning. People had to create meaning.

Whether it's there or not. Which continued to be the problem with true believers of every kind.

With a faint and ironic smile, he continued reading.

> COFAR's calculations show that the artifact's speed is continuing to increase faster than it should, based on all possible variables of which we're aware. That means I'm missing something, and the likelihood is whatever I'm missing is something to do with the artifact. I could be wrong. I've been wrong before. But the AI at COFAR usually doesn't make that kind of mistake. I worry about you, and even the Sinese around the artifact, but mostly about you. As of last night—22 November— at 2030 UTC, we calculated the inbound speed of the artifact at fifty kilometers per second. If the observed rate of increase continues, by the time you reach the "averaged" orbit of Mercury (fifty-eight million kilometers from the sun) on November 30th, possibly late on the 29th, the artifact should be traveling more than sixty-five kps. It might be even faster.

Tavoian frowned. His initial briefing had used the figure of fifty kps. At least, he thought it had been fifty kps.

> By the time it reaches perihelion on December 4th, which we may not be able to see, unless it's very early, because Farside will be leaving lunar day, it will be traveling in excess of 200 kps. How much faster is problematical because we're extrapolating, and those extrapolations are based on the past history of an unknown factor. We're calculating future additional speed by assuming that the artifact is accelerating at a constant rate. Assuming an enormous mass would give the same acceleration, but that amount of mass would have other more obvious effects—such as gravitational attraction and weight if you were standing on the artifact.

> All assumptions are dangerous. Those made on the basis of observing something that is not understood are so much more. I don't know what's involved in what you're engaged in, or even exactly what you are doing, but I would strongly suggest that you give yourself an exceedingly generous margin of safety.

She's worried about you. And it was more than clear she thought staying around the artifact too long and too close to the sun was not a good idea.

Because I've been too lax in skipping past quotes, I thought this one might be particularly appropriate:

Scientists are so often considered cold and calculating. A good scientist is calmly, but fiercely heated and calculating. Cold-ness too often means that you don't care, and above all, a sci-entist should care . . . Especially about being methodical and precise.

That calculation doesn't apply absolutely to people, not for me, although a touch of caution isn't misplaced.

Tavoian thought about Alayna's message, and the last lines, for a time, and about her, how long he wasn't certain, but was diverted from those thoughts by the ship's AI.

THREE SPY-EYES HAVE RETURNED TO THE ISV. THE FOURTH HAS NOT.

"Wait ten minutes."

The errant spy-eye did not return, and Tavoian recalled the ISV to Recon three.

As the ISV headed back toward Recon three, Tavoian thought about accessing the feeds remotely, then decided to wait until the ISV was se-curely docked. While he waited, he called up the Space Command daily news summary and began to read. Almost immediately, he wished he hadn't.

The Indian Defense Minister had issued a warning that if the Sinese at-tacked any Indian installation or territory whatsoever, India would retali-ate with "unstoppable force" and that not even the deepest bunkers nor the most distant outposts would be secure from that force. Tavoian shook his head after he read that President Yates had requested both parties to exercise restraint. From what Tavoian had read, the Indians had exercised restraint, and it had only provoked the Sinese. The Sinese seemed to believe that until the last few days everyone would stand aside while protesting. The Israelis, the African Union, and the Iranians all were backing India.

Tavoian set aside the news summary and considered where else he might send his various remotes that might have some slight chance of discovering something new about the artifact. He hadn't fully investigated all of the passages off the central shaft, not that he'd ever have time to do that, but he had searched and studied the entire circumference of the artifact. After a time, he cleared his throat.

"Plot out on an image of the dark side of the artifact all the areas we've investigated. Highlight those areas less explored and any areas that ap-pear to have any possibility of being different."

The ship's AI actually took almost a minute to reply. PLOT IS READY AND DISPLAYED. ISV HAS RETURNED AND IS DOCKED.

Tavoian was still studying the plot and considering options when he realized that he hadn't studied the feeds from the three spy-eyes that had returned. He accessed the first one immediately.

As with so many of the images Tavoian had seen over the past weeks, the initial image was that of dark green bulkheads, decks, and overheads, as the first ISV threaded its way through the junctions of the passageways surrounding the hexagonal chambers and then through a narrow hexagonal opening into a passageway that appeared to be parallel to the hull. Although Tavoian watched closely, and froze the image a number of times, he could find no trace of an entry along the outboard side of the passage. He even had the AI study the images to see if it could discern any fractional difference in wall coloration or texture, to no avail.

The spy-eye continued past where Tavoian had hoped there might be another ship launching bay and, some fifty meters later, came to an abrupt inboard turn in the passageway. After the turn, the passage continued some ten meters before ending in a blank bulkhead. Again there were no indications of a "door frame" or any means to proceed. On the return, the spy-eye passed two of the other spy-eyes, but did not show an image of the third.

Tavoian watched the feeds from the next two spy-eyes. Both recorded other spy-eyes passing, but neither indicated what might have happened to the missing remote.

Another minor mystery. Mechanical/programming failure . . . or some effect of the artifact? Tavoian doubted that he'd ever discover if either possibility was correct. There were so many interconnecting passageways that it was unlikely he'd recover even one of the malfunctioning units.

He'd been correct about there being a passageway leading to the drive chambers, but any access from the other side of the artifact was blocked. There was no indication of a ship launching bay, even though the passageway seemed to resemble the one on the other side of the artifact. *But with the apparent past plasticity of the material, how can you tell?*

Tavoian went back to the plot of possible areas to explore, trying not to think about the last lines in Alayna's message or what he could say in return to Kit.

Daedalus Base
25 November 2114

Saturday night Alayna didn't sleep well, and she woke up on Sunday early and tired. She hadn't been able to put aside her worries about Chris. She'd tried, and she had even gotten up and tweaked the analytics for her next set of solar observations, but all that hadn't helped, and after fitfully trying to sleep, she'd gotten up before 0530 UTC and fixed coffee, and thought as she sipped it.

First of all, his observation about the change in hull reflectivity had bothered her. To begin with, she couldn't imagine diffraction gratings fine enough to convey a mirror finish to an entire hull while remaining untouched and unscarred for thousands of years. Then to shift reflectivity? She'd managed a brief spectrographic analysis of the artifact, and his report was absolutely correct. That didn't tell her how or why it had happened, but she was fairly certain that the change was linked to the intensity of solar radiation reaching the hull. Abrupt changes in spectral absorption and reflection didn't just happen without cause. To her, that was another indication of either high technology operating while partly destroyed and after at least ten thousand years. And that was scary.

The second problem was the hull "circles," effectively the only circles found anywhere on the artifact. They'd either been changed by whatever the columns that lay behind the hull or designed that way to reflect all visible light wavelengths, except 379 and 380 nanometers. Why did the circle parts of the hull reflect all visible light, except a two-nanometer gap? And why was reflectivity just there one and a half percent lower than the rest of the hull?

The greatest problem, from her personal viewpoint, was where Chris was headed. It wasn't just that he could end up inside the orbit of Mercury sooner than he realized. The problem was the combination of position and the speed at which he'd been carried along with the alien artifact. She didn't know all the details about fusionjets and how they operated, but she did know that most operated best at a one-gee acceleration, and that they were limited to about two hours of continuous acceleration, and needed almost as much "rest" time as acceleration time. If the alien artifact was traveling at sixty-five kilometers per second when it crossed the averaged orbit of Mercury, and it might be closer to seventy . . . She swallowed.

If it's traveling at seventy kps, he can't escape on a direct course, and if a fusionjet doesn't have good shielding, he'll have to take a tangential course outside Mercury's orbit or not too far inside . . . And fusionjets weren't designed for long periods of habitation. He'd already been on his ship for close to a month. If he had to take an elliptical or other indirect return to Earth, which was the closest haven, it might take another month. Even sending someone after him might be difficult.

She needed to get off a message to him. But it needed to be worded carefully, very carefully, just in case. After a time, she began . . .

> Dear Chris,
> Even though I'm the one who's spent much of her life studying the sun, you'll shortly be far closer than I will ever be. I'd like to know what you feel seeing the sun swell in the sky and knowing that you're traveling at such incredible speed. Scores of astronomers will be watching. They, too, will envy you, and many will want to talk to you, especially since you're on a solo mission, all by yourself.
>
> It wouldn't hurt to take some images of the sun just before you reach the orbit of Mercury.
>
> The last person to travel that close was Icarus, but that was mythology . . .

How much more do you dare to say?

> . . . and you have far better "wings" than he did (I know spacecraft don't have wings, but I couldn't resist finishing the comparison), and far better engineers behind you, but it's the only mythological parallel I can think of, and I think it's still valid.
>
> So far as my own work goes, I'm about to try a multi-latitude correlation, or perhaps a multi-latitude negative correlation. We'll just have to see how it goes. We're supposed to be in a solar minimum at present, but over the past month the number of sunspots and other convective activity seems to be increasing, although it's not anywhere near past solar maximums.

But then, even in minimum times, the solar photosphere is an awesome place.

I didn't mention it before, but I'm glad your sister enjoyed the quote about the fractal nature of coastlines. Because I'm squeezing this in between observations, and because I wanted to get it off, Icarus will have to do for a quote.

Do take care.

When she finished and sent off the message, Alayna took a deep breath. She couldn't still have said why, but she'd felt that an out-and-out screaming warning—GET AWAY FROM THE ARTIFACT SOON!—wouldn't have been welcome, and might not have gotten through to Chris, since it had been clear that all messages to and from him were being read.

Since there wasn't anything else that she could do, not that would have much effect, she went through her morning checks, including going to the aeroponics room early, and then checking on the pressure in the cargo lock to see how the seal repairs she'd made were holding up.

After that, she forced her thoughts back to her own problem. She'd gone back and checked to see if there were any instances of the "regular-shaped" mini-granulations, but even Marcel's careful scanning had revealed exactly one possibility in the latest observations, and it also appeared to be another affect of the mini-granulation's impingement on the flux lines bordering the edges of two regular granulations—again. Could it be that most of those only showed up during the times of the solar maximum? Why only then? What might that reveal, if anything, about the multi-fractal mini-granulations?

Once again, the words she'd thought had vanished, at least for a while, were going through her head:

> Yesterday, upon the stair,
> I met a man who wasn't there.

Thinking about what wasn't there, her thoughts drifted back to the artifact, and some of the observations Chris had passed on. It wasn't pitted or scarred anywhere. It had circles on the hull that, again, couldn't be explained in any traditional fashion, and then there was the damned reflectivity shift, indicating that the artifact was now absorbing the higher energy wavelengths. Another form of solar power? Working after tens of centuries, if not longer?

Could something—the alien equivalent of an AI?—still be functioning? Or was it just an intelligent material response, something engineered to work no matter what? Either way, the artifact worried her.

You can't do any more now.

She wrenched her concentration back to her own solar difficulties, hoping that her message wouldn't be unduly delayed and that the message within the message was clear to Chris and didn't scream out too loudly to those reading it before Chris did.

62

The New York Times
25 November 2114

[Ottawa] Last night, after acrimonious debate during a rare Saturday session, in a close vote of 73–71, the Noram Senate approved a supplemental appropriations bill for the Department of Off-Earth Affairs, clearing the legislation for President Yates's signature. The vote was heralded as a victory for the Administration, but foreshadows more bitter infighting over funding in the continuing lame-duck session, despite the looming threat of possible military action by the Sinese Federation against the Indian-UAAS alliance. The vote would not have occurred if President Yates had not called the Senate into session to deal with military issues related to the Sinese/Indian escalation. Conservative Party chair Edward Spalin declared that the loss of three seats in the election earlier this month would not change the calculus of the fight over next year's budget. "The people are tired of their tax dollars being poured into space when so much remains undone here on Earth."

"Pouring money down a rat-hole to perpetuate a global hoax." That was how Senator Riccardo Castenada (CP-NY) characterized the Administration's funding request. He also released documents that purported to show that Space Service officials authorized the Noram manned expedition to investigate the "nonexistent alien artifact" termed the Solar Express, using funds appropriated for other purposes. Castenada's amendment to censure DOEA Secretary Luvalle was defeated on a straight party-line vote of 80–65. Castenada reiterated his contention that the Solar Express was not only a hoax, but a fraud designed to funnel government funds to the military-space combine at the expense of urgent domestic needs.

Senator Craig Savage (CP-ID) attempted to amend the bill to require all funds used for DOEA procurement be spent in North America. That attempt was ruled nongermane by Vice President Saint-Denis, despite a protest by Senator Castenada.

When Senator Kim Greywinter [D-ALB] observed that events had proved Castenada, referred to as the "individual representing New York," had been wrong about the Sinese probe to the Solar Express and the subsequent Sinese manned expedition, Castenada replied, "I don't care if the Sinese pour billions down their rat-hole; that doesn't mean we should."

Castenada was investigated earlier this year by the Noram Inspector-General's office in regard to charges that he revealed classified DOEA material to the media after the Administration failed to provide additional disaster relief to New York City. That investigation was closed without comment by the Inspector General.

In related developments, EC Chancellor Rumikov, recently returned to Vienna, again called on both Noram and the Sinese Federation to share fully any scientific information recovered from missions to investigate the Solar Express. He called their present failure to do so deplorable.

Sinese Minister for Space Wong Mengyi let it be known through ministry officials that it was absurd to think that the Sinese research vessel investigating the Solar Express was a hurriedly converted space warship, since the Sinese refused to be the first to militarize outer space, unlike others who had already engaged in covert militarization . . .

The Yates Administration declined to comment on the veiled Sinese charges about covert militarization. There was no word about whether the President would request additional funds for the Department of Defense to deal with the current international crisis.

63

RECON THREE
25 NOVEMBER 2114

Early Sunday morning, Tavoian checked the CO_2 levels again, up more than slightly to one point nine percent, more than one percent over the recommended SMAC of point seven percent for missions exceeding seven days, but CO_2 levels had been bouncing between one point seven and one point eight for several days, depending on his level of activity. They were up especially after he'd exercised, but the atmosphere system seemed to be handling the CO_2 adequately, if not outstandingly. There was also the continued loss of reserve air, now down to twenty percent, because of all the repairs and equipment refittings requiring use of the lock.

What can you do except worry. Besides, you'll be leaving in a few days. Still, almost a thirty percent increase in a day was something to watch. He knew that the SMAC levels were protective, and that people had survived at higher levels, but that above three percent over several days, there were definite, if minor, adverse impacts, and above five percent the effects were worse. Above seven percent . . . He didn't want to go there.

There were worse things than an elevated CO_2 level. At least, he could breathe without ripping his lungs out, unlike his mother. He didn't like thinking about that, or that Kit was alone with their parents. Not totally alone, but she'd had to deal with so much already. He'd tried to be encouraging, sympathetic, and caring in his last message back to her, but the fact was that he wouldn't have been able to go Earthside even if he'd been on Donovan Base. All that didn't make him feel any better.

He turned from the environmental indicators, considering how much he wanted to use the ISV and the spy-eyes, since his stock of thruster propellant was down to twenty-eight percent. Then he frowned and asked, "When will we reach the orbit of Mercury? Using the averaged orbit figure of fifty-eight million kays?"

AT PRESENT ESTIMATED VELOCITIES, RECON THREE WILL REACH A POINT FIFTY-EIGHT MILLION KAYS FROM THE SUN AT 0721 UTC ON NOVEMBER TWENTY-NINTH.

That was days earlier than anyone had calculated—except Alayna.

A wry smile appeared and vanished. *With three days left, thruster propellant isn't going to be a concern.* It also meant that Tavoian needed to think through what else he could do, what else he and his remotes could possibly discover.

Over the past two days, he had deployed the ISV and the larger spy-eyes to the other four points of the imaginary hexagon where he thought there might be additional other passageways leading to the "drive" chamber. The results had been less than he'd hoped for. One more spy-eye had vanished, but at three of the points, there had been passageways leading in the direction of the drive chamber. Each of those passageways had ended in a closed passage, apparently where the entry to the drive chamber should have been. None of the long passageways had shown any indication of an entry to a possible ship launching bay. The fourth point, although it had been the second investigated, might also have led to the drive chambers, except at a point corresponding to where the other passageways began, there was a solid bulkhead. Whether that meant that there was a passageway, or nothing at all, was impossible to tell.

Tavoian felt as though he were spinning his wheels, figuratively as well as literally, on the smooth, almost-frictionless surfaces of the artifact. He also had the feeling that the Sinese were running into the same problem. From what he could tell, they also hadn't come up with much, for all the spy-eyes and remotes that swarmed over the artifact. There certainly hadn't been any concentration of space-sleds, spy-eyes, or remotes in any one locale.

After studying the map that the AI had constructed, Tavoian began to prepare one ISV, a rover, some signal repeaters, and the fiber-optic spooling device to investigate areas that neither he nor the Sinese had yet looked into.

Shortly after he'd dispatched that ISV, losing more atmosphere in the process, while he was studying the monitors, especially the one focused on the larger Sinese ship, he observed two of the sleds or tugs moving slowly toward the artifact, one towing a large assembly, the other tethered to the assembly and following. The slowness of movement suggested to Tavoian that the equipment—whatever it was—was fairly massive, and that the second sled was there to decelerate that substantial mass so that it would not smash into the artifact.

"Didn't they have that assembly out yesterday, trying to test or cut through the hull?" Tavoian already knew. His question was rhetorical. So far as he and the ship's AI had determined, the Sinese had had no success. *So why are they trying it on the dark material? Or are they trying something different?*

Because he couldn't get that good a view of what the Sinese were doing, Tavoian decided to send out the remaining ISV and a pair of spy-eyes to see what the Sinese were trying, especially since he had had both ISVs investigating passageways when the Sinese had used the laser assembly earlier, and the only images had been from Recon three and not particularly clear. The Sinese had been observing his investigations, and it only seemed fair that he should be able to observe theirs, if from a discreet distance. He wasn't about to hazard the ISV by getting as close as the ten meters that the Sinese spy-eyes had been to his remotes. Depending on the Sinese reaction, or lack thereof, he might ease one of the spy-eyes closer.

He had to hurry to ready the second ISV and spy-eyes, but the Sinese were moving so deliberately that they were still positioning the assembly when the ISV moved out of Recon three's lock and toward the alien artifact. Tavoian halted the ISV roughly a hundred meters from the artifact. From there he dispatched the spy-eyes, as he sat before Recon three's controls and took in the views from both spy-eyes and the ISV. He spread the spy-eyes to each side and halted them around twenty meters from the space-sleds.

Two figures in white spacesuits were working with the large assembly, trying to position it and maintain that position over the slowly rotating artifact. The view from the nearer spy-eye strongly suggested that what it viewed was a high-energy laser, one that had to be powered by a linked chain of supercapacitors. And it was aimed at a center of one of the rectangular sides of a hexagon—which doubtless was an entry point. Tavoian was more than sure that the Sinese had discovered what he had about entries to the hexagonal chambers. The two sleds moved farther apart, the assembly held between them on a cable, with perhaps ten meters separating each sled from the assembly.

Tavoian frowned. *That much distance between them? Are the idiots really going to aim a high-powered laser at that entry point?*

He had scarcely thought those words when energy seemed to flare from the artifact back at the Sinese laser. The images from both spy-eyes blanked. Then the rear of the entire Sinese assembly exploded.

Tavoian immediately had the ISV scanner focus on one sled and then the other. Each of the men piloting a sled seemed to be unhurt, although the shattered and fused laser assembly was hurtling away from the artifact and passed within fifty meters of the ISV.

Neither spy-eye resumed transmitting images.

"Can you control the spy-eyes?"

NEGATIVE. NO RESPONSE TO COMMANDS.

Without an AI rover on board the ISV, there was no way Tavoian could immediately recover the incapacitated spy-eyes. So he eased the ISV back, setting it on a return course to Recon three, then checked on the other ISV, well over five hundred meters away. All indicators were normal. "Can you determine what happened?" He had his own ideas, but the AI had direct access to all sensors, which recorded the entire electromagnetic spectrum.

THE SINESE ACTIVATED A UV LASER. THE MATERIAL REFLECTED IT BACK AND AMPLIFIED IT. THE BEAM SPREAD. THE HEAT EXPLODED THE SUPER-CAPACITORS.

For a moment Tavoian wondered. Then he shook his head. He almost laughed, except it was a wonder the two Sinese hadn't been killed. With the change in the hull's reflectivity, the silver material simply had absorbed all the laser's energy when the Sinese had used the laser on the hull the day before. But the dark material had done exactly what the single thread had done when Tavoian had used a laser to cut it . . . except the Sinese had used a far higher powered laser.

"I'll need those images for my report."

The ship's AI did not respond.

"How are the other spy-eyes doing, the ones with the other ISV?"

THEY HAVE NOT RETURNED.

Tavoian decided against waiting until the end of the day before reporting to the colonel and began to compose a report detailing exactly what the Sinese had attempted to do and what the results had been. He thought about adding a line about how the Sinese attempt suggested that they were feeling thwarted, and that the universal reaction to being denied entry was to use a bigger battering ram or a larger hammer. He decided against it. The colonel could—and would—draw his own conclusions, and if he didn't come to one similar to Tavoian's, a junior major telling him that wasn't going to change a thing.

Once he dispatched the message, with several of the more graphic images, although the laser flashback had been so brief that the only image any of the feeds had was an instant of whiteness, he checked on the Sinese. They had apparently returned to the massive research dreadnought. "Was there any sign of injury to either Sinese pilot?"

THERE WAS NO SIGN OF PERSONNEL INJURY. ONE SLED HAD TO BE TOWED BY THE OTHER. ASYMMETRIC THRUST INDICATED THE THRUSTER UNIT CLOSEST TO THE LASER ASSEMBLY FAILED.

"Let me know if any sleds or large remotes leave the Sinese vessels."

WILL NOTIFY YOU.

Tavoian went back to studying the AI's plot of unvisited areas of the artifact, at least until Alayna's message arrived, which he immediately began to read.

Dear Chris,

Something struck him . . . and it took him a moment to realize that she'd never used a salutation . . . or the word "dear" before. Not once. He read even more carefully, not racing through the words as he often did, and by the end of the first paragraph he had a good idea why she'd written as she had. The first words of the second paragraph, about Icarus, confirmed his feelings.

But why did the colonel let her message go through? Tavoian smiled. *Because it was written in a way that allowed him to ignore what wasn't written in the words.* And who knew? It could be that the colonel might yet order him to depart . . . or leave the departure time to Tavoian's discretion.

Tavoian did smile at Alayna's last three words.

Less than an hour later, the ship's AI reported that the spy-eyes had completed their investigation of the first set of hexagonal chambers and were moving to the second set.

"Will either disabled spy-eye be within easy range of the ISV returning from the artifact when it finishes the next set of investigations?"

ONE CAN BE RECOVERED WITH A MINIMAL COURSE CHANGE. THE OTHER WAS PROPELLED AWAY FROM THE ARTIFACT BY THE MISDIRECTED THRUSTER FROM THE DAMAGED SINESE SPACE-SLED.

"Recover the one, then, on the way back." Tavoian wasn't certain he'd learn anything from it, or even be able to repair it, but it was worth the effort. He still didn't want to send out the other ISV for just a recovery of a damaged spy-eye. Even with only three days left, he was wary about using thruster propellant.

Once he had made certain that the second round of investigation was in progress, he went back to watching the Sinese and keeping an eye on the artifact. He also needed to work on a reply to Alayna.

At that thought, he smiled again.

By early Monday morning, Alayna was even more worried, both about Chris and about the images and data coming from the solar array. The photosphere was showing greater convective activity, as evidenced by the more rapid dispersal of magnetic force lines, and consequently, the more rapid dispersal of the comparatively few sunspots, but conversely there had been a drop in cosmic-ray diurnal anisotropic amplitude over the past days, when it should have been maintaining a higher level, since the sun was in a solar minimum. The solar radiation received at COFAR had increased to almost fourteen hundred watts per square meter, definitely above the average of 1368. While a two point three percent increase wouldn't sound like much to most people, it was definitely impressive and not normal. There were more multi-fractal mini-granulations, considerably more than there should have been under the ambient solar conditions, which had already been at a higher level. While that might help her observations and reveal something new, she couldn't discern anything that might suggest reasons for what she was observing. But then, the sun's activities had never been exactly totally predictable.

You've got better observations and a greater chance for discovering some interrelation . . . and that bothers you?

The question that nagged her most about the alien artifact was something that in some ways seemed minor, compared to the unexplained acceleration, and that was the hull of the artifact, in particular the precision of the difference in light reflection and absorption for the thirty-two circles manifested on the outer hull. Neither she nor Marcel had been able to come up with a scientifically plausible reason for the difference between the circles and the rest of the hull. Given the precision of the artifact's construction . . . there should be a reason. Except Alayna hadn't yet been able to come up with even an implausible reason, let alone a plausible one. That meant she was missing something.

She also kept worrying about Chris, especially how much faster the artifact was carrying him sunward. "Marcel, do you have better calculations on when 2114 FQ5 will reach a point of fifty-eight million kilometers from the sun and its probable speed at that time? Oh . . . and at what distance will it likely reach a speed of seventy kilometers per second?"

"2114 FQ5 has a calculated present velocity of sixty-two kilometers per second. Assuming the present rate of acceleration, it will reach the fifty-eight-million-kilometer distance at 2314 UTC on November twenty-eighth. It will reach a speed of seventy kilometers per second at 0931 UTC on November twenty-ninth."

Frig! Frig! Frig! Now what? All she could do was to send Chris a message and hope that he got it . . . or failing that, that he and his AI could calculate close enough to see the dangers. She could have Marcel calculate a course that would separate his ship from the artifact—

She shook her head. Chris's AI was doubtless far better at that and had more of the necessary data. "What about the artifact's course and perihelion distance?"

"2114 FQ5 will pass closer to the sun than previously calculated. Separation distance at perihelion is now calculated at one point seven million kilometers."

"One point seven?" *That's a huge change!* Or a huge miscalculation, and Alayna doubted that Marcel was that inaccurate.

"That is under present conditions."

"Can you calculate possible changes?"

"Not at the present time."

As she sat down in the control center, she called up Chris's latest message, which had arrived shortly after 1900 the evening before, delayed only a few hours. She read through it quickly and then began her reply.

> Dear Chris,
> You're kind to ask about my work with the multi-fractals, and yes, it is frustrating at times, but at times there are also surprises. The sun has been experiencing a solar minimum over the past several years, and that has meant fewer sunspots and greater photosphere convection. Over the past few days, the convective forces appear stronger and hotter, and there are more of the multi-fractals than I've ever observed before—and I have no idea why. It may be that the greater number of the smaller mini-granulations may provide some insight, but it's too early to tell.
>
> COFAR has been keeping track of the artifact's course and speed. The artifact continues to pick up speed, and our calculations show that it will pass much closer to the sun than

originally calculated. This is probably because of the unknown factors that have resulted in the greater increase in speed than originally figured. This does mean that when it crosses the averaged orbit of Mercury (fifty-eight million kilometers), it will be traveling much faster than originally calculated, and possibly at a rate close to eighty kps.

We don't have the data for that, but it's going to be about that. And that means that to be safe, you need to get out of there. But she couldn't say that, not without risking her message being delayed. No matter what the Space Service might say, with Chris investigating the only alien artifact they'd ever seen, they weren't likely to look favorably upon their one source of possible fantastic new technology departing a moment earlier than absolutely necessary.

Because I'm stealing time from my observations, I have to be short, but I did want to let you know how things are going. A brief quote before I return to the solar array and the mini-granulations . . .

She wasn't that pressed for time, not with Marcel handling the details. Her work would come later, trying to make sense out of the images and data. But she didn't know what else to say in a message that had to get through censoring.

. . . Here is a quote that might apply to pilots as well as scientists and engineers, and I think you know where I feel you belong . . .

Are engineers really scientists? An engineer who's passionate about knowing what's behind what he or she does is a scientist. An engineer whose basic concern is getting something to work well is an engineer. Knowing who is which kind of engineer and the best place for each is where most engineering departments have the most trouble . . .

Please do take care.

She read it over, and then sent it. Just as she finished, another message arrived from her father. She read through it quickly. He was worried. But then, he was usually worried.

She smiled wryly, but fondly. She needed to answer him, but that could wait a few hours. She had another cup of coffee as she checked the rest of the message queue, before turning to her morning duties . . . and checking the cargo lock seals and the aeroponics.

Another day without a single word from the Foundation. Not exactly promising, but at times, no news can definitely be good news.

THE TIMES OF ISRAEL
27 NOVEMBER 2114

(JERUSALEM) "There will be no Sinese Empire dominating the solar system," announced Prime Minister Merav Meir early this morning. "This is the unanimous position of all UAAS member nations. Any military action by Sinese forces outside Sinese borders, in particular against India, will be taken as a military action against all UAAS member states." All Israeli forces are in a high state of readiness, and several nuclear missile submarines have remained at sea past their scheduled return dates.

Indian Prime Minister Ravindra made a similar announcement from New Delhi almost simultaneously, declaring, "India has done absolutely nothing of a military nature within Sinese lands. Nor has India threatened the Sinese Federation. Yet the Sinese persist in making false claims against India. These are nothing more than another facet of Sinese opposition to the Dyaus space elevator. The Federation is attempting to weaken India and the Unity of African and Allied States in undertaking yet another attempt to dominate the commerce of the world and the solar system. If there is any Sinese military incursion on any Indian territory or space installation, India will retaliate with all forces at its disposal." No information is available about the deployment and disposition of Indian armed forces, but sources close to the military high command have confirmed that all Indra missiles, as well as other "defensive measures," are ready to be launched on command, or if any indication of attack on Indian territory or installations is attempted.

The reaction from Sinese Head of State Jiang Qining was equally forceful. "The Sinese Federation has never sought war, but the so-called Dyaus space elevator is nothing more than a concealed military installation in space. We have not militarized space, but if the Dyaus project is completed, we will regard it as a violation of all treaties and agreements against the militarization of space, and we will act accordingly. We will not bow to threats to our way of life. Nor do we believe that other nations have the right to determine what actions we may take to protect our people."

The EC government has made no comment.

Noram President Yates stated that Noram would not be party to "any instigation of hostilities." Numerous sources have noted that the Noram Space Command has canceled all leaves of all its personnel and that all Noram military bases on Earth and all space installations have been placed at the highest level of security . . .

Tavoian woke later than usual on Tuesday morning. After he dispatched one of the ISVs with an AI rover, a large spy-eye and two smaller ones, and the fiber-optic line reel to look at and hopefully into other hexagonal chambers, he found himself massaging his forehead, trying to ease the slight aching in his skull, not quite a headache, or at least not one that was particularly painful. He tried drinking some water, but that didn't help. Then he asked, "What's the CO_2 level?"

THE CO_2 LEVEL IS NOW UP TO TWO POINT FOUR PERCENT. NOTIFICA-TION IS AUTOMATIC IF LEVEL REACHES TWO POINT FIVE PERCENT FOR MORE THAN TEN MINUTES.

Tavoian nodded. That made his headache a bit worse. "Are you certain there's no malfunction in the atmosphere system?"

THE ENVIRONMENTAL SYSTEMS ARE FUNCTIONING WITHIN ACCEPTABLE LEVELS. THERE ARE NO INDICATIONS OF MALFUNCTIONS.

Tavoian didn't believe it. There had to be something that wasn't working quite right. *Didn't there?* Whether or not there wasn't a malfunction, he'd have to watch the air quality. Even if he left the artifact on the twenty-ninth, he wouldn't be back at Donovan Base for another six days, possibly seven. He'd have to check that, based on his inbound speed when he departed. Even if he headed back early, that meant more than five weeks on a system that had only worked constantly for five weeks once. Systems on large installations like ONeill Station or Donovan Base kept the levels below point five percent for years on end, but the systems on a fusionjet weren't as large, and there hadn't been that much experience with extended and continuous use. *And you're short on atmosphere reserves, too.*

He checked the monitors, and scanned the Sinese ships. The two space-sleds were towing another large object toward the center of the artifact. As he ate a ham and cheese omelet sandwiched into the middle of a bagel, he continued to watch as the sleds maneuvered the object down the center hexagonal shaft.

Some sort of drilling apparatus? An ultrasound scanner? Some form of structural sonar? Tavoian hadn't the faintest idea from where the idea of ultrasound had come, except it made a sort of sense. The materials of the artifact were opaque to the electromagnetic spectrum, and while sound didn't carry in vacuum it would carry, theoretically anyway, through solid materials. He just wished he'd thought of that earlier. Although he didn't have anything like that among his analytical equipment, he might have been able to rig something up. Then again, that kind of engineering wasn't his strongest point.

In any case, because he wanted to see if the Sinese were having any success, he swallowed the last of his breakfast, took a long swallow of water, and headed down to the passenger area to dispatch the second ISV with an AI rover and two of the three remaining and functioning large spy-eyes in hopes of learning more about what the Sinese were doing. He hadn't had any success in attempting to repair the spy-eye damaged by the Sinese laser backflash and recovered by the rover and ISV. That had left him with four large spy-eyes and fifteen smaller ones, of which ten were positioned around the artifact.

Once he had sent off the ISV, refitted with the two spy-eyes to observe the Sinese efforts in the center shaft, he returned to the controls and checked on the progress of the first ISV. Since the ISV and AI rover were using the fiber-optic line as a link, only the large spy-eye was investigating, and the view from that spy-eye revealed just another passageway angling sixty degrees at intervals of slightly less than twenty-five meters, with no openings in the hexagonal chambers on either side.

Less than a half hour later, Tavoian was observing the central shaft on the artifact's darker side, although at the moment, it was lit by the sun. Two Sinese sleds were positioning the apparatus at a place where a vertex of one of the hexagons was close to the shaft, about halfway down, some fifty meters from the bottom.

A good half hour followed during which one of the two scientists or technicians positioned and repositioned the equipment, while the other remained with his sled, apparently studying some sort of readout. Neither Tavoian nor the ship's AI could discover any comm traffic, except on a single band, and that was clearly encrypted.

"Can you decipher that?"

NOT AT PRESENT. WITH LONGER CONVERSATIONS IT MIGHT BE POSSIBLE.

Tavoian doubted the two Sinese would be having long conversations.

Then the Sinese handling the equipment returned to the sled, and the two moved the assembly to the bulkhead at the base of the shaft, the one with the hidden symbol that suggested, at least to Tavoian, that the area beyond was forbidden or dangerous, or somehow out of the ordinary. *Assuming that the aliens thought anywhere close to the way we do.*

Tavoian did not move the spy-eye into the shaft immediately, since maintaining signal continuity was a problem for longer periods of time, and since there was nothing to be gained by doing so while the Sinese were setting up again.

CO2 LEVEL IS NOW TWO POINT FIVE PERCENT.

"Thank you." The fact that the level had risen when Tavoian wasn't even exercising was a concern, but not a huge one. *Not yet. Not unless it keeps rising steadily.*

Once the Sinese seemed to have established themselves once more with the equipment, Tavoian continued to monitor the Sinese efforts, which was possible even when the shaft was in darkness because of the lights on the Sinese sleds. After another twenty minutes passed, during which the Sinese seemed to be faring no better than before, Tavoian began to ease the spy-eye down the center of the shaft, trying to get close enough to get a better view of the equipment at that moment when the shaft would be facing the sun.

He halted the spy-eye about fifteen meters away and started to study the image of the equipment more closely when suddenly something appeared, a whitish shape that arrowed from one of the space-sleds toward the lower spy-eye. Tavoian immediately fired the thrusters on the left side, trying to move the spy-eye out of the way, but the blanking of the image indicated he hadn't been successful. He immediately checked the images from the more distant spy-eye and the ISV. The spy-eye was held by a missilelike device with large grabbers, which had already turned and was headed out of the shaft and then toward the larger Sinese ship. Rather than risk losing the other spy-eye, Tavoian recalled both the remaining remote and the ISV.

What was that all about? From what Tavoian had observed, the Sinese had been singularly unsuccessful in whatever they had been doing. Even if they had succeeded, and Tavoian was only guessing that they hadn't, there was no way his spy-eyes could have determined whatever they might have discovered. *Frustration? Anger?*

"Ready torp one. Target larger Sinese vessel. Stand by."

TORP ONE IS READY. POSITIONING RECON THREE. STANDING BY.

Tavoian wasn't about to attack first. He also wasn't about to assume that nothing was going to happen. He hoped that the grabber-device's attack had been the result of a moment of frustration, but . . .

As he watched all the monitors, he sent an immediate message, along with several images of the disabled and captured spy-eye, and the few images he had of the equipment, to the colonel, informing him of the event and his current status. Then he continued to monitor the Sinese ships and the top of the shaft, inside which the two sleds remained.

Fifteen minutes later, the sleds and the equipment assembly emerged from the shaft, clearly returning to the larger Sinese ship.

THE CO2 LEVEL IS NOW UP TO TWO POINT SIX PERCENT.

"Interrogative status of environmental systems?"

SYSTEMS ARE FUNCTIONING WITHIN OPERATIONAL PARAMETERS.

Tavoian was again aware of his headache. *Or is your mind playing tricks on you?* He took a long slow breath, trying to relax.

Eighteen minutes after his message, he had not only a message from Kit, but a response from the colonel.

> Maintain operational readiness to respond if necessary.
> Do not initiate hostilities.
>
> Did the Sinese appear to have made a discovery that they wished to conceal?
>
> Would appreciate more information about likely Sinese use of laser with possible weapons-level power usage.
>
> Request you remain with the artifact and continue investigations as long as is possible, while allowing adequate time for a safe return.

Tavoian smiled wryly at the last sentence. *In short . . . leave too soon and you'll stay a major for life . . . if you're lucky. Leave too late and you'll either fry or die of oxygen starvation because you won't have enough Hel3 for a return to anywhere before the habitability gives out.*

Tavoian's response was immediate.

> There was no indication of a discovery. If the Sinese were trying to gain access to hexagonal chambers, they were unsuccessful. It is impossible to tell if they were attempting to image what lies within or beyond the walls, or if they were successful.
>
> So far they have not attacked other remotes or equipment. The two space sleds and the equipment assembly are returning to the larger Sinese vessel. This withdrawal and lack of continuation would suggest a lack of immediate success.

So would the attack on the spy-eye. But Tavoian wasn't about to say that.

> All information available to Recon three about the power
> levels of Sinese laser has been dispatched to Donovan Base.
> There has been no further use of laser assembly.

Most likely because the Sinese can't repair it.
Once he dispatched the message, he had the ship's AI continue monitoring the Sinese vessels, while he checked the operations of the other AI—only to find that fiber-optic line had been broken or severed, and he'd lost another large spy-eye. He recalled the ISV with the remaining small spy-eyes and AI rover.

While he waited for the return of the second ISV, he opened the message from Kit, dreading what it might contain, and began to read.

> Dear Chris,
> Our thoughts are with you in this perilous time. I can only
> hope that the Sinese will soon—like immediately—understand
> that you can only push some people and nations so far before
> they refuse to be pushed farther. Yet it's hard for those who've
> always gotten their way to realize when they can't push more.
> You will need to do what needs to be done, but I pray—not in
> the religious sense, but in the sense of sending forth thoughts
> of reason—that it will not come to that.
>
> Mother is still hanging on, but it's likely only a matter of days.
> It's been incredibly hard on Dad. I can't tell you how hard, but
> I'm certain you know.

Know . . . how could you not know? And being more than a hundred million kays away when it's all happening?

> I also hope that no harm comes to your friend in Daedalus
> Crater. She sounds like someone you should see more of when
> you can.

Kit . . . always the matchmaker . . . even long distance, even when she hasn't even met Alayna.
When he closed the message, he remained before the controls, unmoving, thinking. There was also the fact that there was no message from

Alayna . . . one from Kit, but not Alayna. Had Alayna not sent another message? Tavoian doubted that. He suspected she had, and that he wouldn't receive it for a while, possibly not at all . . . or not until he'd left the artifact.

That question, and the colonel's "instructions," raised another question. Exactly what was his margin of safety?

"Calculate the current inbound speed of the artifact."

CALCULATIONS ARE NOT EXACT. MARGIN OF ERROR IS BETWEEN THREE AND TWELVE PERCENT. CURRENT INBOUND SPEED CALCULATED AT SEVENTY-SIX KAYS PER SECOND.

Tavoian winced.

"Can Recon three return to Donovan Base with a direct course if we wait to leave until 1200 UTC on November thirtieth?"

NEGATIVE. RECON THREE HAS APPROXIMATELY FOURTEEN HOURS OF HEL3. AT 1200 UTC ON NOVEMBER TWENTY-NINTH, ARTIFACT WILL BE FORTY-SEVEN MILLION KAYS FROM THE SUN. DIRECT COURSE AND STANDARD ACCELERATION/DECELERATION PATTERN WILL REQUIRE A MINIMUM OF SEVENTEEN HOURS.

"Only fourteen hours of Hel3? How did that happen?"

THAT CANNOT BE DETERMINED.

"Are we leaking fuel?"

THERE IS NO INDICATION OF LEAKAGE OR FUEL LOSS.

Abruptly, Tavoian realized what had happened. *All because you wanted to use every drop of Hel3 in the booster.* He frowned. That couldn't have been all of it. Fuel calculations weren't as precise as they could be. The AI had initially had to use fuel to maintain station. But the upshot was that instead of sixteen or seventeen hours of fuel, he had fourteen . . . or possibly slightly less.

"Calculate alternative courses, and a departure time based on a sixty-million-kay distance from the sun."

RECON THREE REACHED A DISTANCE OF SIXTY MILLION KAYS AT 0843 THIS MORNING. RECON THREE IS NOW AT AN APPROXIMATE DISTANCE OF FIFTY-NINE POINT FOUR MILLION KAYS FROM THE SUN.

Tavoian swallowed. "Calculate a course and departure time based on a fifty-nine-million-kay distance." He'd known he'd have to depart earlier than scheduled, just not quite so immediately.

Not exactly the best of days. And it was only early afternoon.

67

[Image Deleted For Off-Earth Transmission]

The new Genghis Khan? Or Alexander the Great? How about Jiang Qining the All-Powerful? Or Qining the Merciless? The Sinese head of state just declared that the Sinese Federation will launch and deploy twenty space dreadnaughts in the next month if India does not immediately drop its plans to complete the Dyaus space elevator. Launch and deploy? How about reveal what's already been built? Minister for Space Wong Mengyi says that's no one else's business. So does Defense Minister Wu Gong. Effrontery squared and then cubed. After all the charges about other nations militarizing space? Oh, did we mention hypocrisy? How about Qining the Hypocrite?

[Image Deleted]

By contrast, there's Noram President Dyana Yates, calling for calm. She was named for a merciless huntress, and our dear Dyana wouldn't know it if a bronzed bow were presented to her with a step-by-step diagram. Calm indeed, with twenty Sinese dreadnaughts about to patrol the solar system? And with hundreds of Indra missiles on hair trigger? Notice she doesn't mention those "refitted" Space Service fusionjets? Or that the Noram Space Service has been shifted for operational reasons to the control of the previously unknown Space Command. Funny thing is that they didn't even have to print new stationery.

[Image Deleted]

This is not a joke. Executives at Twenty-Second Century Fox are planning a biorealie based on President Yates. "It's going to be a serious and tasteful docudrama," announced Mieville Hughes, chairman of the entertainment giant. "No grossity, nothing actionable."

Nothing actionable! How like Prexy Yates, as if action has ever been a part of her persona. Thought, yes, but not action, unlike a few former chief executives who acted without thought. We won't name names.

[Image Deleted]

The sudden death of Noram DOEA Secretary Luvalle might not have been a heart attack. Heart failure, yes...nanobuilt blood clots all through his system. That's the word on the undernet...and in a few other places—like Beijing. Very interesting timing. And you don't hear any heartfelt sympathies from Sinese Head of State Jiang Qining. Can't imagine why. Remember, you heard it here first!

[Image Deleted]

Sacramento, California, is under water! Again. As a result of a late-season tropical storm, the former state capitol is truly submerged with more than fifteen feet of water in places. The old state capitol building has collapsed into a pile of rubble, and the rain is still falling...The last of the Sonoma and Napa Valley vineyards were washed out in mudslides from hillsides destroyed in last summer's wildfires or rotted out in pervasive standing water...

ESCAPE VELOCITY

68

RECON THREE
27 NOVEMBER 2114

Tavoian remained before the controls, almost shaking as he realized that if it hadn't been for Alayna's earlier warnings, he would have been in a far worse position than the merely difficult situation that he was currently facing.

"Present course options. Begin with shortest trip duration."

DIRECT ACCELERATION COURSE WITH STANDARD ACCELERATION PATTERN WILL NOT ACHIEVE STATED OBJECTIVES. NOT ENOUGH HEL3 AVAILABLE.

"Not available?" Tavoian understood even as he voiced the question. His mouth was dry as he studied the figures the AI displayed. Merely reversing course and accelerating Recon three to kill his inbound velocity wouldn't work because the first two hours—all that the drive would take for continuous use, with a slight margin for error—would leave him still moving toward the sun if at perhaps five kays per second, while the drive recovered. Another two-hour burst of acceleration would break him free of the sun's gravitation, but leave him with a lower outward velocity. Two more two-hour bursts, with two hours in between each, would have him traveling at a speed that would take him not quite eight days, with less than ninety percent of the Hel3 he needed to decelerate, even taking Earth's orbital speed into account. Less acceleration leaving the artifact and the sun would stretch the return time to more than ten days, and give him a slight margin in terms of fuel.

All that was a gross oversimplification, but the bottom line wasn't. He didn't have enough fuel for either course. One wouldn't work at all, and the other might well leave him short of fuel for the necessary deceleration. If he dropped another hour from the acceleration phase, that would leave him enough Hel3, but take almost two weeks. And the way the CO_2 level was rising, at the present rate of increase, if it didn't stabilize somewhere . . .

"Calculate the CO_2 level in ten days at the rate of increase over the past two days."

THE LEVEL WILL REACH FIVE PERCENT ON NOVEMBER THIRTIETH. THE CALCULATED LEVEL ON DECEMBER SIXTH WOULD BE NINE POINT TWO PERCENT AT THE CURRENT RATE OF INCREASE.

Almost ten percent, and above that if you take the slow way. At over seven percent, there were definite effects, especially on judgment, and breathing, and at eight percent any lengthy exposure would result in unconsciousness, which if it continued would lead to death.

"Plot a course based on present acceleration and a constantly vectored turn." That wasn't likely the most elegant way of phrasing it, but what Tavoian wanted was to know if he had enough fuel to accelerate along a course swinging away from the sun, in essence trying to swing into what amounted to an elliptical orbital path that would take him toward Earth using the base velocity Recon three already had and vectoring his way onto a return course. He was still too far from the sun to swing around it in a way that would prove helpful, especially given both the time it would add and the fact that Recon three didn't have adequate insulation for a close encounter with Sol.

He thought about trying to collect some of the cubesats, then decided against that, but he did initiate retracting the solar panels, and having the AI lock the two ISVs into the exterior docking stations. As he waited, he had to wonder about the Sinese ships. He hadn't seen any change in their operations. Then again, the converted longliner, as a noncrewed probe, was likely viewed as expendable, and it could be that the larger vessel wasn't so much a converted warship—the ones that the Sinese weren't supposed to have—but a ship heavily shielded in order to allow the Sinese to remain with the artifact longer.

He shook his head, not envying the Sinese team.

After several moments, a very long time for the ship's AI, a course plot appeared, along with figures below it.

THE PLOTTED COURSE WILL TAKE EIGHT DAYS, BUT WILL REQUIRE FOUR IMMEDIATE TWO-HOUR PERIODS OF ACCELERATION, AND AN ADDITIONAL FORTY-FIVE MINUTES, BUT ONLY THREE HOURS OF DECELERATION.

Almost fifteen hours of accel and rest, the same as it took to get to the artifact, to be traveling at roughly half the speed for half the distance. Except, Tavoian realized, it was far more than half the distance given that he'd be traveling farther to avoid initially losing speed in order to use that speed to escape the sun's greater gravitational attraction near the orbit of Mercury. On the outbound trip, he'd also had a boost from the Earth's orbital velocity, while on the return, since he'd be matching speeds effectively with Earth's orbital velocity, he'd only need to decelerate to that, and not to zero. He did feel better about having a margin for error with the fuel, although he worried about the extra time, especially with the rising CO2 levels.

"Plan to begin acceleration in thirty minutes." Tavoian needed to stow more than a few items that he'd left loosely secured in the passenger and cargo areas.

STANDING BY FOR DEPARTURE AND ACCELERATION.

Tavoian had only been working about fifteen minutes, hurriedly strapping down equipment or placing it in storage lockers in the cargo area, and realizing that he still had a number of cubesats that had never been used, when the AI announced, THE CO2 LEVEL IS NOW UP TO TWO POINT SEVEN PERCENT.

"Are the environmental systems functioning?"

SYSTEMS ARE FUNCTIONING WITHIN OPERATIONAL PARAMETERS.

While he knew that he was moving quickly and working to put things away, and that increased his respiration and CO2 output, the fact that as little as fifteen minutes of light exercise had raised the CO2 level worried Tavoian . . . more than a little. But there was little else he could do except finish up buttoning up the ship and get ready to depart.

Ten minutes later he had the spaces secured. He headed back to the control area, where he strapped himself in.

"Beginning checklist," he announced, looking at the screen and checking off the items, until he came to the last one. "Thruster test."

THRUSTERS TESTED AND WORKING.

Tavoian continued with the checklist. When he finished, he ordered, "Begin orientation."

BEGINNING ORIENTATION.

Tavoian had to wait several minutes before the AI reported, ORIENTATION COMPLETE.

For a moment, Tavoian almost requested permission to begin drive ignition, so automatic were the procedures, but he wasn't reporting to an operations controller. Instead, he said, "Commence ignition."

DRIVE IGNITED.

"Activate drive."

DRIVE ACTIVATED.

The gentle pressure began to build, pushing Tavoian down into his couch. He could only hope that the higher-speed course option would work as he had planned. But then, no one had planned for the increase in the speed of the alien artifact, definitely a Solar Express in more ways than one.

He continued to watch the monitors and screens as Recon three accelerated away from the alien artifact—and the two remaining Sinese ships, knowing that, initially, his course line would diverge only slightly from that of the artifact, but that the initial speed would be counterbalanced by the greater distance covered, but not completely. Enough, if all went as plotted, and that the fuel measurements, speeds, and vectors worked as planned, then he might get back to Donovan Base before the ship's atmosphere became too toxic.

Once Recon three was firmly established on course, then, and only then, would he message the colonel, with an explanation about both the artifact's greater speed and the ship's environmental difficulties.

Abruptly, he frowned as he noticed that the separation from the artifact was not as great as projected by the AI. "Are we having acceleration difficulties? Shouldn't we be farther from the artifact?"

ACCELERATION IS AS PLANNED. DRIVE IS FUNCTIONING OPTIMALLY. ARTIFACT HAS INCREASED ITS INBOUND SPEED BY FOUR KAYS PER SECOND WITH A POSSIBLE ERROR FACTOR OF FIFTEEN PERCENT.

That shouldn't be possible. Tavoian didn't doubt that it was happening, though. He also wondered if Alayna had any explanations.

He smiled, faintly. She had enough problems in dealing with her multi-fractal mini-granulations.

69

On Wednesday, Alayna was up early, knowing that she had a half hour in which she could train the main optical array on the alien artifact, the Solar Express, something she hadn't been able to do on Tuesday because of the time commitments already established, some of them years before. When the image came into focus, relayed to the COFAR screens before her, she could only make out three objects.

Has Chris departed? Has something happened to his ship?

"Marcel, what is the position of the artifact with regard to the sun . . . and its current speed?"

"2114 FQ5 is now fifty-two point one million kilometers from the sun. We do not have a position baseline since 1610 on 26 November. At that time, 2114 FQ5 was approximately sixty-three million kilometers from the sun. The artifact's average speed over the past thirty-seven hours has been approximately eighty-four kilometers per second."

"It's speeded up even more. Estimate perihelion."

"If acceleration increases strictly in relation to solar gravitation, perihelion will occur at 1214 UTC on 3 December."

"It's more likely to occur sooner. I can't believe it won't continue to accelerate. The main array will be free again at 1930. Make another observation then."

With the reduction of number of ships around the artifact, Alayna was even more worried about Chris. She hadn't received a message since the night of the twenty-sixth, which wouldn't have bothered her if she hadn't known where he was and the risks involved. *And you don't even know all of them.* She worried about whether her last message had gotten to him.

You've done all you can.

That thought didn't help much, but she forced herself back to her own problems, and the question of why the sun was behaving as it was, becoming hotter abruptly, showing more convective activity, and the lowest number of sunspots in more than a century, if not in historic times.

Are you the only one seeing this?

With that thought in mind, she dashed off a quick message to Emma, just noting her observations on the recent changes in the sun, and asking for a confirmation. While she believed COFAR's observations were accurate, and certainly there was no doubt about the decrease in sunspots, there might well be questions about solar radiation intensity. *Besides, it's a way to bring it to her attention.*

She went back to considering her problem. What was different? The most obvious reason was that the alien artifact was somehow involved, but that was totally absurd. There was no way in the universe that an inactive remnant of an alien spacecraft that measured something like two kilometers by four hundred meters could have any effect on a sun with a diameter of a million four hundred thousand kilometers.

As her day progressed and the solar images she was able to view from the time leased by various Earth-based observatories, one thing became clear. Even at solar latitudes higher than those where she was studying, there were significantly more multi-fractal mini-granulations, and she was even able to identify two absolutely regular mini-granulations, something she'd never captured before.

She still kept thinking about the artifact. What could power something as massive as the Solar Express? Especially with no detectable electromagnetic radiation and no detectable heat? Neutrinos weren't easily detectable, and effectively they had no mass, which disqualified them from any propulsion systems she could envision.

The bottom line was basic—an artifact that was either propelling itself faster than gravitation attraction with no detectable means of propulsion or was acting as if it had a mass in a solar range. Neither was possible according to existing theory and years of observation—or even present observations. Chris and his ship would have been crushed into the artifact if it had that mass . . . and there was no way the artifact could have been carrying, say, a tiny fragment of a neutron star.

Which is least impossible and why?

Another thought crossed her mind, and she didn't know why or from where it came. How about something not quite in the universe . . . or not fully in the universe? What if gravity was merely a small part of something far larger, but less obvious?

Thoughts swirled through her mind. The question raised by the artifact wasn't as Dyson had asked more than a century earlier, whether a graviton could be quantized, but whether it could be used in some fashion . . . A classical gravitation wave could be considered to be a coherent superposition of a large number of gravitons . . . the entire output of thermal gravitons over the entire lifespan of the sun would be four.

The problem remained—an artifact that was either propelling itself faster than gravitation attraction with no detectable means of propulsion or acting as if it had a mass in a solar range.

Chris had postulated that the gray columns in the large chamber represented some form of propulsion system, and there were nozzles above them. But if the hull shared the same controlled plasticity as the interior, then why were the circles on the hull so fractionally discolored? If they were the openings for the drive "exhaust," then the circles retracted and wouldn't be any more affected than the area around the circles.

What if they weren't retracted at all? What sort of drive would that imply?

Gravitons?

Alayna almost shook her head. From what she recalled about gravitons was that until they reached extremely high energy levels, Planck Scale levels, their force over "near space" was negligible . . . at least in terms of doing something like moving a large mass. But at Planck Scale levels . . . except that required energy levels equivalent to a small black hole . . .

How could anything even contain that kind of energy?

Chris's reports showed latent photosensitivity . . . but unidirectional . . . energy in, but not out.

Of course!

Then she shook her head. That wasn't possible. It couldn't be. Still . . .

Five hours later, she had more observations of higher latitude solar multi-fractals, on a scale she hadn't seen before and was still wrestling with the whole question of a graviton drive, her coldly rational side pointing out that even if gravitons existed, they were massless particles both at rest and as manifested as gravity waves, and accelerated particles that had mass couldn't provide propulsion.

At that point, the message from Emma arrived.

Alayna—

And I thought our instrumentation might be questionable! No. We're seeing the same things you are. Your figures are probably more accurate. If this isn't an aberration of a few days, we're on schedule—as if anything solar can be scheduled— for the most restrained solar minimum ever.

Your Solar Express—and I'll always think of it as yours (I've put in a few mentions in a few places, and Jay Mehlin was most impressed with your response)—your Solar Express looks like it will put on quite a show. Send me some images if it's possible.

Dorcaster is playing realiestar as if he knew what your artifact is. When it's all over, do let me know. I know there's more you're not saying. Much more.

Alayna smiled. Emma might come across as a gushy type, but the brain behind that warm exterior was a superchilled quantum computer. *And that means you'd better find a way to let her know some of what you do . . . without letting the world know as well.*

In the meantime, Alayna decided she needed to get on with seeing if any of her correlation programs were showing anything.

70

RECON THREE
28 NOVEMBER 2114

By 1015 UTC, Tavoian was bleary-eyed after almost seventeen hours of alternating two-hour periods of acceleration and zero grav. He'd never been that good at having his sleep disturbed, but that hadn't been a problem when he had been piloting two- and three-hour trips between various Earth and lunar orbit stations. After having an egg bagel sandwich breakfast, and lukewarm tea that should have been hot, but hadn't been and wouldn't be, he stared at the control displays.

He still had a headache, and it didn't help that the CO_2 level was still rising, now at two point seven percent, although he wondered if his headache was as much from worry and fatigue as from CO_2. Two point seven percent wasn't that bad. People had endured those levels for weeks without even long-term effects. *Just so long as it doesn't get too high too quickly.* Because there was no way he was getting back to where he could leave the ship for a bit more than a week. Eight more days, plus close to eight hours of decel and zero grav.

Earlier, much earlier, almost twelve hours ago, he had dispatched a message to the colonel, but only after the first two-hour acceleration leaving the artifact. So far there had been no response. In the meantime, there was little Tavoian could do except go over the last images recorded before he left the artifact and see if he'd missed anything. That, and look at the monitors and screens that showed very little, a reminder of just how empty space was. He did both.

The colonel's daily message arrived at 0817 UTC, along with the news summary, and a message from Alayna, date stamped as being sent at 0814 UTC on November 27, 2114.

So kind of them to delay it a full day.

Tavoian decided to read the colonel's message immediately, if only to gauge just how much trouble he might be in.

Tavoian, Christopher A.
Major, NSC

NSS-21/Recon Three
Understand departure rationale. Regret inability to remain on station longer. SC confirms excessive speed of artifact.

So he actually went to Space Command to see if what you reported was accurate. Tavoian smiled crookedly. In the colonel's position, he probably would have done the same thing.

Maintenance suggests you check the following settings on the atmosphere controls . . .

Tavoian did. He could do that remotely. The settings matched those recommended.

. . . If they match, reset the air heating ten degrees higher and see if this improves system efficiency. Wait at least two hours to determine effect. It is strongly recommended you not increase the air heat more than a maximum of thirty degrees over the recommended setting. Thermostat settings have proved variable in the past.

Variable? Great! What else?
There weren't any other suggestions for dealing with the CO_2 problem.

Your last report did not contain latest images and data. Request you provide those at your earliest convenience.

For obvious reasons, Tavoian hadn't taken the time to report when he had discovered just how fast Recon three had been traveling and how much closer to the sun he had been than anyone had originally anticipated. He'd been more interested in resolving the "small" difficulty of departing before it would have become even more difficult for him to survive the return. After that . . . it had just skipped his mind.

So the next thing he did was head back to the atmosphere control panel, which was behind a security lock in the cargo space. For a moment, he wondered if the techs had forgotten to recode the lock to him, but it finally opened. He made the settings. Out of concern with the sluggish lock, he left the panel unlocked when he returned to the controls.

Next he went to work on composing the report for the colonel, making certain he found and included the most recent images from before he had left the artifact, including one, if from a slight distance, of the Sinese assembly being towed back to the larger Sinese vessel. It was almost an hour later before he sent off the report and turned to Alayna's message.

He smiled as he read the words about her work, but the smile vanished as he came to the part about the artifact's projected speed. *And the frigging colonel held up her message until after you found out that you'd have been fried or asphyxiated if you'd depended on his information and mission plan. And all he'd said was to remain with the artifact as long as it was safe to do so.*

Reading over her message again, Tavoian could sense the worry and concern behind the words. *You're getting more support and better advice from a woman you barely know than from your own organization.* Except that wasn't quite true. After almost a year of messaging, he felt he knew Alayna better than most people. She'd even taken risks, possibly jeopardizing her future, in informing him and the Space Service about the nature of the artifact.

Why had the colonel left it up to him? With no real warning? But that wasn't true. The colonel had to have read Alayna's message. Or had the colonel been under pressure to keep Tavoian looking for the elusive technology of the ancient aliens for as long as possible . . . and leaving it to Tavoian in terms of safety was the most he could do? Tavoian didn't know what to think, and he might never know. *One way or the other.*

He was still mulling all that over, thinking of how to reply, when the message from Kit arrived.

> Dear Chris,
> I haven't heard from you. I continue to hope all is well with you . . .

It's been less than a day . . . He frowned. A day ago had been her last message to him, but when had he actually last messaged *her*? He checked his outgoings. *The twenty-fifth? Three days ago?* Things had been hectic, but still . . . he should have answered sooner, much sooner. He kept reading.

> Mother still hanging on, longer than we had thought, but she's so frail, and so helpless. She still has moments when she's fully alert, but it takes her so much effort . . .

Tavoian continued to read. When he finished, he reread the message. *There's something . . . it's not right.* Had their mother already died, and was Kit keeping it from him, worried that he might already be handling more than he should be? Yet . . . *You've never once suggested you're in danger.* He paused. *You've also never denied it, and Kit knows you . . . and she deserves an immediate answer.*

He began his response.

> Dear Kit—
> I get the feeling that matters are even worse with Mother and Dad than you're letting on, and that you may be keeping things from me because I'm in danger or not in the best position. I hope, probably vainly, because you've done your best to protect me, that this isn't so, but you have a reason for your concerns, although it appears the reasons may be lessening.

THE CO2 LEVEL IS NOW AT TWO POINT NINE PERCENT. ALL SYSTEMS REMAIN WITHIN OPERATIONAL PARAMETERS.

Frig! Maybe the system hasn't had time to respond to the changes. He thought about readjusting the air temperature in the CO_2 removal section of the atmosphere control system once more. *Give it another hour.* He forced himself back to the message.

> You may have read about the Noram mission to the alien artifact, the Solar Express. It required a pilot. You can fill in the details. I'm on the way back now. I couldn't stay any longer, not that close to the sun. I can't say much right now, but it is an artifact, and it's definitely alien, and it's been in orbit around the sun for a long, long time. When we left, I didn't have any idea about Mom. Obviously, there wasn't much I could do at that point, but even if I hadn't been doing what I'm doing, no one was or is getting Earthside leaves, not with all the trouble between the Sinese and the rest of the world . . . and solar system, I suppose . . .

When he finished, he read through it, and then sent it off. Would the colonel let it go through? He had no idea, but Kit certainly wouldn't know if he didn't try. *Even if he doesn't, you'll feel better for trying.* He had his doubts about that rationalization. He should have messaged Kit sooner.

He still needed to reply to Alayna, and he definitely had the time, more than enough time, considering how little real work he had to do . . . although it wouldn't hurt to do a better job of reorganizing the gear he'd so hurriedly secured the day before.

Dear Alayna—

I just received your message a few minutes ago. If you've observed your artifact, you can see where I'm not. If you hadn't made me aware, early on, of the increasing speed of the artifact, matters could have become somewhat problematical, if not worse. My departure was rather hasty.

The construction of the artifact suggests that it is capable of withstanding enormous energies and perhaps even utilizing them. I have to wonder if its course toward such a close encounter with the sun was not planned before whatever happened to the main body occurred and if the fragment that is the artifact is just continuing on a course determined tens of thousands of years ago. If so, it is quite possible that it will survive its encounter. In fact, I would be surprised if it did not. Obviously, my ship is not designed for that. I will be unable to witness what happens, but as you can, I would hope you will keep me informed.

I haven't mentioned this earlier, but just after I left on this mission, I received word that my mother had contracted T3. Kit has been keeping me informed, but the disease is so nasty and so resistant to almost anything that it's not likely I'll be able to return in time . . .

Tavoian couldn't bring himself to spell out directly what he knew was about to happen to his mother, if indeed, it hadn't happened already.

. . . it gives me some better sense of how you must have felt when you lost your mother so suddenly. I'm still a bit numb about it all.

I hope I'm not sounding maudlin, but when you see something as magnificent as the artifact, severed from whatever incredible ship the aliens constructed as if it were nothing and left blindly orbiting a nondescript star, one of possibly two hundred billion suns in our galaxy alone, in turn one of more than three hundred billion known galaxies in the universe, and when at one moment, someone you love can be there, and just as quickly gone, it makes you, or at least me, question why anyone would push to the point of destroying billions of people who would rather live under different governments and systems, not to mention the threat to their own people. The universe could care less, and one way or another, the future, if there is one, will forget. If there isn't a future, what's the point of all that destruction? So what's the point of trying to stop another space elevator by destroying most if not all of civilization? I don't know. Maybe I'm just too tired to see this clearly.

It took Tavoian more than a little time to come up with an appropriate quote, but time was no longer as pressing as it had been just a day before.

On a more upbeat note . . . with what we both are engaged in, I thought this quote from *Observations* was singularly appropriate:

Some things are worth doing because they are worth doing, not because they will generate jobs, profits, or glory, but because they are worth so much more that their value cannot be calculated. Being trustworthy is one of those things, because any high-tech society will eventually fail if trust is breached too often. So, too, is higher education, but only for those who can think, and not use their knowledge as a bludgeon to force others to their way of thinking, because the world always has a surfeit of opinion and a shortage of considered thought. And so is the pursuit of knowledge, because only through knowledge unhampered by the need for repayment can this world reach its full potential . . . and perhaps the stars.

In closing, I cannot tell you how grateful I am for your knowledge, your caring, your willingness, even passion, to strive to do what is right . . . and for just being there.

He hoped he hadn't said too much, but that was the way he felt. He felt even more that way ten minutes after he'd dispatched the message and began to read the grim news displayed in the latest news summary, especially the summary of the latest levels of Sinese and Indian mobilization and readiness.

Now what do you do? Stare at monitors and see nothing? Worry about events you can't control?

He shook his head. At the very least, he needed to write up everything he had learned, felt, or considered about the artifact. He also wondered about the Sinese. What were their orders? At least, the colonel had left it up to him.

"Can you determine anything about the artifact?"

THAT IS NO LONGER POSSIBLE WITH ANY ACCURACY.

Tavoian settled himself before the controls to put down everything that he could recall. At least, it would pass the time. *And keep you from thinking about the CO2 levels.*

THE TIMES OF INDIA
30 NOVEMBER 2114

(NEW DELHI) "We have come to that place from which we cannot return," declared Prime Minister Narahaj Ravindra yesterday. "We cannot and will not submit to another form of imperialistic colonialism." With those words Ravindra rejected the Sinese threefold demand that India stop all work on the Dyaus space elevator, demobilize its armed forces, and re-open its borders to trade and commerce with Sinese bloc nations. He also called on the Federation to provide more details about the ice asteroid reportedly heading in-system toward Mars.

The response from the Sinese Federation was swift and negative. "The nations of the Sinese Federation cannot allow the militarization of space. That is what the so-called Dyaus project is all about. That is its only purpose. That militarization cannot continue, or the Federation will be required to use force—immediate force—to halt the project," declared Sinese Defense Minister Wu Gong. "There is absolutely no need for another space elevator. The Federation has made its space elevator available to all at the same rates as Sinese users are charged." The minister indicated that a timetable for dismantling the Dyaus project had been sent to New Delhi and that failure to comply would have serious repercussions on all of India.

According to knowledgeable sources, the fact that no comment was forthcoming from Sinese Head of State Jiang Qining indicates there is little chance of the Sinese backing down. The Sinese did not respond to the request for information about the ice asteroid.

Sinese officials denied that two Zhou-class force projection ships are missing after operations in the eastern Indian Ocean. "Should any ships be missing," said Sinese Defense Minister Wu Gong, "that would represent the most serious provocation. It could not go unanswered."

Indian military officials denied having anything to do with any Sinese vessels on the open seas and noted that all Indian naval ships had been ordered to give Sinese ships on the high seas a wide berth. That raised speculation that the force projection vessels had been engaged in operations near the site of the converted oil platform that will serve as the ocean base for the Dyaus elevator. India has claimed that platform and the waters surrounding it as Indian sovereign territory.

Claims of not having anything to do with the reputed disappearance of the Sinese vessels would not be inconsistent with past Indian acts. India is known to have more than ten ultra-stealthy nuclear attack submarines based on the design of the never-built British *Seaguard* class, armed with ship-killer torpedoes and boasting maximum underwater speeds in excess of forty knots, and stealth speeds of more than twenty knots.

Noram Secretary of Defense Olassen Trudeau called for a meeting between Sinese Head of State Qining and Prime Minister Ravindra to discuss more peaceful ways of resolving the crisis. The fact that neither President Yates nor Secretary of State Hadfield was the one to make the suggestion was taken as an indication that the Yates Administration believes the suggestion will be rejected.

DAEDALUS BASE
29 NOVEMBER 2114

Chris's message was waiting for Alayna when she hurried to the COFAR control center early on Thursday. She hurried through it, feeling relief as she read about his hasty departure, then anger as she thought about what he hadn't written. *They didn't warn him?*

When she got to the part about his mother, she nodded. She still felt a sense of numbness and loss when she thought about her own mother . . . and a sadness in thinking about the fact that she could never talk to her and hear what she had to say. She'd enjoyed and looked forward to those conversations. *Life can be so fragile.* When she got to the last lines of Chris's message, she had to read them again. *Those words from your self-contained pilot?*

Except he's not yours.

Alayna wanted to send something back, but she also wanted to think about it more . . . especially after the way he'd ended his message. Something had definitely happened out there. *Was it just the artifact? Or a combination of factors?* He hadn't said, and probably wouldn't ever put that down anywhere there was a record.

She pursed her lips. She did need some time to let what he wrote sink in. She also needed to get to work . . . and to see the latest images of the sun.

Abruptly she asked, "Marcel, can you calculate the speed of the artifact?"

"The average speed over the last twenty-four hours was 118 kilometers per second. The present speed is between 130 and 140."

"Perihelion is going to be sometime on the second at that rate of increase."

"The calculations suggest early on the third."

Calculations based on past performance of an unknown artifact are just guesses. She didn't say that. The next few days would bear that out. She also wanted to think more about just what might be behind the even more rapid acceleration.

Now that Chris was safe, or at least on his way back, although she was beginning to question whether anywhere in the solar system was exactly safe, given the current military/political situation, she could concentrate more on her own problems. She couldn't concentrate on what was happening with the Farside Foundation, because she continued to get nothing except routine administrative and scheduling messages.

That left what was happening with the sun, and in a "quiet" fashion, things were occurring. The first images she studied recalled the apparent "quiet sun" paradox. The hotter the photosphere, generally the fewer sunspots and discernible irregularities in the magnetic flux lines, although for some the question was more about the cooling nature of sunspots, and the fact that sunspots and solar pores appeared to be something akin to downdrafts from the surface of the photosphere. Yet for all that, there were still far more multi-fractal mini-granulations and even two possible instances of "regular-appearing" mini-granulations.

Shouldn't there be more regular granulations and fewer of the disruptive smaller mini-fractals?

Whether there should have been or not, the ratio seemed to be remaining constant, even with the higher temperatures. And the temperatures were increasing steadily, if slowly.

"Marcel, please check the temperature records for the latitudes used in the multi-fractal study. I'd like to know how many instances there have been for an unbroken temperature rise as significant as what has occurred over the past week."

Several moments passed. "There are three instances in the COFAR records where temperatures rose steadily without apparent measurable fluctuation. The shortest steady rise was for eight days, the longest for three weeks. None exhibited the magnitude of the current rise, but past models and research indicate that such rises likely have occurred."

"Unusual, but likely not unprecedented."

"That is a logical conclusion."

"Thank you. Please begin providing the enhanced solar images as specified in the multi-fractal protocol."

"The first image was captured at 0505 UTC . . ."

Alayna shifted her attention to the special screen.

She continued having Marcel study and present the images periodically for the remainder of the morning and early afternoon, until the observational time she was piggybacking on shifted to very high latitude observations, which were of marginal use to her.

Her eyes were blurry, and she decided to take a break and reply to

Chris. She began by searching for the right quote to enclose . . . something understanding, warm, but . . . in a way, proper. *Proper? Where did that come from?*

> Dear Chris,
> Your message arrived while I was sleeping, and was the first thing I read this morning. I can't tell you how happy I was to hear from you! Yesterday, when I trained the array on the artifact, we could only make out two ships around it, or rather two points that appeared to be ships. And when I hadn't heard from you . . . I worried even more. I'm trusting that the rest of your return trip will be less eventful than your departure from the artifact.
>
> We are keeping track of it, and according to our best calculations, its current speed is now in excess of 140 kilometers per second. I'm not even going to try to offer an estimate of its velocity just before perihelion. By the way, it's likely to pass much closer to the sun than originally calculated, possibly less than two solar radii. I don't know how good an image we'll be getting, because the sun could be comparatively low, just above the crater walls if perihelion occurs on the third. But I will send what we have, if we can get an image.
>
> My quote to you is much less grandiose than your last, but heartfelt, nonetheless:
>
> *Supposedly, one of the last things Galileo said was, "And yet it moves." Research suggests he said it, but not as his last words or at his trial. He was a passionate scientist. How could an Italian not be? At the same time, he was cautious in displaying his passion. Passion is not just for display, no matter how we like fireworks, but for providing the fuel for both life and science, both of which are necessary. For without science, life has no true meaning, and without life, there is no purpose to science.*
>
> I feel that you're as much a scientist as I am. I don't believe piloting a fusionjet to the alien artifact was just a mission. I wish I could have seen what you did. Even the images are incredible, and when it's possible I very much want you to tell me about it all—in person.

Please take care, as you can. I know your choices may be limited, but I do want to hear about all you've seen.

Have you said too much? Or too little? If Chris was who she thought
he was, she'd said enough. If he wasn't, then it was for the best she hadn't
said more.

She read the message again, and then sent it.

73

RECON THREE
30 NOVEMBER 2114

Tavoian kept running, looking down passageways that turned regularly and endlessly, a three-dimensional maze with each turn at sixty degrees. He kept measuring each turn with a protractor, hoping it would be different, then running to the next turn, past closed doors without handles or locks, doors that he could never open . . . and somewhere a distant drum kept beating, each beat faster than the one before, pushing him to move faster . . .

He jolted awake, breathing fast, his heart pounding, with sweat beading on his face, oozing into his eyes and burning. He immediately blotted his eyes with his sleeve. That helped with the burning, but not the dull aching in his skull. He looked around the control area, then increased the lighting level.

After several moments, he half spoke, half croaked, "Present level of CO_2?"

THE CURRENT LEVEL IS FOUR PERCENT. SYSTEMS ARE FUNCTIONING WITHIN OPERATIONAL PARAMETERS.

Within operational parameters and still slowly failing. Tavoian blotted his face, then reached for the water squeezebottle. It was empty. He made his way toward the dispenser tap, where he began to refill the squeezebottle, but he was clumsy in withdrawing it and squirted water into the cabin, with the result that little globules floated in the air. He didn't try to recapture them. Sooner or later the atmospheric system would collect them, and they weren't the nuisance that crumbs were.

Several swallows relieved the dryness in his throat, and he studied the monitors. Everything seemed normal—except for the CO_2—and he slowly began to fix tea and what passed for a scrambled egg hash, because he'd gone through all of the breakfast bagels, even though he'd begun by rationing them out, knowing that they were his favorite. The not-quite-hot tea seemed to ease his dull headache, and surprisingly the hash wasn't bad and settled a stomach that had been more uneasy than he had realized.

After eating, he turned to the message queue, but there weren't any messages.

"What's our distance from the sun?"

DISTANCE FROM THE SUN IS NINETY-ONE MILLION KAYS.

Almost three days after leaving the Solar Express, Recon three was still some twenty million kays inside the orbit of Venus. *Because you couldn't accelerate any more because you had to save fuel in order to decelerate.* There wasn't much point in arriving sooner going faster if he had no way to slow down, and if he'd used gravity braking around Earth, he couldn't have bled off enough speed, given his approach path, not to have required more fuel than he would have had remaining in order to decelerate enough not to go flying by Earth.

The proverbial catch-22. As he thought that, he wondered from where that particular expression had come.

CO_2 LEVEL IS NOW AT FOUR POINT ONE PERCENT.

As if he needed the reminder.

There was a backup CO_2 removal system, a single lithium hydroxide canister, that could theoretically scrub the air in the ship for six hours. What the documentation didn't show was how much the level could be reduced during that six-hour time period, except that it could drop the level by fifty percent during its six-hour life span, but the instructions didn't say from what level. Tavoian judged that meant it could remove half the CO_2 in the ship's air at a five percent concentration, since five percent was considered a threshold for impairing human performance.

It was a relief of sorts to see the colonel's message arrive, followed immediately by one from Alayna. Tavoian read the colonel's message. The text was as brief as it usually was.

> Request update on CO_2 levels and outcome of adjustments.

> Would appreciate sending additional images and data not previously sent, within transmission procedure limitations. Use your discretion in selecting the most appropriate images to convey the sense of the alien artifact.

Appropriate for what? Justifying a mission to investigate?

> Request ETA L1 area.

Tavoian's reply was brief, if slightly longer than the colonel's message.

CO2 levels continue to climb. Now at four point one percent [4.1%]. Have adjusted air heat recharge levels to the maximum recommended level. Are there any other emergency CO2 removal means besides the one lithium hydroxide canister? Any other possible adjustments to the atmosphere system?

Additional images and data attached.

Among the images Tavoian had chosen were several that showed the artifact and the larger Sinese ship, because he thought the colonel might appreciate that, as well as find it useful, and because the Sinese vessel, for all its size, looked tiny in comparison to the artifact, which it was.

Present ETA is 1830 UTC, 5 December 2114.

Of course, more than a few things could change that, but most that could would probably result in his not arriving at all. He didn't think mentioning that was exactly wise. He dispatched his reply and turned his attention to Alayna's message.

His smile was wry when he read the line about her hoping the rest of his return was less eventful than his departure from the artifact. He hoped so as well, but he had his doubts. He read the quote about Galileo twice before he even thought about replying.

She's quite a woman. His second thought was, *and you're just realizing it now?* Even Kit had noticed it.

When he finished his response, he read it over a last time.

Dear Alayna,
Your message just arrived. I do appreciate your thoughts and the considerate and, I suspect, personal choice of that quotation. I also agree with its substance and spirit.

I would like very much to tell you about the alien artifact—in person. When I will be able to, or when you will be able to be there to hear what I have to say is, I fear, not exactly in either of our hands. You have a tour at COFAR to complete before returning to Earth, and I have no idea at present what awaits me upon my return. That doesn't mean I don't want to or won't tell you in person. I do want to and will. The timing just isn't in my hands.

In fact, at the moment, all I can do is sit/float here before the controls and trust that the systems around me will continue to operate. So far, so good.

Did I ever tell you that I almost didn't apply for the Space Service? I always dreamed of being a pilot. I wanted to go to the edge of the solar system, beyond the Kuiper Belt and out into the Oort Cloud. When I learned that most pilots just flew fusionjets between Earth orbit stations and various lunar stations, and only infrequently to Phobos or Deimos, it didn't seem that exciting. But then I realized that if they did pick a pilot to go farther, they'd pick one from among the existing pilots. So I applied and was fortunate enough to be accepted and good enough to become a pilot. Well . . . I haven't even gotten to Mars, but I got about that far out from Earth, and I've gotten to see and explore, if through remotes, the very first alien artifact. And I met an astrophysicist as well, which, in retrospect, almost seems fated.

It's strange, because I feel that I've known you far longer than I have, as if you've been a part of my life for longer than the year, or not quite a year, that it's actually been. Then maybe it's because . . . except I really can't put words to the reasons, only that's the way it feels.

I've enclosed a few images. They aren't the same as being there, or being able to tell you in person, but for now they'll have to do.

My quote for you is inspired by your efforts to discover what lies behind multi-fractal mini-granulations, although I realize that they are small only in comparison to the sun itself:

Those who can find satisfaction only in having more, experience wonder in only the physically overwhelming, and are astounded by accomplishments solely in the grandiose, and who cannot find marvels in the smallest of things, those individuals are the destroyers of civilization and all that is good because both life and civilization rely on the interplay of the smallest of elements.

I'm still learning this, and you have been vital in helping me understand.

He decided against saying more and sent off the message.

Less than ten minutes later, the AI announced, CO2 LEVEL IS NOW AT FOUR POINT TWO PERCENT.

Another "small" thing that may become very important. Tavoian could only hope that it didn't happen soon.

74

[Image Deleted For Off-Earth Transmission]

Remember those missing Sinese force projection ships? They're still missing, and Sinese Head of State Qining is threatening to "disappear" a few Indian ships and a lot more, if the Indians don't own up to "their treacherous deeds." The Indians told Qining that the ships entered a typhoon and were likely destroyed in a storm that saw waves of seventy meters. Qining's going to raise bigger storm than that if he doesn't get the ships back, or an abject apology along with the immediate capitulation of all Indian military forces and the Dyaus space installation. We'd bet even all that won't satisfy him. Sautéed Earth, anyone?

[Image Deleted]

Former child sex star Eriana D'Bleu—or rather the woman whose image was illegally co-opted by Andrus Entertainment in their realie-sensie breakout *PaniSex*—has declared that she'll be using that MASSIVE settlement she received for her campaign war chest in her quest to replace Senator Johnstone Swallow in 2116. Swallow opposed the settlement and was quoted as saying "entertainment is entertainment, not life." Looks like entertainment is coming to Utah and Senator Swallow . . . as part of life.

[Image Deleted]

The Yates Administration still doesn't seem to get it. Noram Prexy President Dyana Yates keeps calling for calm. Repping words don't stop storms. Her own DOEA Secretary was most likely assassinated with bio-weps. Was that to leave the blame on him for the Space Command militarization? Or a Sinese act because that militarization just might crimp their dreadnaught plan? Words aren't going to stop five hundred Indra missiles. Or stealth subs, or the rumored Sinese fire-eye. Maybe those refitted fusionjets will . . . depending on their refit gear.

[Image Deleted]

A bad week indeed for EC Chancellor Rumikov. Alceste Ciorni, who was acting Chancellor in Rumikov's absence, revealed yesterday a series of separate flashset conversations between Rumikov and unnamed third parties from the Sinese Federation and India. Not only was the double-dexed man double-triple teaming his amorous partners, he was doing the same with the Federation and India. Remember that ADS contract for long-range multispectrum detection systems . . . it was signed right after a flashset that promised that the EC would not back India. Or what about the huge BAE integrated systems support for India's stealth subs. Another flashset promise . . . You have to give the man credit. He will do anything . . . with anyone.

[Image Deleted]

As for Indian Prime Minister Ravindra . . . no one's seen him in days. Not in person. His image, certainly, but not his body, as if he had a body worth watching. Can you spell secret bunker in the Himalayas? He's going to be where he can launch all those Indra scramjet missiles. Whether they'll find and penetrate Sinese Head of State Qining's also secret bunker is another question. Shouldn't we be in the bunkers and those two out in the open?

[Image Deleted]

Astronomers across the globe, and even out in space, are reporting higher temperatures in the sun's photosphere in the past few days. Climatologists just reported that the remaining ice sheets and glaciers in Greenland are calving—that's falling into the ocean, by the way—at a record rate, even this late in the year. One pundit even blames the Solar Express for it all. It's not even a comet. Some people will blame anything . . .

Alayna was up late on Saturday night, December first, working with Marcel to refine the calculations for the exact time of perihelion for 2114 FQ5. That wasn't nearly as easy as it might have been because even with months of observations, the artifact continued to accelerate more than could be determined accurately from those past observations. Getting the time as accurate as possible was necessary because she wanted images with both the main optical array and the solar array. While the solar mirror wouldn't be that much of a problem, since it would be focused on the sun in any case, the main optical array was another question, but Alayna needed the main optical array for another, very simple reason. The solar mirror wouldn't pick up 2114 FQ5 as more than a tiny black spot, if that.

Even with the main optical mirror, the artifact would still be a tiny image, barely more than a dark point against the blazing disk of the sun. But since the main optical array was booked for most of the time, Alayna didn't want to have to divert it for any longer than necessary.

Because there will likely be hell to pay . . . even if you're right. Especially if she happened to be right, because she couldn't explain what she thought she might see. From the logical point of view, one of three things could happen. The artifact could pass through perihelion untouched, which, from the data and observations she'd gotten from Chris, seemed the most likely. Or it could be torn to bits by the combination of heat and solar gravitation. Or it could literally fly into the sun, although that seemed highly unlikely, if not impossible, given the increasing rate of speed at which the artifact was traveling.

As she sat there waiting, she thought about his last message, and especially about what he'd said about becoming a pilot. He'd just said how he'd felt, but he'd never said much about his feelings before, and he'd emphasized how much he wanted to tell her things in person. And the last lines . . .

She smiled, a smile that faded too soon as she considered where he was and where she was.

At 2323 UTC, for what seemed the hundredth time, she asked, "Marcel, what is the best estimate for the time of perihelion?"

"At present and anticipated rates of speed, perihelion will occur at 0143 UTC on December second."

"The current distance?"

"It is calculated at three million kilometers."

"At 0100 UTC, train the main optical array on 2114 FQ5."

"That time is booked, Dr. Wong-Grant."

"Make it a priority override."

"That is so noted."

Meaning that you're really on the hook.

Alayna fixed herself another cup of coffee and tried to sit down to wait. She had two sips, and then stood up. "Make the time for focusing on the artifact at 0030. We don't want to miss what will happen if the artifact speeds up more than calculated."

"That is noted. The main optical array will focus on the artifact at 0030."

Alayna had more coffee. She walked to the aeroponics bay and checked the system. Then she checked the cargo lock seals.

When she came back to the COFAR control center, she composed a message to her father, reassuring him that she was indeed physically safe. *Not necessarily occupationally safe, but that's your own doing.* She revised the message several times, then finally sent it.

Waiting was hard.

Finally, a little after midnight, she began to study the images from the solar array, but could not detect any sign of 2114 FQ5, although it was little more than a solar radius away from the sun.

"Can you enhance 2114 FQ5 on the solar array display?"

"Image is enhanced and enlarged."

With the enhancement, Alayna could see a white-edged point, seemingly less than the radius of the sun away from either the edge of the solar disk or the point of perihelion. "It's moving faster."

"2114 FQ5 is now traveling in excess of four hundred kilometers per second."

Four hundred? That was even more than she'd imagined possible for the artifact. "How far is it from perihelion?"

"One million one hundred thousand kilometers."

Alayna frowned, mentally calculating. *More like forty-five minutes to perihelion.* "We'd better put the main array on it now."

Almost a minute later, another image appeared on the screen wall, this one displaying the full solar disc.

"Highlight 2114 FQ5."

A tiny dark point circled in white showed above the disk, as Alayna expected since the artifact had approached from the beginning with an inclination of some forty-three degrees to the plane of the ecliptic. She really couldn't see it move, except if she looked away and then back, it did appear fractionally closer to the sun. She couldn't tell if the two Sinese ships were still in position around the artifact.

"Marcel . . . are there any ships close to the artifact?"

"There is an indication of one object."

Alayna nodded. *The uncrewed remote.* That made sense.

Rather than stare at the barely moving point, she studied the image provided by the solar array. For the first time in days, it appeared as though the magnetic flux lines were . . . different, not twisted, but somewhat thicker, and there were definitely more of the multi-fractal minigranulations along the edges of the flux lines.

As the time passed, so slowly, it seemed to Alayna, her eyes went from one display to another. The display with the largest change was the one showing electromagnetic effects not visible to the eye in shimmering silvered blue. In one section, the magnetic lines bordering the regular granulations were not only thicker but appeared to be raised from the surface of the photosphere, as opposed to those bordering granulations farther away. The extreme ultraviolet telescope display showed the same differential, except in brilliant yellow-green.

Alayna picked up the light pencil she almost never used. "Marcel, there . . . is that near, will it be anywhere close to directly below the point at which 2114 FQ5 is at perihelion?"

"No, Dr. Wong-Grant. That area of activity is one hundred and eighteen thousand kilometers from the point of perihelion, even taking into account solar rotation."

So much for that idea. Except she had the feeling that she was missing something, but she couldn't come up with it. *You're tired, and you don't think your best when you're tired.* The only problem with that was that the sun and the Solar Express could have cared less that she wasn't thinking at her best.

At just before 0035 UTC, perhaps six minutes before the artifact would likely be at perihelion, a thin filament of plasma erupted from the area Alayna had noted, climbing away from the photosphere faster than any filaments or prominences she had seen or studied. "Can you calculate the speed of the prominence?"

"The calculation indicates a speed in excess of thirty-five hundred kilometers per second."

Thirty-five hundred kps . . . that's one of the fastest ever. While most prominences and magnetic loops didn't extend as far as a single solar radius, a few had been observed extending as far as three . . . and the artifact was well within that range.

The minutes dragged as she watched the solar prominence climb toward the artifact—and slash seemed the only word for the thin filamentlike extension that seemed to move so slowly, yet was anything but slow. Then she could see a faint glow surrounding the artifact. From the main array image, her eyes went to the series of solar array images, including one that showed a massive swelling of matter lifting away from the nominal surface of the photosphere. *That's going to be—it is—a coronal mass ejection!*

"There's an incipient CME at the base of the solar prominence. There's going to be a flare." They didn't always go together, but Alayna *knew* there would be both this time. "Keep an additional separate record and track it. Also track the intensity."

"Additional records being compiled."

Then, improbably, through the center of the filament flare, if only visible in false color on the display showing nonvisible electromagnetic radiation, came an intense beam that struck the artifact. In turn, the artifact flared an intense greenish-purple on the false color screen, and for a moment the displays of all screens blanked.

Alayna froze, then blinked, too stunned even to think.

"Signal overload on all systems."

It took Alayna an instant to order, "Reset and resume tracking."

Almost two minutes passed before the images reappeared. There was no sign of the alien artifact. On the false color screen, stretching from the base of the photosphere through where the artifact had been and farther from the sun was an immense mass of material—the largest coronal mass ejection Alayna had ever seen.

The artifact . . . it's just gone . . . was that a solar laser or particle beam? Or something else? "Did you get a record of that beam?"

"There is a record."

"What was it?"

"A concentration of high energy particles."

"In effect, cosmic radiation. Is that certain?"

"The discharge lasted a microsecond."

Enough for certainty. "And the explosion?"

"The detectors and sensors registered a sharp burst of high energy particles, along with UV and X-rays."

"More than the solar flare?"

"The intensity was similar. The duration was similar to that of the high energy particles."

"Where is the CME headed? Directly toward Earth?"

There was a long pause before the AI responded. "Earth will be on the fringe of the CME's path."

"What's its intensity?"

"The intensity cannot be measured. It is in excess of anything recorded."

Shit! Since the Carrington Effect was likely an X-45 and several past CMEs—that had not come close to Earth—had exceeded X-50, the CME/flare she was looking at likely was a Z class. "Are the notification procedures in the system?" Alayna sincerely hoped they were. Looking them up and trying to go through them by hand would take forever, but Earth had less than a day before that CME would strike its magnetosphere . . . and with the power she'd seen, even a glancing blow could be crippling if satellite and Earthside power and comm systems weren't shielded. *More crippling.* Some satellite systems might already be gone. The odds were that thousands of electrical transformers would be destroyed, melded into slag in places by the currents generated by the solar superstorm, especially in nations still relying on power lines for power distribution. She shuddered to think of the even greater effect if Earth had been in position to take the full brunt of the solar storm.

"The procedures are in the system. You will need to input the data."

"Call them up on one of the screens, and we'll do that." Another thought crossed her mind. "Do we have communications?"

"The backup transmitter is now online. The main transmitter will require repair and replacement of several modules."

"Is the relay satellite operable?"

"You will have to route transmissions through L2. The lunar polar satellite is inoperable. L2 is operating on its backup system."

"And we were on the fringe of that energy burst?"

"That is correct."

"We need to get on with the notifications." She leaned forward. "But keep the arrays on the sun for now."

Once Alayna had sent out the emergency notification of the oncoming CME, as well as a notice to the Foundation that she'd preempted some of the booked time on the main and solar arrays in order to be able to provide information pertinent to the solar superstorm, she just sat in front of the console. Abruptly she had another thought. *What about Chris?* While she hoped his fusionjet had been given extra shielding because of his mission, she didn't know.

She immediately began a message to him.

Dear Chris,

I hope this gets to you in time. A solar flare and some unidentified phenomenon interacted with the Solar Express to create an energy burst and a massive coronal mass ejection . . .

Should you mention shielding? She shook her head. He either had it or didn't, and his fusionjet had already been bombarded with UV and X-rays. But when the CME hits his ship . . .

There's no sign of anything remaining of the artifact, but there might be small pieces somewhere. I have my doubts. The reason for this hurried message is that the CME could play havoc with electronics if they're not turned off or properly shielded. Just in case they're not, I thought you'd like to know. I'm guessing that you have several hours from when I'm sending this for the CME to reach you, but I don't know how long it will take for this to get to you.

I've enclosed a few images, but I don't want to take time to find more or choose from what we have, and a quote will have to wait.

Do take care, as you can.

She sent the message, worrying whether it would get to Chris in time and hoping it wouldn't be necessary, that his ship was shielded enough that the radiation blast wouldn't affect him, and fearing that it wasn't.

For several moments, she sat there. She felt drained . . . exhausted, but she wasn't in the slightest sleepy. *All that adrenaline . . .* She also wanted to know just what had happened. *And why!*

The largest solar flare and associated CME on record, at least from what the COFAR observations showed, in addition to an inexplicable line of . . . something . . . strong enough to destroy an indestructible object, and the only causes she could think of were either an incredible coincidence or an equally unbelievable property of the artifact—something that had only evidenced itself in the increased speed of the artifact . . . until the last few instants.

She looked at the real-time images of the sun, but now what showed was the solar prominence flowing in a gigantic loop, rising out of what appeared to be a sunspot. She focused the image more tightly on the comparative darkness of the sunspot . . . studying the twisted flux lines at its edge. There was something different . . .

"Marcel . . . would you highlight the multi-fractal mini-granulations around the sunspot at the base of the prominence?"

She looked again. There were more . . . but many seemed to be fading as she watched, disappearing far more quickly than was anywhere close to normal. "I'd like to see the images just before the prominence erupted, and then just before the flare occurred."

After a moment another set of images appeared on the screen wall.

There was something about the way the mini-granulations were arranged. *More like the way they aren't arranged.*

"Are you finished with the optical arrays, Dr. Wong-Grant?"

"Oh, yes. Return them to normal operations for now. If you can't transmit the images and data, then store it and transmit when you can."

"Returning the arrays to programmed operations."

Alayna found that her eyes were blurring . . . and she was suddenly exhausted. *Is there anything else you have to do?* If there was, she couldn't think what it might be. Then, she realized one other thing.

"Marcel. Track the CME. Shutter all sensors and electronics at the first sign of its approach. That is an override."

"Understood. All sensitive electronics will be taken off-line and shuttered prior to arrival of CME."

The CME shouldn't arrive in the vicinity of Earth before she woke, even at the unprecedented speed it was traveling, but it was far better to be cautious.

She yawned . . . and yawned again.

"I need to get some sleep."

Marcel probably agreed, Alayna thought, but the AI didn't comment on such statements. She headed toward her quarters, half wondering what she'd overlooked.

RECON THREE
2 DECEMBER 2114

The shriek of the ship's alarm and the full illumination of the control area instantly jolted Tavoian out of an uneasy sleep.

"I'm awake! Report!"

AN UNIDENTIFIED RADIATION SOURCE AT 0031 UTC HAS DAMAGED COMMUNICATIONS AND NAVIGATION SYSTEMS.

"How could—" Tavoian broke off the croaking words of his inquiry, then cleared his throat and asked, "How bad is the damage?" The entire ship was supposed to have been hardened with extra shielding.

NO VITAL COMPONENTS WERE DAMAGED, BUT THE SENSOR DETECTION ELEMENTS NEED TO BE REPLACED AND THE RELAYS RESET.

"We have no navigation radar and lidar until that's done?"

THAT IS CORRECT.

Tavoian almost asked what idiot engineer designed the system until he realized the problem. A series of systems that had to detect extremely faint signals of all sorts but also receive high powered signals at close range had to be both robust and sensitive, and sometimes, apparently, as had just happened, the combination was simply overpowered by a burst of radiation so powerful that it burned out the sensors that were supposed to detect and take the system off-line. In a way, Tavoian reflected, the sensors had done their job, if not quite in the manner they had been designed to do it . . . or perhaps in the backup mode.

"Where are the replacement detection elements?" He hoped that the designers had made access to them easy. He could have dug out the hardcopy manual, but since the ship's AI was operating, it was definitely easier to ask. "And where's the panel where I need to replace them?"

THE REPLACEMENT ELEMENTS ARE IN THE EMERGENCY SPARE PARTS LOCKER IN THE AFT OF THE PASSENGER COMPARTMENT. THE ACCESS PANEL TO THE DETECTION BYPASS SYSTEM IS THE ONE OUTLINED IN GREEN ON THE BULKHEAD TO THE RIGHT OF THE CONTROL COUCH.

They couldn't have made it much easier. Let's see if replacing the elements is as easy as finding them.

The hardest part of the repair, Tavoian discovered, was determining which element went where, because the elements were the same size and shape, and only the symbols on the side, which was in an almost unreadable form of optically recognized lettering, at least theoretically optically recognized, made it difficult to determine which fit into which slots. As a result, the comparatively easy repair took more than a half hour.

ALL COMMUNICATIONS AND NAVIGATION SYSTEMS ARE OPERATING WITHIN ACCEPTABLE PARAMETERS.

Tavoian didn't like that phasing. "How much is their capability reduced?"

NO MORE THAN TEN PERCENT.

"What caused the problem?"

A BURST OF HEAVY MIXED RADIATION. IT INCLUDED GAMMA RAYS, UV RAYS, X-RAYS, AND COSMIC RAYS.

"All together in one burst?"

THE SENSORS RECORDED THAT BEFORE THEY WENT OFF-LINE.

"How much penetrated the shielding?"

THERE WAS MINIMAL INTRUSION INTO RECON THREE.

"Minimal? How minimal?"

THE APPROXIMATE DOSAGE IN THE CONTROL AREA WAS POINT FIVE SIEVERT.

Tavoian winced. That was about half of the total career exposure that would disqualify him from any other long-range trips for the rest of his time as a pilot. "What about other radiation? Was it a solar proton event?"

IT WAS SIMILAR TO A SOLAR PROTON EVENT. YOU SHOULD REMAIN IN THE CONTROL AREA FOR THE NEXT SIX HOURS OR UNTIL NECESSARY.

Until after the CME or whatever the sun has thrown off following that energy surge arrives and passes over Recon three. Hopefully not penetrating the shielding to any great degree.

Tavoian was about to check for new messages before he smiled wryly. *You can't receive messages when your comm system isn't working.* That also meant he needed to send a message to the colonel and Donovan Base to tell them that his comm system had been out and for how long. He doubted that anyone would have been sending him messages in the middle of the "standard" night, but he wasn't about to assume that blindly.

Another thought hit him. The secondary effects of the SPE could scramble his comm and sensors again. "Once I send this message, take all comm and sensors off-line until the SPE heavy storm passes."

THE SHIP WILL BE UNABLE TO DETECT ANYTHING IN ITS PATH.

"If we lose more sensors, we may not be able to navigate back. The command stands."

ONCE YOU SEND THE MESSAGE, COMM AND SENSORS WILL GO OFF-LINE.

After Tavoian sent the brief message, including the fact that he was shutting off comm as a precautionary measure, he dimmed the control area lights and tried to go back to sleep, since he was essentially confined there where the ship shields and magnetic diverters would, hopefully, keep the bulk of whatever had generated the solar proton event from doing excessive damage to his body.

When he woke at 0617 UTC, he had another headache, and he realized that he'd never even asked about the ship's CO_2 level.

"Present level of CO_2?"

THE CURRENT LEVEL IS SIX POINT TWO PERCENT. SYSTEMS ARE FUNCTIONING WITHIN OPERATIONAL PARAMETERS.

Six point two percent and systems are working? Tavoian had some doubts about that. With CO_2 levels exceeding six percent and with almost another four days to go . . . *But people have survived without brain damage at levels less than seven point five percent for days on end.* For all that Tavoian was worried.

"Have we had the secondary storm from the solar proton storm?"

THERE HAS BEEN NO INDICATION OF THAT SO FAR.

He almost asked if there had been any messages before recalling that he'd shut off the comm system.

He took his time fixing something to eat and staring at the largely blank screen wall, before he flipped through the library of music selections and called up a random arrangement of classical instrumental music. He could have read something, but he'd never been fond of reading off the control screens. Somehow they were harder on his eyes than a personal screen, no matter how techs insisted that the control screens could be adjusted to levels the same as personal screens. He'd listened to them and left his personal screen in his quarters at Donovan Base.

He'd only been listening for twenty minutes when the ship's AI announced, A CORONAL MASS EJECTION IS STRIKING THE SHIP.

The fact that the AI could detect it with all external monitors and sensors shut down and shuttered suggested to Tavoian that the CME was indeed powerful.

"Can you tell how strong it is?"

WITH ONLY INDIRECT MEASUREMENTS, ABSOLUTE ACCURACY IS NOT POSSIBLE. INDICATIONS ARE THAT IT IS A HIGH X CLASS OR STRONGER.

"How much is getting through the shields?"

THE CUMULATIVE EXPOSURE DOSAGE CANNOT BE DETERMINED YET.

In short, you're still getting exposed.

By the time the CME had passed, or when the internal detectors could find no trace of increased radiation, the internal monitors showed that Tavoian had taken another point four sievert of radiation exposure.

So much for seeing Mars or anything far from orbit.

THE CURRENT CO2 EXPOSURE LEVEL IS NOW SIX POINT THREE PERCENT.

Then again, Tavoian thought, worrying about long-term health effects was becoming very secondary to shorter-term concerns.

After another half hour, he had the AI unshutter the sensors and communications systems. He immediately sent a message requesting possible other techniques for dealing with the continued rise in CO2.

URGENT!!!

TO: Hensen Correia
        Acting Secretary
        Department of Off-Earth Affairs
FROM: Khelson LeMay
        Lieutenant General
        Noram Space Command
SUBJ: Solar Express/Onyx Hammer Urgent Emergency Actions
DATE: 2 December 2114

Background:

The Sinese "research" ship, a converted prototype dreadnought [code name: Onyx Hammer] that intercepted the alien artifact [Solar Express] on 16 November 2114 departed the artifact late on 1 December 2114. That departure contravened orders issued by the Sinese Space Command. The "research" vessel exploded catastrophically shortly after the Solar Express itself exploded at perihelion. Reports from the Farside lunar observatory [COFAR] and other installations confirm the total destruction of the alien artifact concurrent with a solar flare and a massive coronal mass ejection [CME]. The CME poses a significant and imminent threat to the security, peace, and power infrastructure of every nation on Earth, especially Noram.

Current Situation:

The CME will not strike Earth directly, but an edge will impact the Earth's magnetosphere with potentially devastating physical and strategic effects. Impact time is projected at 1311 UTC today [2 December 2114]. The energy level of the CME is sufficient to degrade or destroy all unhardened communications facilities. It may even severely damage or destroy some hardened facilities. Extremely high levels of radiation are likely for all facilities or facilities in geocentric or lunar orbits and crews and passengers in standard fusionjet transports. Those levels could exceed lifetime safe limits for all personnel who are not fully shielded from the CME. DOD and Continental Security have been notified of the CME and its possible effects.

Recommended Actions:
- Immediately warn all off-Earth personnel and assure they are in shielded locations (as possible).
- Place all sensitive nonessential electronic and communications systems on Earth and off-Earth in off-line status.
- Have all on-Earth and off-Earth electronics disconnected from networks/systems vulnerable to solar effects one hour prior to impact time.
- Disengage all power systems from above ground power lines [as possible] before one hour prior to impact time.
- Immediately disseminate warnings to all power generation and transmission systems in Noram. Also notify all air transport entities.
- Alert National Guard and law enforcement agencies to the likelihood of widespread power system and associated electric and electronic failures.
- Assure that DOEA and Defense facility security forces are in place and prepared as possible for several weeks of continuous service, as necessary.

NOTE TO FILE:
Deputy Secretary and acting Secretary verbally briefed, commencing at 0600 UTC, 2 December 2114. President and Chief of Staff briefed at 0615 UTC.

78

By midmorning Tavoian was getting more nervous, even though he knew there was nothing else he could do, either about the SPE or CME, whichever it had been, but he couldn't not worry. A massive CME or SPE could do major damage to electrical and communications systems in space and sometimes even more to power infrastructure Earthside.

Maybe it will miss Earth. That was possible, according to the figures he ran through the ship's AI. The same figures showed that a direct hit on Earth and its magnetosphere was also possible. With the incomplete data Recon three had, either was possible.

INCOMING MESSAGES RECEIVED.

"How many?"

THERE ARE THREE.

Three? He immediately checked the senders—one from the colonel, one from Alayna, and one from Kit. He started with the colonel's message.

> Tavoian, Christopher A.
> Major, NSC
> NSS-21/Recon Three
> Information received from COFAR and other sources indicates the edge of significant coronal mass ejection will impact Earth's magnetosphere and all facilities in Earth orbit, on the sunside of Luna, and in lunar orbits. Time of impact estimated at 1315 UTC. All communication facilities will be shuttered and off-line. All power generation systems will be off-line during the duration of the CME.
>
> No additional CO_2 reduction strategies feasible for use on Recon three available yet. Will send any feasible strategy when possible.

No problems expected with docking/return to base.

Continue daily reports.

That was it. No CO2 reduction strategies. Nothing else.

While Tavoian hadn't expected much else, he was still irritated. He was even more irritated when he realized that Alayna's message had been sent almost ten hours earlier.

As he began to read and think about it, he got even more angry . . . for several minutes, until he realized that the delay might simply be because the colonel was the only one allowed to read and forward messages . . . and Alayna's message had arrived at Donovan Base in the middle of the night.

He shook his head. Like it or not, he couldn't have done anything any differently even if he had known. He continued to read, his eyes widening as he took in the next lines.

> A solar flare and some unidentified phenomenon interacted with the Solar Express to create an energy burst and a massive coronal mass ejection. There's no sign of anything remaining of the artifact . . .

There's no sign of it? That seemed unbelievable. Material that was totally nonconductive and seemingly impregnable . . . just gone as if it had never been. And how could a solar flare . . . ? When she had time, she'd let him know.

He did appreciate not only Alayna's efforts to warn him, but the words that suggested more than mere responsibility. He still had trouble believing that the artifact was totally gone, but the single image of that ray of light or energy striking the dark spot of the artifact had looked incredible. *But how could that have happened?* He didn't know of any solar phenomenon that looked like that. *You're not an astrophysicist, either.*

But he'd tested and measured the artifact, and the Sinese had used an extremely high-powered laser. Still . . . that light beam looked to have been focused somehow . . . but how? How could the sun focus anything like that?

Tavoian decided he didn't have any answers, and reluctantly turned his attention to Kit's unopened message. He truly dreaded opening and reading it, but he took a deep breath and began.

> Dear Chris,
> Perhaps I've always tried to protect you, but I can tell you already know what I haven't said. Mother died last Saturday . . .

At those words, Tavoian stopped reading. It wasn't that, in a way, he hadn't already known . . . or that he wanted to deny her death. He couldn't even quite say, even to himself, what he felt. Their mother had always been on the verge of fragility, for as long as he could recall, but her vitality, her spirit, her will . . . all had overshadowed that lack of robust physicality. And now . . .

Finally, he resumed reading.

> . . . her spirit was strong to the last, but as we both know, her spirit was always stronger than her body. In the end, the T3 and her body were too much for that spirit. There won't be any service or memorial. That was what she wanted. Dad isn't up to it, either.

Tavoian could imagine that. It wasn't that his parents had been physically inseparable, because they'd each done what they felt needed to be done, but different as they'd been in some ways, they'd always been connected by the need for meaning in life, and the understanding that each needed to find that meaning in their own way.

> Both Dad and I test negative for T3, and if we're still negative next month, we'll likely be out of the woods.

> I have to say that I was relieved to hear that you weren't on what might amount to a military mission and that you're returning. I can't wait to hear what you saw and learned out there. My brother—the first man to see the alien spacecraft . . .

And one of the last as well. Tavoian paused. Alayna hadn't mentioned anything about either of the Sinese ships. He expected that the uncrewed longliner, with its remotes, would have stayed with the artifact. Given what he knew about the Sinese, he wouldn't even have been totally surprised if the larger and apparently heavily shielded ship had attempted to stay with the artifact. If it had, it couldn't have possibly survived whatever it was that had destroyed the artifact.

> Please be careful.

When he finished the message, Tavoian frowned. Kit hadn't said a word about the situation on and around Earth. Her latest message was the first that really hadn't mentioned that. Was that because of their mother's death . . . or something else that had gotten so bad that she didn't want to mention it? Belatedly, he also realized that he hadn't gotten a news summary . . . and, combined with Kit's omission, that was also more than a little worrisome. *Much more than a little worrisome.*

"Present level of CO2?"

THE CURRENT LEVEL IS SIX POINT FIVE PERCENT. SYSTEMS ARE FUNCTIONING WITHIN OPERATIONAL PARAMETERS.

Tavoian massaged his forehead, trying to lessen the dull headache that he'd become more aware of after the AI's response. He was also getting more than a little tired of the phrase "functioning within operational parameters." He hated to think of the situation he'd be in if the systems weren't working within those parameters, if they even were.

There's little enough you can do.

But he could send messages to Kit and Alayna. They might get through before all comm systems were shut down. Later, if necessary, he could resend them.

79

Most of COFAR was already heavily shielded by the very fact that it had been built belowground and designed for exposure to high levels of solar radiation, since the Moon effectively provided no protection. So Alayna hadn't been required to do much to prepare for the impact of the coronal mass ejection except command Marcel to shutter the entire facility and then wait. The most time-consuming part for her was to compose all the messages to various facility users explaining why they'd been precluded from using their time, and offering what time was still available . . . and some time blocks, Alayna knew from experience, would take weeks or even months to reschedule. The good part of that, if anything could be called good, was that no one could blame her for a coronal mass ejection.

Except possibly Director Wrae.

Her other personal concern was that, with the communications systems shut down, and the location of COFAR on the Moon's far side, she had no idea of how great or how minimal the effect the CME had on Earth and the complex web of satellites and orbit stations. If the Carrington Effect happened to be great enough, entire sections of Earthside power grids could be disabled, with transformer and other equipment damage widespread enough to cripple areas for years. But there wasn't anything more she could do. She'd warned everyone she could think of, and it was up to them now.

What she could do—and did—was to study the images from the main and solar arrays of the sun before and after destruction of the Solar Express.

She'd thought that there had been no sign of sunspots, only a rising of the magnetic flux lines that bordered the granulations from where the solar prominence had originated. That turned out not to be entirely so. There had been a definite darkening around the flux lines just prior to the eruption of the prominence. That certainly fit with the understanding that prominences were triggered by a cramping or constriction of the flux lines and the underlying magnetic fields. What didn't fit was the rising of the flux lines and boundaries, since sunspots were essentially cooler places on the surface of the photosphere, in effect downdrafts of plasma.

The most obvious divergence from standard theory was the energy line from the prominence toward the artifact. Unlike the prominence, which had erupted at an extraordinarily high—but finite—sub-light speed, the energy beam—Alayna had no idea what else to call it—appeared more like a laser, except it had not been in the visible spectrum, and she wouldn't have seen it at all if she hadn't also been watching the extreme ultraviolet display. Even that was essentially the by-product of the beam.

Something like a cosmic radiation laser? Except that since cosmic radiation was composed of particles accelerated to almost, but not quite, the speed of light, whatever the beam was, it wasn't a laser, and was more likely the equivalent of the theoretical particle beam . . . and solar plasma at coronal temperatures of over a million degrees Kelvin and accelerated to nearly the speed of light might have been just powerful enough to destroy the artifact. In fact, it had . . . if that was what the beam had been.

Alayna couldn't think of what else it could have been, but she was sure that if any other observations had been made someone else would have ideas.

You might as well write it up and send it . . . somewhere, if just to let the astrophysics community know what you observed. And that you did it first. The downside was that it would take a great deal of effort, particularly making sure the data was correct and presented in the proper format . . . and it would take away from her work with the multi-fractal mini-granulations.

She frowned. She hadn't looked at the mini-granulations, or even studied in detail the charts and graphics she'd asked Marcel to create.

You do have time. With that thought she called up the first of the images showing the links between the multi-fractal mini-granulations in the areas bordering the initial base of the solar prominence. The multi-fractals were so numerous and so close together . . . almost as if they formed a pattern.

She blinked, then shook her head. "Marcel . . . highlight and link the multi-fractals with the same color as the highlighting."

There was something . . . and she knew that she'd felt the same way before. *More of the man who wasn't there, and he's not there again today . . . except he is.*

"Marcel . . . analyze the pattern formed by the highlighting."

"There is no pattern, Dr. Wong-Grant. The lines do not form any recognizable shape, but contain too much Gaussian distribution to be fractal, except for the portions that are discrete multi-fractal mini-granulations."

"Thank you." Alayna continued to study the images, trying to discern what it was that she wasn't seeing. Finally, convinced that, while she was missing something, she wasn't going to find it by staring at the images, she closed the multi-fractal images and turned her attention back to the report she needed to draft on the demise of 2114 FQ5 and the inexplicable solar phenomena associated with its destruction.

For a moment, her thoughts centered on Chris, hoping that he was out of danger and returning safely to Earth . . . or at least to whatever installation where he was based.

After several moments she began to call up data and to organize it in the approved format . . .

80

The Times of Israel
3 December 2114

(JERUSALEM) The massive solar storm that struck the Earth's upper atmosphere yesterday has already accounted for hundreds of deaths across the globe, largely from exploding power lines and the catastrophic failure of electrical equipment linked to outdated and underprotected aboveground power and communications lines. Unconfirmed reports suggest immediate fatalities may run into the thousands, if not higher. Longer-term fatalities in the tens of thousands are "highly probable," according to analysts in the Israeli office of strategic planning, as short-term backup power systems fail in hospitals and in high-rise structures in dense urban areas around the world. The shortage of replacement transformers will leave large areas without power for months or even years.

The entire power grid in the central western states of Noram is reported as inoperable, as are the grids in Southeast Asia, central China, and Australia. The EC authority reports scattered outages, as do the majority of UAAS states. Only defense-related power systems are operating in India, as a result of the separation of defense power systems from the commercial grid two decades ago. Approximately fifteen percent of Noram households have independent renewable energy supplies, but those supplies cannot be utilized by other households or by the power grid as a result of regulatory-generated physical blockages. The WestHem space elevator is expected to resume service this morning, as is the Sinese Federation elevator.

In much of the world communications are spotty, if nonexistent, as a result of electrical failures of communication towers.

Sinese Head of State Jiang Qining declared that any nation that attempted to benefit from the power catastrophe would "suffer the wrath of the Sinese Federation." Scattered sources indicate that most Sinese military facilities are functioning, but that domestic power systems have been "devastated."

In a separate statement, Sinese Space Minister Wong Mengyi declared that Noram and India were jointly responsible for the loss of the Sinese research spacecraft investigating the reputed alien artifact referred to as the Solar Express. That statement was retracted without comment. Requests for explanation were told that the minister was indisposed.

Israeli Prime Minister Meir did not issue a statement, but power in Jerusalem was restored within hours of its disruption yesterday. All Israeli forces remain in a high readiness standard, and cadres of reservists were notified to expect mobilization to maintain order as necessary.

Indian military authorities have announced that all Indra missiles remain in a launch-ready status, and that individual commands have the authority to order launches if any attack on Indian territory or installations is attempted. The orbital Dyaus station is "fully operational," according to General Sanji Gupta. Indian Prime Minister Ravindra has not issued a statement.

The immediate status of power supplies in much of South America is currently not known because of a near-complete blackout of communications and power systems except around Quito, where an isolated power grid is linked to the space elevator.

No comment was forthcoming from Noram President Dyana Yates, but the Noram Defense Forces and Space Command are reported to be on high alert.

RECON THREE
3 DECEMBER 2114

Tavoian woke up with a headache. That didn't surprise him. It seemed like his headache was more or less constant all the time. He also felt flushed and sweaty. He fumbled for the squeezebottle of water and drank several swallows. Then he checked the monitors, asking as he did, "How close are we to destination?"

APPROXIMATE DISTANCE TO DESTINATION IS TWENTY-FIVE POINT FOUR MILLION KAYS.

Just a little less than three days. "Present level of CO2?"

THE CURRENT LEVEL IS SEVEN POINT FOUR PERCENT. SYSTEMS ARE FUNCTIONING AT EIGHTY-FIVE PERCENT EFFICIENCY.

Tavoian almost froze. That was way too close to eight percent. The other problem was that he had his doubts about the reports on system efficiency. If he hadn't been having headaches, sweating, and feeling that his breath was labored, he might have wondered about the accuracy of the monitoring as well. He'd done his own calculations, based on the volume of air in the ship and the amount of CO2 a normal person exhaled every twenty-four hours, and from what he could figure the efficiency of the removal system couldn't be any higher than twenty percent at best, and more like ten percent or less. "Reserve oxygen supply level?"

FIFTEEN PERCENT.

That meant he had enough air in the reserve tanks to replace at most thirty percent of the ship's atmosphere. Replacing that much would drop the level to slightly more than five percent if he didn't run into problems. *Which you will.*

"What is the procedure for venting air from the ship and replacing it with air from the reserve tanks?"

THAT IS NOT POSSIBLE.

Not possible? "Why not?"

ALLOWING THAT PROCEDURE WOULD ALLOW THE POSSIBILITY FOR THE SHIP TO BE TOTALLY DEPRESSURIZED.

"Is it physically possible?" Even if the AI couldn't allow it, Tavoian could override or disable the AI and do it himself.

IT IS NOT.

"Show the schematic that makes it impossible."

Immediately, a diagram flashed on the screen wall.

Tavoian began to study it. From what he could determine, the reason why was simple. The atmospheric system only replaced lost air, and only up to sea-level Earth-norm pressure. There were no venting valves anywhere in the ship. Replacement air could go to the airlock, but interlocks prevented air from flowing into the lock unless both inner and outer lock doors were sealed.

Theoretically, Tavoian realized, he could replace some of the air in the ship by opening the outer lock door, letting the air in the lock escape out into space, then close the outer door, let the lock repressurize, and then open the inner door. The fresher air would then mix with the CO_2-laden air. That would help, except that he was down to fifteen percent of reserve air, and given the lock's capacity, far larger than made sense except for a passenger transport, that would only allow him two, possibly three, uses of the lock to "recycle" air.

He calculated a bit more and came up with figures. If . . . *if* he could recycle twice, saving the third time for an emergency, that would bring the immediate level down to five point three percent. If on the other hand he used the lithium hydroxide canister, it might bring the level down to five percent over the next six hours, if it operated as it should.

Lithium hydroxide it is.

"Activate the lithium hydroxide emergency CO_2 removal system."

THAT WILL TAKE THE NORMAL REMOVAL SYSTEM OFF-LINE.

"Override. It's not working anyway." *It can't be.*

EMERGENCY CO_2 REMOVAL SYSTEM IN OPERATION.

At that moment, Tavoian's uneasy stomach reminded him that he hadn't eaten, which just might be contributing to the headache, or at least its severity. Before he started to rummage through his supplies, of which there were plenty, he took several more long swallows of water. Then he began to look for something appealing. That was harder. There were more than enough instant oatmeal packages, but oatmeal was perhaps Tavoian's least favorite breakfast food. He finally settled on a Mexican omelet burrito, which tasted almost as good as the bagel omelet sandwiches, meaning that the burrito actually resembled its description.

He hadn't heard anything back from Alayna, but that might have been because of the SPE and CME, and whatever they did to communications systems. Earth had been hit by small CMEs before, but never by a large one, at least not in the time where there had been a high-tech civilization to notice. *If not as high-tech as the ancient aliens.*

He still found it hard to believe that the massive and seemingly indestructible artifact was gone. It had seemed so large. *But something two kays in diameter is still tiny compared to the sun.* His lips quirked as he considered that the sun was something like a million four hundred thousand kays in diameter compared to two.

Of course, that did leave the question of why a massive solar prominence and flare had happened on a quiet sun just as the artifact reached perihelion. Tavoian didn't believe in those kinds of coincidences. The problem was that if it hadn't been a coincidence, exactly what had it been?

He wished he could talk it over with Alayna, but talking face-to-face with her wasn't something that was going to be possible for quite some time, not the way things were going—all across the solar system . . . and even in Recon three, which suddenly felt very, very small.

The CO_2 problem still nagged at him.

Then there was always the emergency space suit, which supposedly was good for two to two and a half hours. "Is the emergency space suit standard, with the same oxygen levels?"

THE EMERGENCY SPACE SUIT IS RATED FOR A MINIMUM OF TWO HOURS OF USE.

Maybe, just maybe, between the emergency CO_2 removal system, the reserve air supply, and the emergency space suit, he could get to Earth orbit, decelerate, and reach Donovan Base before he expired from CO_2 poisoning.

He checked the time. It had been almost half an hour since he'd activated the emergency system. "What is the CO_2 level now?"

THE CURRENT LEVEL IS SEVEN POINT TWO PERCENT.

Good. If it kept going down for the six hours it was rated for, and even if it didn't do all it was supposed to, it was better than the alternatives.

He turned his attention to the screens and monitors, not that they showed anything out of the ordinary.

Although the Lunar L2 relay had been operating for more than twenty hours, the first incoming message that Alayna received was at 1032 UTC, and it was from Director Wrae. Alayna studied the second paragraph, not quite shaking her head sadly.

> . . . request immediate report on operational status of COFAR, including but not limited to the number of hours and time slots which were rendered unusable, the number of events that will be required to be rescheduled, those entities whose events were disrupted, and the status of rescheduling . . .

Alayna frowned as she considered the list of what the director wanted, because everything she requested was also in the Foundation databases. *She either can't access that data or the effects of the CME have destroyed those records, possibly even the entire system.* There had to be backups somewhere, but if the power outages were widespread, who knew how long it might be before they could be accessed?

A second thought struck Alayna. *If the damage is that great, who's going to care about observation slots at the moment?* The third thought was one that had occurred to her far earlier—her father's safety. She'd sent a message as soon after the L2 relay had reopened, but had received neither an acknowledgment nor an indication that the message was undeliverable. And then there was Chris . . . and there had been no word from him, either.

She tried not to think about it, but it was still there in the back of her mind. Rather than dwell on what she could do nothing about, she forced her thoughts back to the message from the director and began to compose a reply, which was more reassuring than Wrae deserved, noting that COFAR itself was fully operational and continuing scheduled observations, listing the times and entities that had been preempted, and explaining the reschedulings already made and pending, as well as the interim storage and retention of observational images and data until they could be retransmitted to the organizations that had contracted for those observations and times.

All of that took almost an hour, and by the time she had finished, two other messages had come in—one from Emma and a news summary. Alayna immediately read the news, which dealt entirely with the impact of the "Carrington Effect" on Earth and the various orbital installations, even though what had happened had been the result of more than just a CME. From what she could piece together from the reports, something like two-thirds of Noram was without power, although it was estimated that half of that would be restored within a week. No one was even guessing at how long repowering the remaining third of the country would take. Matters were far worse in Sudam and in Northern Africa. The EC was the least affected thanks to a century of emphasis on decentralized and renewable energy—except in Russia, which was as bad as Noram.

Again, Alayna kept worrying about her father. So when she finished reading the news, she immediately turned to Emma's message, hoping for some distraction.

Alayna!
Thank you so much for the warning! Everyone thought we were crazy, but they listened. They actually listened. The locals even physically disconnected some of the main transformers. The big island mostly has power as a result. It also hasn't hurt that Hawaii has always stored a few transformers because of the problems and shipping difficulties.

Can you send any images? You must have been watching just at the right time. I won't ask how you managed getting the slots. I'm just glad you did. We've been able to follow up. That prominence associated with the CME is the biggest on record! It's a good thing Earth only got the edge. A direct hit, and we'd have been back in the Stone Age. Some of Noram may be before it's over. Sticking to the old ways and having a lot of oil and coal to burn doesn't help much when you don't have operating power lines and transformers . . .

Hope your friend the pilot wasn't somewhere that got slammed by the associated SPE . . .

Alayna winced. She'd tried not to think about Chris, even more than she'd tried not to think about her father.

> . . . at least fifteen satellites are out, that we know of right now. Mostly older ones . . . going to make communications and travel and a lot of things very hard for a long time . . .

When Alayna finished the message, she sent a warm but short acknowledgment. Then, rather than dwell on all her worries, she thought about working on continuing analyzing the solar images and data that the arrays had captured before and after the CME . . . but her thoughts kept drifting back to the alien artifact.

What had happened with the artifact was impossible, according to present theory. But it had happened. Since it had, some aspect of current theory wasn't either inclusive enough, overlooked a possibility, or was wrong. *Or the theory is right, but we don't know how it could apply to the artifact.*

If general and special relativity were right, if incomplete as formulated, then mass deformed spacetime, while still following the curvature of the spacetime it had deformed, which was why gravitational lensing and other effects existed. Although deformation by great mass essentially created gravity, no one had ever either found a way to quantize gravity or to replicate gravitons. Alayna wasn't about to consider dilatons. She began to compose her thoughts, writing them down as she went, along with some very tentative equations. She had the very definite feeling that what she was trying to formulate needed to be written out and sent, before someone else came to the same conclusions.

And she would send it to Chris and Emma as well, if in time. That might help in establishing her provenance in the matter. *You hope.*

First came her general thoughts, put down quickly.

> Effectively mass is energy, but energy confined in defined fields, patterns existing in space-time. Concentration of those patterns creates mass, and the tighter the pattern, the greater the mass. BUT . . . that pattern is also a concentration of energy, and when too great a concentration occurs, the standard patterns of matter collapse . . . and release "free" energy in the process, some of which is manifested in the photons comprising sunlight. That's what happens at the center of a star. In essence, fusion is the forced collapse of hydrogen nuclei into helium, and from there, a star in time builds up heavier and heavier elements.

Gravitons are analogous to photons, in that they are massless, although that's not quite correct because, while photons have a zero rest mass, they do have a relativistic mass determined by their velocity. Gravitons have momentum, in effect never been detected, although gravitational waves have been, but in a crude analogy, that's like trying to describe a water molecule in the ocean by the behavior of waves. The assumption behind gravitons is that they "operate" under the same constraints as photons and other quantum forces/objects. What if they don't? What if they're a property of space-time, and space-time is not an affect of quantum operations, but quantum mechanics, i.e., our universe, is an affect of spacetime?

If this happens to be so, then gravitons, assuming they exist, would have properties outside the limits of quantum mechanics. One of the other nagging questions raised by general relativity is time. Experiments have shown that clocks run more slowly in the presence of greater mass. Why? What property of mass causes this? If gravity is a function of spacetime deformation, and gravity waves are the manifestation of that deformation, with gravitons as the quantized components of gravity waves, then the concentration of gravitons would have the same effect as "conventional" mass. That would explain the acceleration of 2114 FQ5, i.e., the Solar Express. That would also explain why the Noram and Sinese research spacecraft were carried along by the artifact as it accelerated.

What is not so obvious is how a theoretically unpowered artifact accelerated toward the sun . . . and why there was such a solar reaction when it neared perihelion . . .

A slight understatement, Alayna.

One of the early theories dealing with gravitons held that gravity was the weakest of the four fundamental forces because its greatest effect was in another dimension. That idea would also hold true if one regards space-time as the fourth dimension. And . . . if space-time is not fully part of, or fully manifested, in our universe, that would explain several of the oddities involved with the artifact and the solar reaction. Entropy—or time's arrow, if you will—exists because of quantum entanglement. If gravitons do not entangle, and as energy that is massless their entanglement potential in our universe is minimal or nonexistent, then essentially time's arrow does not exist within space-time, assuming as I have that the bulk of space-time is "beneath" our universe. In addition, as a function of space-time, gravitons, or some fraction of them, would always be partially present in any area where they had ever manifested . . . which would also explain the attraction without apparent surface gravity on the artifact. It may also be that time as we think of it does not exist in the "underside," for lack of a better word, of space-time.

All this isn't something that can be laid out fully, but the equations that follow constitute the basis of a possible theoretical approach to the phenomenon displayed by 2114 FQ5 as it approached perihelion and that theoretical basis is consistent with the failure to definitively observe gravitons and the inability to consistently measure gravity waves, not to mention other nagging factors about gravity. This postulate may not be entirely correct, but it would explain the speed increase of the artifact relative to the sun. Assuming that the artifact is in fact the remnant of a larger craft, and that is a very reasonable assumption, and assuming that the artifact used gravitons, which is a definite possibility, as described below, those "residual" gravitons, or the equivalent, exerted the gravitational attraction commensurate with a far more massive body.

The problem with traveling between stars is that we are quantum creatures, and the technology we employ consists of, if you will, quantum structures. All matter, while it is in the quantum universe, is subject to quantum constraints. We can't travel faster than light. In fact, we can't even get close, because at speeds close to that of light, our mass becomes almost infinitely great. That makes sense, because accelerating to the speed of light takes energy, and on the quantum level, energy is mass. That is an oversimplification, but essentially true.

A century or so ago, the physicist Stephen Hawking theorized that one could open a wormhole between points and travel directly from one point to another. He also theorized that the energy required would be equivalent to that of a small black hole. Such travel would also require some means of focusing the wormhole and keeping it open for the time of transit.

The limitations on using a wormhole drive all are based on conventional quantum mechanics. What if our ancient aliens channeled into the underside of space-time, using a wormhole to bridge the gulf between stars.

How did they get and trap all that energy? From the stars they visited. In just the artifact examined by both Noram and Sinese expeditions, there were over ten thousand identical sealed chambers, only a few of which were open. Based on the size of the artifact, and the projected size of the original sphere, the artifact comprised less than four percent of the original craft. Who needs a quarter of a million identical chambers . . . and for what?

For energy storage. Even using a wormhole-graviton drive, it has to require an incredible amount of power to enter the underside of space-time. Almost all of those chambers were likely energy storage chambers, and the passages around them were for the equivalent of insulation. Possibly some even contained quantized gravitons. Why else would the material be so non-conductive?

There was another misconception. The artifact wasn't the drive section. By necessity, it had to have been the forward section and the gray hexagonal columns projected gravitons to keep the Hawking wormhole from collapsing on them during their transit. How the aliens who built the artifact actually quantized gravitons in order to store and/or focus them is another yet undetermined process.

Alayna paused. *Now what?* She smiled. *Finish the equations and see where they take you.*

She'd been working on the conceptual framework of how to integrate space-time and relativity for well over an hour when a set of messages arrived.

The first was from Chris. She didn't even look at the other senders and began to read his message.

Dear Alayna,
I hope this finds you well, but as I recall from your messages and descriptions, COFAR was designed from the beginning to withstand radiation on all levels as well as particle bombardments.

In my case, thankfully, they did put extra shielding around the control area of Recon three. I had to stay in a somewhat small space for several hours, and I did get a slight dosage of radiation even so, probably enough to disqualify me for any more long off-Earth flights, but certainly not enough for any immediate or acute health effects.

Some of the tightness in her entire frame eased, and she could feel herself taking a long slow breath before she continued reading.

I said this before, but if it hadn't have been for you, I probably wouldn't have made it this far. As it is, the return trip is going to take several days longer than planned. That's because . . . well, there were more uses of Hel3 than either I or the mission planners anticipated. I'm also having some difficulties with the atmosphere system. Let's just say that I'm very glad the mission didn't last as long as originally planned.

Difficulties with the air system? Alayna didn't like the sound of that at all.

With very little to do except watch monitors, listen to music, and cringe at what's stored as flat-screen entertainment, and vidloids so bad I just deleted them without looking, I've had more time to think. About a number of things . . . and to think over some quotes, but that comes later.

I didn't mention this before. At least I don't think I did, but just after I left on this mission, Kit let me know that our mother had contracted tuberculosis three—T3. From the tone of Kit's messages and what she wasn't saying, I knew things were bad, and I pressed her in my messages. I just learned a little while ago that Mom died. Even if I'd been at my regular station, with the Earthside crises I wouldn't have been able to get to her. I can say that, but it doesn't help much. I guess there are prices for everything. Sometimes, they're high. I've been privileged to see some of the greatest sights anyone could see. Certainly, the alien artifact, for all its inscrutability, has to be one of those wonders. But I couldn't be with my mother when she so desperately wanted me there. I saw the alien artifact, but I'll never see my mother alive again. I've been closer to the sun and farther from Earth than most people, but my sister was there to support my parents. I wasn't.

The thing is . . . I wanted to be a pilot. I got my dreams, and if I'm going to be honest, I don't know that I would have turned down the chances to do what I've done even if I'd known what I know now. Does that make me incredibly selfish and self-centered?

Alayna looked at the lines again. They almost seemed to blur in front of her. *Were you selfish to take the Farside postdoc post? So comparatively soon after Mother's death? When it was clear that your father missed you terribly?*

We've never talked—or messaged—about things like this before, but I don't know anyone else who would understand, anyone else who looks in wonder at the night sky—or in your case, both the night sky and the blazing sun.

Alayna had to stop reading for several minutes.

While nothing ever goes exactly as planned, maybe after all this dies down, if it does, Space Command will let me take leave on Luna. If not, and if you're willing, we ought to be able to work something out.

Willing? Then again, he was asking. Somehow, she couldn't imagine his not asking, rather than just assuming.
When she got close to the end, she had to smile at what he had written.

I quibble somewhat over the word "pedestrian" in the following quote, but otherwise I agree. I'd never want to assume blindly what you think, but I have the feeling you might agree.

The greatest of all faults in a politician, and in any leader, is the failure to recognize that charisma has nothing to do with ability, excellence, or goodness. In fact, charisma enables far more the evils of the universe than great and worthy accomplishments. Give me pedestrian accomplishment over charisma any day.

Alayna nodded, her eyes lingering over the last words.

Give me an astrophysicist who can not only explain the stars, but wonder at them.

After a time, she opened the next message, discovering it was from Dr. Wrae. The first lines read: "I would appreciate further explanation for the rescheduling required in the early hours of December second, well before the CME struck Earth . . ."

Reading those lines convinced Alayna that she could reply to Chris first, and she did.

Dear Chris,

I just got your message. It was delayed, but the communications nets are anything but in the best shape right now as a result of the CME. I'm so glad that you're on the way back. I can't tell you how glad.

I'm been doing a lot of thinking, about a lot of things. I think I understand how you feel about dreams. My mother died in the flooding caused by Hurricane Ernesto just after I'd defended my thesis at Princeton. My father was devastated, but postdoc positions weren't easy to find, and I jumped at the chance to take the one here. Now, the CME has hit Earth, and I've heard nothing from him. If anything happens . . . But I didn't want to give up the dream of, I'd guess you'd say, making a difference, doing something with meaning beyond money, beyond power. It's not him. He understands and supports what I'm doing. It's me. I suppose one of the prices of wanting to make a difference is guilt. Guilt about all the things people would like you to do, and some that no one asks you to do, but you think you should do if you're a really good person. But you can't do all of those things if you want to make that difference. Does that make sense?

I'm not sending a quote, but I *really* appreciated the one you sent, as if you couldn't tell from what I just wrote. Before long I'll have something else for you to read, something dealing with the Solar Express, but it needs some more work before I do.

Looking forward to seeing you, and yes, I'm willing, and thank you for asking.

Alayna didn't even hesitate in sending it.

She did sigh when she returned to reading the message from Director Wrae, knowing she'd have to be most careful in the wording of her reply. After that, she could answer Emma.

URGENT!!!

CLASSIFICATION: EYES ONLY

TO: Hensen Correia
Acting Secretary
Department of Off-Earth Affairs

FROM: Khelson LeMay
Lieutenant General
Noram Space Command

SUBJ: Sinese Jade Archers

DATE: 4 December 2114

Background:
The Sinese Space Command has undertaken a program to build large spacecraft suitable as weapons platforms [Jade Archers]. Contrary to media reports, only ten spacecraft were planned. Of the ten under construction, only four, including a prototype, are advanced enough to be operable. The prototype dreadnought [code name: Onyx Hammer] was hastily converted to a research vessel and exploded, as earlier reported, after departing the alien artifact, i.e., the Solar Express. It is unclear whether the explosion was remotely triggered by Space Command because the crew had disobeyed orders to remain with the artifact or whether the circumstances of the artifact's explosion in some fashion affected the ship's drives. Of the remaining three Jade Archers, all have received some degree of militarization. Yesterday, at some undetermined time subsequent to the ending of immediate electromagnetic effects on the Earth's magnetosphere caused by the coronal mass ejection (CME), two of the militarized spacecraft were detected moving toward Earth, presumably from the Sinese asteroid manufacturing facility and Sinese off-Earth Space Command headquarters [see asteroid 2031 SJ4].

Current Situation:
The two Sinese spacecraft resembling the prototype dreadnought took a position at 0413 UTC this morning, 4 Decem-

ber 2114, controlling access to L-1 Lunar facilities. Sinese Space Command authorities on 2031 SJ4 have declared that the CME that impacted Earth was caused by actions of the Noram research craft observing the alien artifact, and that such actions were an act of war against the Sinese Federation. The off-Earth Sinese Space Command is demanding a negotiated turnover of all near-Earth space installations to the Sinese Federation. It has also indicated that any spacecraft leaving any L1 facility will be considered as initiating a hostile act of war, and all L1 facilities will be immediately destroyed. Earthside Sinese Defense Force command does not respond to any communications. All indications are that the two craft report to Sinese Space Command located on asteroid 2031 SJ4. Any direct action by Donovan Base, regardless of success, will likely result in the loss of all L1 civilian facilities and damage to or loss of Donovan Base, with concomitant loss of life.

Noram Earthside defense assets cannot be committed at this time. ONeill Station only possesses three fusionjets with limited military assets. Donovan Base has four moderately adapted fusionjets, but it is likely any movement will trigger Sinese action against L1 installations.

Indian authorities have the capability to take out the Sinese Federation geostationary military installation, but have advised that they do not have any spacecraft with military capability currently able to reach L1 area in the "immediate future."

Recommended Actions:
- Immediately prepare all L1 personnel for possible attack.
- Determine if any defensive capabilities possessed by Donovan Base can be adapted to determinative offensive action.
- Attempt to open talks with Sinese Space Command authorities, both on and off Earth.
- Investigate all possible alternatives.

NOTE TO FILE:
  Acting Deputy Secretary and acting Secretary verbally briefed, commencing at 0445 UTC, 2 December 2114. President and Chief of Staff briefed at 0625 UTC.

84

RECON THREE
4 DECEMBER 2114

Tavoian was sweating and breathing hard when he woke. A few swallows of water helped some with the feeling of being overheated, but didn't do anything for his headache.

"Present level of CO2?"

THE CURRENT LEVEL IS SIX POINT FIVE PERCENT.

Too high too soon. After almost six days after leaving the alien artifact, Tavoian had to admit he wasn't feeling as well as he'd like. In fact, not anywhere near. He hadn't dared exercise, not and put even more CO2 into an environmental system that had ended up unable to scrub much if any of it out. The emergency CO2 removal system had brought the levels down to five point seven percent before shutting down, and while the regular system had resumed, Tavoian couldn't see that it was doing anything at all, since the CO2 levels had increased by eight-tenths of a percent from the time the emergency removal system had shut down.

After a while, he felt well enough to eat and tried something called a Mexican omelet. He almost wished he hadn't, but his stomach settled after a while. The monitors and screens showed nothing near Recon three, at least not within the roughly five-million-kay range of the radar—five million kays for comparatively large objects like the artifact, and less for smaller ones.

INCOMING MESSAGE.

It couldn't be from Alayna. Not early in the day. It wasn't. It was from the colonel, and it was short.

Tavoian, Christopher A.
Major, NSC
NSS-21/Recon Three

Report status immediately. No report received for 3 December 2114.
Interrogative CO2 situation.

Tavoian frowned. Hadn't he sent a report? He checked the outgoings. He hadn't. He certainly had more than enough time on his hands to have done so. *You aren't thinking as well as you should be.*

"What is our current ETA at Donovan Base?"

CURRENT ETA REMAINS 1830 UTC ON 5 DECEMBER 2114.

Thirty-six hours . . . thirty-six long hours. He shook his head. *You'd better see about dealing with the CO2 level.*

He left the message unanswered and made his way to the main lock. "Open the outer lock."

THAT IS NOT RECOMMENDED AT PRESENT SPEED.

Neither is asphyxiating. "Priority override."

OUTER LOCK IS OPENING.

"Let me know when the pressure in the outer lock is zero."

PRESSURE IS ZERO.

"Close the outer lock." If he had calculated correctly, by venting the outer lock, and repressurizing it, and then opening the inner lock, he should get a reduction in CO_2, perhaps getting the ambient level down to around five point four percent.

At that moment, Tavoian realized something, and he could have kicked himself. The lock air had been separate from the air in the rest of the ship. If he'd opened the *inner* lock door first and let the lock air and ship air mix, that would have dropped the overall concentration in the ship's atmosphere by maybe half a percent, since the lock air and ship air would have mixed, and the last time the lock air and ship air had mixed had been back when the ambient level in the ship had been significantly lower. Even if he didn't have the numbers quite right, it would have helped. Then he could have waited for another four or six hours before cycling the lock.

Stupid! Stupid! But he couldn't undo what he'd just done.

After fifteen minutes, he had the AI open the inner lock door. The air that rushed into the passenger space felt cool and refreshing. Part of that might have been his imagination, but the coolness definitely wasn't imagined.

He made his way back to the control area. He might as well begin his reply to the colonel while he waited to see what the effect of the lock cycling had been.

A second message had arrived, this one from Alayna. He decided to answer the colonel first and methodically composed his reply.

Recon three operating status within parameters, with the exception of CO2 removal system. CO2 system is nonfunctional. Emergency CO2 removal system deployed. Successfully lowered ambient CO2 to five point seven percent. Level returned to six point five percent at 0600 UTC. Cycled lock and reduced CO2 level to . . .

"Interrogative current CO2 level?"
CURRENT CO2 LEVEL IS FIVE POINT EIGHT PERCENT.

. . . five point eight percent. Anticipate future rise to seven percent by 0600 UTC, 5 December 2114. Will attempt to cycle lock before beginning decel at 0800 UTC, 5 December 2114.

Recon three remains on schedule ETA of 1830 UTC tomorrow (5 December 2114).

Tavoian didn't know what else to add. So he sent the reply as it stood.

Then he turned to Alayna's message, the first lines of which brought a broad smile to his face. The smile was replaced by a thoughtful frown as he began to read about her mother's death, and then about her worries about her father.

Was that why Kit had never married or had a partner? *Because she worried so much about you and your parents?* Or because she just didn't want any more worries? Tavoian had to admit that he'd never worried that much about his parents. They'd both seemed so capable, almost invulnerable. *Was that a childlike view, one that you never gave up because it was so convenient?*

His eyes went back to the message screen, wondering exactly what she had to say about the alien artifact or ancient spacecraft that she was having to work on. That suggested something professional and complicated, but beyond that Tavoian wasn't about to guess.

Her closing lines stunned him. He definitely wanted to see her, but had he really asked? Or had he assumed, and half asked? Either way, he was glad she'd taken it as asking. *Very glad.* Unfortunately, it was likely to be a long time before anything could happen.

He recalled an ancient myth about lovers separated by a strait of treacherous water and how one of them drowned when someone put out the light he was using to navigate. That strait was as nothing compared to the gulf between Alayna and him, even when he was where he was theoretically stationed.

An hour later, another message from the colonel arrived. The rapidity of the colonel's reply bothered Tavoian, and he immediately called it up and began to read, not that he wouldn't have anyway.

Tavoian, Christopher A.
Major, NSC
NSS-21/Recon Three

Received status report. Request you attempt lock cycling prior to 0600 UTC on 5 December for maximum effectiveness.

Be advised that unidentified spacecraft are operating in the vicinity of your deceleration corridor. Believed to be militarized Sinese craft. Do not open hostilities. If attacked, respond with all available force.

Further orders may be forthcoming. Request you assess possible additional offensive capabilities.

Frig! Frig! Frig! Not only did he have to worry about being asphyxiated in his own ship, but now he had to pass through a gauntlet of "unidentified spacecraft," which had to be Sinese, and if they were built anything like the one he'd seen at the Solar Express, they'd dwarf his fusionjet. And besides two torps, exactly what sort of additional offensive capabilities did his hastily converted fusionjet have?

He thought about returning Alayna's message immediately, but his stomach was still uneasy, and he had time, a good twenty-four hours of doing little but waiting.

85

The first message to come in on Tuesday was from Alfen Braun, the first communication Alayna had received from the Director-Generale of the Farside Foundation in months. Alayna opened it and began to read with great trepidation.

> Dr. Wong-Grant:
> I have just finished reviewing your actions following the impact of the coronal mass ejection. You should be pleased to know that your timely actions in sending advance notifications of the event to a wide range of professionals have not gone unnoticed or unappreciated. The Foundation has benefited greatly from those actions.
>
> In addition, your initiative in dealing with scheduling and information and data transfers has also been noted. Your actions have been a credit to your expertise and professionalism and have resulted in maintaining the high standards for which the Foundation has become known. While times may be trying in the weeks and months ahead, we look forward to your continued efforts to maintain COFAR operating as close to full efficiency as is possible.
>
> My congratulations and appreciation.
>
> Alfen Braun
> Director-Generale

Obviously, something in what Alayna had done had rebounded to her credit. Just as obviously, either Director Wrae hadn't wanted to tell Alayna, or the Director-Generale wanted to do so herself . . . for political reasons, Alayna had no doubt.

Alayna smiled faintly as she made sure a copy of the message went to her very personal and locked files.

She'd hoped, definitely hoped, that she'd hear from her father. It had been days, and while Lincoln was normally a fairly safe locale, with power still out across much of Noram, and projected not to be restored for weeks or months, no place without power would stay that safe for long. She didn't know, and couldn't find out, the status of power in Lincoln. And no source she could find could even project when that information might be available.

Knowing that she couldn't do more, but still worrying, she went back to work, trying to make sense out of her solar images. Now that COFAR was immersed in lunar night there were no new solar images to study, but that did give Alayna more time to study the last ones the solar array had captured, and when Braun's message had arrived, she had been in the process of comparing the later ones to those just after the solar prominence had erupted.

There was something about the way the mini-granulations were arranged. *More like the way they aren't arranged.*

"Marcel . . . connect all the mini-granulations . . . I mean highlight them and then link them with the highlighter."

A good minute passed before the enhanced and adjusted image appeared.

There's something . . . "Can you analyze the pattern, the line?"

"It approximates a fractal, Dr. Wong-Grant . . ."

"But it's not. It could be, couldn't it?" That was a stupid question, Alayna realized. Anything could be tweaked into something approximating a fractal, but that didn't make it one. "Is there a section of the flux lines bordering the multi-fractal mini-granulations that is a fractal?"

"There are three sections."

"Highlight them, please."

Alayna studied them, then frowned. The three were all close enough that a larger, regular granulation could have enclosed all three. "They look similar. Are they?"

"At the highest enlargement, they appear to be identical."

"Save a highlighted image to my research files."

"The image is saved."

"Now . . . highlight any fragments of smaller flux lines that would fit within that same fractal pattern."

Alayna watched as the image emerged, something that appeared to be almost a fractal-edged sunspot, with fainter lines across the middle. It reminded her of something, something specific, but what exactly she couldn't recall. "Save that enhanced image as well."

Next. Alayna studied the image of the same section of the sun captured by the main optical array just after the massive CME had burst from the photosphere. Again, there was a similar pattern of magnetic flux lines, clear for only one image. "The main array image I've got on the center screen. How does the flux line pattern compare to the enhanced pattern you just saved?"

"The defined flux lines are fractal. The pattern in those sections is identical to the fractal sections in the images you had enhanced."

What are the chances of that fractal emerging by chance twice at random? The word "astronomical" came to mind, and she almost burst out laughing. "Save that image to my research files as well."

None of the later images showed that level of fractality, not even with Marcel's greater ability to find and enhance.

Alayna was still comparing and puzzling over images at 0946 UTC when she received the one message she'd worried about not getting, the one from Chris.

Dear Alayna,
Your message definitely has me intrigued. I'll be looking forward to the mysterious document that you're working on. Whatever it is, it's bound to be good.

If all goes according to plan, in little more than twenty-four hours I'll begin decel and the final approach back to my station. It should be routine, and after that, and once I'm settled, maybe I can get a decent night's rest. Let me tell you, sleeping in weightless conditions doesn't make for uninterrupted sleep . . .

Sleep? He's talking about sleep, after what he's said before . . . Alayna frowned. Something was not right. Had he even written what she was reading?

I still can't fathom why the artifact exploded. That's not my field, though. It's yours. Do you have any thoughts on that . . . or will they be part of that mysterious document?

But that part sounds just like him.

I've been asked to take an inventory of what's left of all the equipment I carted out to the artifact, and I've been surprised both at how much isn't left and how much is. I suppose that's the result of the Space Service's version of packing heavy . . .

understandable considering no one knew what might be there when they sent me off . . .

At times, I do feel that you have a higher opinion of me than I may deserve. You're a brilliant astrophysicist. I'm a pretty bright Space Service officer and pilot. That doesn't compare. I guess I worry . . . Then again, maybe it's just because it's been a long mission and I'm just plain tired.

Tomorrow's going to be a big day, and I'm not too scintillating now . . . but I do want to take you up on getting together—very much, and whenever that is, even if it's months or longer.

Alayna blinked. The message was so like Chris . . . and so unlike, almost bouncing between cheer and reflection. *He's worried. He's really worried, and he's trying to be cheerful.*

And that worried her. The more she thought about it, the more she worried.

Finally, she set aside her work and sat down to write a message to him. Whether or not he would get it before he began his deceleration and approach to wherever he was stationed she didn't know. But she needed to write as much for her sake as his.

When she finished, she immediately sent it.

She was still concerned, but she tried to put those concerns aside and concentrate on the other puzzling aspect of what happened to the alien artifact. Just what had that direct line of energy been? The scant amount of data that COFAR's systems had been able to detect and record suggested that whatever had struck the artifact had aspects of an X-ray laser and what amounted to focused high energy particles at temperatures approaching a million degrees Kelvin, in essence the science-fictional idea of a particle beam consisting of hadrons. The problem with that was that it wasn't consistent with quantum mechanics because experiments had shown that even stable protons tended to become unstable at extremely high temperatures.

What if confined instability was what gave that beam its destructive force?

Alayna shook her head. That just added problems at another level. How could one confine unstable hadrons in what amounted to a vacuum. Inside the sun was one thing, with incredible gravitational/mass pressures, but in the corona?

What if the beam originated below the photosphere and the instruments only picked it up when it reached the corona?

She went back and followed the images, and the timing. The beam, for lack of a better word, had only lasted seven seconds and had never extended beyond the artifact. That suggested it *could* have originated somewhere below the surface of the photosphere. But there was no evidence to prove where it had originated.

Between her struggles with the multi-fractal mini-granulations and the very real but inexplicable beam, not to mention her worries about Chris, it was a relieving distraction when the message from Emily arrived in mid-afternoon.

> Alayna—
> Thanks for the follow-up! And those images. They're spectacular, but I'll keep them private.
>
> Pleased and then some to hear your friend survived the SPE and CME. Maybe I'll get to meet you both together some time.

If that isn't both hint and suggestion . . .

> The big island is still cleaning up, but we're fully operational here. Hope all the Earthside mess doesn't translate into problems for you.
>
> Looking forward to whatever you're working on. Knowing you, I won't be expecting whatever it is.
>
> Emma

When Alayna went back to work, after touring the aeroponics section, she was still worrying about what her solar observations had shown, but even more about her father, from whom she still had not heard, and Chris.

86

Tavoian wasn't even certain that he actually slept, not with all the thoughts and dreams that swirled through his head, especially about weapons. The thought that lingered and was with him when he woke was the definition of a weapon. It was simple enough. Projection of force. Most weapons were projectiles of some sort. Even lasers projected something, even if what was projected were essentially photons at the speed of light. In essence, projectiles were a combination of velocity and mass.

As he took several swallows of water from the squeezebottle, he stiffened. Velocity and mass! He currently had a great deal of velocity . . . and there were a number of cubesats and several spy-eyes that he hadn't used. Plus there were two ISVs, both with AI rovers still attached, that might allow limited maneuverability.

He had barely finished eating the last Mexican breakfast burrito, which left something to be desired, such as flavor beyond excessive chilies, when the latest message from the colonel arrived. He read it slowly.

> Tavoian, Christopher A.
> Major, NSC
> NSS-21/Recon Three
> This is to inform you that two Sinese spacecraft with military capabilities have taken positions as noted in the attached data plot. They have demanded that all Noram off-Earth facilities be surrendered. They have also declared that any craft or weapon leaving any facility will result in that facility being immediately destroyed . . .

Tavoian reread that again. The words didn't change.

> ONeill Station currently incommunicado.

Sinese Space Command headquarters does not respond. Ships at L1 appear to be under control of off-Earth Sinese Space Command military authorities.

Any action that you can take to disarm or disable Sinese spacecraft would be appreciated.

That was the entire message. Tavoian doubted that the last line had been approved by higher authority. But it appeared that Sinese higher authorities had been rendered mute by the CME, as had Noram commands . . . or at least the ability of Noram to respond to the threat.

He was still thinking about the colonel's request when the message from Alayna arrived, which he immediately began to read.

Dear Chris,
After reading your last message, even if you may be back at wherever you are stationed before you get this, I had to message you. Your thoughts and comments have come to mean so much to me. Some might say that it's just because I'm running CO-FAR alone, and I'm lonely. I don't think so. I like people, but I don't need them, not in the sense of absolutely having to have them around. The very few with whom I'm friends are those who think and who have something of worth to say. I've enjoyed so much exchanging comments and quotations. I want those exchanges to go on, one way or another, even if it takes time before we can do so in person. I wanted you to know that.

Tavoian swallowed. *She cares, and she wants you to know it.* His second thought wasn't as cheerful. *She's read through what you said, and she's really worried.* After a moment's thought, he realized that he wasn't all that surprised.

I'm still working on what you called my "mysterious document." I will be for a while yet, but I promise that you'll get to read it.

Take very good care of yourself.

Short and sweet. Very sweet.
After several moments, and belatedly, he checked the CO_2 level. It stood at six point nine percent. At the current rate of increase, it would reach seven point five percent around 1200 UTC, and that was a definite

danger level. He'd hoped to keep it below seven percent . . . and somehow he definitely had to keep it below eight percent, although he was running out of options.

He thought about cycling the lock, as the colonel had suggested, but something held him back. The last time he'd been too hasty, and a few minutes more of reflection wasn't going to change anything measurably one way or the other.

His thoughts went back to the colonel's message. The first thought was that it was clear the colonel didn't think Donovan Base was going to survive without outside intervention. The second thought was that even if Tavoian could provide only a distraction, then the colonel could launch the converted fusionjets at Donovan Base, and that might well change the calculus of the situation.

Tavoian, on the other hand, had no desire to provide a distraction that would prove fatal to himself. He also couldn't afford to have the L1 facilities destroyed for quite a number of reasons, and with ONeill Station incommunicado and possibly inoperative, his own options were limited, to say the least.

After several moments, he asked, "Distance to L1 when we begin decel?"

TWO MILLION ONE HUNDRED TWENTY-EIGHT THOUSAND KAYS.

Tavoian thought. That was quite a ways away for accurate plotting to have objects even generally get close to a target. But if the Sinese ships remained comparatively stationary with regard to L1 . . .

"Do we have enough thruster propellant to do two turnovers?"

THERE IS ENOUGH FOR FOUR TURNOVERS AND A STANDARD APPROACH TO DONOVAN BASE.

Recon three would be traveling at roughly eighty-five kps for two hours after the first two-hour decel. Tavoian did more mental calculations. At eighty-five kps, any object released from Recon three would be traveling at over five thousand kays a minute. "What will be the distance from L2 just before we begin the second decel burst?"

SEVEN HUNDRED EIGHTEEN THOUSAND KAYS.

"How accurately can you program the torps from that distance?

THEORETICALLY, ACCURACY IS WITHIN ONE HUNDRED METERS FOR A TARGET TRAVELING ON A STABLE ORBITAL PATH.

"What about unpowered objects?"

THERE IS NO DATA ON WHICH TO BASE AN ANALYSIS.

Another guess. What he had in mind *might* work, and he couldn't think of anything else. And it was a very good thing he hadn't cycled the lock, because that cycling was going to have to do double duty, so to speak.

HOTNEWS!
5 DECEMBER 2114

[Image Not Available Due to Technical Limitations]

Power's back on in the EC. Mostly, that is, except for Russian and the black glass area on the north side of the Black Sea. Who needs power there? It still glows. Chancellor Rumikov would be pressing everyone else, but he can't. The others are too busy with not enough power, not enough transport, and soon, not enough food.

[Image Unavailable]

No one's heard from Jiang Qining the All-Powerful? Might be that one of those scattered explosions across the Sinese Federation rumored to be Indra scramjet strikes silenced him. Or maybe Qining the Merciless is still in his deep bunker hoping for mercy? The silence hasn't stopped some of his space dreadnoughts from demanding the turnover of all Noram space assets to the Federation. A deep space coup, perhaps? No word from Ottawa, but silence has always suited Prexy Dyana.

[Image Unavailable]

An AAZ delivery drone got misguided, but it did pick up images of what's happening in Ulaanbaatar. Mongolia First has brought out the horn bows. They don't require any power but muscles. The remaining Sinese security forces have dispersed. Fled— that's the word. Now that all the maglevs are down—they take LOTS of power—Beijing can't send forces there. Well, they could airlift them, but there's the small problem of air control. Also it's hard to refuel when there's no power for the fuel pumps.

[Image Unavailable]

The top dog at Twenty-Second Century Fox already plans a full-scale production based on the recent solar superstorm. That's right. Mieville Hughes, chairman of the entertainment giant, has it all planned. The best thing of all? He can tell the truth— mostly, anyway. What an amazing idea!

[Image Unavailable]

Noram's acting Secretary of DOEA—that's the not-so-lovable Hensen Correia—he's got two converted and militarized fusionjets in striking position to take out the Sinese EastHem space elevator, if the Sinese attempt to move against the Noram L1 facilities. Talk about a standoff. Only problem is . . . our would-be standoffer can't find any Sinese authority who'll talk to him. Or even talk back.

[Image Unavailable]

This just in! New York, the Venice of the North, is totally without power. Situation's getting worse by the moment. No power . . . no pumps. Everything's flooded, and there's a strong probability that the waterlogged not-so-big apple might take a hit from late-season Hurricane Tomas . . . which did a number on Savannah and just finished the demolition of the west end of the old Mall in the ruins of Washington, D.C. What's next? The obliteration of the Balt—

[Signal Lost]

At 0745 UTC, Tavoian initiated turnover, and at 0801, deceleration began. Immediately, he felt heavy, very heavy, and his head began to throb. His vision was fuzzy as well, but after several swallows of water, he could see better. He still felt like shit, but he was sitting in the control couch, not floating.

"Current CO_2 level?"

CURRENT CO_2 LEVEL IS SEVEN POINT ZERO.

He just hoped he could hang on until 1145 UTC, or thereabouts. Sitting, watching the monitors, and waiting made him even more worried. Less than twenty minutes later, he was in the aft compartment, the one that had been filled with gear, surveillance, and measuring and analytical devices, many of which he had used, and some of which he had not, but there was still quite an array of items and still unused equipment.

To begin with, Tavoian sorted out the smaller items he had not used, such as the spare cubesats and spy-eyes, and other small items, such as spare thruster paks, and moved them all to the space adjoining the main lock. He'd hoped that there might be items like steel screws and nuts and bolts. There were all of three small packages. Unsurprisingly, the rest of the fasteners and the like were of lightweight composite.

As the deceleration continued, Tavoian took all the other detachable things that were of small and moderate sizes, among them the carbon extruder and the broken tunable laser, and moved them as well. He thought about the space anchors, but realized that they were still attached to one of the ISVs docked to Recon three.

After the deceleration stopped at 1202 UTC, Tavoian asked, "Are the Sinese spacecraft still in position at L1?"

THEIR POSITION HAS CHANGED. THEY APPEAR TO BE STABLE.

At least they were stable in that position some four seconds ago. "Calculate course line for Sinese craft, and indicate how much fuel it will require to put us on that course line with no tangential vector component." The last words might not have been necessary, but Tavoian wanted to make certain.

ADDITIONAL FUEL REQUIRED TOTALS FOURTEEN MINUTES.

"Will Recon three have enough fuel remaining for decel and approach?"

RECON THREE WILL HAVE SUFFICIENT FUEL FOR DECEL AND APPROACH WITH A MARGIN OF EIGHTEEN MINUTES. THAT IS LESS THAN THE REQUIRED MARGIN OF THIRTY MINUTES.

It was getting so that everything was coming up a little short. Tavoian paused. Hel3 requirements were affected by the mass of the ship. It just might work. Especially if he got rid of everything he could. *The colonel did suggest all available weapons.*

He'd still have to wait almost another two hours, and he'd never been good at waiting when there was something to do. So he went back to the aft compartment to see what else he might be able to add to the pile of parts, equipment, and objects that now floated in reasonable proximity to the inner airlock.

When he had done all that he could, he returned to the controls, and began to program the two ISVs to home in on any vessel with the profile similar to the Sinese ships. That was probably an exercise in futility, given the speed at which the ISVs would be moving and the comparative minimal power from the ISV thrusters thrust from, but . . . if they just happened to be close . . .

Another hour passed. By then he was feeling even less well, and he asked, "Interrogative CO2 level?"

CO2 LEVEL IS AT SEVEN POINT TWO PERCENT.

Just a little longer.

As he waited, Tavoian couldn't help thinking that it had taken him sixteen hours of accel and rest, the same as it took to get to the artifact, to reach a speed that was half of what his outbound velocity had been. Now he was traveling at half that speed for half the distance, and it was taking almost as long. Except, Tavoian realized, it was far more than half the distance given that he'd been traveling farther to avoid initially losing speed in order to use that speed to escape the sun's greater gravitational attraction near the orbit of Mercury.

Finally, after heading aft once again and adding more to the stack, pausing, and rethinking his plans, and rethinking again, and adding more small items, at 1355 UTC, Tavoian asked, "Are the Sinese ships still in the same position?"

THEY HAVE SHIFTED POSITION SLIGHTLY, BUT ARE STABLE.

"When the drive is ready, do a turnover and make the course change to a straight-on intercept of the Sinese ships."

THAT REQUIRES AN OVERRIDE.

"Make course change with minimal fuel usage. Priority override. Compensating factors will decrease fuel mass ratio."

Eight minutes passed before the AI announced, BEGINNING TURNOVER AND MAKING COURSE CHANGE.

Even before the AI replied, Tavoian could sense the ship moving around him.

"When on new course, slew the ship so that the airlock is aligned with the course line."

Slightly more than fifteen minutes later, the marginal acceleration stopped, and the AI declared, OUTER AIRLOCK DOOR IS ALIGNED WITH PRESENT COURSE AND HEADING.

"Open the inner lock."

The inner lock opened, and a brief wave of chill air rushed past him. As the lock air mixed with the compartment air, Tavoian felt slightly less flushed and his stomach was less uneasy. *That could be your imagination.* Whether it was imagination or not, the improvement in the way he felt was welcome, and he began to shift everything he had determined that was unnecessary for his return to Donovan Base into the lock, wondering if it would all fit.

It did, with barely enough room for him to slip inside as well.

He extracted the emergency space suit from the wall locker next to the airlock and struggled into it, not the easiest of tasks while weightless. Within several moments of sealing the helmet, he definitely felt even better. His headache wasn't throbbing so much, and he didn't feel as flushed. *Auto-suggestion ... or real physiological relief?* He didn't know. He wasn't sure he cared.

He stepped into the main lock, and attached the tether to the suit's equipment belt, not that he had any equipment attached. "Close the inner airlock hatch."

OVERRIDE REQUIRED WITH CODE.

Tavoian had to struggle to remember the code. "'Tiger, tiger, burning bright.'"

INNER AIRLOCK HATCH CLOSING.

Tavoian waited. "Open the outer lock."

THAT IS NOT RECOMMENDED AT PRESENT SPEED.

Neither is asphyxiating because you don't have a home base to return to. Any home base. "Priority override. 'In the forests of the night.'"

OUTER LOCK IS OPENING.

Several of the loose and lighter items were carried out of the lock as the air dispersed into space. Tavoian edged forward to the opening and looked out, taking in the view, restricted as it was by his helmet.

He could see his destination, or rather both the Earth and the Moon . . . and the approximate position where the L1 facilities were. He thought he could make out several small points of light, but whether those were station lights or distant stars in the same position, he couldn't tell.

For a moment, he just looked. In all the time he'd been a pilot, he'd been where he could physically see the stars and Earth and Moon directly, not through a screen or a sensor, only a handful of times, mostly in various training exercises. Finally, he took a last look, trying to fix in his memory the image of Earth and Moon, half a million kays away, a not-quite full blue orb and a smaller dusty white crescent, against a star-splashed black velvet depth.

Then he turned and began unloading the airlock by lifting the broken laser and pushing it out. Then came the carbon extruder, followed by the spy-eyes and the small cubesats and thruster-paks, and all the other paraphernalia. The smaller items he eased out awkwardly, trying to give them some tiny amount of separation, but as little as possible.

All in all, it took him almost fifteen minutes before the lock was emptied.

"Undock and launch ISV one on current heading and course. Minimal ISV thrust for two minutes only." Tavoian waited until the first ISV was clear, then ordered the launch for the second. When he was certain it was on its way, he stepped back and pressed the stud to manually close the outer airlock.

He had to wait more than five minutes before the airlock was pressurized and he could open the inner hatch. As soon as he was in the passenger area, he took off the helmet and made certain that he turned off the suit's air supply as well.

"Interrogative CO_2 level?"

CO2 LEVEL IS SIX POINT SEVEN.

Tavoian wanted to take a deep breath. With roughly four hours to go, he *should* reach Donovan Base before the air in Recon three became unbreathable enough to knock him out.

"Initiate turnover and reorientation."

INITIATING TURNOVER AND ORIENTATION.

Tavoian slowly struggled out of the emergency space suit, then replaced it in its locker. Within minutes of when he reached the control couch, the AI declared, TURNOVER AND ORIENTATION COMPLETE.

"Commence deceleration."

COMMENCING DECELERATION.

Since Tavoian had used fifteen minutes of drive availability for the course change, that meant Recon three would only actually decelerate for an hour and forty-five minutes, and that would add more than twenty minutes to the final decel—after another two-hour break.

He just lay back in the control couch for several minutes, thinking. What he'd attempted was an incredible long shot, but with all that he'd launched out of the lock, if any of it hit either of the Sinese ships it would do significant if not catastrophic damage. Considering that each piece would be traveling at close to three hundred thousand kays per hour, even a carbon fabric fastener could likely punch through most spacecraft hulls. And if something like the ISV or the broken tunable laser hit one of the Sinese ships, it would render the ship inoperable if not destroy it. On the other hand, he'd launched at most two or three hundred objects, less than fifty of which had significant mass. He'd attempted to create almost no spread, but he had figured that just his own actions would create a little spread. The two ISVs would remain in the center of the spread.

It might work . . . and from this distance what else could you have done?

He still had two torps, but those would have to wait until he reached the L1 area, and he hoped he wouldn't have to use them . . . but feared he would.

His thoughts drifted . . . and then he woke with a start when the deceleration stopped and he became weightless once more. He checked the time—1605 UTC—and immediately worried about the Sinese ships, but when he tried to ask the AI, his mouth and throat were so dry that all he could do was croak. He fumbled to find the squeezebottle. It took several mouthfuls and swallows before he could clear his throat.

"Can you pick up the Sinese ships on RCS?" The AI should, since Recon three ought to be around a hundred and seventy-five thousand kays away, almost next door in astronomical terms.

THAT IS AFFIRMATIVE.

Tavoian wanted to shake his head. His debris should have struck the ships some fifteen minutes before the end of decel.

ONE VESSEL IS RADIATING EXCESS HEAT. THE OTHER IS CLOSING ON IT.

Yes! "Can you determine the severity of the damage?"

THE DAMAGED VESSEL APPEARS TO BE MISSING A LARGE SECTION OF ONE END, WITH LESSER DAMAGE MIDSHIPS.

The "good" thing about the damage was that at the speeds involved, it would be difficult for the Sinese to discover anything but the fact that the ship had been struck by a high velocity object . . . and meteors and cosmic debris did occur. The bad thing was that one of the ships appeared to be intact. The other problem was that Tavoian really didn't have any choice but to complete a standard deceleration, because he didn't have enough Hel3 for anything else.

Except it doesn't have to be exactly standard. "To what speed can we decelerate to reach firing range on the two Sinese ships, execute turnover, fire torps, and then turnover and complete decel at two gees and still have enough thruster propellant and Hel3 to reach Donovan Base?"

THE OPTIMUM SOLUTION WOULD BE TO CONTINUE AT PRESENT VELOC-ITY FOR AN ADDITIONAL TEN MINUTES BEFORE EXECUTING TURNOVER AND FIRING TORPS, THEN EXECUTE A TURNOVER AND COMMENCE DECEL-ERATION AT THREE GEES FOR TWELVE MINUTES. THAT ALLOWS TEN MIN-UTES FOR EACH TURNOVER, WITH THE STANDARD MARGIN FOR ARRIVAL DISTANCE.

Rotten as he felt, Tavoian had no doubts that he could take three gees for twelve minutes. "Prepare to execute that solution. Program the torps accordingly. Display the approach profile."

The approach profile appeared on the screen wall, and Tavoian immediately began to study it. He almost swallowed when he saw the distances. When Recon three released torps, they'd be less than seven thousand kays from the target, and the torps would be traveling almost twenty-two kps, fast enough to cover the distance in roughly five minutes. While that sounded incredibly fast, defensive fire-control systems operated in nanoseconds, and they likely had Recon three already in their system.

There wasn't anything he could do about that, and the AI's solution would give the torps far more velocity—and less reaction time for the Sinese—than his own would have. The plain fact was that he didn't have anywhere else to go and the Sinese would likely target him as he approached Donovan Base if they could. So his only choice was to take them out first. *If you can.*

After a time of trying to think of a better way to handle things, he thought he dozed, but he wasn't certain. Then, slowly, he became aware that he was sweating more, flushing, and that his stomach was getting uneasy. "Current CO2 level."

THE CURRENT CO2 LEVEL IS SIX POINT EIGHT.

He checked the time—1736 UTC—still almost an hour before commencing the attack on the Sinese ships and then beginning decel. Another thought struck him. Why hadn't he heard anything from the colonel?

Because the Sinese ships are in an ideal position to intercept anything sent from Donovan Base to you. There was also the fact that even if the Sinese couldn't break the encryption, the direction of the transmission might call attention—or greater attention—to Recon three. That suggested that, first, the colonel was putting a great deal of faith in Tavoian and, second, that the colonel didn't have many options. It also explained why he hadn't gotten any more messages from anyone.

"Is there any change in the position or actions of the Sinese ships?"

THE SINESE SHIPS REMAIN IN POSITION. THE DAMAGED VESSEL IS NO LONGER ACTIVELY RADIATING HEAT OR ENERGY. ITS HULL IS COOLING.

"Can you detect communications?"

THERE HAVE BEEN NO DETECTABLE TRANSMISSIONS.

All that meant was that no transmissions had been directed anywhere in Recon three's general area. There was no way that the AI could detect a tight burst beam to or from the ships, not from Earth or near-Earth orbit installations.

After what felt like an hour of checking the monitors he looked at the time readout—1751 UTC.

His headache was worse, and he felt even hotter, although he was shivering. *Time for remedial measures.* He pushed himself away from the control couch and then pulled himself down to the locker beside the inner airlock door. It seemed to take forever to get into the emergency space suit, but he was finally suited up, except for the helmet. He pull-floated himself forward to the control area.

Because he was feeling even more light-headed, he asked, "Interrogative CO_2 level?"

CO_2 LEVEL IS SIX POINT NINE PERCENT.

Tavoian decided not to wait any longer. He turned on the suit's air supply and donned the helmet. Within minutes, or so it seemed, the light-headedness vanished, and some of the uneasiness in his guts subsided. Except, when he checked the time, it was 1810 UTC.

He shivered. *Closer than you thought.* "Time to turnover."

EIGHT MINUTES TO COMMENCING TURNOVER.

Nineteen minutes to releasing torps. "Status of Sinese ships?"

STATUS AND POSITION ARE UNCHANGED.

Something about that bothered Tavoian. Why hadn't the undamaged ship moved? Or were they still trying to rescue the crew of the damaged ship? He couldn't say he liked what he'd done or what he was about to do . . . but with the Sinese threatening to destroy all the L1 facilities if any ship so much as moved, he didn't see that he had any real options. And with the CO_2 toxicity problems, and the lack of Hel3, he also couldn't afford to wait around to see what was happening. He was literally running out of air, time, and fuel.

"Combat screens." Even with a clearer head, Tavoian had to concentrate on the screens arrayed before him, even though the AI was directing the attack as programmed. The target, the still-functioning Sinese ship, was almost dead ahead—zero zero one relative.

Each second felt like a minute to Tavoian as he watched the screens. At 1818 UTC, the AI announced, COMMENCING TURNOVER.

And there was still no movement of either Sinese ship. Surely, they must have detected Recon three. How could they not, with all the energy expended in deceleration over the past hours?

ORIENTED ON TARGET. REQUEST OVERRIDE AND CODE.

"'What hand or eye could frame' . . . Code Ultra."

TORPS AWAY. ON TARGET.

The two torps were no sooner away from Recon three than the AI declared, COMMENCING TURNOVER.

As the ship shifted for the final deceleration, Tavoian continued to watch the combat screens, expecting some sort of reaction from the Sinese ships, but nothing occurred. He could see the torps streaking toward the larger ship, except that the screens just showed two points of light moving toward a larger point of light.

The minutes passed while the AI reoriented the ship. The torps closed, then touched the larger point of light. He expected something—a flare, a flash of light—but there was nothing. All three points of light vanished.

TARGET SUCCESSFULLY DESTROYED. Just like that . . . two huge, at least by human standards, ships just gone, shredded by debris and two not terribly powerful torps. *Except they were moving at twenty-two kps.*

TURNOVER AND ORIENTATION COMPLETE. COMMENCING DECELERATION.

The gee force began to build, and build, pressing Tavoian back into the couch. Even with the better air from the emergency suit, he felt as though he struggled to take each breath, that each inhalation was an effort, and that he had to force the air back out of his lungs.

Tavoian felt like the deceleration lasted forever . . . and then it was gone.

DECELERATION ENDED EARLY. WILL RESUME IN THREE MINUTES FOR ONE MINUTE.

"Why?"

THERE WAS EXCESSIVE DISTANCE TO DONOVAN BASE. THE BASE WAS NOT WHERE IT WAS BEFORE.

Not where it was before? Tavoian smiled. Trust the colonel to try something. The Sinese had said no ship could leave, but they hadn't thought about the base moving. *But what good would that do?*

"Is the base where the storage station was, and the storage station where the base was? With dummy ships locked to the storage station?" Tavoian was guessing.

AFFIRMATIVE.

"But how did . . . ?"

The AI did not reply. Tavoian had not framed a complete question because there were too many unknowns . . . and he was still thinking about the Sinese ships.

COMMENCING DECELERATION.

Tavoian doubted that the final decel lasted even a minute.

NEARING DONOVAN BASE.

Tavoian cleared his throat, then keyed the suit into the comm system. "Donovan ops, Recon three. Request immediate docking assignment."

"Three, opscon. Request you stand by."

"Opscon, request immediate docking assignment. Ship's atmosphere toxic. Space suit running low on air."

"Three, wait one."

Another voice broke in, the voice hard and cold. "Opscon, Anson here. Clear lock five. Clear it now."

"Yes, sir." After a pause, opscon continued. "It will be just a minute or two, three. That's as fast as we can clear. Proceed to lock five and stand off until it is clear."

"Opscon, proceeding to lock five." Tavoian turned the ship back to the AI, certain that it would be more deft than he would be in locking in.

The two minutes turned into five before the space tug locked there moved away.

As soon as Tavoian felt the ship settle into the grapples, he began to move toward the airlock. He had the inner hatch open when the AI declared, SHIP DOCKED AND SECURE.

"Open the outer lock and commence shutdown." Theoretically, Tavoian was supposed to do that, but there were times when "supposed to" just wasn't suitable or appropriate.

As soon as the outer lock opened, and Tavoian saw the two uniformed spacers standing outside in the docking corridor, he stepped through the lock, then unlatched the space suit helmet and took it off.

He took a deep breath of the station air . . . and everything went black.

89

HOTNEWS!
6 December 2114

[Image Deleted For Off-Earth Transmission]

Sinese dreadnoughts smashed by high-speed meteorites? Or by a Noram or Indian mystery weapon? Early this morning the Sinese Defense Ministry declared that its ships had been attacked in an unprovoked fashion by ultra-high-speed missiles. They're accusing Noram of secretly militarizing space. Seems like the Sinese wanted their military ships to be the only ones out there. They've also accused the Noram research ship that returned from a Solar Express mission of using those mystery missiles. Acting DOEA Secretary Correia denied the charge and offered to have a multi-nation team inspect the battered fusionjet that barely escaped the sun's gravity and the explosion that claimed the Sinese research ship. Maybe the Sinese are mad that the smaller Noram ship made it back and their big monster didn't.

[Image Deleted]

The power's back on in Beijing . . . and Sinese Head of State Qining is nowhere to be found. No one's talking. Not about the ten scattered deep craters in various parts of China, or about the mysterious illness—that's the polite term—that led to the death of Defense Minister Wu Gong. Space Minister Wong Mengyi is acting head of state. That's because he's the only minister anyone could find. He's declared loudly and publicly that he will not retain the post. He's also denied knowing anything about that secret asteroid base where those not-so-dreadful dreadnoughts were built. Maybe he doesn't want to be the next victim of Indra-cide.

[Image Deleted]

Vistaar Limited plans a realie based on the Solar Express! That's the word out of Mumbai, less than a week after the catastrophic coronal mass ejection that crippled the world's power grids and transmission facilities. The as-yet untitled realie will be "a cross between *Veda* and *Nova!*, with shades of *Alone in the Void*," according to chief exec Amir Lagaash.

[Image Deleted]

When it rains, it pours . . . No! Deluges are cascading down on the British Isles. Forecasters say they won't stop for days. The Thames is over its banks—again—in London and there are no banks downstream, nothing but water and more water. No operating banks of the other kind upstream, either. Between the solar superstorm and the weather not much of anything is operating in England. But has it been lately, anyway?

[Image Deleted]

Disasters are great business! Paramount Realies has jumped into the solar fire. Yes, the third oldest entertainment producer is going to do its version of the Solar Excess, pardon us, the Solar Express. Working title of this all-too-realie? We've heard *Deathstar Extreme*, *Alien Annihilation*, and *Sunstorm*. Let's hope the realie's better.

90

Tavoian was drowning, struggling trying to swim up toward the surface, but that shiny surface where there was air kept retreating . . . no matter how much he tried . . .

Suddenly, he was awake . . . sweating, lying on a bed, wearing only his underclothes. As he sat up, he looked around, but there was little to see in the small chamber, except the bed, a chair, a side table, and a clothes locker. The bulkheads and overheads of pale blue meant he was indeed inside Donovan Base. At least, Donovan Base was the only off-Earth station he'd been where pale blue was used.

Within moments, a spacer3 appeared, carrying a tray. Tavoian didn't recognize the man, who smiled as he set down the tray on the table. "Good morning, Major. How are you feeling?"

"Fine, thank you," replied Tavoian automatically, before he realized that he didn't feel anything of the sort. His head still throbbed, and his entire body ached. "Not as well as I'd like," he added.

"That's not surprising, sir. Dr. Cattertyn will be here in a few minutes. She thought you might feel better if you had something to eat and drink. If you need to wash up, the facilities are in the next compartment."

Tavoian realized, belatedly, that he wasn't weightless, but that the gravity was less than that of the main levels of the base. "Low gee?"

"Yes, sir. If you'd excuse me, sir."

Tavoian smiled. "Don't let me keep you. Thank you." He moved to the table and moved the chair into place before sitting down. His entire body was sore. *Just from twelve minutes or so of three gees?*

The breakfast wasn't remarkable—scrambled eggs with cheese, something that resembled and tasted like ham but probably wasn't, sliced fresh tomatoes, toast and marmalade, and a pot of steaming hot tea. Tavoian ate it all.

He was thinking about seeing if he had any clean uniforms or the like and then taking a shower or washing up when the door to his small quarters opened and a lanky, gray-haired woman with the collar insignia of the medical corps and the gold eagles of a light colonel stepped inside, gently closing the door behind her.

Before Tavoian could say a word, she gestured for him to remain seated. "You gave us a bit of a scare, Major."

"I gave myself a bit of one, sir," Tavoian replied.

"Did you report the correct CO_2 levels?"

Tavoian frowned. "I reported the levels that the ship's indicators showed."

"I was afraid you'd say that."

"Weren't they reading correctly?"

"We don't think so. They may have been reading a percent too low. That's what the preliminary tests show. That wouldn't make much of a difference in regular operations, but . . ." Cattertyn shook her head. "We'll need to do some tests on you."

"To see if I suffered brain damage?"

"It doesn't seem likely, but under the conditions . . ."

"You'd like to make sure. Why the low-grav quarters?"

"You need some gravity, but we didn't want to stress your system. We'll need to increase that gradually."

"How gradually?"

"That depends on the results of the tests."

"Do you know if we're on restricted comm now?"

"No. We're under regular screening. Nothing special."

"I'd like to see any messages and send some."

The doctor smiled. "I'll have Salazar bring you a terminal. Right now, I'd like you to stay on this level. I've already sent him to get a clean shipsuit for you, and a few other things. Your personal gear is in the locker. When you get cleaned up, I'll be back to run over the tests with you." She rose.

The spacer3 returned within minutes after the doctor left, bringing a terminal and one of Tavoian's shipsuits and clean underclothing, and taking away the breakfast tray on his way out.

The shower, shaving, and clean clothing helped, although Tavoian still had a slight headache when he sat back down at the side table and called up his messages on the terminal.

There was only one, and that was from Kit. For a moment, he was disappointed that there wasn't one from Alayna—until he remembered that she'd sent him the one telling him to take care just the day before. *How could you forget that?*

After a moment, he decided that he hadn't so much forgotten as wanted another message from her, and the best way was to send her one.

Dear Alayna—

I'm back at base now, and apparently whole, but somewhat the worse for wear, since my atmosphere system decided to stop removing CO2, and I spent the last several hours in a space suit, during which times circumstances required that I make a higher than normal gee-force deceleration. I've got to go through some medical tests before they tell me how soon I'm returning to duty, but it's pretty certain I will . . . I just don't know exactly when.

Tavoian hoped he wasn't stretching the truth there, but despite the lingering headache, he didn't feel all that bad. *Especially after all that happened.*

I can't tell you how much your last message meant to me, but I hope I'll be able to in person, and I can only hope that it won't be as long as since I last saw you, but with the unsettled state of events . . . who can tell? I'd like to say more, but I need to get those tests, and I wanted to let you know that I was back . . . and that I wouldn't be if it hadn't been for you.

My hopes that you've made great progress with the multifractals and the mysterious documents. More later.

Once he sent his reply, he read Kit's message.

Dear Chris,

I know I should wait like a good big sister. But it's been almost a week, and I've heard nothing from you. I worry. I'm just hoping that you're fine, but not in a place where you can reply.

Despite the power system going down, the solar cells, the ground tap, and the wind generator have kept the house here in good shape, and there's even a comm system with satlinks, that works most of the time, although I have no idea why one works here and not in Salt Lake . . .

Tavoian closed the message at the knock on the door. "Yes? Come in."

Colonel Cattertyn entered, followed by Spacer3 Salazar, who pushed a small console on wheels.

"Ready for some tests, Major?"

"As ready as I'll ever be."

"I doubt that." Her words were dry.

First came a thorough physical examination, including the drawing of blood, then inhaling and exhaling into a face mask, followed by several minutes of breathing oxygen and then exhaling. After the physical examination came questions, verbal word puzzles, mental mathematics, and various memory tests.

Less than five minutes after the doctor had left, the door opened, and Colonel Anson walked in.

"Sir." Tavoian immediately stood.

"At ease, Major. Dr. Cattertyn says that there are no signs of permanent damage. Your system will need some readjusting to gravity. We'll talk about that in a minute. I have my own ideas, but what happened to those Sinese ships?"

"They were hit by high-speed space debris." Tavoian paused. "It might be better said that way. I was short on Hel3. It struck me that the less mass was in the ship, the longer the fuel would last. So I tossed out everything that was either broken or not of further use before we entered the second decel—"

"What was your speed at that point?"

"Eighty kays per second."

"So . . . did you have any idea that any Sinese ships were nearby?"

Tavoian knew what the colonel wanted. He wouldn't go that far. "I knew there were Sinese ships near L1, but the way I jettisoned the excess equipment was designed to avoid the L1 installations." *Which it was.* "I had so little Hel3 remaining that I couldn't make any major course changes."

The colonel nodded. "That's perfectly understandable. The fact that nothing hit any L1 installation shows just how accurate you were under very stressful circumstances. The data and images you brought back will prove invaluable."

"I doubt it, sir."

"Oh?"

"The only thing that all the data, observations, and images will show is that it is theoretically possible to design a starship with an almost impregnable hull out of common materials reconfigured on the hadronic level in a way we know nothing about, powered by a technology we can't even guess at. With the only hard physical evidence being a 38 millimeter chunk of an impregnable substance, I have my doubts how invaluable what I did was."

"What you did was invaluable." The colonel smiled. "Invaluable enough that I've put you in for the Medal of Valor. You will receive it. Both the DOEA Secretary and the Secretary of Defense have signed off on it."

Tavoian understood that part of the reason for the medal would never be mentioned directly.

"Once we wade out of this current morass, Major, you'll be very much in demand, and you're going to be the voice for interplanetary exploration . . . and beyond. I assume that meets with your approval?"

Tavoian did not reply, thinking about that magnificent fragment of a giant ship. *Who else could talk about it . . . and be believed?* "I take it that my health is good enough that I can do almost anything—except long space voyages?"

"You take it, correctly, Major. Rather, your health will be . . . once you complete gravity reacclimation. We'll talk about that tomorrow. We've talked enough today." The colonel nodded, then turned and left the small chamber.

Tavoian's mouth dropped. *What was that all about?*

When no one appeared, he decided that he'd better finish reading Kit's message and send a reply.

91

Even though Alayna had known from Chris's message that he wouldn't be back until late in the day on Wednesday, when she went to sleep that night, she'd still heard nothing. Nor had there been anything in the news summaries. There had only been a notice that all travel to and from all lunar and L1 and L2 locales had been suspended due to the presence of armed Sinese spacecraft.

On Thursday, she woke up early and worried. As soon as she was in the COFAR control center, she checked her messages, but there was only the news summary, just the second one since the CME had hit Earth's magnetosphere. Because of her concerns about her father, from whom she'd still heard nothing, and Chris, she opened the news summary first. She knew what she was about to read would be anything but encouraging, and she wasn't in the slightest surprised by the long litany of areas of the world where the power grids were nonfunctional, including most of the midwestern Noram states. She didn't worry about power in the case of her father because he had both solar and wind power systems at his house outside of Lincoln. What worried her more was the report of heavy snow across the area. Snow and overall power shortages were not a good combination, especially in early winter. That New York was flooding and failing was no surprise, either, not when there wasn't enough power for all the pumps that kept everything dry.

The tiny blurb at the end caught her attention, and she froze for a moment, then read it once more.

> Two Sinese spacecraft were destroyed within several thousand kilometers of various L1 installations around 1830 UTC yesterday. Noram sources declared that the two craft were warships destroyed by high-speed natural space objects. Sinese Space Command sources insist the ships were unarmed and were the victims of an unprovoked attack by a single mil-

itarized fusionjet of Noram origin. Whether there was a ship
in the vicinity at the time, and if there was, what became of it
is unknown at this time.

"Unknown at this time" doesn't mean destroyed. Alayna also knew
that just because Chris had been scheduled to arrive somewhere around
that time, the unidentified craft didn't have to be his. But she also knew
that if the Sinese ships were holding L1 installations hostage, that they
had likely been warships, since travel had been suspended. Under those
conditions, Chris was the type to try to do something. *Even if you did*
tell him to be very careful.

She sent off a short message to her father, not knowing whether it
would reach him, just saying that she was fine and that she hoped to hear
from him.

Finally, she fixed herself coffee and breakfast, then began to eat while
she considered her day, which was actually lunar night. The scheduled
observations were continuing, although the system was still having
to store some of the data and images for later transmission. The monitors
showed everything operating normally, even the extreme ultraviolet telescope, for which she was thankful, since she'd had to replace several components the day before. She wondered if that might have been a possible
aftereffect of the concentration of the system on the destruction of the
Solar Express.

She still had no idea of how the high-temperature particle beam had
been generated, or why it had focused on the alien artifact. In thinking
about the alien artifact, another thought popped into her head, this time
about the "circles" Chris had observed on the outer hull. If the alien ship
had been using a graviton drive or gravitons as a way to traverse a wormhole, were the circles merely an affect of the gravitons projected due to
scattering from the hexagonal columns that were projectors? *How would*
you know? And what would it imply?

It might . . . she began to think in terms of how to express that in mathematical theory.

At least, that would keep her mind partly off worrying about her father
and Chris.

Less than an hour later, another message arrived, and Alayna immediately dropped what she was doing and called up the message, hoping it
was from Chris or her father.

She couldn't stop smiling as she saw it was from Chris, and she immediately began to read. When she finished, she read it again to make certain that she wasn't missing anything. He sounded well, but she could

sense that he was worried about the medical tests, worried that he wouldn't be able to continue as a pilot, or even in the Space Service. *That would be hard for him. But he's back. He's back safe.*

Alayna was still thinking about what she might say that wasn't excessive when another message arrived. She hoped it was from her father. It wasn't. She didn't recognize the sender. At least, she didn't think she did. The name was Caldwell Blaakner. She immediately began to read.

> Dr. Wong-Grant:
> It's been a number of years since we met. It was, just after your second year at Princeton, when you returned to Lincoln to visit your family . . .

Who is this Caldwell Blaakner?

> . . . and your mother was kind enough to introduce you to my son, who was interested in either astronomy or astrophysics and wanted to know more . . .

Now . . . Alayna recalled the name . . . and the face. A tall stern-faced woman who had been her mother's physician. *A doctor? What's happened to Dad?*

> . . . You may have learned that Lincoln suffered a sudden devastating blizzard in addition to the failure of the power system. That's why I'm contacting you from the hospital. I wish there were another way to convey this . . .

Alayna swallowed.

> Your father knew that his neighbors, the Kalimpuras, were not so well provisioned or powered as he was, and he made his way through the snow to offer them a warmer place to stay. Unhappily, two others had gone there before him. He surprised them as they were attacking the couple. Both the Kalimpuras were injured, Yakob more so than Isbella, but with your father's assistance, they subdued the attackers. Your father did not realize that he had been as severely wounded as he was. When the couple realized that, they managed to stop most of the bleeding and rushed him to the hospital in his own vehicle . . .

Of course, Dad was prepared for everything.

> . . . I can't be certain, but I believe he died before he reached
> the hospital. We tried everything . . . I'm so sorry.

Alayna just sat before the controls and screens. Finally, she read the
last lines.

> Your father had mentioned to Dr. Neher that you were the res-
> ident director of COFAR, and a friend managed to find the
> address for us. I did think you would want to know . . .

The rest of the words washed over Alayna. In a way, she'd almost
known. Her father would have tried anything to let her know he was all
right. *So like him . . . thinking of others . . .*

How much time passed, she wasn't certain, but it was well into early
afternoon when she realized that another message had come in. She almost didn't want to open it, especially when she saw it wasn't from
Chris . . . or anyone else she knew, but from the Department of Off-Earth
Affairs.

Now what? Was it terrible news about Chris? She shook her head.
Even if something had happened to him, no one was going to notify her.
They weren't related.

Thinking about her last encounter with the Noram government and
the rather intrusive and overbearing nature of more than a few members
of the Inspector-General's investigatory team, she didn't even want to
open the missive, especially after the last message, and particularly one
addressed to her as Dr. Alayna Wong-Grant, Resident Director, Combined Farside Array, Daedalus Base. The first lines weren't any more
reassuring.

> Director Grant:
> All lunar entities receiving funding, whether partial or full,
> have certain obligations to the government, said responsibili-
> ties being administered by the senior DOEA official in the area
> under whose jurisdiction such entities fall . . .

Alayna took a long deep breath. The last thing she needed was another
run-in with anyone, especially DOEA, since the DOEA funding that Farside Foundation received was critical to maintaining COFAR. *And your
appointment and future.*

At that moment, Marcel announced, "You have an urgent message from the Director-Generale, Dr. Wong-Grant."

Why now? Can't they all just leave me alone? After a moment, she sighed. *No doubt a directive to comply with whatever DOEA requires.* It had to be something like that, because Alayna couldn't believe DOEA would require something without notifying the Foundation. She switched to the Director-Generale's message. While it took two paragraphs, the bottom line was simple: Do what DOEA wants and make them happy.

Alayna wouldn't have expected anything else. She nodded and returned to finishing the DOEA message—more like a requisition, she thought. But, upon further thought, probably not unexpected with everything that had happened in the wake of the Solar Express and the CME.

Whether or not you like it, you don't have any choice. Slowly, she began to compose her replies, first to the local DOEA authority and then to the Director-Generale.

Later . . . when she was more settled, she'd reply to Chris.

92

At precisely 1000 UTC on Friday Tavoian entered the colonel's sanctum sanctorum on the main level and seated himself.

"We'll keep this meeting short," the colonel said. "Dr. Cattertyn doesn't think you should be spending more than an hour at a time in half gee right now."

"She won't tell me why, except that I didn't get enough exercise, and my blood chemistry is out of sorts."

"That should be sufficient, considering you were operating on the edge of consciousness for more than a few hours. You're very durable, Major. You were also very fortunate. Now . . . let's go over the mission. You can skip the outbound trip. Just begin from when you took station on the artifact. Don't bother with anything that's logged into the system. More about what you saw, any conclusions or observations that you've kept to yourself . . ."

Tavoian was more than happy not to have to dwell on his stupidity in trying to use every gram of Hel3, although those details were certainly in the AI's records, and if the colonel didn't know already, which he likely did, he would before long. "One of my first impressions, sir, was just how damned big the artifact was . . . and how perfect and untouched everything was . . ."

Tavoian had talked for close to forty minutes before saying, "I really can't think of anything more that I haven't already reported."

"If you remember anything else you think might be important, just make a note on it, and we'll go over it when you get back."

"I'm leaving soon?"

"In about three hours." The colonel paused. "You're not to mention where you're taking your low grav reacclimation to anyone, particularly to your friend the astrophysicist."

"But—" Tavoian started to protest.

"No 'buts,' Major. We can't risk anyone knowing where you're headed. Even our burst transmissions might not be perfectly secure.

That's another reason for your early departure, and why we've already dispatched all the information you brought back to DOEA HQ and Space Command. It will blow over, especially after the Sinese understand the position they're in, but they're still furious about what happened to their ships, and not all their dispersed elements are necessarily under the full control of the new government."

"You make me seem like a wanted man."

"As far as the Sinese are concerned, you are."

"Can I at least say that I'll let her know more about my therapy when matters are settled?"

The colonel smiled. "That would be appropriate. Also very misleading if any transmissions are intercepted. Now . . . get back into lower gravity. Otherwise, I'll have to apologize to Dr. Cattertyn. I'd rather not."

Tavoian stood, realizing his legs were in fact a little shaky. He tried not to show it.

By the time he returned to his temporary quarters, he found two messages waiting for him, one from Kit, and one from Alayna. He decided to read Kit's first.

> Chris!
> I'm so glad to hear you're back. There's been no word in what news we've been able to get about your return. You'd think that someone would be interested in the only man to actually see the alien artifact.
>
> Are you sure that you're all right? Dad and I don't need any more sudden—or gradual—surprises. I hope you've let Alayna know. I still think she'd be good for you, if only as a friend if you're not romantically interested.

You don't give up, Kit.

> I suppose it will be some time before you're back on Earth. The way things are here, you may be better off where you are than most places in Noram. The good thing about Brian Head is that it's not easy to get to, especially for the unsavory types. The bad thing is that there's no easy way to get what you don't already have. But Dad had laid in enough stuff to last all winter and then some.

That doesn't sound good. But then, Tavoian realized, what could you expect after massive power system failures in a country that had never believed fully in infrastructure that didn't turn an immediate profit?

The rest of the message was cheerfully chatty, without even a hint of what Kit and his father had just gone through.

He almost felt guilty when he opened the message from Alayna and began to read,

> Dear Chris,
> You're not saying everything. I can tell that. The fact that you're worried about medical tests tells me that you went through more than you're saying. I'm just so glad you're back.
>
> I'm sorry to be late in replying to you. I was going to do so sooner, but just after I got your message I got another one. It was from a doctor my mother knew. She'd treated my father after he'd been wounded in saving a neighbor couple from looters. In all the snow, I think the couple had trouble getting him to the hospital. He lost too much blood, and the doctor couldn't save him . . .

Tavoian stopped reading. *She's lost both parents . . . and she's worried about being late in messaging you.*

> . . . I wasn't much good for anything for a while after I got Dr. Blaakner's message. It was so like Dad. He had all the backup power, and his house was secure, but he knew the neighbors might be having trouble. So he went to see if they needed anything.

And she's just like her father. He finished reading the message and immediately began to compose a reply, knowing that he didn't have that much time.

> Dear Alayna,
> I just got your message. I understand. I hope I do, anyway. I won't claim to know exactly how you feel, but you know I lost my mother, and I couldn't even get to see her because of where I was. Unlike you, I do have my father and sister, but I wish so much that I could be with you right now.

There are too many similarities between what's happened to and around us over the past year, and we need to talk about them, or message until we can talk in person. Unfortunately, this message will have to be shorter than I'd like, because right now I'm under orders, and I don't have much time. I *promise* to explain everything to you in great detail as soon as I possibly can. That won't be too long.

In the meantime, please, please take care of yourself.

As he sent the message, Tavoian hoped that she would understand. He needed to make what preparations he could for his coming stint in low-grav therapy.

The Times of Israel
8 December 2114

(JERUSALEM) The aliens were real! After releasing a series of stunning images of the alien spacecraft destroyed by the solar prominence last week, the Noram Space Command finally admitted that its mission to study the so-called Solar Express has returned safely to an undisclosed location, with a massive amount of data and images. Once the material is processed, the Noram DOEA will make the bulk of the material available to all "cooperative space agencies" and research institutions. DOEA acting Secretary Correia declined to clarify what constituted a "cooperative" space agency.

Although the NSC mission was crewed by a single pilot, Noram sources have indicated that for reasons of health, including a prolonged period of weightlessness, the officer will not be immediately available for appearances. The pilot is expected to recover completely in a relatively short time.

The massive solar storm that struck the Earth's upper atmosphere was an aftermath of the prominence that destroyed the artifact, a crescent-shaped section of a larger craft that "probably" was destroyed in some fashion more than ten thousand years ago, according to noted astronomer John Dorcaster.

In the meantime, the death toll from the aftereffects of the solar superstorm has now reached into the tens of thousands, and looting and violence continues to occur sporadically in areas of the world where the power disruptions were the greatest and where hundreds of millions remain without access to any centralized form of electric power...

At present, all sections of the Israel power grid are operating, although sporadic local outages have been reported in Gaza...

Alayna didn't sleep well on Friday night and woke early on Saturday, thoughts swirling through her mind. Would things have been different if she hadn't taken the COFAR position? Of course, they would have been. Someone else would have discovered the Solar Express, but with the same result. The CME would have occurred, and the odds were that she still wouldn't have been anywhere near Lincoln, not in time to change what had happened with her father.

That doesn't help . . . But it was true.

Chris would still have been assigned to the mission, but he might not have survived without her concerns and warnings.

He might have talked to another postdoc . . . Alayna smiled wryly. That most definitely wouldn't have happened. She'd learned later that the other top two candidates for the COFAR position had been men, and it had been clear to her from the beginning that Chris was strictly interested in women.

That didn't help much, either, because she felt like she'd had to pay, somehow, because she'd jumped at the opportunity offered by COFAR . . . because she'd been attracted to Chris from the moment he had briefed her and the others before leaving ONeill Station, and she had been forward in lingering to talk to him at the end of the transit to the Lunar Low Orbit Station. *But you've both paid. He paid for following his dream of being a pilot . . . and seeing the stars.*

Knowing that if she stayed in her bunk, she'd only stew, she struggled up and dressed, then straggled to the kitchen and made a large pot of coffee. She was going to need it. And then there were her worries about Chris, which hadn't been fully abated by his last message, although she'd been touched by the way he had promised to explain everything. Finally, she wasn't looking forward to the DOEA requisition of space at COFAR for two weeks for no more than five DOEA personnel for quarters and use of common facilities for operations in the area that would not interfere with COFAR operations.

She'd already received a second message from the Foundation, this time from Director Wrae, requesting that she report on the arrival of DOEA personnel and the requirements imposed on COFAR, as well as reminding Alayna that the Foundation could invoice DOEA for all supplies and food consumed by the DOEA team.

As she sat at the mess table and sipped her coffee, she turned her thoughts to what she could control—at least, a little—her work.

Her clearly speculative theorizing about the basis of the alien spacecraft was coming along as she expected. Slowly. That was always the way it seemed matters went after the initial inspiration. The intellectual grunt work to fit the pieces together took forever. *If they will even fit.* There was a Sinese proverb or the like about a journey of a thousand kilometers beginning with a single step. Well, in trying to figure out the theoretical basis of the graviton drive, she'd taken a few steps along the way on a journey that might take millions of light-years.

The other problem that nagged at her was one that was far closer to her own studies—the source of the pseudo-particle beam that had destroyed the alien artifact.

She couldn't help thinking that, somehow, "the man who wasn't there" was somehow involved. Maybe, if she saw the images again . . .

She thought about eating, shook her head, then picked up her mug, carefully, and walked from the mess to the control center, where she seated herself in her usual position.

"Marcel, please display the fractal construct based on the multi-fractal mini-granulation array—the one that was visible right after the solar prominence and the event that destroyed 2114 FQ5."

The image appeared on the screen wall.

"Can you construct a three-dimensional image based on the construct?"

"That is possible, but it will not be a fractal."

Alayna recalled the time, as an undergraduate, when two of her classmates had attempted to create a Mandelbulb—a mathematical attempt to re-create a Mandelbrot set of fractals in three dimensions. Marcel was politely telling her that he couldn't do that, either.

"Cancel that." Instead, Alayna studied the existing construct. Surely, it should remind her of something. She kept looking, but she couldn't think of a thing.

"Marcel . . . would you see if you can find a fractal image anywhere in the database, any of them . . ." She paused. "See if you can get a link to the National Science Center and request a match." Using Earth-Moon links was frowned on, but if the NSC was up, there actually might be less traffic.

While Marcel waited for a reply, or possibly even for a link, Alayna realized that another message had come in, from Harris at Lunara Mining. She frowned as she opened it and began to read.

> Pack train will be leaving here at 0830 with DOEA contingent and supplies. DOEA is paying for the extra power. Enjoy.

The fact that the AI-guided series of lunar rollers was being sent during lunar night meant DOEA was serious about whatever it was, and that was another concern Alayna didn't really want to dwell on.
She immediately replied.

> Thanks for the heads-up.

The response was even shorter than usual.

> Our pleasure.

Alayna smiled wryly. *Their pleasure at your having to deal with another DOEA contingent.*
"Dr. Wong-Grant," said Marcel, "we did obtain a link. This is the closest to the one you indicated. It may not be what you wanted. Please note the source."
Alayna did—"Fractal Structure Failure as Indicator of Dysfunction," Kellana M. Dukes, M.D., *Journal of Neurology*, April, 2109. She immediately studied the image—which did indeed resemble the construct. Then she began to read the article, and a section leapt out at her.

> ... *natural fractals do not exist in three-dimensional form. Three-dimensional natural biologics do have a two-dimensional fractal representation in certain biological structures, particularly in the human nervous system* ...

Could it be? Observations over the past century had shown that AGNs at the center of certain galaxies appeared to exercise some form of regulatory control over the ebb and flow of gases and matter in a way that kept those galaxies intact and functioning. Even the Earth shifted its magnetosphere to block certain types of CMEs. The problem with the last CME had been that the magnetosphere had been essentially overpowered.
And then there were the ancients. Had Akhenaten been right in his

belief and speculations that the sun was more than a natural phenom-enon?

That's stretching, Alayna.

Still . . . why had the sun reacted so violently to the approach of the artifact . . . unless it could somehow sense the gravitons. Even so . . .

Energy! All those energy storage chambers had to be filled—energized—somehow. What if the sun, or whatever the multi-fractals represented, opposed having energy being drained?

That's preposterous. You're grasping at straws . . . or the man who isn't there.

Nonetheless, she shivered for a moment. Should she send a copy of the reconstructed solar image, along with a copy of the image from the article, to Dr. Dukes?

Abruptly she smiled sadly and then shook her head. She'd write it up, if only in her personal records, but for the present, the Solar Express had been enough of a shock to the poor inhabitants of Earth. Equally impor-tant from a professional point of view, first, she wasn't a neurologist, and second, the near-matching solar fractal was a theoretical construct, not a complete observation.

If you can ever capture a complete image . . . But that would be like imaging the man who wasn't there.

Perhaps . . . later . . . but only with better evidence. *Much better evi-dence.* A lingering thought remained. *But no one else has a better expla-nation, not yet anyway.*

In the meantime . . . she did have a base to run, and she only had a few hours to make certain it was presentable to whatever DOEA contin-gent was about to descend upon her.

Something else that was likely another price to pay.

LRT [AI2]
8 DECEMBER 2114

Tavoian stood by the airlock door, holding his kit bag in his left hand. His knees were shaking, despite the low gravity, as the lock doors opened. He stepped out toward the woman who stood there, her mouth opening.

"Chris . . ." Her voice caught. "You . . . you're . . . the DOEA contingent?"

"All of it . . . for better or worse. The colonel couldn't think of a better place for my low-grav rehab. I did promise you . . ." He didn't know what else to say.

He didn't have to.

Her smile, brighter than a lunar day, was more than enough as she stepped forward, her intense green eyes meeting his as she took his hand.

Alayna Wong-Grant
(2085-2197)

Nobel Prize–winning scientist Alayna Wong-Grant died in her sleep at 0131 UTC on this date. The Noram-born astrophysicist received her doctorate from Princeton University at the comparatively young age of twenty-eight. After taking a postdoctoral appointment as the resident astronomer at the Combined Farside Lunar Array (COFAR), she pursued her interest in solar dynamics and, in particular, a study of solar multi-fractal mini-granulations. As part of her other duties at COFAR, she discovered what appeared to be a comet, an object classified prosaically as 2114 FQ5, which became the Solar Express, the only alien artifact yet discovered. Her studies of solar dynamics and the interaction of the Solar Express led to the formulation of her Gravitonic Theory of Spacetime [GTS], for which she later received the Nobel Prize for Physics, and which is the basis of the Gravitonic Drive. After several years with a number of observatories, she succeeded Dr. Jay M. Mehlin as director of the Williams Observatory consortium, and as professor of astronomy at Williams College. Upon her retirement from direct observational activities, she remained as Director Emerita until her death.

She was predeceased by her husband of seventy-one years, Brigadier General Christopher A. Tavoian, who served as the Noram Space Command's director of outer planet studies for nearly fifteen years, and who was the only survivor of the expeditions sent to investigate the Solar Express, for which he received the Medal of Valor. The couple had two daughters and five grandchildren.